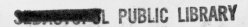

NORTH FROM THURSDAY

JON CLEARY

North from Thursday

WILLIAM MORROW AND COMPANY

NEW YORK, 1961

To Richard Beynon

This book is entirely a work of fiction. Several actual place names are mentioned in it; as are also certain official positions in those places. None of the characters in the story has ever lived in or passed through any of the places mentioned; the men occupying the official positions in the story are characters I have invented. Anyone who sees himself or anyone else in this book is, I assure him, mistaken.

The customs featured in the story occur in New Guinea; but not all of them in the one area as I have them occur. I have tried to tell a story of what life is like in New Guinea in the outer regions; I have therefore drawn a composite picture, if one that is not geographically factual. But every patrol officer, I hope, will recognize some aspect of the story I have told here. This is primarily the story of the patrol officers.

The book could not have been written without the considerable help of District Commissioner Bill Seale, District Officer Bill Tomasetti, Senior Patrol Officer Bob Greeney and Education Officer Syd Neilson. I want to thank them; and at the same time absolve them from any opinion expressed by any of the characters in the story.

NORTH FROM THURSDAY

1

SHE WAS AFRAID, more afraid than she had ever been in her life before. She sat with her eyes closed, her stomach constricted not only by the seat belt, and tried to remember being afraid in the past. And remembered only too clearly, till the sweat broke in her palms again. But fear was like pain, she told herself: you couldn't compare the present feeling of it with that of the past. Even so she knew that this fear now, being different from any she had ever experienced before, was something for which the past fears had not prepared her.

Ten thousand miles from Prague, above the green tangled mountains of New Guinea, she uttered a cry of terror, but it was lost in the roar of the plane's engine. She opened her eyes, blinking in the grinning glare of the sun, and glanced cautiously at the pilot. But he was not looking at her, sitting casually at the controls, wheeling the Cessna around the mountain peaks as if he were driving a car around the hills outside Cieszyn. He was a good-looking young Pole who had been eight years in Australia. His accent and outlook were now Australian, and soon, he had confessed to her, he would be changing his name from Stanislaus Hlasko to Stanley Hall.

He turned to her now and pointed away to the right. He leaned close to her ear. "Mount Wilhelm! The highest mountain in New Guinea. Or, anyway, the highest they have discovered so far!"

Before she located the mountain, she had remarked what he had said: *the highest they have discovered so far.* It was astonishing to her that there were still some parts of the world not yet explored; Peter had written her that there were still considerable sections of New Guinea where no white man had yet been. Reared in a civilization that, over the past two years, she had come to believe was dying, she found it almost impossible to believe in places where civilization had not yet even begun. Yet Peter had told her that in this wild green land over which she now flew, the Stone Age was not ten thousand years but perhaps only a mountain range away.

She saw the mountain rising like an iceberg out of the sea of cloud that surrounded it. The snow on it, in the bright glare of the sun, blazed like a white fire; a plume of cloud trailed from its summit like wind-whipped smoke. Accustomed to snow-topped mountains, to the Tatras with their jagged peaks that glittered like Czech crystal in the northern air, it was some moments before she remembered that this was a tropic mountain; and then the sight of the snow-covered peak somehow became incredible to her, as if her eyes were deceiving her. She looked away from the white-topped mountain, at the green forested mountains immediately below; they were forbiddingly real, promising nothing but death if the plane had to land amongst them, and then she knew that Mount Wilhelm was real. In that moment she knew New Guinea itself was real and Czechoslovakia, another life, was behind her forever.

But if Mount Wilhelm was real it was also unexpected, and she had not yet come to expect the unexpected in this strange land. She had landed in Port Moresby only last night, seen nothing of the coast, flown on to Goroka early this morning, remained there on the strip only half an hour, and now was on her way in to Kundavi. New Guinea was still nothing more to

her than an endless torment of green mountains over which the
shadow of the plane moved like a dark bird of death. And death,
Peter had also written, was part of the climate of New Guinea.

Her shoulder was touched by a black finger and she turned to
look into the smiling face of the plane's other passenger. Sergeant
Beraki was a big muscular man whose dark blue shirt and lap-
lap, piped with red, was too tight for him; he was from Buka, in
the Solomon Islands, and he was proud of his physique above
that of the small mountain men amongst whom he was stationed.
Vanity was his one fault, but the Kiap never chided him for it:
he smugly knew that his well-trimmed hair beneath the rakishly
slanted beret, the mirrorlike shine on his belt and harness, and
the scrubbed look of his muscular body was an example to the
other members of the Kiap's small police force. Sergeant Beraki
was a man who was very sure of himself, but he was a good police boy. He would not have lasted long with the Kiap if he were
not.

Elisabeth stifled a reflex to lean away from the friendly black
man. One did not meet many colored people in Prague; she could
not remember ever having met any at all; and she had been surprised to find that the natives, even this clean, well-scrubbed
policeman, smelled so different from white people. The thick
musky smell of them did not sicken her, but she knew it would
take her some time to become accustomed to it. It was a small
thing among the many strange things to which she would have
to become accustomed.

"Dis pela hap bilong Kiap Narvo." Sergeant Beraki waved an
expansive hand; she noticed that two fingers of the hand were
missing. His smile was suddenly gone and his black face was
stiff with an almost childish pride. "Bilong Kiap Narvo and me."

It was not the first time she had heard the name Narvo. At
Moresby last night, sitting in the hotel dining room at a table
with a coffee planter and his wife down from the Central Highlands, the wife, talkative on rum and the thought of tomorrow's

trip South, had warned her to tread carefully with Roy Narvo—
"He's the A.D.O., assistant district officer, that is, and A.D.O.'s
are God in their own particular district. Especially Roy Narvo
at Kundavi. And he hates women in his district. I think he hates
women, period, blast his arrogant hide." At Goroka the young
Pole, standing on the strip and looking across the valley to the
mountains that marked the way to Kundavi, had told her: "He
hates any outsiders coming into his district. He does not think
the kanakas in his district are ready for white men just yet. He
is a kanaka-lover, in his way. Some people in the Administration
think he is crazy, and that is why he is not a district officer, although he should be. Watch your step." And when she had settled herself in the plane Sergeant Beraki had leaned forward and
said, "Missus come Kundavi? Kiap Narvo, he know, eh?" And
when she had said, No, Kiap Narvo did not know she was coming,
he had sat back and smiled and shaken his head almost pityingly
at her.

The plane suddenly banked steeply and went down into a
gorge. She knew they must be approaching Kundavi, judging
by the time they had been flying, but she could not imagine their
putting down anywhere in this green wrath of mountains. A black
cliff rose sheer on their right, blocking out the sun; they flew
through purple shadow and came abruptly out into a blaze of
sunlight. Then she saw the strip for the first time. It was laid
out along the top of a narrow-spined ridge that separated two
immensely deep gorges, a patch of flattened *Kunai*-covered earth
that from the air looked no larger than a strip of green-brown
carpet. A grass hut stood at one end of it and from a pole in the
roof of the hut a windsock fluttered like some native totem. As
they circled, the Cessna bumping on the rough air, she saw that
the windsock stood straight out from the pole but never in the
same direction for more than a few seconds at a time. The pilot
had mentioned to her that winds in these mountains were a major
hazard, but, ignorant of flying conditions, she had not been much

impressed by his remark. Now, however, she looked at him for some hint of concern, but he looked as casual now as he had all along the trip. This was a taxi run for him, just a job of work.

He took the plane in a steep bank along the side of a mountain, and Elisabeth looked down through the side window of the cabin. At the bottom of each dark gorge she could see the white water of a swift river; the two rivers joined below the narrow-spined ridge in a tempest of wild water and went as a boiling torrent down the third gorge up which the plane had just flown. Mist came up from the gorges, supporting pale fragile trellises of rainbow that excited the eye; even the shadows on the dark sides of the gorges seemed to have color in them, black, purple and a dark green that was almost luminous. The plane was now well below the peaks of the mountains and she turned her head to look up at them. They did not appear to rise against the sky so much as fall from it, coming down from a long white pelmet of cloud in great green folds that, in the shining light, seemed to have no more solidity than drapes of green crêpe paper. Native gardens were stitched against the precipitous sides of the mountains in abstract patterns; a moth of smoke fluttered in a narrow fold and a loose thread of waterfall flickered in the wind. On a narrow outcrop a native village of round houses looked like a row of buttons; an antlike figure ran out from beneath one of the buttons and disappeared beneath another. Beyond the far end of the gorges the mountains stretched away to the horizon, range upon crumpled range looking like the wreck of the world, their dark narrow valleys indistinguishable from the cloud-shadow that moved with slow grace over their shimmering sides. Above it all the scalding blue sky rose in splendor, its immensity pointed by the dark speck of a cruising eagle. Accustomed to city horizons, Elisabeth's heart leapt and she forgot her fear, past and present, in the wild magnificence that surrounded her. She had long ago lost her belief in God, but some memory out of her childhood told her there had to be a Creator for all this grandeur.

Then they were coming in toward the strip, and all at once she was afraid again. The strip loomed *above* them, looking almost perpendicular; the plane went in as if it were going to dive straight into the ridge itself. "Steepest strip in the Territory!" the young Pole yelled, not taking his eyes off the task ahead, holding the plane steady against the sudden winds that blew up from the gorges. "Fifteen per cent angle! Never need brakes to pull up!"

The wind caught the plane, they swung up and out of line, the pilot corrected quickly, then they were touching down, running swiftly up the hill of the strip, and a moment later they had come to a stop. Elisabeth sat for a moment, sharply aware that at last her journey was over. Prague to Kundavi, ten thousand miles of hope and fear, but no regret. She had come all this way, and whatever the future, she was glad she had come. It was positive, the first meaningful personal thing she had done in years.

A large crowd of natives was congregated by the side of the strip. There was first a bunch of them, closed tightly together in a mass of brown and black and vivid varied color that splintered the gaze till nothing was clearly distinguishable. Behind this first group there was a sprinkling of natives against the side of a small hill, all of them moving in a shifting pattern, so that they, too, could not be distinguished as individuals. And finally, strung along the line of the hill, there was a dark frieze of them against the burning sky. The bunched natives began to move closer and she saw now that they were armed: they all carried spears, some had bows and arrows and one or two had beautifully decorated shields. But she was only half aware of their armor: her artist's eye could not get past the color that they wore. Nearly all of them wore headdresses of such magnificence as she had never seen before; she knew at once that the feathers in them could come only from the birds of paradise about which Peter had written her. Brilliant reds, purples, greens danced in the wind that blew up the strip; they waved above the glistening bodies like colored reed grass above a dark swamp. A cluster of spears was held high above the milling throng by a long brown arm; their tips, streaked with red mud or blood, shone like spiky flowers. Then the pilot switched off the engine and she heard the monotonous meaningless chant of the converging natives, and the soft thud of their stamping feet on the dust of the strip, and somewhere in the background the nervous beat of a hand-played drum. The crowd came close to the plane, hemming it in till she was sure it would be crushed under the surge of bodies, and an incredibly ugly face under an incredibly beautiful headdress glared up at her through the side window of the cabin. She looked wildly about for Peter.

"There's your friend," said the young Pole, and nodded across the shimmering dazzle of waving plumes.

Peter, with two white men and a woman and a small boy, stood beside the round hut from which the windsock fluttered. She saw a tall thin figure in white shirt and shorts and socks, looking so different from the Peter she remembered and yet recognizable even after so long. His hair seemed blonder, or perhaps it looked so because his skin was burned so much darker; and he looked thinner, or perhaps the white shorts and socks made him appear so. He raised his arm in the curious gesture she remembered so well, half welcome, half challenge; and she felt a thrill pass through her, of excitement, of love (or was it fear in another form?). Then he was pushing his way through the natives, handling them roughly, he was pulling open the door of the Cessna, and she was falling, laughing a little hysterically and crying, too, into his arms.

"Elisabeth!"

He held her tightly against him, and all at once all her fear had gone. She kissed him and something brushed against her lip. "Oh, Peter, you've grown a mustache!" She laughed again, like an embarrassed schoolgirl; she was so glad to see him, and laughter released her nervous tension. "It makes you so hand-some!"

"I always was handsome. You used to tell me so." *He hasn't changed,* she thought; *he is still vain, and yet it is one of the things about him that I love.*

He held her away from him, admiring her, oblivious of the natives who crowded around them, their dark faces wide open with frank curiosity of the new white woman. "You are more beautiful, if that is possible."

"Oh, Peter, darling." She went to kiss him again, then was aware of the other white people pushing their way through the throng of natives. She blushed and Peter saw the direction of her gaze and turned around. His thin face, which had been tight for a moment with some secret thought, almost a doubt, broke open with a sudden smile.

"Father Shawn. Eric, Bernice and Harry Macy." He and Elisabeth had been speaking in Czech to each other, but now he spoke in English. "Elisabeth Palyardi. Father Shawn is our Roman Catholic missionary. Eric is my medical assistant."

"Welcome to Kundavi." Father Shawn was a small thin man with close-cropped curly hair that was already almost white, al-though he was only in his early forties. At first glance, before he took off his straw hat, Elisabeth had taken him to be in his twenties; there was a certain boyishness about him that gave a wrong first impression. Then the tired look of the gray eyes be-hind the steel-rimmed spectacles became apparent; and when he turned his face the long scar down his left cheek made him look suddenly old. His voice was light and soft and unmistakably American. "Peter has been telling us for days of your coming. We had begun to think you were another of his fancies."

"That's just the sort of complimentary remark a priest would make!" Bernice Macy dug Father Shawn with her elbow and put out a hand to take Elisabeth's. "His fancy what? Hello, Elisabeth. It's so nice to have you. Don't take any notice of the men. None of them here at Kundavi know how to treat a woman."

Bernice Macy looked at her husband, smiling at him almost maliciously; but her glance at him was so quick that Elisabeth was not certain if the remark had been meant for him. Bernice moved so swiftly, both in gesture and expression, that it was almost impossible to pin down the exact meaning behind anything she said; even her words tumbled out of her as if they were no more than a jumble of sound, her quick light voice bouncing against the ear with no more inflection than the pinging of a tuning fork. She was in her mid-thirties, still a good-looking woman but running a little now to plumpness: in ten years, if she didn't change her habits, she would be fat, and irritable and petulant because of it. Her hair was black and cut short: long hair was a nuisance in this country, too hot for comfort and too hard to keep clean: she had vowed secretly that when she finally got back South she would let her hair grow down to her waist. She glanced again at her husband, who would have still loved her if she had been bald, then looked back at Elisabeth.

"It's good to have another woman here. Joan Duggan, that's the nursing sister, and I, we've been longing for another girl to come along. Just so's we could pick on her, instead of picking on the men all the time." She laughed, and Elisabeth recognized the last remark for a joke. Or was it a joke? Again there was the quick glance by Bernice at her husband. "Well, come on, let's get you over to the post. . . ." They pushed their way through the crowd of natives, Bernice talking all the time and the men grinning good-humoredly at her chatter. Even the natives seemed amused by her continuous talking, but she was oblivious of them. She pushed her way through them as if they were no more than a clump of tall *kunai* grass.

"Don't shake hands with them!" she suddenly cried, and Elisabeth jumped with alarm. Several of the older natives had put out thin dark hands to offer a greeting to the new white woman.

Elisabeth had put her own hand into one pale palm and at once felt the dirt and grease with which it was caked. Bernice was saying, "By the time you've gone the rounds you'll feel you've been dipping your hand in a barrel of dirty lard. Give them just one finger. They don't know the difference. They're only aping us whites. One of Roy Narvo's symbols of progress."

But her back was to Elisabeth, she was pushing on through the natives, and her words bounced away on the air, no more emphatic than a sneeze. Only the swift darkening of Eric Macy's big red face underlined what his wife had said.

Then they had come to the two Landrovers, and Elisabeth saw the lifeless body of the native woman lying in the back of one of them.

2

"It is *kuru*," said Peter. "The newspapers that got hold of the story called it 'the laughing death.' At an advanced stage the patient giggles or even laughs outright."

"Pours ice water down your spine the first time you hear it," Father Shawn said, lighting a cigarette. "I still don't like the sound of it. It's an unearthly sound, and I don't mean it's a heavenly one."

"You won't hear this woman," Peter said. "She is past that stage."

"Is she dead?" Elisabeth stared at the pitiful wretch: naked, the shrunken body seemed somehow more horrifying: clothes were a modesty, but perhaps they were also a defense against the truth of death.

"Not yet, but she will be within the week. When they go into this coma, they don't come out of it. The kanakas were waiting here with her this morning when we came over to the strip. There is nothing I can do for her, and they know it. But they were glad to get rid of her. We'll take her over to the hospital, wait till she dies, then hand the corpse back to her sub-clan—to her relatives, that is. Righto, hop in." He said *righto* in two syllables, in the precise way foreigners have when they imitate English colloquial speech; he had always been an admirer of the English and, as a precocious schoolboy, had even defended them after Munich. His father had given him a hiding for his views, and it had been the beginning of the coolness between father and son. He had begun to wonder lately if his father remembered those opinions and had repeated them to someone else. "Come along, we don't want to be late for lunch."

Elisabeth had been staring at the dying woman, and now she looked up quickly to see if Peter had made some tasteless joke. But he had opened the door of the Landrover for her, and there was no hint of humor in his face. Then she remembered: *death is part of the climate of New Guinea;* and he was acclimatized.

She heard the plane's engine start up and she turned to see the young Pole waving to them as he swung the plane around and went down the long steep slope of the strip. The natives broke into a high-pitched roar, a shrill yell of childish delight that was still mixed with awe: Peter was to tell Elisabeth later that only months had passed since the natives had given up worshiping the plane as a god. The Cessna went down the hill, plunged off the end of the strip, already airborne a thousand feet without rising, then it was climbing, a small blue bird against the green wall of the mountains, and a moment later had gone from sight around the corner of the gorge.

Native carriers were packing supplies into the back of the Landrovers. Cases of beer, frozen meat in brown paper parcels, a bundle of magazines, a carton of phonograph records, a small canvas mailbag; the dying woman's face lay against the words, *Carlton Beer,* her sightless, slightly crossed eyes staring at the stenciled letters like those of a myopic person trying to comprehend a language she had never met before. Sergeant Beraki was shouting at the carriers, hustling them along, glad to be back among these mountain kanakas where his authority was undisputed. Down on the coast, at the police school he had been attending, he had been just another police boy and the knowledge had bruised him. He shouted louder now and swung his stick; the mountain boys, just as proud, made only a pretense of moving faster. The mountain men and the islander were of different nations, of a different time: a civilization separated them. The color of Sergeant Beraki's skin meant nothing to them. He, like the white outsiders, was one of the "others."

Elisabeth got into the front seat of the Landrover and Father Shawn followed her. Two natives, their bright cotton lap-laps distinguishing them from their wilder brothers, who wore only strips of grass around their loins, clambered into the back of the vehicle, both of them turning their backs on and sitting well forward of the dying woman. Peter let in the gears and they started down the narrow road just as rain began to fall.

"It comes up out of nowhere in the mountains," said Father Shawn, seeing the surprise on Elisabeth's face as the rain spattered against the windshield. "It can rain out of just one cloud. You'll get used to it, won't she, Peter?"

"If she wants to," said Peter, and Elisabeth was aware of a note in his voice, of something like bitter apathy, that she couldn't remember from the past.

The rain had increased and the road had already turned slippery. It was not really a road, but just a red soil track hacked out of the side of the mountain. It wound down the mountainside in a series of tight-angled bends; across the gorge, on the neighboring mountain, the pattern was repeated as the road climbed to the distant patrol post. Native gardens bordered the road in places, their fences of sharp stakes running down the chest of the mountain like a necklace of yellow pointed teeth.

The Landrover crept down onto a narrow bridge. It was no more than two stout tree trunks laid across a crevice and topped by a platform of slimmer tree trunks lashed to the supports by vines. Above the bridge a waterfall leapt out from a great spout of black rock. It came down in a thin white fall, the rock of the mountain glimmering behind it like black glass, ripped through the crevice beneath the frail bridge and plunged onto the river a thousand feet below. Spray joined the rain above the bridge, and the Landrover crept forward into a diamond-glittering mist lit by a shaft of sunlight from across the gorge.

The wheels bumped on the corded surface of the bridge and the vehicle inched its way across. On the other side of the bridge the road rose steeply, and beyond the frantic metronomes of the windshield wipers Elisabeth could see the water rushing down the red mud of the road. Peter had changed into four-wheel drive and now he urged the Landrover forward to take the steep ascent. The front wheels bit into the mud, lost their traction, and at that moment the rear wheels began to slide sideways on the slippery logs of the bridge.

For one awful moment Elisabeth's heart stopped beating. She felt herself as part of the vehicle, suddenly without any grip on the world and sliding slowly toward death. The motor was roaring and the tires screeched as they fought for adhesion on the greasy surface. Elisabeth looked past Father Shawn's tightly stretched face, his mouth open in what could have been a curse of anger or a prayer of despair, and saw the tiny figure of a native working unconcernedly in the sun in a garden on the mountainside on the other side of the gorge. She was aware with a terror that chilled her that there was nothing between them and the methodically working native but shining space into which the Landrover would plummet like a hurtling rock.

Then the front wheels tore at the mud of the track, took hold and the Landrover lurched up off the bridge. And at once Father Shawn turned quickly in the seat and flung himself headlong over the back of it. Elisabeth, startled, still feeling reaction from their narrow escape, jerked her head around. Father Shawn lay stretched over the cases of beer, the parcels of frozen meat and the mailbag, his thin arms holding tightly to the even thinner arms of the native woman, who had slipped almost out of the back of the Landrover.

He was yelling at the two native boys, cursing them in pidgin, but they were shying away from him and the native woman. Peter took the Landrover up the steep rise and brought it to a halt where the road flattened out below another sharp bend. He switched off the engine, jumped out and ran around to the back of the Landrover. Elisabeth slid out beneath the driving wheel and followed him. Her legs were unsteady, her knees weak, but she would not have complained if she had collapsed into the red mud beneath her grateful feet. The earth felt solid and safe. The rain had stopped now and steam was already rising from the mud under the fierce heat of the sun. She was sweating profusely, but she knew it was not from the heat. She leaned against the side of the Landrover, sick with relief.

Peter pushed the native woman back into the truck. She lay like a rag doll out of which most of the sawdust had run; her head lolled as if her neck were broken and the sightless eyes stared at them and beyond them. Father Shawn got out of the truck and came around and stood beside Peter and Elisabeth. He looked in at the two natives still in the vehicle and said something in pidgin.

"These two are from my mission," he told Elisabeth. He took out a cigarette and lit it; his hands shook as if he were in the grip of fever. He had done many brave things in his life, but they had almost invariably been reflex actions; he was a retrospective coward and for days after would suffer spasms of chilling fear, amazed at what he had done and that he had managed to survive. His biggest wonder was that he had had the courage in the first place to come out to this country as a missionary. It had been a planned action, not a reflex one, and he knew it had been a brave one; he was too humble to believe he had been divinely inspired, and he had continued to be amazed at himself.

"I've kidded myself I've made Christians of these fellers, but when it comes to a thing like this"—he patted the arm of the dying woman; the arm flopped like a loose end of rope and he picked it up and put it back beside the crumpled bag of the body— "when it comes to this, I know how little I've achieved. I've only been here since the end of the war. I'm up against ghosts who have been here since the beginning."

The two natives stared back at the priest with blank faces, never for a moment looking at the dying woman. Elisabeth all at once felt an unaccountable pity for them; then she heard Peter say, "Here come the Macys," and she turned and saw the other Landrover approaching the bridge. She held her breath, feeling fear rise in her again; but a fear she recognized this time and had known in the past, fear of seeing other people go to their death. The second Landrover moved slowly onto the bridge, crept like some huge steel animal across the corded logs, then accelerated and came up the steep rise in a flurry of mud and the angry whine of its engine. Eric Macy took it past them, negotiated the sharp bend and went on along the mountainside. In the back of the vehicle, seated between native boys, young Harry Macy waved back at them, as unconcerned as a city youngster passing on his way to a beach picnic. It was only then that Elisabeth realized that neither Peter nor Father Shawn had mentioned their narrow escape crossing the bridge. To them it was only another part of their day. They had been upset only by the fact that they had almost lost the native woman.

"I'll ride in the back," Father Shawn said, as they prepared to get back into the truck. "Just in case she slips out again." He looked at the skin and bones that, for want of a better name, still had to be called human. "Poor devil. The Lord sometimes makes me wonder." Then he looked up and blushed, as if he had not meant Elisabeth to hear the last words. "Forgive me. No one should hear a priest talk like that."

"You are honest, at least," said Peter Traxal. "It is better to be doubtful than to delude oneself."

"Spoken like a true agnostic," said Father Shawn, and Elisabeth looked at Peter and wondered when he had become an agnostic. That was something else in him that had changed.

They got back into the Landrover and went on up the road. It curled up over a shoulder, then dropped suddenly and they went down in a long coil of agonized bends to the bottom of the misted gorge. Here it was impossible to hear each other talk. Words were lost against the roar of the water as it tore beneath another log bridge and went plunging on down beneath luminously shining cliffs. They crossed the bridge and climbed slowly out of the aqueous light, like submariners rising out of a lake whose waters were only mist. The thunder died away, the mist dropped below them, and they came up into a blaze of sunlight.

Up ahead of them a long line of native carriers was strung out along the track. At the head of them a tall white man in tattered shirt and shorts and a battered broad-brimmed hat was holding a bush native by the throat, lifting him off the ground and shaking him violently.

"Roy Narvo," said Father Shawn from the back of the truck. "Meting out white man's justice."

2

THE MACYS went past in the Landrover, slowing to call a greeting to Roy Narvo. He smiled and waved at them, tired and irritable, but glad to be back among white people. He was well aware of his reputation as a kanaka-lover, and he was sincere in his belief that this area was not yet ready for the influx of whites, either as visitors or as settlers; but he was neither a hermit nor an exile, and his mind was too educated, too civilized, to sustain itself interminably on sensuality, superstition and the simple jealousies of a people whose language he spoke but who could not speak his. He always felt this way at the end of a long patrol. He would leave on a patrol with a feeling of excitement, of anticipation; sometimes he would smile at himself, as if he were a boy setting out on an adventurous camping trip. But he knew it was more than that: he had read Rimbaud and Conrad, and he knew of the urge in some men to go back to the beginnings of themselves, to try to trace the thread that bound all men, primitive and civilized, together: if he did not go with that thought uppermost in his mind, he knew he went with more than just the excitement of setting out on a walk into strange country. Then as the patrol wore on the excitement wore off: he was no longer interested in finding the ancestral heart of himself among these

17

savages. They were people of another world and he wanted to return to his own world, even to the trivialities of it and the meringuelike minds of many of those who lived in it.

He would even be glad to see Bernice again, even though he put her in the meringue-brain class. She did not like him, he knew, and it was his own fault; she would probably never like him, because he was incapable of adjusting his personality to those who could not take it. But he liked Bernice, although she was unaware of it, and when she waved to him as the Landrover went past, he waved back with genuine pleasure. Then he saw young Harry yelling to him from the back of the truck, almost falling out in his excitement; and his face lit up, and he took off his hat and waved it vigorously. Two years ago he would not have believed that he could find the company of an eleven-year-old boy agreeable and satisfying. Each time he went out on patrol he looked for things to bring back to Harry; he brought back stone axes, carved arrowheads, even decorated phallocrypts, like a favorite uncle coming home with Christmas gifts. Some of his gifts had not always pleased Bernice, but he had ignored her disapproval in the bright shine of Harry's excited pleasure at them.

He waved vigorously to Harry, grinning widely and yelling at the boy. Then the Landrover had gone around a bend in the road, and he turned and saw the police boy struggling with the bush native. He ran back down the road, his rifle bumping against his shoulder, and grabbed the native and pulled him away from the police boy. He held the native by the necklace of cowrie shells he wore and turned to the police boy and asked in police Motu what had happened.

The police boy was straightening his beret and dusting down his lap-lap and vest. His dignity had been hurt by rolling in the dust with the bush native, and he was as much disturbed by that as by what the other man had done. But if the Kiap wanted to know, this kanaka (the term uttered with the scorn that only a town or post native can use toward a bush one) had been following them since early morning and had just tried to steal the Kiap's rain cape from one of the carriers.

Narvo was a big man. He stood six feet three and last time he had weighed himself, on leave in Sydney nearly three years ago, he had pushed the scales up to 217 pounds. Tramping these mountain pads had allowed no fat to grow on him, and all his bigness came from the bone and muscle in him. The bush native, too, was all bone and muscle, but like most of these mountain natives, he was a small man, only a little above pygmy height. At the end of Narvo's long muscular arm he looked no more than a half-grown boy.

Narvo swore at him in English, then switched to the local dialect. With over five hundred mutually unintelligible languages in Papua and New Guinea, the usual *lingua franca* was pidgin or police Motu; but Narvo had always made a point of learning the dialect of the area in which he was stationed. It helped him to *think kanaka,* and he was a better administrator because of that. But *thinking kanaka* meant that he sometimes acted in a way that would not have been condoned by Administration headquarters back in Moresby. He lifted the native by the throat, holding him at arm's length, and shook him violently.

"What is your name? Where do you come from?"

The native's eyes bulged with fear and the strangling hold on his throat. Narvo lowered him to the ground, repeating the question, and the native gasped, "I am Kasin, Kiap. From Vaikaka."

"Get back there then! And remember, he who steals breaks both the black man's and the white man's law! And I am here to see that both are kept!"

He let go the man's throat, and as the native turned to scuttle away into the bush, Narvo kicked him where his peace plant hung down behind. Then the second Landrover came up the road and pulled to a halt.

"You treat these kanakas too gently," said Father Shawn, getting out of the truck. "You remind me of St. Francis of Assisi."

"In your priestly eye," said Narvo, grinning and throwing his arm about the priest's thin shoulders. "How've you been, you old God-botherer? Making headway with the heathen?"

Then he saw the girl sitting in the Landrover beside Traxal, and he straightened up. His brows came down in angry puzzlement, and he walked around Father Shawn and strode across to the Landrover.

"Hello, Peter," he said, and looked straight past Traxal at the girl. "Who is our visitor?"

"My fiancée, Elisabeth Palyardi," said Traxal flatly.

Narvo took off his hat. "Are you staying long, Miss Palyardi?"

Elisabeth looked at this man who, even before she had met him, had promised to be one of the major obstacles to her settling in here at Kundavi. She was first aware of his size, of the suggestion of brute animal strength in him. There were no buttons on his shirt and it gaped open, exposing a massive hairy chest; the long thick legs beneath the torn shorts were dark with long black hair. His hat, streaked with mud and with a ragged hole in the crown, had a band of possum fur. He hadn't shaved for two days and his cheeks and jaw were covered with a stubble of black beard. The only clean thing about him, oiled and shining, was the rifle that hung from his shoulder. He looked more like a fugitive from justice than the symbol of government in this area.

"As long as Peter stays," she said. "His plans are my plans."

"That's nice. I'm an admirer of loyalty and devotion." He was tired, but he managed a good-humored smile. "I just would have liked to know you were coming. As the A.D.O., I'm responsible for everyone in this area."

"I got word that Elisabeth was coming less than a week after you went out on patrol." There was no antagonism in Traxal's voice, but Elisabeth, sensitive all at once to changes in him, could find no hint of apology, either. He spoke flatly, as if he were reciting facts that did not really concern him. "I got in touch with Neil Figgins at Goroka, since he is district commissioner for the whole area, and he gave me permission to bring Elisabeth in here."

"Well, that's fine," said Narvo, still smiling. "I take it Neil is responsible for her, then, till I'm ready to shoulder the burden."

"I should like to think I am Peter's responsibility," said Elisabeth tartly. "That is, if it is all the same to you and Mr. Figgins."

"You're elected then, Peter. Don't let the lady down." He winked at Traxal, who inclined his head with a cool smile; then Narvo looked back at Elisabeth. "Anyhow, welcome, Miss Palyardi. I hope you like it here. It's lousy country for women."

"I'm sure it is," said Elisabeth, straight-faced; and beside her Traxal kept a smile hidden behind a face equally straight. He started up the Landrover, looked at Father Shawn, who shook his head, then drove on up the road. He said something in Czech that Elisabeth didn't catch, and she looked at him.

"You do not like this Narvo?" she said.

"He could make it difficult, having you here." They were speaking in Czech again: New Guinea went by outside, alien and forgotten for a moment.

"You should have warned me about him."

"Perhaps. But there seemed no point in spoiling my letters by mentioning him—somehow I never really believed you would get here."

"There were times when I did not believe it, myself. But it was the difficulties in Prague, not the thought of someone making me unwelcome at this end."

"Never mind." He took his hand from the wheel and squeezed her arm, smiling at her. He looked at her, a stranger, and tried to put in her place the girl he remembered, the girl he had loved. He had stifled love, or passion, call it what you liked, for so long, that now it did not come easily to the surface and he was forced to make a pretense of it. And because he had to pretend, this girl beside him became a stranger whom he had to learn to know again. "Darling, it is wonderful to have you here. That is all that matters now. Forget Narvo."

Elisabeth had the feeling that that would be difficult, but it would not be the first time she had tried to forget people who had been objectionable or who had interfered with her attempt at happiness. As a child she had tried to forget, or anyway ignore, the gauleiter who lived in their street behind the Smetana Embankment: the man who, despite the fact that some of the neighbors said he was cheerful and kindly, represented the Nazis who had arrested her father and taken him away and shot him. Later she had tried to forget the Communist official who, every three months, like a debt collector, called and questioned her on the habits and behavior of the British diplomatic family for whom she had worked as governess. Beside those two men Narvo would be just a minor obstacle in her pursuit of happiness. She squeezed Traxal's hand in return, promising him her future and seeing in him the promise of her own future. Then she was aware again of the two natives in the back of the Landrover, sitting with eyes still averted from the woman dying of *kuru*, and she was aware of the woman herself, her life already gone and waiting now only for the mercy of death. And she felt a stab of conscience, as if happiness had somehow become something of which to be ashamed.

Back down the road Father Shawn stared after the disappearing Landrover. "I wonder if Peter's mood will improve now his girl has arrived?"

"His might. Mine won't. He'd better marry her soon, otherwise she goes back to Goroka."

"You sound very moral. I thought I was the one who should throw up my hands at people who live in sin?"

"I'm not being moral, and you know it, you skinny little hypocrite," said Narvo, grinning affectionately at the priest. "I'm just

being practical. If he marries her, I can't object to her being here. If he doesn't, then she is just a visitor on the post, a woman visitor at that, and I don't encourage visitors."

Father Shawn took out a cigarette and drew heavily on it. He looked at his fingers with distaste: they were dark with nicotine. He was glad that he had always smoked with his left hand, so that his right hand had remained clean for passing out the Host: he had ideas on hygiene, but mostly he figured the Lord wouldn't appreciate being tainted by nicotine. He sometimes wondered if the Lord looked upon those who died of lung cancer as suicides; but the thought hadn't been able to make him give up smoking. He fell into step beside Narvo, walking fast to match his pace against that of the taller man. "How'd the patrol go?"

"Pretty bloody. We got jumped four times." He took off his hat and fingered the arrow hole in it. "I had to kill one kanaka. The bugger was just about to bash in the head of one of the police boys."

"Where was this?"

"Up beyond Wabut." Narvo waved a hand to the west, where the mountains lay like gray-green iron beasts under the harsh blue rim of the sky. He spoke casually, a man grown accustomed to long treks into unmapped country, a commuter to the suburbs of the wilderness: home was the patrol post up ahead, and not the house in Randwick back in Australia, where his father sat amongst sardonically grinning dentures writing his history of dentistry that would never be published, and his mother played her collection of Gilbert and Sullivan records and never understood the satire of them. "Bloody awful country, full of leeches. I'm practically bloodless. I didn't blame the kanakas for jumping us. I'd be bloody-minded, too, if I lived in that country."

"How'd the carriers go?" Father Shawn looked back down the long line of carriers, sixty of them, all of them walking a little straighter now and throwing off their weariness as they got closer to home and their women.

"A lazy lot of bastards. These mountain blokes don't like work." He looked back at the carriers and swore obscenely at them. Then he looked down at the priest. "Sorry, Mike. I promised not to use that word, didn't I?"

"You better be careful with your tongue now we've got *three* women on the post. The place is getting civilized. Do you swear like that in front of young Harry?"

"Don't insult me. I'm not entirely uncouth."

"Peter thinks you are," Father Shawn said, smiling.

Narvo made a remark that proved Traxal's point, and put his arm about the priest's shoulders again. "It's good to see you again, you skinny little bastard. I missed our arguments. You can't argue with a kanaka who just shakes his head and says he doesn't understand you. Every time I picked a leech off me, I thought of you sucking the blood of my brain."

"I missed you, too. I had to invent another hair shirt."

They walked up the road, steam rising from the red mud, and the mud itself caking on their boots, and came out on the tiny plateau where the post had been built. At the edge of the settlement a man in a red lap-lap and an old straw hat came out of a hut and raised his arm in welcome. He was a white man, but from a distance, skinny and burnt almost black, he looked like a native. He came clumping across the road to them, the old army boots he wore loose and laceless about his skinny ankles.

"G'day, Jack!" Narvo slapped the man on his naked shoulder. With people he liked, Narvo's greetings could at times be overpowering: he threw his arms or his hands at them almost as if trying to demolish them. It was a sign of their affection for him that neither Father Shawn nor Jack Bermingham had tried to dodge his dangerous welcome of them.

Jack Bermingham winked his good eye: the other stared glassily at the two men. He was almost as tall as Narvo, but only half as broad; above the bright red lap-lap his ribs showed plainly beneath the wrinkled brown flesh, and his arms were

corded with sinew. His face was long and bony and mottled with sun cancers; his brows were bleached almost white by years of sun, and strands of gray-blond hair stuck out from beneath the straw hat. But when he smiled, his teeth were those of a young man, white and strong and with none missing. His smile seemed to take years off him, if one avoided looking at his body, which was that of a man in his late fifties.

"I heard you were on your way in. The wife's old man came in ahead of you."

"How's Mary?" Narvo said. "Still happily married?"

"Oh, my word, yes. But she's—she's pregnant again." He took off his hat and ran a long thin hand through his hair; his hair was thick and long, lying on his head like a silver pelt. He had once been a handsome man, but the years and his own neglect had taken toll of him. He looked at Father Shawn, his good eye squinting into the sun and his glass eye blank and innocent. "I'm sorry, Mike. I didn't tell you—I was hoping she might've made a mistake."

Father Shawn shook his head. "It's Roy's worry, Jack, not mine. The Church doesn't worry about the color of souls. I've baptized your other two, I'll do the same for this one. I just worry for the kids when they grow up, that's all. So far the Territory is too young to have had a half-caste problem. I hope for the sake of your kids it never does have one."

Bermingham looked at Narvo. "What do you reckon, Roy?"

Narvo shrugged. "I gave you permission to marry Mary. I can't very well forbid you going to bed with her. But it might be an idea if you started practicing birth control. Even if Mike here doesn't like it."

"I appreciate the problem," Father Shawn said, lighting another cigarette from the butt he had just finished. "Just don't expect me to condone *that* solution to it."

The three men walked up the plateau, past the huts of the unmarried police boys, past the stockade where three prisoners waved to Narvo and grinned widely at him. He waved back, swearing good-humoredly at them, and said to Bermingham, "What else has been going on?"

"Has Mike told you about the *kuru?* There's been another outbreak."

Narvo swore again, this time with ill-humor. "I thought we'd seen the end of that. Peter told me there hadn't been a case in six months."

"We've had five in the past week," said Father Shawn. "Six. I forgot the woman we brought up this morning from the air strip."

They passed the married police boys' quarters. Each hut stood in its own garden; one or two of them were speckled with the pink flower of the climbing *antigonon;* clumps of bamboo were a windbreak behind them. Women in bright lap-laps sat on the steps, chattering like brilliantly plumaged parrots: they gossiped about the white men as they passed, and screamed at their children as they played in the mud: the native women were less removed from civilization than their menfolk. Some of the older women, faces wrinkled as empty gourds, slack breasts hanging like satchels from their bony shoulders, were cutting the grass of the parade ground. They swung their *sarifs* in a rhythm that had no relation to time: the grass would still be growing when they were long dead. One could read the thought in their faces. A bush native, bark cloak hanging down his back, three vivid plumes stuck in his dyed hair, the polished metal badge strung on a cord gleaming like a Cyclopean eye in the middle of his forehead, gave a caricature of a salute as he went by. He was a *tul-tul,* the clerk of a village and aide to the *luluai,* the government-appointed headman: he represented the government, he was a *man bilong Gavman,* and he threw the salute as much to impress the women as to acknowledge Narvo. The latter saluted in return, and the *tul-tul* went strutting down the path, the green plumes in his hair waving like those of a proud cock.

"I'll talk to Peter later," Narvo said. "He's going to have his hands full. *Kuru* and that woman of his. I hope he appreciates which is the more important."

"Which is?" said Father Shawn, and Narvo looked at him scornfully.

He came to his own house and Father Shawn and Jack Bermingham went on up the road. He took off his hat and rifle and bandolier, gave them to the houseboy who had been waiting for him on the veranda, and slumped down in a canvass chair. Three mongrel dogs came around the corner of the veranda in a bumbling rush and flung themselves at him; he gathered them in his arms as he might have a trio of children and his laugh mingled with the dogs' barking in a loud reunion. He pushed away the dogs, still laughing and swearing, dragged off his boots and lay back, yelling to the houseboy to bring him a beer. Paiwo, the houseboy, came out with two cans of beer, a glass and the mailbag that had been dropped off by Traxal as he had gone past in the Landrover.

Narvo punctured a can, poured the beer and drank half a glass in one swallow. Then he opened the bag and took out the letters. He skimmed through the letters, putting half a dozen aside with his own name on them. There were letters for Traxal, the Macys, Frank Rossi, the cadet patrol officer, Joan Duggan, the hospital sister, and Father Shawn. There was none for Jack Bermingham; there never was. Narvo cursed, feeling an unreasonable anger at the relatives and friends who had forgotten Bermingham and turned him into an outcast. Inured to loneliness himself, Narvo yet could not bear to see the loneliness of others. He knew that Bermingham, like himself, preferred to live here in New Guinea; yet, contrarily, what helped make life bearable here in the wilderness were the letters from outside. A man could choose to live alone, but he did not choose nor could not bear to be forgotten. Nostalgia was a natural partner to memory: a man remembered and liked to be remembered. Yet Bermingham even at Christmas did not receive a card, that smallest most insincere token that one is loved and remembered. It was the knowledge that he had been forgotten that had in the end led him into marriage with a native woman. Narvo himself had performed the marriage, reading the words of the ceremony in a loud bitter voice, as if they might be heard back on the mainland where Bermingham had been closed out of the family circle.

If Narvo's anger could be deep and violent, his compassion had the same intensity. His anger was notorious; only a few knew of his compassion. He had always been an angry man, reacting violently to anything with which he disagreed. He had been twice demoted in the army because he had refused to obey what he had called stupid orders: on both occasions events had proved him right, but he had not endeared himself to his superiors who believed good discipline was as important as good sense. The same tendency to quick anger had gone against him in the Administration service in New Guinea; he had not always been right, but the chastening experiences hadn't calmed him more than temporarily.

If he had ever thought about it at all, he could not have told when compassion had entered his make-up. He had started life as an intolerant boy and taken the same fault with him through to manhood; down South there were many people whose lives were still dark with the bruises of his opinions of them. The impulse to kindness, to feel the suffering of others and be hurt by it, had been something that had come slowly like the day-by-day picking up of a new language; now it was part of him, but for some reason which he did not examine, he never advertised it and indeed tried to hide it. It was as if he were afraid that this sympathy for others, this capacity to share their suffering, which had come so late to him, might be a weakness. And in this job and in this country no man could afford to be weak.

He picked up the letters addressed to himself. One of them was a slim official envelope and he slit it with the knife he had taken from his belt. He opened the letter and read it slowly.

Then his bellow of rage was heard on the other side of the parade ground.

2

"This is the guest hut," Traxal said, and carried Elisabeth's two bags, all she had been able to bring with her from Prague, into the hut. It was a small hut of one room with a shower cubicle built in one corner. Sparsely and primitively furnished, the one modern convenience was the electric globe hanging from a roof timber.

Traxal saw her looking up at it. "Narvo salvaged an old generator down on the coast. A talent for improvisation is one of the few virtues of the Australians." He said it grudgingly but sincerely: he knew that he owed all his comfort and amenities over at the hospital to Narvo.

He put his arms around Elisabeth and drew her toward him. She kissed him as she had not kissed a man in a long time; she moved her mouth over his as if taking from him the breath of life she needed. There was hunger in her kiss for him, and a certain relief: the kiss was not an act of love, but the climax of a journey. She was a passionate woman, but her passion now was not all of the blood. His hands moved over her searchingly, remembering the body they had once known so well, but she was hardly aware of them; sex just now would be a desecration: one didn't thank God with an act of fornication. It was a moment before she realized she *was* thanking God, that what had gone through her mind as she kissed Peter was a prayer. She could not remember when she had last prayed.

"I missed you, Peter. Sometimes I almost gave up hope——"

"I, too." They were still speaking in Czech: the language of their youth, the time when they had first fallen in love. "I wanted to come home to you——"

"No. That wouldn't have brought us happiness. We could not be happy in Prague, darling."

He let her go and walked to the door of the hut. "We shan't be happy here. This is no place for a civilized man."

"But we shan't stay here! Not forever. You wrote me that you had to stay up here only two years and then you could go back to Australia and practice. You have only three months more here."

"I don't mean just here in New Guinea. I mean Australia. I've tried, Elisabeth. You have no idea how I've tried to like Australia. But I can't."

"Why not?" She could feel her relief and her new-found happiness beginning to crumble: the foundations of her future were cracking before it was even built. "You chose Australia to come to. You said it offered opportunity——"

"I know, I know." He had had arguments like this with Narvo; he hadn't expected to have to defend his point of view to Elisabeth. "I got off to a bad start, perhaps I expected too much. I don't know. They wouldn't let me begin practicing right away—they wanted me to do a postgraduate course at one of their universities. Who do they think they are? We had universities and doctors when this country, Australia, I mean, was just as wild and untamed as that out there. . . ." He waved a hand toward the distant ranges. "All they want is to protect the interests of their own doctors. Australians are afraid of real competition, of anyone who works really hard. We foreigners are thrown the crumbs. If we join the New Guinea Health Service —jobs their own doctors don't want—we can practice in Australia after we've spent two years up here. They make you earn the right to be an Australian. As if it were some sort of honor." His voice was bitter with sour anger; he thumped a fist against the doorjamb. A nation of upstarts, still wet behind the ears, demanding that he, a Czech with fifteen centuries of Bohemian blood in his veins, earn the right to be one of them!—he felt dizzy with anger and insulted pride, and thumped the doorjamb again.

"But you have earned it now, Peter! You have only two or three months to go. Then we can go to Sydney or Melbourne——" They were only names to her: she knew nothing about the country.

He shook his head, looking out at the mountains across the gorge; he saw Narvo and Father Shawn and Jack Bermingham come up the road, the line of carriers strung out behind them like a long mottled snake. He envied the three men their companionship: they had mutual interests, even if by his own standards those interests were worthless. He looked across at the mountains and tried to remember the Tatras, and couldn't: he felt cheated, deprived even of homesickness. "It's not only that. I don't like the life down South——" He spoke like an Australian without realizing it: the expatriate Australians, for most of whom *down South* was synonymous with home. "It is too—too vulgar. There is no refinement." He felt prissy and pompous: *I'm beginning to think Australian,* he thought, *five years ago I wouldn't have felt that way about using those words.*

"Do you think there is still refinement back home, Peter?"

"There must be relics of it. Even that is something. A Communist coup doesn't wipe out a tradition of culture just like that." He gestured with his hand.

"It can tarnish it. People back home are dispirited, Peter. They don't care very much about anything. Tired minds don't add much luster to a tradition."

"It won't always be like that. They must have accepted the Communists by now. They'll come awake again soon."

"Do you mean you want to go back to Prague?" It was like asking an innocent man if he wanted to go back to prison: she did not expect him to take her question seriously.

"I don't know. My father still writes to me——"

"He came to see me before I left. He sent his love. He works for Cedok now. The State tourist organization," she said, as if he might have forgotten how the State now ran everything.

"I know. He sends me travel propaganda—as if I were a tourist, instead of his son. Come to Gothic Prague, Visit the bohemian Paradise——" The trite travel slogans came up in his mind. The pamphlets were hoarded in his room, like souvenirs of a home destroyed by some disaster: he felt a sudden spasm of homesickness and welcomed it as a man might welcome relief from pain. "Does Prague still look the same, still beautiful?"

"It looks the same. It doesn't *feel* the same."

He was silent for a while, still staring out across the parade ground. An old man walked down the path past the hedge of wild hibiscus, a skinny sunken-bellied old man leaning on a stick and trailing a small pig on a string behind him. A pig was wealth in these mountains, and the old kanaka reminded Traxal of the old men who, before the coup in 1948, had walked in the Wallenstein Gardens, the gold watch chains on their sunken bellies, brought out now the Nazis had gone, glinting in the sun: they had spent the war in the Terezin ghetto, and now they walked with a pitiful pride, telling a world that no longer cared that they had once been the rich men of Prague. Where were the rich old men of Prague now? And who would come to conquer the old native and take away his pig? Traxal looked across the parade ground and saw Narvo stop by his house; but he saw no conqueror there. Conquerors could never afford to love the conquered, and Narvo did love the natives of these mountains.

"I have to go across to the hospital," he said, not wanting to argue any more with Elisabeth: she had let him down, had failed to bring the breath of home with her. "Lunch will be in half an hour. We are eating with the Macys."

"Peter, darling." She came to the door and put her hand on his arm. "Perhaps it will be different now I have come. Oh, that sounds conceited—you know what I mean——"

"I know, darling." He smiled, a little tiredly, and bent and kissed her cheek. "Perhaps things will change. One never knows the future."

Then they heard the bellow of rage from across the parade ground and a moment later saw Narvo come down the steps of his veranda in one leap and come striding across toward them.

"What is the matter?" Elisabeth was puzzled, and afraid that Narvo's rage was aimed at her.

"I don't know. He blows up suddenly like this." Traxal could feel her trembling, and he was angry at Narvo for making her like this. "We are used to it. You'll get used to it, too."

Narvo's boots were unlaced and his shirt open to his shorts. He had considerable less dignity as a representative of the government than the *tul-tul* who had saluted him a while back, but he either ignored the fact or was oblivious of it: his anger was not the sort that could ever be hidden by a show of dignity. "There is another bloody United Nations party on its way here!"

"They are entitled to come here," Traxal said reasonably. "New Guinea *is* a UN Trust Territory."

"It isn't three years since the last one was here! What do they expect us to have achieved in that time? Turned the kanakas into businessmen, made them into trade unionists? What about you—what are you going to say when they ask you why you haven't cured the kanakas of *kuru?*"

"What do you want me to do? Spirit all the *kuru* cases away into the mountains? Roy, you should calm down. These UN parties are going to continue coming here. You may as well learn to live with them."

"I'll never learn to live with stupid prejudiced clots!" He looked at Elisabeth, and for a moment she thought he was going to turn his anger on her. Then abruptly he grinned, and she was surprised how it altered the set of his face. He would never be called handsome, his face was too broad and rugged for that and the broken nose did not help; but there was a sympathy about the dark eyes that she had not noticed before, and when he smiled she saw there was also deep humor in them. "Did I swear in front of you, Miss Palyardi?"

"I do not know. My English does not contain any swearwords —yet." She returned his smile, hoping this break in his black mood would continue.

But it didn't: his smile went. "It will if you stay around here," he said, and looked back at Traxal. "I'll see you, Eric and Frank after lunch. We'd better have a natter about this."

He went back across the parade ground, his boots flopping about his ankles, his shirt almost hanging out the back of his shorts. He looked more of a derelict than Jack Bermingham. Bermingham had gone almost completely native, and the natives had dignity.

Suddenly he stopped and looked back. "There's a bloody Czech in this party!" he yelled. "You'd better watch out, Peter!"

He gave a bellow of laughter, then went on across the parade ground, shouting to his houseboy to lay out clean clothes for him, yelling at the old woman to *katim garas kwiktaim* or he'd *katim* their bloody heads off. The police boys and their wives and children stood outside their huts chattering happily, the old women smiled with betel-stained gums, even the prisoners in the stockade capered gleefully. The Kiap was back and things were always happening when the Kiap was around.

"I'll come down for you in twenty minutes," Traxal said, kissed Elisabeth on the cheek and went up the path to his own house.

She stood in the doorway and looked after him. She felt a sudden pity for him: pity was a strange feeling to her, one she hadn't experienced in a long time: self-pity, the familiar feeling of the past five years, was another sensation altogether. She looked after Peter and recognized that, though she herself was now free, he was still a prisoner. He wore his Czech nationality like a birthmark; the umbilical cord of home had stretched ten thousand miles and still held him. He disappeared into his house and she was aware, after a moment, of the blinding glare of the sun against her eyes that saw nothing.

She closed her eyes, suddenly exhausted, suddenly afraid again.

3

"I'M JACK BERMINGHAM," the one-eyed man said. "If there is anything you wanna know about New Guinea, I'm the bloke to tell you. My word, I am."

After Traxal had gone, Elisabeth had unpacked her bags. She had put her things away in the chest of drawers with the feeling that it might all be just a waste of time; her stay at Kundavi had all at once taken on a temporary prospect and she might be repacking in a few days to leave here. Peter had said nothing specific to give her that idea, but she had had so many disappointments she had become almost habitually pessimistic. She was not disappointed nor unhappy. She had had no particular anticipation of Kundavi itself: she would go wherever Peter wanted to go. But it had shocked her to find that after five years on this side of the world Peter had put down no roots here. She set the photo of her dead parents on top of the chest of drawers, and wondered if she would miss them more here in New Guinea or in Australia than she had back home. She was too newly departed from home to feel any nostalgia just yet.

She undressed and went into the shower cubicle. She was surprised to find that there were hot and cold taps. Smiling skeptically she turned on the hot tap—and had to jump hurriedly from beneath the spray of scalding water. She regulated the two taps, then stood beneath the spray and washed the dirt and tiredness from herself. She was a tall woman, full-bodied and graceful; she took a certain sensual delight in the contemplation of her own body. She moved her arms with lazy snakelike grace as she washed her pale golden hair; the lifted breasts had the full firmness of a woman who took care of herself. Her shoulders were broad, and her back had the hollow of a woman of passion; the rounded arms and thighs and slim wrists and ankles were those of a woman made for love. She had been called beautiful by too many men not to know that they spoke the truth; the compliments had not made her vain but only glad that she was as she was. Her face was not every man's ideal of beauty: the cheekbones might have been too wide and prominent, the eyes too dark for the color of her hair, the lips too full; but there was a lush bloom about her that transcended the features, a suggestion of warmth and passion that men remembered long after they had forgotten the shape of her nose or the color of her eyes. It had been an effort for her to remain in love with the one absent person for five long years. That she had was possibly due to the fact that to her Traxal had been as much a symbol of freedom as he was of love.

She changed into fresh clothes and walked out onto the veranda, and the one-eyed man was sitting on the steps.

"I been up here thirty years," he said. "I was one of the first pilots they had up here. I used to fly Junkers into Bulolo. That was the first air lift in the world. Flew in everything—timber, houses, dredges for the mines, food, everything. I flew for fifteen years with only one eye and I never had a crash. A kanaka's arrow took my eye out back in '31. Like I said, I never had a crash. Then after the war the Civil Aviation johnnies, they come in here. They made me read a card on the wall, and when I couldn't, they said I couldn't see well enough to fly. So they grounded me. It's always the way, you know. The first thing progress eliminates is the pioneers." He looked out across the parade ground and the gorges to the airstrip on the distant ridge: a cloud shadow moved slowly up it like the ghost of a lost plane. "But I like the country, it gets you in, sort of, and I stayed on. There ain't many left like me. White men have been coming to this island since the beginning of the sixteenth century. Explorers first, then the sandalwood men and the blackbirders——"

"Blackbirders?"

"Yeah. Slavers, if you like. Oh, this was a great place for law-breakers back in the last century. A hundred years ago New Guinea was about the only safe place in the whole Pacific for blokes who had no respect for the law. Then the missionaries started to come in, and when they appear on the scene that's the end of it for the crims. They just give up in disgust and fade away. The crims hate the missionaries more than they do law and order."

"How do the natives feel toward the missionaries?" Elisabeth asked, thinking of Father Shawn, the little man who had the look of defeat in his face.

"It's a toss-up. You ask a missionary, a bloke who's been here for years, like Mike Shawn, for instance, ask him for an honest answer and I'll bet he'll shrug his shoulders and tell you he dunno whether he's made any real progress. Course, that ain't what he writes home to the bishops, oh my word, no. But I can back him up—it's a heartbreaking job trying to make Christians outa these kanakas. Putting 'em in Mother Hubbards don't make Christians of 'em."

Elisabeth knew what Mother Hubbards were: she had seen the shapeless dresses worn by some of the women down on the coast. "I haven't seen any of the women here in Mother Hubbards."

"The men would take 'em off the women and tear 'em up and use 'em to decorate themselves. These mountains are just like a fowl yard. It's the cocks who are the vain ones."

Then Traxal came down the path for her and she went up with him to the Macys' house. "What about him?" she said when they were out of earshot of Bermingham. "Does he eat with any of you?"

"Narvo has him up occasionally. He's got a native wife," Traxal said. "It's not a love match. I think Jack was just lonely and had nowhere to go. There are a lot of old-timers like him up here. Lonely and with nowhere to go. Some of them take native wives, others drink themselves to death. Jack treats his wife well and he loves his kids. But he lives on the other side of the fence, as it were. Joan Duggan, she's my nursing sister, and Bernice won't have him in their houses. The women are always the worst when it comes to drawing the color line. They take it as a personal affront if a man doesn't marry one of their own kind."

"I wouldn't," Elisabeth said. "Not if I knew it was the man's only alternative to loneliness. I know what real loneliness can be."

"That's all over now, darling," he said, and squeezed her hand. "You won't have to marry a black man."

She laughed, feeling a surge of happiness, and they went up the path toward the Macys' house. The post was laid out in a rough square about the grassy parade ground. On one side were the prison stockade and the police boys' huts; on the opposite side were the hospital and the sister's house. Against the slope of the mountain were Traxal's house, the Macys' house and the guest hut. At the end of the tiny plateau, looking out over the gorge, were Narvo's house, the cadet patrol officer's house, and the House Paper, the office and administration building. This last was perfectly round, its roof rising to a twisted cone.

"That was Narvo's idea," Traxal said. "With these mountain people a round house is a symbol of authority. That is the biggest round house for miles. It impresses the kanakas very much."

"Mr. Narvo seems a very impressive man," Elisabeth said, and looked at Traxal for reaction, but there was none.

Lunch, to begin with, was a gay affair. Even Traxal seemed to throw off the moodiness that Elisabeth had begun to fear might be habitual with him now; he was more like the Peter who had said good-by to her five years ago. Besides the Macys, at the lunch table there was also Frank Rossi, the cadet patrol officer. He was a short stocky lad, only just turned twenty, with dark crew-cut hair and a tan that made him almost as dark as the two houseboys who served the meal. He sat quietly looking at Elisabeth all through the meal, till his gaze began to embarrass her. Past attention from men had never embarrassed her; indeed, she had enjoyed it; but then Peter had not been sitting on the other side of the table, next to the man paying attention to her. It struck her only then that she did not know whether Peter was jealous or not.

"I'm sorry I can't offer you wine with lunch," Bernice said sitting at one end of the table, wrapping the party in a tinsel of words. "We can only bring in so much by the plane, and the men insist all the grog has to be beer except for a little rum and gin. Or Roy Narvo insists."

"If Bernice had to tramp these hills like Roy does," said Macy, sipping his beer, "she would realize that beer is more practical. A man needs to put the salt back into his system."

"Beer for medicinal purposes," said Bernice. "Some men will cook up any sort of excuse. I'd just like to escape just for a while back to Moresby. For some wine and a little bit of gracious living, for a change."

Macy almost choked on his beer with laughter; Bernice cut his throat with a glance. Then young Harry Macy said suddenly, "Miss Palyardi, did you have to escape from the Communists?"

He was a good-looking boy, and unless some woman spoiled him he would grow into a man unaware of his looks: he was a man's boy and he would be a man's man, and his idol right now was the big roaring-voiced man in the house across the parade ground. He was eleven years old and had all the frank curiosity of a child; but he was old enough to know he could hurt his father by being too frank in his worship of Narvo. And he did not want to hurt his father: his mother did enough of that. What troubled him and sometimes seemed sinful to him was that he loved both his mother and father, but did not worship them in the same way that he did Roy Narvo.

"You shouldn't ask such questions, Harry." Macy cleared his throat, getting the last of the beer out of it. He was a tall man and heavily built, but a good deal of his heaviness came from fat. He had begun drinking beer at an early age and now it had little more effect on him than water; but it had softened his flesh and given him a belly at which his wife constantly jabbed, both with her finger and with words. He had once been reasonably good-looking, but the sun and beer had mottled his complexion, and his jowls had thickened. He was balding quickly and over the past year he had taken to wearing a hat almost constantly, even when working in the hospital pharmacy. One of his few saving graces, in his wife's opinion, was his cleanliness and neatness. He shaved twice a day, his big freckled hands were as impeccably manicured as Bernice's own, and he changed his starched white shirt and shorts three times a day. It saved him from being a slob in his wife's eyes. "Miss Palyardi may not want to talk about it."

"No, I do not mind." Elisabeth recognized the terms of escape in which Harry thought. It was the way most people thought of escape: the flight through the darkness, the dash across the border, the dogs snapping at one's heels. She knew that was the way some people had escaped, that dogs were used on the borders of Germany and Austria, that barbed-wire fences ran for miles along the frontier and watchtowers crowned every hill; but no dogs had barked at her, no bullets had been fired at her, and at the airport the Customs officials had wished her a pleasant journey. After a long wait for her exit visa, she had been surprised at the ease and quickness with which her departure had been facilitated once the visa had been granted. She had first applied two years ago, right after her mother's death, but in the succeeding months, each time she had inquired how her application was faring, she had been brusquely told it was still under consideration. Then, suddenly, one day it was granted; a week later she was on the plane. In her happiness at the thought of rejoining Peter, her surprise had not turned into curiosity but had soon been forgotten. Over the past twenty years it had become a Czech habit never to query good fortune.

"No," she said, smiling at Harry. "They let me come."

"Why? Mr. Traxal had to escape, didn't you, Mr. Traxal?"

"It was different then, Harry." Traxal seemed embarrassed by the sudden turn in the conversation. He looked over Harry's head and said to Macy, "Roy wants to see us after lunch. You, too, Frank."

Harry recognized the rebuff. He dipped his head to his plate, biting his lips and red about the ears. Elisabeth felt an instant sympathy for the boy; why had Peter wanted to cut him off like that? He *had* had to escape, and dangerously: she remembered the long agonizing weeks of waiting before she heard that he had reached London and safety. She looked across at him, but his face was averted, as if he had expected her to query him and wanted to avoid the question. Then she saw that Rossi was still watching her, and she lowered her eyes to her own plate.

"That Roy!" Bernice's bosom jumped with annoyance in her low-cut dress. She and Macy had argued for years about the dresses she wore in front of the houseboys; he always lost the argument when she taunted him with the fact that it had been her revealing dresses that had attracted him to her in the first place. "He comes back, six weeks away, and back in the place an hour, and already issuing orders for people to see him. I'd like to give him a piece of my mind!"

"You already have, hon," said Macy. "It was water on a duck's back. He doesn't think women have minds."

Then Rossi said, "Are women respected in Czechoslovakia, Miss Palyardi?" He had a surprisingly deep voice for one so young, yet it went with the serious cast of his round, dark-eyed face. When he spoke he had a habit of biting his bottom lip, as if he regretted what he had said: it gave a tentative air to everything he said, as if one expected him to retract it.

"Now there's a good question!" Bernice cried. "Don't let me down, Elisabeth, even if you have to lie to him. They can't be less respected than they are in this part of the world!"

"I think we are respected," Elisabeth said to Rossi, knowing that *he* would respect a woman. "If you mean have things changed since the Communists took over—no, I do not think so. The Czech has always had time for his women." She looked across at Peter, testing him for jealousy; she felt perverse, but all at once she *wanted* him to be jealous. "I was never neglected in Prague."

He looked up, and she thought: he *is* jealous; and felt ashamed of herself, as if she had scored some sort of mean victory over him. Love, for five years, had been such an abstract thing; she was relearning that the desire to hurt is part of the act of loving. Traxal said, "Prague doesn't seem to have changed. I am glad of that."

Only she recognized the double edge to his voice. She knew then that what she had taken for jealousy in his face was something else again, another misery just as deep that went under the name of homesickness.

2

"I know these UN committees, Mike, I tell you. They come out here just looking for faults. I'm waiting for the day when one of them stands up in New York and criticizes us because we haven't yet taught the kanakas how to make the hydrogen bomb. The yoke of imperialism, they'll say. Denying the downtrodden black race the fruits of progress. All men are created equal for their own self-destruction."

"You're drunk," said Father Shawn.

"That's a priest for you. Never anything but the truth. Don't you ever get tired of the truth, Mike? Wouldn't you, just once, like to tell a whopping bloody great lie?"

"I've thought about it," said Father Shawn, telling a whopping bloody great lie. "You need more talent than I have."

Narvo filled his glass and threw the beer can over his shoulder. It hit the wall and dropped with a clatter onto the others that lay in the corner. "Paiwo! Where are you, you downtrodden black bastard?"

The houseboy came to the door that led from the kitchen, pushing aside the bead curtain and letting it fall with a soft hiss behind him. He was taller than the average mountain native and thicker in the chest and shoulders: muscles moved like snakes beneath his black skin. Tribal marks were cut into his cheeks and on both shoulders; cicatrices marked him like the hieroglyphics of manhood. There was a large hole in the septum of his nose, and holes in the lobes of his ears; without the pigtusk in the nose and the cane bangles in the ears, the pierced flesh somehow looked obscene. Narvo had brought him to the patrol post eighteen months ago, his blackpalm bow and arrows in his hand, his bark cloak hanging down his back, and his long hair caked with mud and laced with grass fiber. Now he carried a broom, wore a lap-lap, and his hair was cut close to his scalp and, under Narvo's orders, washed twice a week with kitchen soap.

He moved to the corner of the room and began to sweep the beer cans, rolling them across the room in front of the broom. Narvo looked over his shoulder at him. "Liklik Bandi? You tok i come!"

Paiwo shook his head. He had not succeeded in mastering

pidgin, although he could understand the gist of anything said in that language; he always replied to Narvo in his own dialect, a language of epiglottal sounds at which few white men, other than Narvo and Bermingham, had become expert. "My son is over at the village with his mother, Kiap. I shall bring him to this house in the morning."

He turned and went out of the room, his arms full of beer cans, the bead curtain hissing again as it fell into place behind him. In his bare brown arms the beer cans had a degrading look, but no expression showed on his scarred face: he had inherited ten thousand years of simple dignity.

"He's my prize exhibit for that UN party," said Narvo. "Eighteen months ago a head-hunter, now a cook, butler and valet. I haven't taught him anything yet about self-government, but what do they expect in two years? I've stopped him from eating his enemies—isn't that progress?"

"I can't remember if protection from being cannibalized is covered in the Bill of Human Rights," said Father Shawn. "Maybe it isn't an inherent right to remain uneaten."

"Have you seen the newspapers that came in today?" The question was rhetorical: everyone else got the newspapers only after Narvo had finished with them; it was one of the few selfish habits he had, as if he were trying to prove he was boss of the patrol post. "The Russians are yelling again for independence for New Guinea within ten years. And all the Red bloc and India and even some of the South Americans are backing them up. They're all talking through their necks. Colonialism has become such a bogey word, they can't see straight for it. A man with ten kids, he's an imperialist in their eyes. Mike, do you reckon you could trust those kanakas out in those mountains to govern themselves in ten years? As soon as we'd move out, they'd go back to bashing each other's brains out and eating each other. Out on this patrol I came across two kanakas who'd been cut up for Sunday joints."

He got up and began to move restlessly about the room. He fingered three spears fastened to the wall; he twanged the string of a bow fastened to another wall. He took down a stone club from a shelf and swung it: Father Shawn shuddered, hearing in his imagination the sickening sound of a skull cracking beneath the blow. Narvo brushed his hand against a *bilum* net bag of bones: Father Shawn knew they were leg bones of a cassowary, but they made the same sound as a rattling of human bones.

"I'd like a couple of weeks in New York at the UN. I'd get up and demand that India domesticate all its tigers in ten years. They'd have an easier job than we'll have civilizing these kanakas in ten years." Narvo drained his glass and dropped back into his chair. "I get tired, Mike. Sometimes I wonder if it's worth all the sweat and trouble. Who thanks us for it? Sometimes I feel like chucking it all in."

"Where would you go?" said Father Shawn quietly, lighting another cigarette.

Narvo shrugged. "That's it—where would I go? I'm like Jack Bermingham—I'm married to this country. I don't bed down with a black Mary and I haven't got a lot of little brindle bastards running around after me—but I'm married to it just as much as he is. More. I've got more responsibilities than he's got. And more conscience, damn it."

"I'm glad to hear that last bit."

"Don't raise your hopes, sport. I'm not clamoring to get back into the Church."

Father Shawn smiled and absentmindedly stroked the long scar on his cheek. He was not drinking tonight. He had had a touch of the shivers today and he wondered if he was in for another bout of malaria: he would pray for himself tonight and let the heathens look after themselves. He blew a plume of smoke up toward the gecko lizard on the rafter above his head; the gecko click-clicked as if in annoyance and slid up into the thatch out of sight. Narvo's three mongrel dogs lay in a heap by

the door, like a jumble of near-empty potato bags: every time
Narvo raised his voice their tails would thump the floor and they
would lift up their heads as if expecting him to throw them a
bone. Beyond the open door the mountain opposite was bathed
in bright moonlight; a scarf of pale-blue cloud encircled it and
on the upper ridges native fires burned like angry eyes. *I'm
married to this country, too,* Father Shawn thought; *even more
so than Roy. There is no divorce at all for me, and not just because of the Church.*

Narvo stood up and crossed to a small portable phonograph.
Despite the chill of the night air he wore only shirt and shorts;
his bare feet slithered softly on the pandanus leaf mat that covered the floor. He put a record on the turntable: Louis Arm-
strong playing "St. Louis Blues."

"There you are, Mike. Let's forget the UN. Our favorite piece
of music. Better than any of your national anthems and hymns.
More truth in it." He hummed the song in a flat, deep baritone.

"Don't talk like that, Roy. Let me enjoy it. Don't ask me to
compare it with sacred songs."

"Can you whistle a sacred song?" Narvo demanded. "No!
Well, there, you see!"

These two had been sparring for almost two years now, ever
since Father Shawn had followed Narvo into this Kundavi country and set up his mission. They had never come to open argument, although there were certain things on which they could
never agree. Narvo had once been a Catholic: he had admitted
that to Father Shawn almost at once and with some belligerence;
but Father Shawn had never pressed the point of reconversion:
he valued Narvo's friendship more than the latter's soul. It was
another of the secrets he contained within himself, a priest who
knew he had failed.

"What are you going to do about Miss Palyardi?" he said, to
change the subject.

"What can I do?" Narvo was prowling about the room again.

His big toes stuck up like horns; his large feet slap-slapped on the mat. His shirt was hanging out and occasionally he lifted it and scratched his belly. *He's a real hillbilly,* Father Shawn thought, *a New Guinea mountains hillbilly.* Yet he knew the extent of Narvo's education: the degree in economics that he held, and the paper he had been working on for the past twelve months to obtain his doctorate of philosophy; and he had experienced himself, and seen others embarrassed by, the cold analytical quality of Narvo's mind. Father Shawn knew that Peter Traxal's opinion of Narvo was wrong. The man was uncouth in manner and appearance, but twelve years of living on the far reaches of civilization hadn't helped him there. What Traxal had never appreciated, because he and Narvo had never reached a lasting point of communication, was that Narvo's mind was sophisticated and civilized to a high degree. The well-thumbed books on the shelves attested to that fact: a man could not remain untouched by Plato, Locke, de Montaigne. And only a highly intelligent and civilized man would be as unhappy as Narvo was in his sense of failure. For Father Shawn knew that Narvo also thought of himself as a failure.

"What can I do?" Narvo repeated. "I can't send her out. Not after the D.C. gave her permission to come in here. I'm in the gun enough with headquarters without shoving my neck out by countermanding the D.C.'s orders. This is no place for a woman, but I got kicked in the behind when I objected to Bernice and Joan Duggan coming in here."

"Bernice doesn't like it here. I feel sorry for Eric." Father Shawn lit another cigarette. "Have you ever thought of getting married?"

"Don't be bloody silly." Narvo walked to the door and stood looking out. The dogs stood up and rubbed themselves against his bare legs. Then, still looking out at the night, he said, "I did think of getting married, once. I don't think I was in love with the girl—it just seemed a good idea at the time."

"That's always a good basis for marriage," said Father Shawn. "Like taking a bath or having a beer."

"None of your blunt priestly sarcasm. Why is it all you priests have to be so unsubtle? Are you taught at the seminary never to credit the congregation with intelligence? The Church and Hollywood have a lot in common."

"About this girl," said Father Shawn, unruffled.

"Oh, her. I can't even remember what she looked like, except that she was a blonde. I think I'd make a bloody good husband for some girl, if ever I got around to it. At least I'd be faithful. That's something."

"You're talking to a priest, bub. I've been taught it's meant to be everything."

"Well, you want to come out of the cloisters, sport. That idea hasn't been fashionable since they gave up burning adulterers at the stake." He turned around, still leaning against the doorjamb. "I'd like to get married, Mike. I'm not dedicated to the chaste and lonely life, like you. But with me it's not just a question of finding the right girl. I have to find the right girl, the right time and the right place. I'm a man who wants his happiness to be perfect."

"Which means you'll never be happy on earth."

"And you could be right at that. But it means I shan't make anyone else *un*happy. I shouldn't like to lay the odds on that girl's chances of happiness with Peter." Then he looked over his shoulder. He had heard the boots on the gravel path a hundred yards away across the parade ground. In the clear mountain air sound traveled long distances, but even so Narvo's hearing was better than the average white man's; he had trained himself to hear like a bush native, and several times the sixth sense he had developed had saved his life. But there was no danger this time: he recognized the footsteps as those of Traxal. "Speak of the devil."

"I always do," said Father Shawn, rising and coming to the door. "Every Sunday."

"Not this one," said Narvo, and stepped out on to the veranda. "What's up, Peter?"

"Can you come down to the hospital?" Traxal halted at the bottom of the steps. His face was in shadow, but the urgency in his voice was plain. "One of the *kuru* patients has just been murdered."

3

"Eric found her. It was the woman we brought over this morning from the airstrip." The three men hurried across the parade ground, their shadows long before them. Narvo had pulled on his boots and was now tucking his shirt into his shorts; every now and again he uttered a short curse as Traxal told him what had happened: "The kanakas don't know of it yet. That's why I came up to tell you myself."

"Who killed her?" Narvo asked. "Someone from the post?"

"No. One of the other patients. You'll see."

Narvo cursed again, and led the way into the low long hut that was the hospital. The hut had sacsac walls, a *kunai*-thatch roof and an earth floor; the beds were boards laid on rough trestles, and each patient had two gray bush blankets. One end of the hut was screened off by a laced-cane wall; behind this were the *kuru* patients, silent but for an occasional high-pitched giggle. Eric Macy and Joan Duggan, the matron, stood beside one of the beds, talking in low voices. A bloodstained blanket covered the body on the bed, looking in the dim light of the electric globe like a mound of soft gray earth.

Macy looked up as Narvo and the others came into the *kuru* ward. "He bashed her head in, Roy. Just one blow. He didn't need any more."

"What did he do it with?"

"The usual." Macy held up a bloodstained stone club. "We didn't take it off him when he came in here. He had no record of being dangerous."

"All patients will be disarmed when they're admitted, from now on," Narvo said. "Tell 'em it's a new rule."

"Locking the stable door——" murmured Joan Duggan.

Narvo heard her, but said nothing. He knew she was right in a way, but he had always hesitated to take a mountain native's arms from him unless he had to: they would instantly suspect Narvo of treachery, and he had spent many patient months trying to build up their trust. But to explain that to Duggan would be a waste of time: she herself trusted no one, black or white.

Narvo looked around at the figures on the other beds. They lay like lumps of clay, misshapen figures that resembled the discarded models of an experimental sculptor: *if this is one of God's experiments*, Narvo thought, *I wonder what Mike thinks of it.* Light gleamed on dull eyes, as on blobs of jelly; a head rolled and for a moment a pair of eyes seemed to gleam with intelligence, but it was only a trick of the light. A grotesquely thin arm, patterned with tribal markings, rested on a blanket, thin and sheenless as a long-dead snake. A giggle sounded from one of the beds, as if the patient had remembered a long-forgotten joke; it went on, increasing to something that resembled a laugh, a laugh that chilled the blood of the silent white people; the wasted body shook convulsively, the arms threshing till it seemed they must snap off; then the laugh died abruptly away, and there was just a sound like labored hiccups. Then they, too, died away and there was just silence and the sweet-sour smell of dying flesh. Narvo, conscious always of the skull beneath the skin, the sigh of death as the echo of the shout, shivered a little and blinked in the dim light: the beer he had drunk was sour now in his mouth and he could feel it coming out of him in sweat. Death was familiar to him after twelve years in this country, but not so familiar that he had lost his fear of it nor his pity for those who suffered it.

"He didn't touch any of the others," Joan Duggan said, her voice rasping in the silence. She was in her mid-forties, a gray-haired woman whose face was her misfortune and who had a manner to match; she had long ago realized she had no natural charm and, matter-of-fact as she was, had given up the struggle of trying to develop any. She had been in New Guinea five years and would have been matron of one of the coastal hospitals if, like Narvo, she had not had a talent for treading on the toes of authority. It was the one thing she did have in common with Narvo. "But that doesn't say he won't if he gets the chance. Eric came in just in time to prevent what might have been a massacre."

"You're too imaginative," said Narvo, straight-faced, and Joan Duggan gave him a sour look: the exchanges between these two had the dry astringency of wit laced with malice. Each resented the other, but both realized the need of each other: authority and medical care were equal partners in the battle to win the natives away from such practices as the one that had brought the government officer and the nursing sister together right now. "Where is this bash artist?"

Narvo followed Duggan through into the other ward of the hut. Behind them Father Shawn had begun to pray over the dead woman. She had never been a mission native, but he prayed anyway: he was like a workman afraid of being sacked, keeping his nose to the grindstone just to earn his keep.

"There he is," said Duggan, and Narvo sat down on the empty bed beside the murderer's. He waved away the two native medical orderlies who had been standing guard, and waited till they had gone out of the hut.

"Do they know what this feller did?"

"No," Duggan said. "Dr. Traxal called them in and told them

to keep an eye on this man. They know there's been trouble, but they don't know what."

Narvo looked at the murderer. He was a man past middle age, his face and his whole upper body laced with scars: the dim light made a hatched pattern on the brown skin, so that he looked as if he wore a shirt of net. He did not look at Narvo as the latter scrutinized him, but stared down at his clasped hands, muttering to himself as if in prayer. From the other side of the screen came the whisper of Father Shawn's voice: the long hut murmured with the litany of Christian and pagan.

Narvo spoke to the man in dialect. "Why did you kill this woman?"

The native did not look up, but went on muttering. Narvo leaned closer, trying to catch what the man was saying. Then he stood up. "He's convinced all the *kuru* patients have got the evil spirit in them. What was he in here for?"

"He had a touch of pneumonia. But he's all right now. We were going to send him home tomorrow. He comes from Vaikaka."

Narvo bit his lip. "This changes the pattern a bit. Is the dead woman a Benamaua?"

"Naturally," said Duggan acidly. "Do you know of any other people that suffer from *kuru*?"

Narvo grinned at her, but without humor. "Have the Benamaua committed *tukavu* while I've been out on patrol?" Duggan shook her head, and Narvo looked back at the still-muttering native. He stared at the man for a while, still biting his lip. "This is the first time another tribesman has got in first. Up till now they have waited till the Benamaua have committed *tukavu*, then they've gone all out for revenge. I think this bloke must be a bit touched in the head."

"What are you going to do with him?"

"I'll lock him up in the bastille. Give him time to come to his senses and see then if he is soft in the nut."

"Are you going to charge him with murder?"

Narvo looked at her, his face expressionless. "What would you do? Have you been able to cure *kuru* with white man's medicine?"

"You know we haven't a clue even to what it is."

"Maybe this kanaka knows what it is. Maybe it *is* evil spirits. And how does white man's justice deal with evil spirits?"

"So you'll let him go?"

"I didn't say that. I shan't hang him, that's all. That was what you wanted, wasn't it?"

"You've got to teach them a lesson," Duggan said, felt in her pocket for her glasses and remembered she had left them in her office: she peered myopically up at Narvo, smelling the beer on his breath and hating it, annoyed that she couldn't tell whether he was joking with her or not.

"He won't learn anything if I hang him. Nothing of any lasting value."

"Don't joke about such things, Narvo. You treat them all too soft. We might all be murdered in our beds one night."

"What evil spirit inhabits you?" said Narvo, and Duggan turned and went back to the *kuru* ward, her starched white uniform swishing angrily. Narvo *did* treat the natives too softly and they *would* all be murdered one day: she would almost welcome an attack upon herself just to prove Narvo wrong.

Narvo walked to the door and bellowed for Sergeant Beraki. Before the sergeant appeared two police boys who had been on picket duty materialized out of the moonlight. They saluted smartly, thumping their bare feet into the gravel path: they enjoyed the ceremony of a police boy's lot as much as the authority. They stood waiting for orders, but Narvo gave them none. He knew how much Sergeant Beraki was a stickler for protocol: the senior natives were born public servants in that respect. Beraki came loping across the parade ground, buckling on his leather as he ran: he would as soon be caught without his lap-lap as without his police belt and strap. He came to a foot-stamping halt and threw up a salute that would have bruised a less-hard head.

Narvo was both amused and impressed, but he kept a straight face; Beraki took himself too seriously, but he could be depended upon. Narvo jerked a thumb at the muttering native in the ward. "Bringim man ia long kalabus. Em i kilim i dai pinis wanpela meri."

"Yes, Kiap." Beraki saluted again, and barked an order at the police boys. The latter showed no surprise at what Narvo had said. Murder was part of their natural climate: they had probably indulged in tribal killings themselves before they had become police boys. They moved into the hut, roughly took the Vaikaka native by his arms and bundled him out of the hut and across the parade ground to the stockade. The murderer went without a struggle, still muttering to himself, still lost in the trance that had prompted him to kill the woman inhabited by the evil spirit. Sergeant Beraki saluted again and followed the police boys and the prisoner across the parade ground. There had been no surprise, no queries, no fuss: *oh, for a couple of these boys on that UN party*, Narvo thought. But life was never so simple as that, and he shrugged and turned as Traxal and Father Shawn came out of the hut. A moment later the three of them were joined by Eric Macy.

"I'll send word down in the morning for the relatives to come and pick up the body," Macy said. "They're not going to like it when they hear how she died."

"Why don't we just bury her ourselves?" Traxal said.

"They'd dig her up," Narvo said irritably: Traxal had never made any attempt to understand how the native mind worked. "We'd better cook up another story. Say she went mad and tried to kill this bloke from Vaikaka and he had to bash her head in to protect himself. They believe in the evil spirits just as much

as he does. That's why they were glad enough to send her up
here till she died."

"What are you now?" said Duggan, who had come to the door
of the hut. "Counsel for the defense as well as prosecutor and
judge? Very versatile."

Narvo sounded more patient than he felt. "All I'm trying to
do is avoid trouble, at least till this UN party has come and gone.
Justice can wait."

"You are beginning to sound like a dictator also," said Traxal.

"Maybe that's what this Territory needs. It's an uphill battle
for anyone who believes in democracy. Sukarno can't get it to
work over in Indonesia, and the Indonesians are two thousand
years ahead of these kanakas here. Democracy doesn't recognize
killing as a social custom. These kanakas do. For the time being,
I'm going to play the game their way. They don't recognize the
merit of truth, so I'm not going to waste my time telling them
the truth. I'm going to be a bigger bloody liar than Ananias."
He looked carefully at the three men and Duggan. "And you're
all going to be liars with me. Understand?"

Duggan, Father Shawn and Macy hesitated, then all nodded
their heads. Narvo looked at Traxal. "Well, Peter?"

"It will depend upon what the UN committee asks me," said
Traxal slowly.

"What about your medical report?"

"I shall report only on the woman's death. I do not have to
tell *why* the kanaka killed her. You forget, Roy—I am not yet an
Australian. I cannot afford to tell lies, not on official matters.
Not if I want to become a naturalized Australian."

Narvo did not miss the mockery in the quiet voice, but he
knew that Traxal had him beaten. The federal government, new
to such authority, handed out naturalization papers as if they
were Queen's Birthday honors; a man who lied couldn't possibly
be accepted as an Australian, even though the greatest confidence
men, the most professional liars of all, had been Australians.

Narvo had never been convinced that Traxal wanted to be an Australian, but this was least of all not the time to ask a man if his intentions were honest. It might be one time when Traxal would feel justified in lying.

"All right," Narvo said. "Just don't say anything to the kanakas, that's all. Can you stretch your conscience that far?"

"It has been stretched before," said Traxal, "on your behalf."

4

ELISABETH LAY in her bed, listening to the sounds in the roof of the guest hut and, across the parade ground, the murmur of the voices by the hospital. She heard Narvo yell for Sergeant Beraki, and she felt a shiver of fear: shouts in the night in Prague had always meant trouble. She got up, putting on her trenchcoat over her nightgown against the chill of the air; she had been surprised to find how cool the night was here in these tropic mountains. She went out on to the veranda and in the bright moonlight that was almost like early daylight saw the four men coming across the parade ground. Traxal detached himself from the group and came toward her.

"What is it, Peter?" She could not help the fear in her voice: once, it had been an habitual note. "What is wrong?"

"Nothing, darling, nothing." He put his arm about her and led her back into the hut. "One of the *kuru* patients has been killed."

"That is nothing?" She looked at him, afraid again of a tasteless joke: she remembered his conversation about the woman dying of *kuru* and his comment that they must hurry back for lunch.

"It *is* something, darling. But it happens often here in these mountains. We become used to it." He practiced the lie on someone who would never recognize it. "The woman went mad and attacked another of the patients. He killed her to defend himself."

"A woman? Was that the woman we brought over this morning?" He nodded; and then she said, "But where did she come by the strength to attack a man? You said she would never come out of her coma."

He kissed her, unable to think up another lie on the spur of the moment. He felt another sudden spasm of anger toward Narvo: the man who ran his whole life, even bending Traxal's ethics to suit his own ideas of how to deal with the kanakas. "I have given up trying to understand or anticipate the kanakas. They are Narvo's concern."

She took off her coat and lay down beneath the blankets again. He sat on the bed beside her and she put her hands up and held his face in them. "Oh, my dear. I thought the time would never come. It has been so long——"

"Did you ever give up hope?" He kissed the palm of her hand and ran his own hand down her bare arm. He felt beneath the thin nightgown for her breast, and was relieved when she did not push his hand away. They had been lovers before he had left Prague, and he could still remember details of their last night together five years ago. But now they were like lovers newly met; or worse still, divorced lovers trying to start over again. He remembered her passion, but what if she had changed? The cynic who had described love-making as an act of chemistry was closer to the truth than he had meant to be: it had all the unpredictability of a chemical experiment.

"Once or twice I almost gave up." She was more practiced in lying than he, had had to be to survive; but it never entered her head to lie to him now.

"I used to wonder what you were doing. I can still remember what we used to do together." She smiled at him in the dim light of the room, putting her hand on his as it held her breast, and he said, smiling back at her, "No, not only this. The other ordinary things."

They would walk over the Charles Bridge, dawdling beneath the statues that lined each rampart of the bridge. They would stand beneath Brokoff's group of St. John of Matha, St. Felix of Valois and St. Evan. It was not the saints who had interested them, but the pensive figure of the Turk leaning on the pedestal: within the pedestal itself, as within a cave, Christians writhed in stony agony, but the Turk looked into the distance, undisturbed by their cries, dreaming of some Turkish delight.

They would walk over the bridge, past the long stone pageant of saints that the Communists had not dared remove because they were as much part of Prague as the Vltava that flowed beneath the bridge. They would stand looking down on the Certovka, the Venice of Prague, and dream of someday owning a house whose front garden would be just a quiet stretch of water in which only reflections flowered. Then they would climb through the sun and shadows of the twisting streets to the Cathedral of St. Vitus: the saint, one of the Fourteen Holy Helpers, had never helped them very much, they would cynically comment. They would lean on the wall there, looking out over the domes and spires, the landmarks of religion that had now only become symbols of the past, and love the city as much as they loved each other. Prague was part of them and they were part of Prague: they were brother and sister to the Good Soldier Schweik. In those days they had not believed that they and the city could ever be separated. They were not the first who were to find out that the one thing not marked on the map of a city is the imprint of its citizens.

"I cannot ever forget Prague." He lay down on the bed beside her, he above the blankets, she below them: the blankets separated them like five years of forgotten intimacy. He said, not looking at her, "Was there anyone else, darling?"

Something landed with a thump on the roof, and she jumped with fright. "A cus-cus," he said. "Like a small possum."

"It frightened me," she said, but she had been more startled by his question. In the roof thatch a gecko lizard clicked monotonously, like a loud cheap clock: one hoped for it to break down and stop, but it never did. In her room in the house in Prague there had been a rat that had made itself heard in the ceiling every night; whether it was the same rat or not, she never knew, but every night for five years it had been there in the ceiling, scratching away as if at time itself.

"No," she lied: how could she tell him that what the other men had given her had not been love but only respite from fear and loneliness? There had been only two, two lovers in five of her ripest years. Promiscuity was not a matter of degree, she would not excuse herself on that point, not even to herself; but she had no intention of telling Peter of the two men, nor of asking him if there had been any women for him in the past five years. Those years contained enough bad memories; why add ghosts to them? "No, Peter, there were no others."

He stood up and began to take off his clothes. She watched him in the dim light of the room; he could have been a stranger, and all at once she was afraid again. But she could not deny herself to him. She had not denied him in Prague; how could she say no to him now? Morality did not enter into it: they had both grown up in a time when morals had become devalued, like the coinage of a realm that had crashed. She wanted to be loved, was hungry for it, and she could not understand the sudden trembling doubt that had assailed her.

He was gentle at first, but he had waited too long. He was with her suddenly, almost brutally, and with something like despair she surrendered. She tried to answer his passion, but it was only with her body; her mind remained cold, a spectator of the act of love. When he had finished she pulled his face to hers and kissed him savagely, but it was a deceit: she was like the traitor who cheers loudest of all in the moment before he shoots the king. Then she was crying, and again she had to lie: "I'm so happy, Peter."

He lay beside her stroking her face. He was exhausted and wanted to sleep, but he forced himself to caress her, gentling the passion he had aroused in her: where was it he had read that all men are liars in the act of love? Did one really only love up to the moment of consummation, then have to begin falling in love all over again? Conscience pricked him (he smiled to himself at the thought, and was ashamed: love was not a matter for joking; one could joke about sex but not about love), and tried to revive some of the love that lay exhausted within him. He kissed her, as passionately as she had kissed him, and dug his fingers into her flesh; they lay together, liars who didn't recognize the lies of each other. The fragility of love, he thought, was never more apparent than in bed. "I love you, Elisabeth."

"Darling, I love you." In the roof the gecko lizard clicked: disapprovingly? she wondered. Up on the hill behind the huts she could hear the hum of the generator; it faltered for a moment, like a missed heartbeat, then went on. It reminded her of how much was improvised here on the patrol post; and she wondered if love could be improvised. "You had better go. We must not fall asleep."

Wanting to do nothing else but sleep, he reluctantly slid out of bed and began to dress. Across the parade ground a phonograph was playing; he recognized a blues tune, the only sort of music Narvo played. When he had first come here and learned that Narvo had a phonograph, he had looked forward to some shared hours of perhaps Bach or Beethoven; but he and Narvo had not been able to agree even on their choice of music, and for eighteen months now he had been listening to music that offended his ear as much as the singing of the mountain natives.

He bent and kissed her again; reawakening desire held him like a rope to her bed. "Must I go?"

"Please, Peter." She kissed him back, and he made no further argument. He went out of the hut, closing the door softly behind him, and she heard his footsteps going away down the gravel path. A voice challenged him and she heard him say something in pidgin. She giggled, comparing the police boy to the matron at the university: she remembered the night she had been held up in the corridor outside the dormitory, when the matron, shocked as an abbess, had demanded to know with whom she had been. The matron had been a staunch Communist, and staunch Communists were often rabidly puritanical. The police boy barked his challenge now and Peter reassured him; but she wondered if the native was puritanical and what he would think of white men who stole out of white women's huts in the middle of the night. Were promiscuity, fornication and adultery frowned upon by these people or were they only sins against civilized convention? She would ask Peter in the morning.

Then she knew that she would not ask him. Something made her—ashamed?—of what she had just done. It wasn't the act itself. She was not promiscuous, she told herself, but virtue had never been one of her vices: it was an old and worn joke between Peter and herself, one she doubted he would remember. No, she was ashamed because, even while she had been with Peter, it was as if she had been unfaithful to him. *I didn't love him,* she thought with something akin to horror. *I accepted his love, gave myself to him, the physical pretense, and I didn't love him in return.* It had happened before, with the two men in Prague; but that had been different, she told herself. The men had not loved her and she had not loved them: there had been no deceit there. But she had deceived Peter. All at once she began to weep, and was further ashamed because she knew the tears were as much for herself as for him. For she knew that her journey had been in vain, she had waited five years and come ten thousand miles to exchange one loneliness for an even greater one among these wild mountains. She no longer loved Peter.

She heard footsteps on the gravel and heard the police boy bark another challenge; he was answered by a voice that she recognized as that of the American priest. Then she heard the priest go on up the road, whistling. He had a beautiful whistle, and the song he whistled was a strange one for a priest, sad and profane: *St. Louis Blues. I hate to see the evening sun go down* . . .

Did the priest, too, have a sadness and loneliness that came to him only in the night?

2

Michael Shawn zipped his old army jacket up to the neck and walked up the road toward his mission. It was cool tonight and he liked cool nights; they were good nights for whistling. And they reminded him of home: the nights when, as a boy, he had gone for walks along the shore at Woods Hole. But Cape Cod was another life away: *whistle me up a memory,* went the words of a popular song; but it was hard to do even that.

He whistled now, but he was hardly aware of what he was whistling: the tune could have been any blues tune, but the sadness was his own. Tonight he had been witness to the disintegration of a man, or anyway the beginning of it. Narvo was losing the battle to which he had dedicated himself. . . .

"They've given me notice, Mike. I didn't tell you, it was in the mail today. Unofficial notice, that is. Neil Figgins sent me a private little note." Figgins was the district commissioner at Goroka, the senior officer in the area. "This UN crowd has got Moresby and Canberra jumpy. If the UN party doesn't like what it sees when it gets here, I'm going to be the bunny. I get the boot and someone else comes in here."

"They can't do that," Father Shawn had said. "They just can't do it, Roy."

"They can and they will, sport, make no mistake about it. My

record goes against me—I've trodden on too many toes because
I haven't worked according to the book."

"What will you do if they do transfer you?"

"I dunno. Leave the service, become a beachcomber, go prospecting with old Jack, I dunno. I love these bloody kanakas,
Mike!" he said fiercely, and went out through the bead curtain
into the kitchen. Father Shawn heard him at the kerosene re-
frigerator, then he came back with an armful of beer cans. "I
go out to their villages like on this patrol, and I see the poor
beggars living and dying like animals. Rotten with t.b. Kids
with bellies swollen by too much *kau-kau* because they've got
nothing else to eat. Women torn out of shape by bad births or
too many births. Babies with their limbs burnt off because they
rolled into the fire in the dog-kennel huts they live their whole
lives in. Men with bloody great scars disfiguring them, scars
they got fighting because fighting is the only thing that relieves
their miserable bloody existence. I want to help them! I don't
mean civilize them or Christianize them—I'm not a missionary
like you, I don't even agree that what you're trying to bring
them is what they want, is any good for them. All I want to do
is help them live better—and everybody is against me! The busy-
bodies in Canberra who couldn't tell the difference between a
Kukukuku and a boy from the Trobriands, the stinking nationalist
prejudice of some members of these UN committees who see
New Guinea only as a question of whites and blacks, even the
ignorance of the kanakas themselves! Here is this UN crowd
coming in here demanding some evidence that the kanakas are
being civilized—and here's the kanakas themselves setting the
clock back to taws, killing because of bloody evil spirits, wiping
out everything I've tried to teach them in the two years and a
half I've been here!"

He drank savagely from his glass; Father Shawn almost expected him to bite on it. A huge moth tried to commit suicide
against the electric globe; it fell onto Narvo's shoulder, then to

the floor, but he didn't notice it. Father Shawn had the feeling the roof could have fallen in and Narvo would not have noticed it.

"There must be some other job a man can do! Something where he sees some return for what he does!" He shook his head, and there were tears in his eyes, something Father Shawn had never seen before. He stood in the center of the room, a huge unkempt figure, his hair hanging down over his brow, his face shining with sweat, his shirt wide open and his massive chest a glistening mat of black hair: he looked as if he possessed no more feeling for humanity, white or black, than an ancient slave driver. He raised his arm and hurled the glass across the room; it exploded against the doorjamb and glass fragments sprayed like shrapnel about the room. "You're a priest! Tell me—was this how Christ felt?"

The question was rhetorical: it could have been melodramatic, even ridiculous, in anyone less serious about his work. But then Father Shawn knew the extent of Narvo's dedication to his job: he was a secular missionary, as committed as Father Shawn himself to his own doctrine. There was no other job for Narvo but this one.

"Who knows how Christ felt? If I'd known, I might have achieved my own ambition." He lit another cigarette and picked a crumb of tobacco from his tongue. Dispirited by the other man's dejection, he felt in the mood for confession: a failure who recognized a kindred soul. "I wanted to be a saint, I ever tell you?"

Narvo was searching for another glass. "I never wanted to be anything. You never met such an ambitionless bastard. Where are the bloody glasses? Paiwo!"

"He's gone home," said Father Shawn, and thought: *even a kanaka is more fortunate than I am, even he can go home.* Even Jack Bermingham, the derelict, who had come to dinner earlier in the evening, had gone *home:* a grass hut, a native wife and three half-caste children, but *home* still. "My birthday is St. Patrick's Day. A big day among the Irish in Massachusetts. I took it as an omen that I was going to be a saint, too. Was I saintly! I must have driven people out of their heads with my damned holiness!"

"You're not holy, Mike." Narvo had found another glass and was pouring beer into it. "Don't kid yourself, sport."

"You think I do? I know what I am, Roy. Not even a good priest, let alone a saint. I stay on here as a missionary because I'm too damned scared to go back where a civilized congregation would recognize me for what I am. A failure. My only consolation is that I know God's mercy extends to failures."

"Move over, sport. The queue for failures forms on the right."

Father Shawn looked up at the big man standing over him. "You're in the wrong queue, Roy. You're not a failure so long as you're still battling on."

"Aren't you still battling on?"

Father Shawn shook his head. "I'm just a good actor. You gotta be if you're going to make any sort of show as a priest. Why do you think I stay on here at Kundavi? Because I'm winning the battle to convert the heathen?" He shook his head again. "I stay on here because Kundavi is about as remote as I can get from Cape Cod. My conscience worries me, but I manage to live with it—which only goes to prove further that I'd never have made it as a saint."

Narvo patted Father Shawn's scrawny shoulder, a comforting pat that was more like a punishing thump: there would be a bruise there tomorrow as a mark of his sympathy. "You poor miserable little bastard! You're worth a dozen of those plump sanctimonious coots in their pulpits back home. You want a good word said for you with the Lord, you let me know, sport. There'll be no hellfire for you while I'm around."

He was drunk now. He had forgotten his own problems; he had searched in the bottom of his glass and found oblivion. In another five minutes he would be maudlin, ready to weep and to curse the world for Father Shawn's troubles. The latter recognized the moment, and he recognized the cause of it. The crack in Narvo's control had not been caused by despair over Father Shawn's troubles, but over his own. He was ready now to weep for anyone, to camouflage the tears for himself.

Father Shawn stood up, butting his cigarette. "Come Judgment Day, Roy, I'll call on you. Look for me at the bottom end of the line of Christians, down among the tax-deducting philanthropists, the God-is-on-our-side statesmen, and the other hypocrites."

Narvo threw an arm about the priest's shoulders; he leaned on the small man as they walked to the door, and Father Shawn had difficulty in remaining upright. "We'll form our own bloody line, Mike!" His words were slurred and he spoke belligerently: he would have picked a fight with the first man who walked in the door. "Me and you and maybe one solitary kanaka, if we can find one, just to say a good word for both of us——!"

He stood in the doorway of the house, waving to the priest as the latter went up the path to the road that led up to the mission. A string of flying-foxes cracked the face of the moon, and on the mountain across the gorge a scream rent the silence: a bird, a human, nobody cared. Over in the hospital hut a light still burned: Joan Duggan sat there, dead as the murdered *kuru* patient. *Another failure,* thought Father Shawn; but felt no pity for her as he did for the battered giant still standing in the doorway of the House Kiap.

A police boy stepped out of the shadow of a rain tree, and Father Shawn answered his challenge.

"Yu pela sambai long Kiap," he said, telling the police boy to take care of Narvo, and the native's answering smile was a white dagger in the gloom.

Father Shawn went on up the road, whistling the song that was his and Narvo's hymn. *Oh God,* he prayed, and the tears came to his eyes, *save Roy from failure.*

5

ELISABETH STOOD on the veranda and watched the morning mist rise out of the gorges. The sun was already bright on the mountain opposite; a native fence of newly shaved pickets hung like a golden ladder down the mountainside. Elisabeth looked at her watch: eight o'clock; then tried to remember what day it was and couldn't. She was having her first taste of the anonymity of days in the wilderness. There were only yesterday, today and tomorrow: the pioneer and the prisoner had that in common, they were without need of a calendar. She could not think of herself as a pioneer, and she knew that she was no longer a prisoner. It suddenly became important to know what day it was, as if by knowing she would give herself identity. A police boy went past and she said, "What day is it?"

He stopped, saluted and shook his head. He said something in pidgin: he might just as well have spoken in Chinese. Then Harry Macy appeared beside him, trailing a young but large bird on a rope. "What you want, Miss Palyardi?"

"I asked him what day it was."

"He wouldn't know, even if he could understand you." He spoke in pidgin to the police boy, who grinned broadly, saluted and marched off. "What you wanna know the day for?"

Her answer would appear ridiculous, even to a small boy. "I —oh, it is not important. What is that?"

"This? Oh, it's a cassowary." He held out his hand and the bird put its head in it, as a dog might do. "Roy brought him back from the coast for me. I gotta watch him, though. He's a bad-tempered bugger."

He used the word unself-consciously: somehow it didn't even sound vulgar on the young lips. He had gone to the limit in his worship of Narvo: he spoke like his hero without realizing it. Elisabeth didn't know the meaning of the word, but she had heard the British consul in Prague use it when angry, and she guessed it was one of Narvo's swearwords.

"I'm going down to the salt-making. You wanna come?" He was self-conscious in his invitation: strange white women were part of the great outside world.

"The salt-making?" Elisabeth said, and stepped down off the veranda.

"Better put your hat on. The sun can burn holes in your skull if you ain't used to it." She put on the straw hat she had bought at the Chinese store in Moresby; and the three of them, the woman, the boy and the cassowary, walked down the path. "Yeah, there's a salt spring down in the gorge. Roy says what the kanakas do with it, it only goes to prove they're just as intelligent as we are. Roy says——"

A procession was coming down a side path from the hospital. Four men carried a rough litter on which lay a blanket-covered body. The men were walking slowly, singing as they went; a song that had no music and seemed to have no words, but was full of an ineffable sadness: the song was abrasive, rubbing against the ear of memory, telling of the devil that danced in everybody's sleep. Behind the litter half a dozen women and children walked, keening the same song. At the rear walked a figure that Elisabeth at first had difficulty in recognizing: gray, misshapen, something inhuman and frightening. Then as the

procession came closer Elisabeth saw that the figure was that of
an old woman thickly coated from head to foot in gray mud.
She looked like something primeval, risen out of the slime of
ages, out of the dead gray mud of a million graves. The gray
mud caked her hair, her face, the whole of her body and her
limbs: she carried the smell of the grave with her. Wound
round and round her neck and covering her chest were strings
of gray seeds; from her chin to below her breasts she looked as
if she were covered in cheap chain mail. She sagged beneath
the weight of the beads, but made no attempt to ease the burden
of them by taking the load of them on her arms. As she went
past, Elisabeth noticed that even the old woman's lips and eye-
lashes were caked with the gray mud.

"She's the mother of the woman who was killed last night,"
said Harry. "That's how the women show they're in mourning,
they paint 'emselves with that mud. She pongs, don't she? Those
seeds, they call 'em Job's Tears. She'd have fifty yards of 'em
strung round her neck."

He watched the funeral procession go on down the path ahead
of them, untouched by what he saw, another one acclimatized
to death. Elisabeth was suddenly angry at the boy for his indifference; then just as abruptly she realized it was not his fault.
He had been brought up in this country and he had learned by
instinct how to live with it. It might not be right by the standards of a civilized world, but this boy, with his pet cassowary,
his rough words and his familiarity with pagan death rites, was
a stranger to a civilized world. Elisabeth was glad she had not
let her momentary anger show; she had the feeling this small
boy was going to be her friend, and she was in need of friends.
He looked up at her and smiled wryly.

"That didn't upset you, did it? I'm sorry if it did——"

"I have to get used to such things, Harry."

"Yeah, that's right. Roy says that's the only way in New
Guinea, you gotta get used to everything in it. Roy says——"

Harry talked about Narvo all the way down the steep winding path into the gorge. They passed natives working in the precipitous gardens, heaping the soil into mounds beneath which the sweet potato, *kau-kau*, grew. Small patches of corn waved greenly in the bright sun; banana palms were a wild hedge bordering one garden. Some of the gardens were fenced with *tangket* stakes and these had taken root: the fence grew its own leaves, so that it looked like a long thin line of bush running down the slope. *Pit-pit*, wild sugar cane, waved gracefully, like dancers' arms, in the breeze that blew up from the gorge. They passed beneath a dripping outcrop of rock, and Harry, thrusting the cassowary's string into Elisabeth's hand, clambered up the rock and returned with a bright pink flower.

"It's an orchid," he said, handing it to her. "Mum likes to wear 'em in her hair."

"I'll wear it here," she said, pinning it with a brooch to the bosom of her blouse. "If I take my hat off, I may get holes burned in my skull."

He grinned, and they went on down the path: they were friends. Natives called to Harry and he answered their greeting with a casual wave of his hand, sure of his place among them: an eleven-year-old Kiap. By the time they reached the bottom of the gorge they were expected: all the way down the mountain the word had gone ahead in a telegraph of ululant voices, crying in the tongue without consonants that the mountain natives use as the mountain people of another land use the yodel. Down at the bottom of the gorge the roar of the cascading river drowned any other sound, but somehow the message had got through, even though Elisabeth knew no one had run ahead of them down the path. She had read of the telepathic gift of certain wild peoples, but even now she found it incredible. She would ask Peter about it. Then she knew that if she wanted to learn anything about this country and its people, Peter would be the last one she should ask. She would have to ask someone who had

learned to live with the country, had become used to it. Someone like Harry or Jack Bermingham. Or Roy Narvo.

They turned off the path and clambered over shining black
rocks to the spring. Elisabeth was soaked, both from perspiration brought on by the walk down the steep path and by the
mist that hung in the bottom of the gorge, but she soon forgot
the dampness of her clothes in her interest in what she had
come to see. Women, dressed only in sporran-like skirts of grass,
their dark skins glistening so that every movement they made
caused a small accident of light, were the only workers at the
spring. They came down in a long file from a path across the
river, crossed a swaying vine-rope bridge, and with huge bundles of grass balanced precariously on their heads came sure-
footed over the rocks to the spring.

"That's kangaroo grass." Harry had to shout above the roar
of the river. "They bring it from away up there." He pointed
to a spur that ran out from a distant mountain. "Three hours
walk. Roy says——"

But Elisabeth didn't hear what Roy said. She had turned
away, too engrossed in what she was witnessing, amazed at the
ingenuity and the patience of these wild people. The women
brought their loads of grass to the spring, and each woman
dropped her bundle of grass into the long trough cut in the rock
below the spring. She would then move on, pick up a soaking
bundle of grass from farther down the trough, and carry it up
to a small flat clearing above the mist of the river and which
looked as if it would be in the path of the sun for most of the
day. Harry motioned to Elisabeth and, still trailed by the cassowary, he led her up the short steep path to the clearing. Pandanus palms backed the clearing, and their glistening green
fronds contrasted sharply with the barren red earth of the clearing. In Elisabeth's eye the black figures of the women added
to the color of the scene; white people would have spoiled it,

made it anemic and without the drama that the dark figures somehow gave it.

"That's Paiwo's wife," Harry said, and pointed to a woman who seemed to be the supervisor of what went on here in the clearing. "Paiwo is Roy's houseboy. These people come from Vaikaka."

The woman looked across at them and smiled shyly. She was a small sturdy woman, well proportioned and cleaner-looking than the other women. When Paiwo had first come home from the patrol post and told her that she should bathe more frequently, she had accused him of learning bad habits from the Kiap: if she washed off the pig grease and the dirt, she would die of cold. But Paiwo had insisted, telling her that if he, on the Kiap's orders, had to wash every day, then she, Kabu, and the child, Bandi, were also going to wash every day. It had taken her some time to become accustomed to the frequent washing, and sometimes when she shivered in the chill morning air, the members of her sub-clan, smug and warm in their pig grease and dirt, sat and smirked at the woman who tried to ape the foolish customs of the white people. Only once had she been the envy of the other women: Paiwo had brought home a bottle of perfume he had stolen from Bernice Macy's house, and Kabu had doused herself in it and for three days, remaining unwashed despite Paiwo's threats, had gone around smelling like a tree-load of orchids.

But washed or unwashed, she was still the best woman worker in Vaikaka, better even than Kerami, the wife of the fight-leader, Wangamunggu. She made the best salt here in the mountains, and the salt had made Vaikaka the richest village for miles around. Aware now that she was being watched by the boy Harry and the new white woman, she went about the task of supervising the salt-making with an added air of pride and authority. The other women looked at her resentfully, but said nothing. She was Paiwo's wife and Paiwo was the Kiap's houseboy and the Kiap had his own way of dealing with quarreling women. They would get their own back on Kabu when the boy Harry and the white woman had gone.

They brought up the bundles of grass dripping with the salt water from the spring and laid them out in neat rows in the bright sunlight. Then they picked up bundles that were already dry and carried them across to the fire, burning at one end of the clearing. This fire was kept low and burning only in the one place; the grass was fed slowly into the fire and never allowed to blaze. On the other side of the rock-ringed shallow pit that was the fireplace, other women were carefully scooping up the dry ash of yesterday's fire and carrying it to troughs cut in another large rock. These troughs were lined with banana leaves, and the ash was laid on these. Then water was poured slowly on to the ashes, dripping out of bamboo pipes, and the water, carrying the salt from the ashes of the burnt kangaroo grass, dripped through matted fiber strainers at the ends of the troughs into hollowed-out rock pans set above low fires. The water boiled and evaporated and the salt, the wealth of Vaikaka, was left like gray-white gold in the bottom of the rock pans.

"It takes a long time," Harry said. "But Roy says these kanakas have all the time in the world. He says the one civilized thing he don't wanna bring into these mountains is a clock. You know, he don't own a clock or a watch."

"Do you own one, Harry?"

"No," he said, and Elisabeth knew that he wouldn't, at least not till Narvo owned one.

Elisabeth sat down on a rock and lit a cigarette. The women tramped by her, looking at her out of the corners of their eyes. She felt pity for them, but she knew, without being told, that they would not understand nor want her pity. Aged by work and hardship, their breasts slack and cumbersome, their legs and feet covered in sores, some of them already halfway to death with tuberculosis, they had no pity for themselves: this was their life and they knew no other. Elisabeth wondered how they would have reacted to life in Prague, and for a moment felt a stab of shame. She had hated the life there, but at least it had been *living*. This was only existence.

She looked up across the gorge to the top of the path that wound up the steep mountainside. The funeral party had come down into the gorge, crossed the bridge, climbed the path and now stood at the top resting. The litter-bearers had put the corpse of the murdered woman down on the ground, and the bead-burdened, mud-encrusted mother stood above it, like the materialized figure of some spirit from the Spirit Land to which the woman had gone. A small band of men carrying spears and bows and arrows came up from the other side of the ridge on which the funeral party stood, and the whole group stood looking down on the women working at the salt spring.

Elisabeth touched Harry's arm and pointed. The boy looked casually up across the gorge, squinted and remained staring, then abruptly straightened up and yelled something in dialect. The women stopped, looked up across the gorge, and all at once screamed and began to run.

The men with the spears and bows and arrows were already halfway down the path, running swiftly toward the junction of the two paths on the other side of the vine-rope bridge, the one path that led to Benamaua, the village of the dead woman, and the other path that led to Vaikaka, the village of the man who had murdered her. Vengeance came down into the gorge like another, thicker mist.

2

Bernice Macy watched Harry and Elisabeth disappear down the path to the gorge. The Czech woman had a slow, graceful walk, the sort of walk which Bernice wished she herself could cultivate; she knew, even as she wished, that she was possessed of too much nervous energy ever to do anything slowly and gracefully. As Elisabeth disappeared down the path, she saw Peter Traxal come out of his hut and walk down toward the hospital. She watched his tall, thin figure as he walked down the path deep in thought, and she felt envy and the stirring of an old desire. Envy of Elisabeth, because she knew that last night the Czech woman had had Peter make love to her. And the stirring of an old desire because Peter had once made love to her.

Eric Macy came out onto the veranda from the bedroom, his hat already settled firmly on his head. "Where's Harry?"

"Gone down to the salt spring with Elisabeth."

"Why didn't you go with them?"

"I'm not that soft in the head—yet. I've got better things to do than walking my legs off down a mountain to watch a lot of kanaka women doing work their men should be doing."

"A suffragette. Are the kanaka women going to vote for you?" Macy was tired enough to want to flop down in the chair beside his wife and just make irritable remarks till he fell asleep: last night's business down in the hospital had kept him up till the early hours of this morning. "What better things have you got to do?"

"Reading a book, for instance, improving my mind. I got six new mysteries in the mail yesterday."

"I dunno what you'd do without Agatha Christie."

"Neither do I," she said, and succeeded in her attempt at an enigmatic smile. Macy, unsure if he had lost the argument or even if there had been one, stomped down off the veranda and made his way across to the hospital. Bernice watched him go and tried to remember what desire she had felt for him. There had been desire once, because she had loved Eric once, passionately and with all the single-mindedness of which her shallow mind was capable. They had been married now for fifteen years, and in the early years Eric had been good-looking, attentive and, as far as her limited experience could tell her, a good lover. In those days she hadn't wanted much more.

They had been living in Melbourne then and there had been enough social life to keep her busy. Even when they had come north after the war she had been busy and content: at Rabaul, at Moresby and at Madang there had always been something to do after her household chores were finished. There had been six months at Goroka and she had enjoyed that, too: the rounds of gossip, golf with the other women, the dances and films at the club, dinner down at the hotel with visitors from Moresby and the mainland. She had not really become discontented till Rob, their elder boy, had gone off to school on the mainland and Eric had told her they would not be able to afford to send Harry, her favorite, when it came his time to go. Only then did she begin to realize that Eric's job, and that meant their whole life, had no real future. The social life of the towns, the one compensation for staying in this climate, was eating up the only spare money they had, the money they needed to educate the boys. She had still been smarting under the discovery that Harry, the bright one, the one she had hopes for, was not going to get the education he deserved, when Eric was offered the job of European medical assistant at Kundavi. They both knew, from the experience of others, the money that could be saved on an isolated post, and she had joined in Eric's willingness to accept the offer. That was twenty months ago and now she thought as much of her own future as she did of Harry's. And she had come to resent fiercely Eric for not being more than a European medical assistant and for what seemed to her a stupid dedication to such a lowly job.

Across the parade ground, outside the House Paper, she saw that Narvo was about to begin a court. Because there hadn't been a court in the weeks Narvo had been away and because she had nothing better to do, she went down off the veranda and strolled across the parade ground. She would never have ad-

mitted it to anyone, but she felt a certain sadistic delight in seeing the kanakas sentenced for their crimes. It was some sort of
compensation for her own imprisonment here.

Narvo was sitting at a table, and Frank Rossi sat beside him;
above their heads, from a whitewashed pole, the Australian flag
fluttered in the morning breeze. In front of Narvo and Rossi
stood the prisoners and complainants, none distinguishable by
expression from the other. Sergeant Beraki, spruce as a recruiting advertisement and as stiff as a clockwork toy in his efforts
to impress the bush natives, was acting as court bailiff. On either
side stood the crowd of spectators, chewing on betel nut, smoking
cigarettes of trade tobacco rolled in newspaper, morbidly curious
as any crowd in a city court, having a day out watching other
people in trouble. They giggled as Sergeant Beraki stamped his
feet and threw his salute, and every time sentence was passed
they slapped their palms against their thighs and laughed outright, as if Narvo had made a joke. There was no sympathy at all
for the prisoners.

As Bernice arrived two complainants were standing before
Narvo. He said something to them in dialect, then turned to
Rossi. "These fellers say their village was raided last week by
men from Kunyamya. They want us to take a patrol over to
Kunyamya and hand out some punishment."

"I haven't heard anything about any raids," Rossi said.

"There hasn't been any," Narvo said. "These blokes are
just trying their luck, hoping we may get a bit tough with the
Kunyamya." He looked back at the two natives and spoke to
them again in dialect, this time with some force. The natives
drew their bark cloaks about them, as if they suddenly felt cold,
and shifted their feet uneasily. Narvo waved his hand in dismissal, and Sergeant Beraki barked a command that almost blew
the two small natives off their feet. They turned and made their
way out through the jeering crowd, smiling bashfully but not
hurt by their summary dismissal. Narvo said, "They'll be back

again in a month or two. They'll chuff back to their village and all the elders will get together and cook up some other charge against the Kunyamya. It's a kanaka refinement of the welfare state—let the government do your fighting for you."

He looked up then and saw Bernice. "Hello, Bernice. Where is Harry?" There was almost a note of disappointment in his voice. "I thought he'd be over to watch this."

"He went down to the salt spring with Miss Palyardi," said Bernice, and smiled a little maliciously. She resented Harry's worship of Narvo, but did not blame the boy; she felt that Narvo went out of his way to impress the boy, and she resented Narvo the more because she knew that she, and Eric in particular, could offer nothing in competition. Narvo, by deed and reputation, was a hero; she knew deep down he could have been her own hero, if he had not so obviously thought nothing of her.

Then she looked over Narvo's head, beyond the crowd of natives, and saw first the cassowary and then the screaming women come running up the path from the gorge. In that moment she was glad that it was Narvo and not Eric who was on hand to answer her own scream for help.

3

Elisabeth's first reaction to the attacking natives was one of disbelief. The scene beside the salt spring, with the women working and gossiping, had been too peaceful, almost domestically so. True, the roar of the river in the gorge had a threatening sound to someone accustomed to the gentle murmur of the Vltava; but Elisabeth had been surprised at how quickly she had become oblivious of it. When she had lit her cigarette and leaned back against the rock behind her, it was with a feeling of almost complete relaxation. A memory had come out of the past of a holiday she had spent at Olomouc with Peter; the native women reminded her of the peasant women bringing in the harvest. Even when she had pointed out to Harry the tribesmen running down the path across the gorge, she had felt more curious than afraid.

"Quick!" Harry grabbed her hand, and in doing so let go the string by which he held the cassowary. The bird stood for a moment, then, frightened by the screams of the fleeing women, it leapt over the rocks and went running up the path that led to the patrol post, its thin legs moving so fast that its body seemed to be traveling suspended above only a dark shimmer in the bright morning light. Harry and Elisabeth, still clutching hands, began to run after the bird.

The vine-rope bridge was swaying violently as the women raced over it. The first of them had reached the other side and turned up the path that led to Vaikaka when the tribesmen came down the other path. Elisabeth, pausing for a moment as Harry helped her down a steep shelf of rock, saw one man raise his club and saw the young girl die beneath it. On the other side of the river, across the roar of the torrent, the young girl seemed to die in silence: the fleeing women on this side of the river uttered her death scream for her. Elisabeth herself uttered a cry, but she never knew if it had any sound; she was only aware of the chill horror that swept through her and left her paralyzed. Harry tugged desperately at her hand.

"Come on! Miss Palyardi, come on!"

A pregnant woman stumbled by them, hampered by her heavy belly and breasts; she ran with her hands clasped over her belly, as if trying to protect the unborn child. An old woman tried to run, couldn't, and collapsed; she sat down with a look of resignation on the wrinkled nut of her face. Another woman, still carrying her bundle of grass, slipped on a rock and fell; she lay beneath the spray of grass, and it was impossible to tell whether she was unconscious or was just lying there hoping to avoid discovery.

The bridge was jammed now with women and children; it

swayed and bent beneath the weight of them. Those in front, closest to the killers, were trying to retreat, but were hampered by those behind them, who seemed unable to turn quickly on the narrow catwalk of the bridge. The tribesmen stood along the bank of the river and hurled their spears at the women on the bridge, and two natives, their plumes bobbing furiously with their efforts, hacked away at the vines that held the flimsy structure. Farther up the river, where the path on the opposite bank was above the path that led up to the patrol post, four men were shooting arrows down into the fleeing Vaikaka women.

Elisabeth, pulled by Harry, jumped down off the rock and went to follow him up the path. A woman brushed by her, moaning incoherently with fear, her face and body shining under a skin of sweat, and ran on up the path. She came to the spot opposite the bowmen, hesitated a moment, then kept running. Ahead of her was an outcrop of rock; once beyond that she was safe. She ran desperately, her arms upflung before her as if she were about to grasp safety and clutch it to her. She never saw the arrow that killed her: it went in behind her ear and jiggled in the air behind her as she ran. She kept running for another five or ten yards, then she slowed, as if exhausted, and sank to the ground. Her hand came up to clutch at the arrow, then seemed to realize the uselessness of it all and dropped back to the ground. Elisabeth, about to follow Harry up the path, pulled up sharply and looked in terror across at the bowmen. And then, above even the roar of the river, she heard the scream of the women and children.

She turned at the moment the bridge began to fall. For a split second it seemed to hover above the river, as if held to the opposite bank by the willpower of those clinging to its hand ropes. Then it fell, like the long branch of a tree darkened by human foliage; a baby fell away from it, a shrieking clump of leaves, and disappeared into the white torrent beneath. Then the other figures began to fall. They clung to the trailing bridge, the cobweb that held them to a world they did not want to leave; they strove furiously to clamber back up it, but even the frenzy of terror did not give them enough strength. Their grips relaxed and they fell off the bridge, some falling spreadeagled as if crucified on the rainbows that hung in the mist above the river, others plummeting down as if welcoming the swiftness of inevitable death. They went down into the roaring savage water and were gone from sight in a moment, only a dark arm showing occasionally in what could have been a desperate effort to keep afloat or just a last despairing gesture of farewell.

An arrow hit the ground beside Elisabeth and, still horrorstricken by what she had seen, she felt herself pulled behind a large rock.

"We'll be all right now. They can't get across, now the bridge is gone. And they're lousy shots with their arrows. Roy says——" An arrow hit the rock above them even as Harry spoke. He ducked down, and huddled close against him, Elisabeth could feel him trembling as much as she was herself. He looked up the path, biting his lip. He was acclimatized to death, but not to the possibility of his own: this was the first time he had ever been in real danger. Then he saw Narvo, Rossi and his mother running headlong down the path toward them, and he couldn't stop the tears that burst from him. "Mum! Mum!"

He left Elisabeth and rushed up the path and flung himself against his mother. Bernice, weeping hysterically, grabbed him to her almost savagely. Narvo and Rossi went past them, and a moment later Rossi's pistol rang out as he shot at the killers, now fleeing up the path across the gorge.

"Hold it!" Narvo yelled, and Rossi lowered his pistol, puzzled and angry.

"What's the matter?" he said.

"You won't hit them with a pistol at that distance," Narvo said. "And I don't want one or two of them dead. I want the whole bloody lot of them. Alive!"

Then he saw Elisabeth, still cowered behind the rock, and he came on down the path to her. "You all right, Miss Palyardi?"

She nodded, and sank down on the slope behind her. There was no strength in her legs, she could feel them trembling violently, and she was afraid that if she opened her mouth to speak she would be sick. She raised a limp hand and pointed, and only then did Narvo see the destroyed bridge.

He uttered an obscenity for which he made no apology to Elisabeth, and went on down to the bridge. Some women lay about on the ground near it; they were the ones who had managed to struggle up the hanging bridge to safety. They lay exhausted by fear, relief and their desperate efforts to save themselves; only their eyes moved in their dark gray faces, their fingers dug into the earth as if they were afraid of sliding off it into the river below. Narvo spoke to them in dialect, but could get no answer. He squatted down on his haunches and gently lifted up one woman. She stared at him, still fear-stricken, and he spoke to her as he would have to a terrified child. Slowly the fear went out of the woman's face and at last she answered his question.

He sat for a moment on his haunches, staring at the wrecked bridge and the cascading river below it. A bird went as a dark flash down through the mist and its whistle, in the steep walls of the gorge, was a thin long drawn-out scratch against the ear: the last echo of the screams of those who had died. Gently Narvo released the woman and stood up. Slowly he went back up the path, took Elisabeth's arm and, without a word, led her up to where Rossi stood with the still-weeping Bernice and Harry.

"All right, Harry?" he said, and the boy turned a tear-stained face toward him.

"Geez, it was terrible, Roy! I didn't even see 'em till it was too late——"

Narvo patted the boy's shoulder. "It's all over now——"

Then he saw the native woman lying in the bush beside the

path, her face buried in a wreath of orchids and the arrow growing from the back of her neck. He let go Elisabeth's arm, knelt down beside the woman and turned her over.

It was Kabu, the wife of Paiwo.

6

"EIGHTEEN DEAD, as far as I can make out," said Frank Rossi. "Eleven women and seven children. And Paiwo's wife makes nineteen."

They were standing outside the office of the hospital: Rossi, Narvo, Traxal and Macy. Joan Duggan came to the door of the hut and, squinting without her glasses, blinded by the glare of the sun, said, "Well, what are we going to do, Mr. Narvo? Do we find excuses for these murderers, too?"

Narvo looked steadily at her, and Traxal waited for the big man to erupt: why did Duggan always have to bait Narvo so bluntly? "There are no excuses for these killers," Narvo said evenly. "I know why they did what they did, but there are no excuses for them. What I'd like to know is, how did they get word about what really happened to that woman with *kuru*? Did any of you say anything to any of the kanakas?" He looked about him, pausing to look longest at Traxal.

"I didn't have time to tell you," said Macy, pushing his hat back and wiping the sweat from his face. "It was one of the orderlies we had standing guard over that bloke last night. It was my fault—I'd forgotten he was a Benamaua man. He went through during the night—hopped it back to Benamaua and told them what had happened."

"It couldn't be helped, Eric. Forget it," Narvo said kindly, and in the background Duggan sniffed loudly: he wouldn't have spoken kindly to her if *she* had been the one at fault. Narvo turned to Rossi. "We'll leave straight after lunch. Twelve police boys and enough carriers to hump supplies for an overnight stay."

"You think you'll have it all cleaned up in a day?" said Traxal.

"I shan't have it cleaned up in a month," said Narvo. "Those blokes have already chuffed off into the hills. I'm going out to Benamaua, call the roll from the Village Book, and those that don't answer their names I'll put down as being in the killer party. Then I can spread the word as to whom I'm looking for." He looked at Rossi without smiling. "I've got my stool pigeons. You'll learn to cultivate yours. There's never been a policeman in history who got along without a stool pigeon."

Rossi looked disgusted. "Will these kanakas sell their own kind out to a white man?"

"They'll sell their wives if the price is right," said Narvo. "And I always see that the price *is* right."

"Mug copper," said Joan Duggan sourly, and Narvo raised his hat. Then he turned and walked away from the group and down the path. He had seen Paiwo and his son coming across from the House Kiap. Paiwo was carrying the boy, a chubby five-year-old whose big brown eyes sparkled when he saw Narvo.

"I'll take Bandi," Narvo said, and took the boy. "Sergeant Beraki is down at the bridge with your wife. The bridge will take a few days to repair. You can bring your wife's body up here to the post."

Paiwo shook his head. "I shall take her back to Vaikaka. I shall go downstream to the ford and cross the river. I shall be away two days. Will the Kiap care for my son?"

"I shall care for him. I have to go out and arrest the men who killed your wife and the other women and children. But Bandi will be cared for."

"Thank you, Kiap." Paiwo's face was expressionless: there was no hint of grief or any other emotion. He turned and went down toward the path that led down into the gorge. He did not hurry, but walked with an almost deliberate step, as if he knew that nothing he could do now could help his wife, that she was now beyond the dictates of time, that all he had left of her was memories, and they had no urgency.

Narvo watched him go; then still carrying the boy he went up toward the Macys' house. But as he reached the steps leading up to the veranda, he could hear Bernice crying inside the house. She sounded still a little hysterical, and he could hear Harry, his own voice tremulous, trying to comfort her. Narvo hesitated, then turned back: he was in no mood to face an hysterical woman, one who might even go so far as to blame him for the massacre. He stood at the bottom of the steps, still holding the boy Bandi and wondering where to take him for the present. Then he heard his name called by the Czech woman.

She was standing on the veranda of the guest hut, and clearly she had got over her frightening experience and had regained her composure. With the sound of Bernice's weeping in the house behind him, he found himself reluctantly admiring Elisabeth Palyardi. If he had to have women in his district, he preferred those who had control of their nerves.

"You look lost, Mr. Narvo," Elisabeth said as Narvo walked toward her. "I cannot see you in the role of father."

Narvo put down Bandi, and the boy instantly ducked behind him, peering out shyly at Elisabeth. "This is my houseboy's son. His father has gone to take the mother's body back to Vaikaka."

Elisabeth approached the boy and knelt down, talking around Narvo's legs to him. She looked up at Narvo without rising. "May I take care of him till his father returns?"

Narvo hesitated. He looked back at the Macy house, then

he said, "I'd be grateful if you would. I have to go out to Benamaua——"

"He will be safe with me," Elisabeth said, straightening up. "I was a governess in Prague for two years. I looked after the children of the British consul."

"Bandi has no diplomatic status," Narvo said, running his hand affectionately over the crinkly scalp of the child. "But if he lives long enough, survives the fate that caught up with his mother, isn't driven to suicide by civilized do-gooders, he could wind up as president of the Republic of New Guinea."

"Perhaps much the same was said of Thomas Masaryk."

"Perhaps," said Narvo dryly. "Although I doubt if Masaryk's mother died with an arrow behind her ear. And I've never heard of the Czechs being cannibals." He patted the boy's head, and Bandi smiled up at him lovingly and trustingly. "Bandi comes of a long line of gourmet anthropophagi, don't you, sonny boy?" The boy nodded eagerly, ignorant but happy in the shadow of the Kiap. Then Narvo looked back at Elisabeth. He smiled, and for the first time she noticed the gold tooth at the side of his mouth. "Would you care to come down for a drink?"

Elisabeth managed to hide her surprise at the invitation. "I should like that, Mr. Narvo."

In Narvo's living room, with a glass of gin and tonic in her hand and with Bandi sitting on the floor on the other side of the room staring at her with wide eyes, she said, "Do—things like this morning's happen very often?"

Narvo sipped his beer. "Very rarely in controlled territory— which is what this area is supposed to be. I've been here at Kundavi two years now and nothing as bad as this has ever taken place before."

"What do you think caused it?"

Narvo pondered for a moment, gazing at her as if he wondered whether to trust her with his answer. The three dogs and the little boy sat at his feet; with his free hand he caressed whichever head happened to be closest. "I wouldn't tell you this, Miss Palyardi, except that I think you have made a mistake in coming here. I have nothing personal against you, but I think you would be well advised to get out as soon as you can. This area isn't ready for white women. It isn't ready even for some white *men.*"

"Do you mean Peter, Mr. Narvo?"

"I mean a lot of people. I'm not naming names—that would mean calling practically the whole electoral roll of Australia. I mean every white man who doesn't know how to handle these kanakas."

"You do know how to handle them, Mr. Narvo?"

"I think I do," he said flatly, unoffended by her direct question: he had given the same answer to the same question more times than he could remember. "If I hadn't been away on patrol these last six weeks, this morning's trouble wouldn't have happened. I have my own way of knowing what capers these kanakas are up to—*before* they happen. This morning's massacre was the culmination of a lot of things. Tribal revenge, fear of evil spirits, dislike of governmental authority, restlessness and some of it just sheer bloody-mindedness. It wouldn't have happened had I been here."

"Are you blaming Mr. Rossi?"

"I'm blaming myself for staying out on patrol so long. Yet the patrol had to be done, and Frank couldn't have done it. He hasn't the experience—and that's what let him down here, lack of experience. The kanakas can scent out an inexperienced officer as soon as he's in the area—and they reckon he's fair game for them."

"So this morning's massacre was part of the game for them?" Elisabeth was having a second reaction to the horror she had seen. She could feel herself beginning to tremble, and the ice in her glass rattled as her hand shook.

"I didn't say that. What happened this morning is part of the kanaka's long history, something he was doing long before we came here, something we want to stamp out and that he sees no reason for discontinuing—" He rose abruptly from his chair, treading on the tail of one of the dogs, which yelped and skittered across the room. He crossed to Elisabeth in three swift strides and took the glass from her hand. "I'm sorry! I shouldn't be talking about it—I'm used to it—" He yelled for Paiwo, then remembered that the houseboy wasn't here. He looked down at her solicitously. "Are you all right?"

Elisabeth lay back in the cane chair, her head resting on the cushion Narvo had pushed behind her. For a moment she had feared she was going to faint or be sick, but now she could feel control of herself gradually returning. Bandi hadn't moved from his place on the floor, but his eyes widened till they seemed ready to fall out of his head. For some unaccountable reason she felt resentful of the small boy; then reason returned, and she tried to smile reassuringly at him. He was a kanaka, one of a long line of cannibals and murderers, but she knew he was the symbol of Narvo's hope for the future.

"I am all right, thank you. Please relax, Mr. Narvo."

He continued to stand close to her for a moment, still studying her; then he went back and picked up his glass from the table where he had set it. He drank, then stood looking at the empty glass in his hand. "You see what I mean about this area not being ready for white people? You need a strong stomach and a certain deadening of the sensibilities to survive up here—at least for the first two or three years. After that, you're conditioned—and if you aren't by then, you'll never be."

Elisabeth was slowly feeling better. But even if she hadn't been, she would have stayed anyway. Her interest was quickening in this big man who was such a mixture of arrogance and tenderness, intolerance and patience. Accustomed to only one standard, she wondered how he would have fared under the Communists back home. "Why did you come here to New Guinea, Mr. Narvo?"

"Call me Roy," he said, and she recognized the second concession: the first was to have invited her in here for a drink. "I don't know. Escape, I suppose. Well, partly that. My folks wanted me to be a doctor or a dentist. My dad was a dentist, he's retired now, and my elder brother, he's one. Very successful, too. Four kids, on his third Jaguar, his wife gets her name on the social pages every week—the week she doesn't make it, she rings up the papers to find out why." He looked at her, grinning: the gold tooth flashed. "You still interested?"

"Not in your family. In you, yes."

"My family sounds dull? Yeah, they are. They're nice, and they're all solid citizens, but they're dull. I saw that, even my last year at school. I left school the beginning of 1940 and went straight into the air force. Had to put my age up. I was always big and looked older than I was. The air force was dead hungry for recruits in those years, and so was the army. They never looked to see if you were old enough to shave—so long as your voice had broken you were okay. You Czechs never wanted to fight—don't be offended, it's the truth. You're always saying we sold you out after Munich and again in 1948, but you're a bit like these kanakas—you'd like someone else to do your fighting for you."

Elisabeth contained her anger: the argument would be pointless here in these New Guinea mountains, on the other side of the world from the Hron Valley where the Nazis had shot her father. Some Czechs might not have wanted to fight, but not all of them. "My father was killed by the Nazis. They didn't shoot him just because he happened to be in the way. He had a price on his head."

He stood looking at her for a moment, sucking on his bottom lip. Then he gracefully dipped his head. "I apologize. I scatter generalizations like buckshot. If it is any compensation, let me say there were also a lot of Australians who didn't want to fight, either. You ask some old recruiting sergeant who had the toughest job back in 1940 and '41."

"You were telling me what brought you to New Guinea." He had offended her and she was not going to forgive him easily.

He accepted the rebuff with only a raised eyebrow, then went on, "My folks dragged me out of the air force because I was under age. I finally got into the army in 1943, came to New Guinea and, well, fell in love with it, if you like. I came back right after the war and I've been a patrol officer ever since."

"And you believe in what you are doing?"

He looked at her with what seemed to be surprise; she had thought he was a man beyond surprise. "Of course. Do you think I would stay on here if I didn't?"

"I'm sorry I asked that," she said. "I think I, too, am suffering from a form of conditioning. I have just come from a city where the only people who believe in what they are doing are the Communists. It is difficult to believe in anything when your life has no meaning."

"I'm no Communist, but I admire their dedication. We could do with some of it, especially down in Canberra." Then he looked at her frankly. "Is Peter a Communist?"

She shook her head. "No. Why do you ask?"

"Because he wants to go back to Czechoslovakia."

"Did he tell you that?"

"No. But you get to sense certain feelings amongst people after you've been up here awhile. There's Father Shawn wants to go back to America, Mrs. Macy wants to go back to civilization, as she calls it—it wasn't hard to recognize that Peter had much the same sort of feeling."

She took the subject away from Peter: it was too close to her right now, there were too many points to it that she hadn't the courage to discuss just yet. "And you? What do you want to go back to?"

He grinned and again the gold tooth flashed. "Maybe I'm one of the lucky ones. Maybe I've got nothing to go back to."

"Perhaps Peter has nothing to go back to," she said, and did not hear the footsteps on the veranda outside. "He has a lot to worry about."

"Who has a lot to worry about?" Traxal was standing at the door.

Elisabeth turned sharply; there was no mistaking the tone of Traxal's voice. He stood in the doorway and even against the light one could see the stiffness of his stance. Elisabeth stood up, feeling a little giddy still. "We all have, Peter. You came in only on the end of the conversation."

Traxal knew he had been rebuffed, and felt foolish. He had come up here to see Narvo on an official matter, and had not expected to find Elisabeth lying back in one of Narvo's chairs with a drink on the table beside her. He had been unable to control the jealousy that flashed through him, and the words had been out of him before he was fully aware of what he was saying. He could have used the same words in a bantering tone, but even when there had been no jealousy there had been no banter between him and Narvo. He did his best now to get out of the situation gracefully.

"That is all I am good for, the tail end of conversations." He came into the room, away from the light, so that Elisabeth could see his smile. "I am just a full stop. Period, as Mike Shawn says."

"You're wrong there, Peter," said Narvo, his own smile not as self-consciously wide as Traxal's, but just as dry. "One thing you'll never be is a full stop. You'll never put period to anything."

"You make me sound like a perpetual irritant," Traxal said still smiling.

"I don't make you anything," said Narvo, picking up Elisabeth's glass, showing that his hospitality was over. "You were whatever you are long before I met you."

He is wrong there, Elisabeth thought; but said nothing. She walked to the door and Traxal took her arm. "Thank you for the drink, Mr. Narvo. Will you bring Bandi to me this afternoon, before you leave?"

"You had better move in here while I'm away," Narvo said. "There won't be room for Bandi over at the guest hut. I'll dig up another houseboy to look after you."

Crossing the parade ground Elisabeth explained to Traxal her offer to look after Bandi. "I feel I must do something useful around here. I don't think Mr. Narvo is in favor of parasites."

"Narvo is in favor of nobody but himself."

"I think he is in favor of the natives," said Elisabeth. "Even this morning's murderers."

2

Eric Macy stood up after he and Paiwo had lifted the body of Kabu on to the litter. He looked across at Father Shawn and said, "Got any prayers you want to say, Mike?"

"I've said them. Privately. Paiwo isn't a mission boy and he wouldn't welcome my intrusion."

"It's a pity all missionaries aren't as tolerant as you."

Father Shawn shrugged deprecatingly. "I know a brick wall when I see one. I'm a percentage man. I concentrate on the not-so-difficults and leave the others to the fanatics." He cocked an eye heavenwards. "God forgive me."

Three other men from Vaikaka had appeared and with the widower they each took a corner of the litter. Then walking slowly and carefully they began to make their way downstream along the bank of the river. The three other Vaikaka men were also widowers, but their wives were lost somewhere in the river. They would go looking for them later and, if found, bring them back to Vaikaka. In the meantime the body of Paiwo's wife had to be taken back to the village to be smoked.

"That's what sickens me, the smoking of the body," said Father Shawn, gazing after the retreating funeral party. "Not just spiritually, either. It revolts me physically."

"I've got a strong stomach," Macy said, as they began to walk back up the path. "A lot of people don't recognize how necessary that is if you're gonna be a good doctor. If my brains had matched my stomach, I'd've been a top specialist." He peeled a stick of gum and began chewing it. "That's the theme of my life. If."

"Did you fail badly at college, Eric? I mean, so badly it wasn't worth trying again?"

"I was bottom of the class. The professor knew about my strong stomach—I was the only one of the class who didn't turn green at our first anatomy lecture. After the exam results came out he took me aside and recommended that I get a job in an abattoir or a morgue."

"A mordant sense of humor."

"No, really, he was trying to help me." There was no ill-will in Eric Macy's make-up: it was another doctor's talent he had, although one he had never recognized. They walked up past the hospital, *kunai*-thatched, cane-walled, a caricature of what he had once aspired to; he had dreamed of being the superintendent of a huge medical center on the American plan: he had even had a name for it, the Macy Clinic. Medical care at bargain prices: there had been a time, when the dream was still a dream and therefore still possible, when he had been able to make such jokes.

"Well, you're almost a doctor now. I heard about some of the operations you performed when you first came in here, before Peter came."

"Those don't count. The Department of Health officially has to turn a blind eye to them. Now Peter's here—" He stopped outside his own house, took off his hat and wiped the perspiration from his brow, then quickly replaced the hat. "You make the best of it. That's all you can do."

"My sentiments exactly," said Father Shawn, and scratched his skinny chest through the gaping vent of his buttonless shirt. He wore a hat made of palm leaves, a pair of faded blue jeans and a pair of rope sandals. Christ hung on a leather string around his neck, surrounded by poverty. "Strangely enough, I believe they're good enough to get most of us into heaven."

"I'll see you there, then," said Macy, and went up the steps into his own private hell: the abuse of his wife and the unspoken disappointment in the eyes of his son.

"We've got to leave here," Bernice said as soon as he came in the door. "It's too dangerous——"

Macy sat down, still with his hat on. "Darling, it's just as dangerous down South. He could be run over by a car——"

"For God's sake, stop chewing!" She struggled to keep control of herself. "Harry, go out and see if the cassowary has come back——"

"Wally! I'd forgotten all about him!" The boy was a better actor than his parents knew: he put on a face to save theirs. He went out of the room calling to the bird, not caring for it, caring for the two people in the room behind him but knowing they did not want him around while they settled their argument.

Macy took the gum from his mouth, looked about for a place to put it and went to drop it in an ash tray. "Not there! Don't be filthy. Throw it outside."

Macy hesitated, then put the gum back in his mouth. "I'm too tired to get up. Go on—what were you saying about Kundavi being dangerous?"

"Well, don't you think it is? How can you sit there, after seeing your son almost killed—" Bernice was pacing about the room, her hands making nervous patterns in the air, like birds trapped in an invisible cage. Her make-up, about which she took such care in the mornings, was streaked with tears; the cosmeticians had learned to camouflage pimples and age, but they hadn't learned how to counteract woman's oldest weapon. Her dress was crumpled and stained with dirt from Harry's hands when she had hugged him to her. "You've got to write to Moresby tonight, do you hear? Tell 'em you want a posting back there, that this is no place for a married man with a family——"

Macy took off his hat and dropped it on the floor. The long strands of red hair which he so carefully combed over his bald patch, hung down about his ears: he had the battered look of a clown, one who had been sacked, who had no jokes left. He chewed slowly on the gum, not reflectively but automatically: the gum moved in his mouth like the cud of his own futility.

"Bernice, we might as well get it straight. I'm not going back to Moresby. They wouldn't want me, for one thing. The only job they'd have there for me would be clerical, and I'm no good for that. And I *like* being here at Kundavi. Here I get the chance to do some medical work—the closest I'll ever get to being a doctor, the one thing I've ever wanted to be."

"What about me and the boys? What about what we might want to be?"

"You never wanted to be anything but a social success." He had never been so truthful with her before; he was surprised at his own bluntness. He saw the look of shocked anger on her face, but he didn't care this time: he was bankrupt of grace, and he was no longer capable of peace at any price. "As for the boys —I can't help it, hon. I'm not the first father who's let his kids down."

"You—you spineless—!" She shook with fury; their rows in the past had never reached this peak. "I'm going and I'm taking Harry with me! We'll go out on the plane next week! You can stay here and play at being a doctor——!"

But he was past being hurt by her cheap jeers. He watched her storm out of the room, and marveled at his own calmness. *I'm still in love with her,* he thought, *but why can I take all this*

from her without shouting back at her? Had New Guinea done
that to him—taken all the fight out of him? He had met plenty
of beachcombers in his time here in the Territory: almost without exception they were men who no longer had any fight in
them, who had been beaten by the climate, the conditions and
the general ennui that trapped you if you were not careful.
Was he on his way to becoming a beachcomber?

"Dad." Harry stood in the doorway.

"What's the matter?"

The boy came slowly into the room. "Dad, Mum was talking,
I mean before you came in, she was talking about us going back
to the coast. Are we, Dad?"

Hope jumped in Macy's breast. "Don't you wanna go?"

"Gee, no, Dad! I mean, I like it here. Back on the coast, it'd
be just like being down on the mainland. I'd have to go to
school, wouldn't I?"

"Oh, too right, you would. But it might be easier to learn
things than the way you have to learn lessons now. I mean,
from correspondence lessons——"

"I don't mind that, though. Roy says I'm the best-read kid
he's ever met——"

"Roy hasn't met many kids." *There* was the hurt: Bernice
hadn't been able to touch him with her abuse, but Harry could
stab him just by mentioning another man's name. "But you'd
really like to stay here, eh?"

"Oh, gee, yes! Dad, don't let Mum talk you into going back
to the coast."

"She's got no hope of that." He looked at his son with love:
he didn't even now resent the boy's worship of Narvo. "Just
don't let her talk *you* into it."

The boy winked at his father: they were fellow conspirators,
the closest they had been since they had first come here to
Kundavi; Bernice, wanting to take the boy away from Macy, had

given him back to him. "She's got Buckley's hope of that, Dad. We'll stay here, all right."

3

Paiwo and the other three men lowered the litter to the ground. The three men, without a word, went out of the hut and almost immediately Kabu's mother came in. She dropped on her knees beside the corpse and began to bang her forehead on the earth floor of the hut. Paiwo watched her for a while, then he bent and took the old woman by the shoulders.

"We must prepare for the mourning," he said. "The others will be coming soon."

He went out into the village and found two young men, and the three of them went into the nearby bush and gathered armfuls of branches. They brought the branches back to the village and stripped the leaves from them. Kabu's mother then made a bed of the leaves in the hut and Kabu's body was laid on it. Another woman brought a bark cloth and this was laid over the body, only the head being left uncovered. By this time the first of the mourners had begun to arrive.

The mourning would go on for four days. The mourners, particularly the women, would beat their foreheads with stones till the blood came. Kabu's mother had already lost another daughter and two sons: her forehead was marked with scars, grief inscribed on a living monument to the dead. The wail of sorrow had already begun and would go on for the four days; the sound of sorrow would keen through the grass huts of Vaikaka like a mountain wind and would be heard in the other villages. It would be heard in the village of Benamaua and the people there would not be able to sleep because of it. For the people of Benamaua knew that revenge followed grief: they had followed the same pattern themselves.

Paiwo went to Wangamunggu, the fight-leader of Vaikaka.

These mountain natives did not have a chief, but a council of elders and a fight-leader; the government appointed a *luluai,* a mayor from one of the elders, but the natives accepted his authority only in government matters. This was a tribal matter, one of honor, and Paiwo knew that the government would be ignored. The fight-leader, not the *luluai,* was the man who counted now.

Wangamunggu was a small man, muscular and unafraid: his body was marked by the hazards of his deeds. His nose and teeth had been broken by a stone club; a trade ax had taken a piece out of his shoulder blade; knives and spears had scarred his ribs and legs. He would die fighting, and he would be ashamed to die any other way.

"The mourning must be done first," Wangamunggu said. "The Benamaua people did not wait to mourn their woman killed by Sangiap, but wanted their vengeance at once. We of Vaikaka are not like that. We have more respect for our dead. Besides," he said, and his broken nose spread across his face and the broken teeth showed in a betel-stained smile, "the Kiap will be on his way to Benamaua now. We do not want to fight him at the same time as we fight the killers of Benamaua."

"I do not want to fight the Kiap at all," said Paiwo.

"It is your decision," Wangamunggu said, sitting cross-legged on the ground, filing methodically at the spearhead he held almost affectionately. His own life had escaped the massacre and he had no grief to weigh him down; he looked forward to the coming fight with unadulterated pleasure. "But remember—it was the Kiap who asked us people of the mountains to trust each other. If we had not trusted the Benamaua, if we had not relaxed our guard, this would not have happened."

"It was our brother Sangiap who did the first killing," said Paiwo, still troubled.

"Did he not kill the woman with *kuru,* the woman inhabited by evil spirits?"

"Who put the spirits into the woman? Perhaps the Benamaua think we of Vaikaka did it."

"Would they not have come to capture one of us and commit *tukavu* on him if they had thought the sorcerer lived amongst us Vaikaka?"

Paiwo knew that what Wangamunggu said was true. If the Benamaua had thought a sorcerer from the Vaikaka had put the evil spirits into the woman with *kuru*, they would not have committed this morning's massacre. They would have sneaked up on the village of Vaikaka, grabbed a suspect, preferably an old woman or an old man, and spirited him away into the bush. There they would have performed the ritual of *tukavu* on him or her, pulverizing the muscles with heavy stones and biting out the jugular; the sorcerer would have died and with him the evil spirits, and the Benamaua would live in peace till the next *kuru* victim was possessed.

"What you say is true," Paiwo said. "But who knows if there was not an evil spirit in Sangiap? His brain has always been weak."

"It is your decision," said Wangamunggu, working on the spearhead with a bamboo knife, carving out the barbs that would stick in the flesh like the thorns of a bush, running his fingers over the barbs with the same sensual delight as he would run them over the nipples of his woman: life was only fighting and loving, and there was nothing else. "But remember—Kabu was a woman of Vaikaka. We all grieve for her and feel her death, as we do that of the other women and children who died. And no one in the past has killed our women and gone unpunished."

Paiwo went back to the hut and knelt down with the women and wailed, as much for himself as for his dead wife. He wondered if the Kiap would hear his wailing and would guess at the trouble that, like an evil spirit, now inhabited him.

7

NARVO AND ROSSI arrived back on the morning of the third day. They came up the path from the gorge, walking slowly at the head of the line of police boys and carriers.

"They caught no prisoners," said Traxal.

"Did they expect to?" Elisabeth had some sewing in her lap. She was a poor needlewoman and disliked sewing, but the job had to be done; she had never been able to afford to employ someone else to do it for her. She had seen photographs of dresses in magazines at the British counsul's house and wished she had been capable of making copies of them; instead of which she could only buy the uninspired dresses at the State shops and hope that she looked better than she felt. She had admired Bernice Macy's dresses and soon she would pluck up courage and ask where Bernice got them. In the meantime the torn blouse and the split seam in the skirt, her own scars of the massacre down at the bridge, had to be mended.

"Not really." Traxal stood up, not wishing to look too much at home here on the veranda of Narvo's house. He absent-mindedly picked one of the dahlias that grew beside the veranda rail; then remembered it was one of Narvo's flowers and Narvo was proud of his garden. He held the flower in his hand, looking for a place to dispose of it: he was like a kleptomaniac who had suddenly come to his senses with the stolen goods in his hand. He dropped it over the side of the veranda and hoped Narvo wouldn't notice it. "But he has to show the flag. Myself, I think the whole thing is a lost cause before it is properly started. I mean this attempt to civilize the natives. Why should they be made to live according to our rules and conventions?"

Elisabeth looked at the boy Bandi playing on the grass in front of the house. The boy trusted her now and she had enjoyed playing mother and nurse to him. The mother instinct in her, at least toward other people's children, was not strong; but there was a warm sincerity about her that could win the trust of a child, this small native's as much as that of the English children in Prague. "Perhaps children like Bandi will grow up to see something worthwhile in our rules."

"I doubt it," said Traxal, and stepped down off the veranda as the patrol came up to the parade ground.

"The children back home are growing up to see something in communism," Elisabeth said, putting down her sewing and coming to the top of the steps. "It is only a question of education. Of environment and lack of other standards."

Traxal looked up at her. "Are you trying to tell me it is safer to stay here than to return home?"

"Were you thinking of returning home, Peter?"

But before she could get his answer, Narvo and Rossi were coming toward them. "Hello, Bandi," Narvo said, and picked up the boy. He said something in dialect and the boy laughed and pointed at Elisabeth. Narvo grinned up at her. "He says you have been a good mother to him."

Elisabeth laughed: she was surprised at how much she welcomed Narvo's return. Already the natives of the post were coming across the parade ground, laughing and chattering, to welcome back the Kiap. *I must have caught the virus,* she thought, amused at herself; *why does this man have such an effect on us all here at the post, making some of us glad to see him and upsetting the others?* She looked sideways at Traxal, who was obviously one of those upset.

"A good son makes it easy to be a good mother," she said.

Then Harry Macy came running across the parade ground and in a moment Narvo was giving all his attention to his two sons by other parents. Traxal turned to Rossi. "How did it go?"

"No good. Nobody knew anything. There were eight men missing from the village, but no one had ever heard of them. I don't know whether it's because you can't see them blush because of the color of their skins, but these fellers can look you straight in the eye and lie themselves blind. We showed them the names in the Village Book, but they just shook their heads and said we must have made a mistake."

"What happens now?" Traxal said.

"It's up to the boss." Rossi shrugged and nodded at Narvo: it was obvious that he had expected more to be done than had been done. He was not a vindictive boy, but he had gone out on what he had thought was a punitive patrol, and all that Narvo had handed out had been a few harsh words.

Elisabeth looked across at Narvo and wondered how the man could be so lighthearted with the two boys. Then he looked up at her, unmasked for a moment, and she saw the pain and weariness in his eyes. She smiled at him, but he had already looked away, retreating behind his small talk with the excited Harry.

"I'll carry your things back to the guest hut," Traxal said, and went up onto the veranda and picked up Elisabeth's two bags. He came down from the veranda and began to walk up the path. Elisabeth hesitated for a moment, embarrassed by Traxal's stiff-necked exhibition of possessiveness and annoyed by it, too; but Narvo was still talking to Harry, and Rossi had turned away to speak to Sergeant Beraki, who had just come down from dismissing the police boys and the carriers. Then Narvo looked up at her, looked after Traxal, then nodded at her.

"Thank you for looking after Bandi, Elisabeth. I'll see you later."

She had gone four or five yards after Traxal before it struck her that Narvo had called her by her first name. He had spoken to her as if she were now a friend and not an intruder. It was even possible that he had accepted her as part of the permanent population of Kundavi.

Traxal put down the bags and motioned to a native to come and pick them up. Then he took Elisabeth's arm and they began to walk up toward the guest hut. "Elisabeth, would you like to go back to Moresby?"

"Alone?"

"It would only be for a month or two, darling. I have friends down there you could stay with——"

"What happens after two months?"

"I shall be coming to Moresby for a conference with head-quarters. We can talk then about our plans——"

"I had only one plan when I came to New Guinea, Peter. To be married."

They had come to the steps of the guest hut. Behind them a clump of *gora-gora*, the ginger lily, stirred in the breeze. Elisabeth had liked its sweet scent and wondered if it had grown wild or been planted there by Narvo. Then, knowing Narvo's dislike of visitors, she had decided that he had not been the one to scent the breeze for strangers.

"We can't be married here, darling." Traxal watched the big goura pigeon preening itself in the casuarina tree beside the path; everything in this country was bigger than life-size, even the pigeons could be as big as roosters. It would be late summer in Czechoslovakia now and the birds would be flying south, the gray-lags trailing their long V-formations across the sky and the white storks rising in exclamation from the lakes. "I don't want to start our married life here. To me, it would be—it would be unlucky."

"You think I care about good or bad luck after the last five years? I take what I can when I can, Peter. You offered me the chance to marry, darling. I want to take it."

"You make it sound like a business proposition," he said, smiling to take the edge off his words. "Something without love."

She stifled the confession on her lips: there was no love. Something had happened in the five years they had been separated, either to Peter or to herself, and she knew now that she no longer loved him. But what was she to do? She had no money, nowhere else to go; she had been allowed into Australia because Peter had sponsored her. Love was not a convertible currency. Love was happiness, they said; but happiness was relative, and, she guessed, so was love. At least she had been unhappier alone than she would be with Peter, even without love.

"I don't mean it to sound like that, Peter. But after waiting five years—" She tried to joke, to ease the pain she felt at lying to him: "I am almost ready for the shelf, Peter."

"Nonsense," he said, squeezing her arm and kissing her cheek, looking over her shoulder and seeing the goura pigeon flying off in panic, pursued by the hawk. "You are beautiful enough to get any man you want."

"Are you hoping another man might grab me down in Moresby?" She was still smiling, still joking; but now there was fear behind the smile, the joke was hollow. Was he no longer in love with her, did he regret sending for her? *Serves you right*, she told herself; but she was too afraid to ask him how he really felt.

"Not hoping," he said, smiling at her with all the old charm. "Afraid."

"But you would rather take that risk than have me stay up here with you?"

"Yes, darling."

"But why, Peter? It can't be because you think it might be unlucky—you never were superstitious before. You used to laugh at me for walking around ladders, at how I used to hope to find fern-seed blooming on St. John's Day——"

"You never did find it."

"If I had—" Then she stopped. If she had found the mythical blooming fern-seed it would have led her to the treasures of the world, and then she would not have needed Peter. She felt ashamed of the thought, and as compensation, surrendered: "Give me time to think, Peter. Must I go to Moresby right away?"

"No," he said, and saw in the distance that the hawk had caught the goura pigeon: feathers fell like blue snowflakes as the pigeon died in a flurry of wings. "The plane doesn't come in till next week. I think you should be gone before the UN party arrives."

"What has the UN party to do with my staying?"

"They will need the guest hut," he said, but she knew that was only half the answer that lay behind the smile and the kiss he laid on her cheek, a kiss that all at once felt cold.

2

The next morning Narvo finished the court that had been interrupted on the morning of the massacre. Reluctantly he sentenced the man who had murdered the *kuru* patient to be kept in custody till a plane came in to take him out for trial before the Supreme Court. He was convinced that Sangiap, the murderer, was mentally backward, and he was also convinced that the man had been in a trance at the time of the murder; the killing had not been as cold-blooded as had been the massacre down at the bridge. If it had been in his power he would have given Sangiap a short sentence in the Kundavi stockade, then let him go back to Vaikaka. As it was, he made up his mind to speak in defense of Sangiap when the latter came up for trial before the Judge of the Supreme Court.

Narvo's outlook on Sangiap did not impress the district commissioner when the officer flew in from Goroka that afternoon. Neil Figgins was a small dapper man with a mustache that he continually brushed with the knuckle of his forefinger: the gesture made him look pensive or vain, depending upon one's experience of him. Actually he was neither vain nor pensive: his mind was too quick and incisive for either indulgence. "These blighters need to be taught a lesson, Roy."

"Not this feller," said Narvo. "The Benamaua mob, yes. But locking this feller up for a couple of years, or stretching his neck, won't teach *them* a lesson. This bloke Sangiap is a bit light in the head. I saw him right after he had killed the woman. He no more knew what he had done than a sleepwalker. It's the *kuru* that's right at the bottom of this, Neil. If you've got the answer to that, I'll gladly make use of it."

"How do you mean the *kuru* is at the bottom of it?"

"It has them scared. It's always had them scared. And while they're scared, they'll always be looking for evil spirits. And you'll never educate or civilize these kanakas while they believe in evil spirits."

"So you think once you've got rid of the *kuru,* you'll have a clear go?"

"Hell, no. It's only one of the troubles we have to face. But it's the cause of the immediate mess, the one we have to get tidied up before this UN party comes in."

Figgins looked at Traxal. The meeting was taking place on the veranda of Narvo's house. Besides Figgins and Narvo there were Traxal, Rossi, Macy and Jack Maugham, the district officer from Goroka; and grouped about the bottom of the steps some fifty natives, staring at the conference with the frank curiosity of children at some demonstration. Now and again Sergeant Beraki went through the group, shouting and wielding his stick; the group broke up, then reformed behind him without taking its eyes off the men on the veranda. It was like trying to disperse a mudhole.

"What about this *kuru?*" Figgins said to Traxal. "You any further advanced?"

Traxal shook his head. "No more than I was six months ago. I've sent blood and brain specimens to Melbourne and to various places overseas, but we still haven't found a clue to what causes it."

"How does it affect them?" Maugham, a tall red-headed man with the biggest belly Narvo had ever seen, had been district officer at Goroka only three months; he had spent all his time down on the coast and in the islands, and he was still learning about the mountain people.

"Well, to begin with," said Traxal, "it strikes only at this one people in this area. It isn't known outside this particular district, nowhere else in New Guinea or anywhere in the world. The area, as far as I can trace it, is bounded by those two gorges over there and that mountain range right at the back. Perhaps ten thousand natives live there. No native from this side of the gorge has gone down with *kuru,* and as far as I can see it isn't infectious."

"Is it some sort of mountain sorcery?" Maugham asked.

"No, it is certainly a disease. It can affect a child as early as four years. As children, it affects twice as many girls as boys, then in adults the ratio becomes fourteen women to one man. I'll take you down and show you the disease in its various stages. We have eleven patients right now, they're coming in practically every day. This is the worst outbreak we've had."

"All of them bound to die?" Figgins said, stroking his mustache, looking more pensive than ever.

"I'm afraid so," Traxal said. "I don't think a doctor could be faced with anything more frustrating and depressing."

"Is that why you're leaving us?" asked Figgins, and both Narvo and Macy looked up sharply.

"No," said Traxal, looking straight at Figgins and avoiding

the gaze of the other men. "My time is up here in a couple of months. I am not bound to renew my contract."

"We were hoping you would," Figgins said. "Because we can't get a replacement for you. If you go, Eric will have to run the hospital on his own."

Macy kept the hope from his eyes. "I could do it, if I had to," he murmured, unable to refrain from chewing a little faster on his gum.

"I know that, Eric." Figgins knew Macy better than the latter realized; an ambitious man, he recognized ambition in others. He was just not prepared to be as self-sacrificing, to work for nothing, as he knew Macy would. He believed in what he was doing, but he also believed in fair payment. He was a trade unionist in the trade of idealism. "I just don't like to have a setup in my district where a man is underpaid for the job he is doing. You would be underpaid, and there would be nothing I could do about it."

Macy didn't argue: he did not want to appear too eager for Traxal to go. At the back of his mind he wondered how he would tell Bernice of the prospect that had suddenly come up. The first question she would ask would be how was it going to better their financial position; whatever her reaction might be, right now it wasn't important. The important thing was that very soon he might realize his ambition. He would not be a doctor and he would not be in charge of a medical center; but he would be responsible for the health of a large number of patients and he would be running a hospital, even if only a native one. It was typical of the thinking of New Guinea men that he, and all the others, had completely overlooked Joan Duggan.

Later Narvo walked down to the Landrover with Figgins and Maugham. "I didn't know Peter was thinking of leaving," he said. "When he brought that girl of his out here, I thought he was planning on staying."

"I believe you weren't happy about my letting her come in here," said Figgins.

"How did you know that?"

"Grapevine," said Figgins, and stroked his mustache. "The kanakas aren't the only ones in these hills who are telepathic."

"What does your grapevine tell you about this UN crowd?"

"Just to watch your step. This particular crowd is coming looking for faults. Every member of it is anticolonial."

"So am I," said Narvo. "That's what makes this job so bloody difficult. But no one yet has come up with a system for civilizing these kanakas that is as good as the old colonial system. There has to be a boss to begin with, and we're stuck with the job. I think I might kidnap one of these UN johnnies and keep him here for a year to let him see how tough things really are."

"Just don't put him on your ration list," said Figgins, and climbed into the Landrover beside Maugham. "I've got my own troubles back at Goroka, keeping out the coffee speculators."

"We're picking up another little trouble over at Okantu. Did Neil tell you we have a visitor from Canberra?" Maugham was arranging his belly, getting ready for the rough trip over to the airstrip.

"He mentioned something about it," Narvo said offhandedly. Figgins had told him all about the visitor from Canberra in the note in which he had warned that he, Narvo, was to be the scapegoat if anything displeased the UN committee. "What's he like?"

"A trier," said Figgins. "Just the bloke to send up here to write a report. Doesn't know a thing about it, but he's a trier."

"Do you think we Aussies should have taken on this job?" Narvo said. "I mean, trying to get this country out of the Stone Age?"

"No," said Figgins. "By experience and history—which may be the same thing—we were the least fitted to do the job. It's only a little over fifty years since we stopped being a colony ourselves. We haven't yet really learned how to run our own country. But who else would have come in here if we hadn't? The Indonesians, the Indians, the Chinese? They've got their own problems at home. And in any case, the truth is that at this stage we wouldn't want any one of them as such close neighbors. We haven't yet learned to trust each other—it's just a question of color, but it's a fact and it's there. The Yanks wouldn't have taken it on because they're traditionally anticolonial, although they at least don't go gunning for us in the UN. The British— well, they're trying to get rid of their colonies, not take more on. And the Dutch have got their own headache over in West New Guinea without taking this one on. No, we had to come in here because these kanakas, civilized or uncivilized, are our best bet as neighbors for the next hundred years. Nobody back home worries much, I mean the ordinary bloke in the street, but Australia's real problems are up here. They begin north from Thursday Island. And we're the bunnies who have to do what we can to solve those problems. Some of us are going to get it in the neck, without any justification, but that's the price of progress when you're trying to please everyone. Especially when you're dealing with so-called intelligent men who divide the world into white and black." He motioned to the native driver to start up the engine. "So long, Roy, and good luck. Bring in those Benamaua killers if you can."

"Yeah," said Narvo, and watched the Landrover go down the road. The natives ran after it, yelling *Aiyo!* the greeting that meant *I should like to kiss your genitals,* and which Figgins, a man with respect for local customs, acknowledged with a like cry and a straight face.

Narvo looked across the gorge to the mountain opposite, and beyond it to the ranges under their battlements of clouds. In the village on the mountain opposite, which was Vaikaka, a column of smoke wavered like a trembling finger; Narvo wondered if the smoking of Paiwo's wife had already begun, and his nostrils crinkled with the memory of slowly roasted flesh. Two

women went by, their *bilum* bags on their backs supported by
cords around their foreheads; their net bags were full of *kau-kau,*
and they were so far bent over against the weight of their burden
that they could not raise their eyes to greet the Kiap. An old
man, one-armed and half blind, went shuffling by, leading a
small pig on a string; he spat out betel-nut juice, and the spittle
fell to the ground like a red petal. A young man, hair sprouting
a coronet of red parrot feathers topped by bird of paradise
plumes, came up the path. A breast-plate of gold-lip shell hung
from his neck, and he wore a chain of large white cowrie shells
down his back. A cresent of cassowary bone hung from the hole
in his nose, and loops of bamboo dangled from the lobes of his
ears. The fur of a tree-climbing kangaroo, dyed yellow, was
twisted around one arm; the other upper arm was wound around
with string made from the fiber of an orchid stem. His decorated
belt carried an empty *bilum* bag in front, and a strip of dyed
bark hung down at the back. He carried two spears, a heavy
warrior's spear and a light hunting one. He pushed the old man
out of the way and came striding up to Narvo.

"Why did you push the old man aside?" Narvo said.

"He is weak and useless," said the native. "He clutters up the
path of those who are young and strong."

Narvo knew that this was the social philosophy of these natives: life was too hard in these mountains to waste time and
sympathy on those unable to fend for themselves. But that
didn't make him less angry. "Who are you, strong one?"

The native did not miss the sarcasm. He had to look up at
Narvo, but he was able to give the impression that their gaze
was level. His thick lips curled. "I do not give my name to the
Kiap."

Narvo did not press the point. Some of the tribes still believed
that to give one's name to a stranger was to give power to the
stranger over oneself; and this native, proud and unafraid, was

not going to give that power to the Kiap. "All right, then. Where do you come from?"

The native waved an arm; the spearheads glinted in the sun. "From Kagata."

"I know the village. What do you want?"

"I come with news for the Kiap. He wants the killers of Benamaua. I know their names. They are led by Nudgil, the fight-leader."

"This I know," said Narvo. "Why do you tell me this?"

"Does the Kiap know that the men of Vaikaka are going to look for the killers of Benamaua?"

Narvo was not going to show ignorance in front of this arrogant informer: he knew why the man was here, but he repeated the question anyway: "Why do you tell me this?"

"The Kiap does not want war. He is like the people of Kagata —they want peace."

"What else do the people of Kagata want?"

The native stared up at Narvo. "The lands of the Benamaua and the Vaikaka. When they have all killed each other, the Kiap will give the lands and the salt spring to the peaceful people of Kagata."

"Like hell I will," said Narvo in English, then reverted to dialect. "We shall see. There is no certainty that the Benamaua and the Vaikaka are going to war."

But he could put no note of certainty into his voice even as he said it.

3

Elisabeth was washing Bandi's head when Narvo came up the path from the guest hut. The boy, his head topped by a wig of white lather, didn't know whether to laugh or to cry; he crouched with his eyes tightly shut and his mouth wide open, while Elisabeth poured water over him from a battered enamel pitcher.

Children from the married police boys' quarters stood around in a laughing circle, happy that they were not being subjected to the rigors of civilization: they shrieked with glee as the soap ran down into Bandi's eyes, and urged Elisabeth to throw more water on him.

"I'm taking him back to his village," Narvo said.

"Do you have to do that?" Elisabeth began to towel Bandi's head. "I don't mind looking after him till his father returns."

"That's why I'm going to Vaikaka. I don't know if his father is going to return."

"If you keep Bandi here, won't that ensure Paiwo's coming back?"

Narvo smiled. "Did you learn that little bit of blackmail in Czechoslovakia?"

"It works," said Elisabeth. "I know of quite a few escapees who have returned home because the Communists would not allow their families to follow them."

"Does Peter have a family?"

She had not expected such a blunt question. "Why, yes. His father and mother and two sisters all live in Prague. And he has a brother at the university in Olomouc."

"He has plenty of reasons, then, for going back to Czechoslovakia."

"Has he told you that is what he intends to do?"

"No," he said. "Has he told you?"

She hedged on the question, giving all her attention to the drying of Bandi's hair; the boy's head wobbled on his shoulders under her vigorous toweling. "I should not have come all the way out here if Peter had told me he was returning to Czechoslovakia."

"Probably not," said Narvo, but noted how she had phrased her reply: she had neither answered his question nor told him a lie. "Anyhow, I'm taking Bandi over to Vaikaka with me. Keeping him here won't bring his dad back if he doesn't want to come. Parental love is a controllable urge amongst these kanakas. They have other urges that are less controllable."

"Such as?"

"The urge for revenge. The urge to prove you're just as good a fighter as the man on the other side of the mountain."

"If Paiwo is not at the village, will you leave Bandi there?"

"That remains to be seen," Narvo said, and ran his hand over the boy's now dry hair. "In these hills I've found it pays never to make a decision till you are confronted with it."

"I gathered that, had you known I was coming, you would have made your decision on me before you were confronted with me."

He looked at her without replying for a moment, then he said dryly, "You must have given the Communists in Prague a lot of headaches."

"On the contrary," she said, "I was always welcome in Prague. Even Communists like to have women around them."

"Which is another point, then, on which they and I disagree. Although perhaps, in different circumstances, they might see my point. The Communists have been fortunate so far. Unlike the colonial powers, they have never yet been called upon to educate a really savage people. Backward people like the Turkmen, yes, but never savages like these kanakas. When they do, they may find they'll have to amend a lot of their ideas. Including that of having women share the work."

"Just why do you object to women, Mr. Narvo?"

"I don't object to them in general. I am anything but a misogynist—when I am away from Kundavi. I just think this is not the place for them."

"But why? Is it because you think Kundavi is too dangerous? Women have shared danger before with men. Your own country was built on the partnership of men and women sharing the hardships of the pioneering days."

Narvo hesitated, then he said, "Do you want to come over to Vaikaka with me?"

"Yes," she said, then relented a little: "I should like to do that, Roy."

Twenty minutes later Narvo, Elisabeth, Bandi and Sergeant Beraki went down the road in the Landrover. Traxal, standing on the steps of the hospital, saw them go and forgot for a moment to hide the annoyance and jealousy he felt.

"You can't expect her to sit twiddling her thumbs," said Joan Duggan, putting her glasses on and looking after the disappearing vehicle.

"Where are they going?" Traxal tried to sound as if he hadn't heard her comment.

"Your guess is as good as mine," said Duggan, taking off her glasses and polishing them: it was as if she were removing an expression that might show, might give her away. "Except that I wouldn't be bothered to start guessing. What Roy Narvo does, doesn't worry me."

She turned and went into the hut, and not for the first time Traxal wondered about her. Did she really dislike Narvo or was she in love with him, and knowing she was handicapped by her ugliness, preferred not to show any weakness? Traxal had never been any good at reading women's minds or anticipating their reactions: it had been the one fault that had let him down in his love affair with Elisabeth. All their quarrels had been the result of his indifference or insensitivity to Elisabeth's moods; her moods might not have been caused by him, but he had never been able to anticipate any cause at all. He had not been selfish or brutally callous, but, like so many men, had been born with complete ignorance of what motivated a woman in anything she did. Only his charm and natural sympathy had saved him from being a boor. It was these latter qualities, plus his looks and his talent as a lover, that had made Elisabeth fall in love with him. She had fallen in love with him at eighteen, when her experience of men had been negligible, and she had remained in love for the next two years, till he had escaped abroad; and the five years since, although Traxal didn't know and Elisabeth herself was only just beginning to realize it, had been his best insurance that she had continued to remain in love with him. In different circumstances their love might not have lasted. He had never really appreciated that Elisabeth's best quality was her loyalty.

Which perhaps was why he was not disturbed by Bernice's lack of loyalty. She came down the path to him, bosom bouncing, smiling brightly, chattering before she had even reached him. He looked at her and thought that, like so many Australian women, she was as unsubtle as a flirtatious cow, but there was a healthy sensuality about her that he liked. He had enjoyed the weekend, spontaneous and unplanned, that he had spent with her in Moresby; but he had accepted no invitations and given none once they had returned to Kundavi. They had never spoken of the weekend; sometimes they shared a secret smile, but that was all. He could not think of themselves as lovers, but only as two people who had shared a bed in an effort to dispel loneliness and seek distraction. He had been afraid at first that Bernice, with her endless chatter, would sooner or later let the cat out of the bedroom, as it were; then, as time went on, he had been continuously surprised at Bernice's talent for masquerade and secrecy. If it had not been for the occasional smile, to show that she still remembered, he might almost have believed that she looked on him as a man she knew no better than Father Shawn or Jack Bermingham. For, though he did not want a recurrence of the affair, Traxal was glad of that occasional smile: it saved his ego from complete prostration.

"Peter, I want to talk to you. Now, I mean, not later. It's important——"

"What about, Bernice?" He looked back over his shoulder, to make sure Duggan had disappeared. Was Bernice suddenly going to spoil a good record and bring up that weekend in Moresby?

"About Eric. And you leaving here. Look, where can we go? I don't want Eric to hear me——"

She had told him things at Moresby that she hadn't wanted Eric to hear. But this was different, and he recognized the difference and wished for escape. He was being ensnared, entangled in other people's lives, something that right now he wanted to avoid as much as he wished to avoid getting *kuru*.

"Come on, Peter. Let's walk down to the cliff. Come on, why are you holding back? I'm not going to push you over. Eric is the one I'd push——"

They went down the path together, and from the window of her office, behind the bamboo blind, Duggan watched them go. She had her glasses on, and her eyes behind the thick lenses glittered with tears that could have been tears of hate, of envy or plain self-pity.

4

"We have to walk from here," Narvo said; and leaving the native driver with the Landrover, they began the climb up the steep path that led to Vaikaka. Narvo walked ahead carrying Bandi, now and again turning to see how Elisabeth was negotiating the steep ascent, and Sergeant Beraki brought up the rear. The path was bordered with stakes that fenced the precipitous gardens. Elisabeth, stopping to get her breath, saw the gardeners bent over against the slope of the mountainside and wondered how they kept their balance.

"Why do they stay on these mountains?" She was panting, the breath catching in her chest: the altitude, as well as the climb itself, was affecting her. "Why don't they move out to some of the valleys?"

"It's a question of survival, mostly." Even though he had been carrying the boy, Narvo was breathing easily. He sat on a rock, his hat tilted back on his head, and drank water from the palm leaf cup Beraki had brought him. "Up here on these spurs they can keep an eye on their neighbors—the Good Neighbor doctrine hasn't penetrated to these parts of the world yet. Living up here, too, they dodge a lot of the fevers from down in the valleys— malaria, for instance. And scrub typhus. On top of that, these people don't like change, either of place or custom. They've lived up here for centuries, so why change? These blokes are the original reactionaries."

"What are they doing up there?" Elisabeth pointed farther up the mountain, where smoke wreathed up to join the low clouds.

"Burning off to make more gardens. They're killing the land and the timber around here, but they won't listen to me. Survival for these bods means only for themselves and their kids—they just don't understand why they should have to worry about their unborn grandchildren. Progress has its drawbacks when you bring it to these people. You bring them medicine, improve their health, lessen the infant mortality rate—then find in ten years that the population has nearly doubled but is still living on the same area of ground. And you can't get them to move. We are having that problem over in the Chimbu district now. So far it hasn't come here, but it will."

"Do you ever get disheartened by all these problems?"

He sat looking down the slope at her. He was regretting now that he had brought her: she was going to see something that would probably make her sick, might even have a permanent effect on her. His decision to bring her had been a spur-of-the-moment one: he had hoped, by shocking her, to prove his point that these mountains were no place for white women.

He stood up, picking up Bandi. "I do get disheartened occasionally. But maybe I'd get just as disheartened outside—" He waved a hand beyond the ring of mountains. "There are just as many problems out there. At least in here I can try to solve these in my own way."

"Except when United Nations committees come in?"

He nodded. "I believe in a united world, but I'm cursed by being an individualist. That's my own particular problem."

They climbed on up the path and came to Vaikaka. The village, surrounded by a stockade of head-high stakes, their tops sharpened so that the fence had the threatening look of a regiment of raised spears, lay on a tiny flat stretch at the end of a narrow spur. Its houses were all of the same type: low walls, only three feet high, of sacsac, topped by a conical roof of *kunai*-thatch; a man of Narvo's height would not have been able to stand up even in the very center of a hut. Pigs, chickens and some mongrel dogs roamed about the stockade; a white cockatoo sat on a pole outside a hut and screeched at the visitors. A flat space, its surface trodden hard by generations of dancing feet, was at the far end of the village. Here a hut without walls had been erected, and beneath its *kunai* roof the smoking of the body of Paiwo's wife was taking place.

Narvo stopped and put Bandi down. "Do you want to stay here?" he said to Elisabeth. "This business often makes people sick when they see it for the first time."

The villagers, silent and curious, were clustered about Elisabeth; but even above the smell of them, she was aware of the other odor that she had never smelt before. "You brought me up here to show me something. Was this it?"

He hesitated. "Well, yes. But you don't have to see it if you don't want to. You won't be the first to turn your back on it."

"The first woman, you mean?"

"Both. Man or woman. Father Shawn never comes up here when this is on. Says he prefers to wait for the hereafter to put up with the burning of the dead. He has a fifty-fifty chance of avoiding it, he reckons."

"I should not like to bet on my chances. The odds may not be so good."

Narvo smiled, looking at her approvingly for what she thought was the first time. "Are you a betting woman?"

"I used to go to the races in Prague. It was another means of escape."

"A lot of people down in Sydney look on it the same way. My father escapes from my mother every Saturday afternoon." He turned Bandi over to one of the native women, saying something in dialect, then he took Elisabeth's arm and led her through the crowd toward the hut at the end of the village. "Don't breathe too deeply, that's the trick. And don't let your imagination run away with you. This was once a human being. It's just dead flesh now."

A platform of banana palm trunks had been built beneath the shelter of the *kunai*-thatch roof. The body of Kabu was propped in a sitting position, the feet and hands tied to the platform, and a piece of bark cloth had been passed between the legs and was kept in place by a waistband of thick vine-fiber: Elisabeth had been surprised at the odd quirks of modesty these people seemed to have. A slow fire burned beneath the platform, and two women, Kabu's mother and sister, sat beside the fire.

"They don't smoke all their dead," Narvo said. "Mostly village leaders, young men and young women, and battle victims. If Kabu hadn't been a victim of that massacre down at the bridge, when she died she would have been taken to the caves over there on that mountain and just left there with all the kids and the old folks who died from natural causes." He looked at her with concern. "How are you feeling?"

She nodded, not trusting herself to speak: she knew he had invited her here to test her, and she was determined not to fail. She kept her mouth shut, her nostrils tight, her mind as dead as she could make it, and gazed steadily at what went on before her. The heat of the fire had raised blisters on the skin of the corpse and the two women were wiping the skin with bark cloths; they worked carefully but with no show of emotion, as if this were no more than another of the thankless tasks women got in this savage life. Occasionally one of the women would turn her face away from the smoke of the fire and spit, but they appeared unaffected by the smell of the smoked corpse.

"They never mention the corpse's name while this is going on. All smoked corpses get the same name. Amabiaka." Narvo had moved upwind from the fire; the breeze from the gorges took the smell away. "They wipe off those blisters because if the fat drips to the ground, then the spirit of Amabiaka is lost forever. They believe in hell, too."

They walked back to the other end of the village, the natives crowding around them. They were all smiling now and when Narvo smiled back at one of them, the man pointed to his own mouth, then at Narvo's.

"It's this gold tooth," Narvo said to Elisabeth. "It's the bane of my father's life, he being a dentist. But it gives me prestige here amongst the kanakas. Now they're all saving up to buy a gold tooth and get up to my social level."

"That particular man seems impressed by more than your gold tooth," Elisabeth said.

Narvo grinned at the man. "He and I are old friends. His brother once put a trade ax into my shoulder. I had to kill him— blew the top of his head off. It impressed the rest of them. Especially that feller there. He thinks I'm God Almighty. Father Shawn hasn't yet succeeded in convincing him otherwise. I'm half hoping he never does. Not for the elevation to the divinity —just for the protection. If ever he finds out I'm mortal he might try to finish off the job his brother started. He's not too bright to begin with, and his idea of his own immortality would be to kill a Kiap. Wouldn't it, you blood-thirsty bastard?" he said, and the native, grinning widely, not understanding a word, nodded vigorously.

Then Narvo turned to the crowd and asked for Paiwo. The *luluai*, an old man, his skinny body marked by scar tissue over an old burn, his badge of office glinting brightly in the middle of his forehead, stepped forward. Everyone had tried to answer Narvo's question, but the *luluai* barked an order: he was the government's representative and they had better not forget it. At least not while the Kiap was here.

"Paiwo is not here, Kiap." His face was too scarred and wrinkled to be impassive; but the same wrinkles and scars disguised the thoughts that went through the cunning old brain. "He grieves for his loss."

"Where does he grieve?"

The old man waved a hand: the wide, wide world was Paiwo's grieving ground. Narvo looked around at the crowd, then back at the *luluai*. "Where is Wangamunggu? And the young men? Bring me the Village Book." The old man hesitated, then moved slowly away, and Narvo reverted to English: "Get a move on, you old devil, or I'll toe you up the rudder!"

"Something is wrong?" Elisabeth said, and felt the tension in the crowd around her.

"I don't know." Narvo seemed only half aware of her. He spoke to Sergeant Beraki in police Motu: "Beraki, I'll have a roll call of all the men. Round 'em up!"

The *luluai* brought the Village Book. "This is like a Gutenberg Bible to these fellers," Narvo said to Elisabeth, taking the cheap cardboard-covered book. The books showed the usual governmental lack of imagination, and Narvo always tried to make up for the humdrum official approach. This Vaikaka book was decorated with a colorful picture of the Queen, cut from a woman's magazine, on the front cover; the back cover bore a picture of Keith Miller in action, not because Narvo was a cricketing fan but because he had been running short of colored pictures. A neighboring village's book was decorated with a picture of a racehorse, a species of animal the natives had never seen; had the original horse of the photograph been brought to the village, it would have been an object of idolatry, although the natives, in that respect, would not have been departing far from the customs of their more civilized brothers down South. Narvo held the Vaikaka book out for Elisabeth to see. "To have their names in here means government protection. They haven't yet woken up to the fact that it also means government authority and the means of enforcing it. Righto, Beraki, line 'em up!"

Besides Paiwo and Wangamunggu there were twelve young men missing from the roll call. Narvo slammed the Village Book shut and handed it back to the *luluai*. "Tell Paiwo and Wangamunggu I want them over at the patrol post before the sun is in the top of the sky tomorrow."

"I shall tell him, Kiap," said the *luluai*, and gave a salute that, if it had not been so naturally inept, could have been a derisive gesture.

"What do we do about Bandi?" Elisabeth said.

Narvo looked down at the boy standing between two native women. The boy stared up at him with what he knew must be trust: Bandi was too young for deceit. Or was he? At what age did deceit start amongst a people who had learned through countless generations that one could not live by trust alone? Suspicion, deceit, treachery were born in the blood of these people: it was part of their inheritance of the means of survival.

"I don't know. If his dad comes back, then everything will be all right. If he doesn't come back—" He looked around at the silent natives, up at the mountains, across the gorges at the distant patrol post, then back at Elisabeth: he had just taken in the whole of his world, where he was king but where his head would fall if things went wrong. "If he doesn't come back, I'm going to be too busy to be raising children. There'll be a war on."

"Will this village be attacked?"

"It could be. The pay-back is part of the mental make-up of these kanakas. A man hurts another man, the second man pays back the first, the first man in turn pays back the second—it goes on *ad infinitum*, till someone gets tired or they're all dead.

Unless I can stop it before they really get into the swing of it."

"Do they resent your interference in their tribal wars?"

He grinned. "Both sides would do me over if they got the chance. This is just like the United Nations—internal squabbles are no concern of outsiders. Although I might have some trouble convincing the members of this committee of that."

"Where do you think Paiwo and the other men are now?"

"They could be anywhere, but I'd hazard a guess they're on their way to Benamaua. We'll get back to Kundavi, I'll get together a police party and we'll go over there. If I went over there now on my own, I'd be gone in a moment and nothing would have been achieved. I can't prevent the fight, but I can arrest the winners afterwards and maybe teach them a lesson."

"I'd like to take Bandi back with us," Elisabeth said suddenly. "I don't like the thought of his being involved in all this. I shall look after him——"

"You'll be gone from here in a few months. When Peter goes."

"The trouble may all be over by then. Paiwo may be back at the post." She took Bandi's hand, and the boy gave it to her without demur. "Please, Roy."

Narvo hesitated, then he shrugged. "Righto, we'll take him back with us. I don't want to see the poor little beggar massacred, either. I don't want to see any of them massacred, if I can help it." He looked over the heads of the natives to the end of the village where the corpse sat on its smoking throne. "If this thing gets out of hand, these mountains will be covered in smoke. We shan't need the Village Book. Everyone will answer to the name of Amabiaka."

8

HIGH UP on the mountain, above the ledge where the smoked dead sat and looked out with sightless eyes over the gorges, Paiwo saw the Kiap leave the village and go down the path to the road far below where the Landrover was parked. Cloud was drifting across the face of the mountain and occasionally the party below was cut off from view; but Paiwo had recognized that the Kiap had with him the new white woman, the arrogant island police sergeant and Paiwo's own son. The Kiap was carrying Bandi, and Paiwo watched the two-headed creature go down the path: love and loyalty struggled within him, but tribal law and custom were too strong. He drew his bark cloak about him, feeling cold, not yet warmed as the others were by the excitement of the coming battle with the Benamaua.

"We go now." Wangamunggu crouched beside Paiwo. He carried his shield, his bow and arrows and his bone-tipped fighting spears: he was like a child on its way to a party, carrying his deadly presents. A *bilum* bag swung under one armpit: it held some *kau-kau* and two roasted rats: he and the other men had gone farther up the mountain, where the women were burning off the *kunai*, and caught their food. One or two of them had a small cus-cus in their bags; two of them had been fortunate enough to catch a small wallaby and had divided it. The warriors would go into their battle well fed.

"The Kiap has gone. We go now," Wangamunggu repeated, and stood up. He wore no ceremonial headdress, but just a single green parrot's feather stuck in his hair topknot; a necklace of pig tusks clicked coldly as they swung against his breast. The curved pig's tusk in his nose was turned upwards, the sign that a man was on the way to kill.

Cloud had now obscured the valley and Paiwo could no longer see his son and the Kiap. "It is not good weather for fighting." He pointed across the valley to where a rain cloud hung like a spreading bruise against the white thigh of a towering cumulus. "One cannot fight in the rain."

"A true warrior can fight in any weather," said Wangamunggu, and Paiwo knew the argument was lost: the question of courage was the final answer to everything in these mountains.

The party, led by Wangamunggu, began the march over the ridges to the village of Benamaua. They went down through the cloud, past the resting place of the smoked dead, keeping their eyes averted, not wanting to take the spirit of these dead with them on this march: these dead had not been killed by the Benamaua, and the strength of the Vaikaka men must be kept pure, fired only by the spirits of those dead they were now going to avenge. They went down into a gorge, keeping away from the worn paths, crossed the river, climbed through a grove of dripping casuarina trees, and came up behind a long line of pandanus palms. Beyond the palms, at the end of a garden-covered spur, stood Benamaua.

"The men are in the village," said Wangamunggu, peering through the screen of palms. "They have returned now they know the Kiap has come and gone. But they will have guards posted in case he should come back."

"They will have guards looking out for us, too," said Paiwo, wanting to return to his own village.

"That is to be expected. We do not want the fight to be too easy. The women are working in the gardens, but we have not come to kill women. That is for the likes of the Benamaua."

It was also for the likes of some of the younger Vaikaka men who had not yet killed. They stared at the unsuspecting women among the *kau-kau* domes, trying to imagine the feel of a spear in the hand as it went into a back or a belly. But Wangamunggu was the fight-leader, and none of them dared challenge his authority.

"The rain will be here soon," Wangamunggu said. "The clouds are coming down the mountain. We shall use them for cover."

Paiwo, silent and troubled, watched the thick clouds rolling down the mountainside like a gray landslide. A few drops of rain fell and he shivered as they hit his skin; he drew his cloak about him, but he knew he would need more than a bark cloak for the cold that lay inside him. Down in the gardens the women had brought out their pandanus umbrella mats; they crouched beneath them in the rain and to Paiwo they had the look of women already in grief. The rain spattered on the broad leaves of the pandanus palms that hid the fighting party, making the leaves shine and turning the *marita* fruit of the palm into a long glistening cob of bright red crystals. Then the rain abruptly stopped, the air turned cold and the cloud rolled down over the men of Vaikaka. Wangamunggu stood up and the other men rose with him.

The cloud was thick, and as the Vaikaka men moved down through it one flank man could not see the other. Paiwo, unhampered now by his *bilum* bag and his bark cloak, which he had left behind the screen of palms, moved in the track of Wangamunggu. They ran swiftly down the path that led between the gardens; beyond the garden fences the women still crouched beneath their umbrella mats. Paiwo caught a glimpse of one woman, looking like the dim shape of a bush; the broad leaves of the mat hung over her, dripping water. The earth of the path was greasy with rain, and Paiwo had to run carefully. The cloud swirled about them, cutting out all sound but the soft pad of their feet as they ran; shapes appeared out of the gray mist and were gone before they could be recognized. A bird whistled through the cloud, and Paiwo faltered, thinking for a moment that it was an arrow.

They were at the gates of the Benamaua stockade when Wangamunggu, running faster than the others, proving his title as fight-leader, slipped and went down in a flurry of arms and legs. In that moment the cloud rolled on and the sun came out in a blinding burst.

Paiwo, running behind Wangamunggu, had to leap over the fallen fight-leader. He was some ten yards ahead of the other Vaikaka men, well inside the gates, when the first arrow went by his head. The Benamaua men, at the far end of the stockade, were ready and waiting for them.

Paiwo faltered in his run, then cut sharply to his right behind a hut. He saw one of the younger Vaikaka men go plunging past, running with chest bared into an arrow; his battle cry changed in his throat to a death scream, and he lurched and fell with a look of hurt surprise on his face. Then Paiwo saw the two Benamaua men hidden by the gate, and he turned and went at them. They were about to swing the gate shut, trapping the Vaikaka men within the stockade, when Paiwo hit the first of them with his club. Then two other Vaikaka men appeared, and the Benamaua men died with the gate still open.

Paiwo turned and, crouching on one knee, sent an arrow in the general direction of the main Benamaua party. He had come into this battle without enthusiasm or excitement, and his mind had not reacted quickly to the unexpected resistance of the Benamaua. It was a long time since he had last fought, not since before he had gone to live with the Kiap. His hands were shaking and he was amazed and ashamed at his own fear.

An arrow thudded into the wall of the hut beside him. In the gardens outside the village he could hear the screams of the women; in one of the huts a child was wailing in a thin, pitiful voice. A pig squealed and went rushing across the open space in the middle of the village; three fowls followed it, their squawking like a long-drawn-out echo of the pig's squeal. A young woman holding her arms across her bouncing breasts came out of a hut and ran toward the Benamaua men. Paiwo saw the arrow appear suddenly in her shoulder, like a miraculously sprouted wing bone, but she kept running and disappeared behind the line of the enemy.

The Vaikaka warriors were now all inside the stockade and had split up. Wangamunggu had regained his feet and sped behind a clump of bamboo. He was working his way slowly along the fence of the village, not firing his arrows till he was sure of his shots. He had reached the second last hut when the Benamaua man leapt out at him with stone club upraised. Wangamunggu threw up his shield, but he was too late. The club came down and Wangamunggu's skull split open and was crushed; he fell forward and lay with the red cabbage of his head like an offering at his enemy's feet. He died without a murmur, a fighting man not surprised by nor angry at his fate.

Paiwo saw Wangamunggu go down, and saw at once the indecision that gripped the young Vaikaka men. Instinctively they all looked toward him, and just as instinctively Paiwo looked toward the open gates behind him. Then he heard the yell from the Benamaua men, and he knew it was too late for retreat. He saw the fight-leader of the Benamaua coming toward him, spear upraised and the threat to kill marked plainly, like another tribal scar, on his yelling face. In that instant Paiwo realized he was now the Vaikaka fight-leader and the result of the battle depended on him.

There was not time to fit another arrow into his bow. He dragged the stone club from his belt and, flinging up his shield, leapt out to meet the Benamaua. He was hardly aware of the battle yell that tore its way out of him; it was instinctive, like the snarl of an animal going in for the kill. The Benamaua fight-leader hurled his spear; it hit Paiwo's shield, splintering it and twisting it aside. Paiwo stood exposed, head-on to the onrushing Benamaua. Paiwo braced himself, his club arm raised; he saw the swung club of the enemy fight-leader and at the last moment he stepped aside. He brought his own club down and it went in against the side of the neck of the Benamaua. Paiwo felt the club go home, the muscle and sinew yielding beneath it; then the blood lust boiled up in him, like an old forgotten fever. He hit again and again, yelling frenziedly; then he spun away and went leaping in long strides toward another of the enemy. Behind him he heard the suddenly excited yells of the Vaikaka young men, following their new fight-leader into action.

The battle was over in five minutes. The Benamaua suddenly broke through the ranks of the Vaikaka and ran out through the gates. They went up the path between the gardens, swung to the right and were soon lost to sight behind a long line of bamboo. The women, seeing their men flee, all at once turned and went down the steep slopes of the gardens. Some of them fell and rolled, others slid on their buttocks down the steeper slopes; in a moment they, too, had disappeared to join the Benamaua men. The Vaikaka warriors were left in the village, among their own dead and the dead of the Benamaua and with the old men and old women and the very young children cowering in the huts.

Paiwo stood breathing heavily, shivering a little with excitement: he had killed three men and proved himself a worthy successor to Wangamunggu as fight-leader. His club was red with blood, and his cane shield was splashed crimson. His cheek bled where an arrow had grazed it and his shoulder ached where a club had struck it a glancing blow. But these were part of the glory that was his and the pain of them was part of the excitement he felt.

Two young Vaikaka men came out of a hut dragging with them an old woman, a young girl and a child who could barely walk. "No!" Paiwo stepped forward as one of the young men raised his club. "We did not come to kill women and children. Wangamunggu said so, and now I say the same!"

The young men stared at him for a moment, then reluctantly they let the prisoners go. Paiwo looked at the young girl, still feeling the heat in his blood. She was betrothed: a line of betrothal marks had been burnt into the flesh above her breasts. She was a comely girl and later might be beautiful; she had the long nose that was considered beautiful, and the sunlight struck blue on her black skin. He ran his eyes over her and was reminded of Kabu; and he turned away and left the girl untouched. And saw the young man cutting the flesh from the buttocks of the dead Benamaua fight-leader.

He crossed quickly and grabbed the young buck by the shoulder. "No! We do not eat the flesh of the Benamaua!"

The young man stood up, the blood-dripping piece of flesh in his hand. "But if I eat the flesh of this Benamaua, who was a brave man, I shall inherit his courage and strength——"

"No!" Paiwo wasn't quite sure why he went against the custom of ages; there had been a time when he, too, had eaten the flesh of an enemy. But that had been before he had gone to work for the Kiap. "Leave the Benamaua in peace. Our women and children have been avenged."

He stared at the young man, aware of the other bucks standing around them. The young man looked down at the piece of flesh in his hand, then slowly his fingers opened and it dropped beside the body of the Benamaua fight-leader. Paiwo drew in a deep breath, knowing he had just won some other sort of victory, then he turned and crossed to where the body of Wangamunggu lay.

He gave orders and some of the young men went away and soon returned with a rough litter. Wangamunggu was laid on it, his battered head wrapped in a banana leaf. Paiwo picked up the dead man's arrows and broke them across his knee; the sound cracked loudly in the stillness of the village. The splintered shield was laid on the body, and the broken arrows on top of the shield. Then two men picked up the litter and the party began to march back to Vaikaka.

Paiwo walked at their head, the fight-leader. He took some betel-nut from the *bilum* bag that swung beneath his arm and began to chew on it. When he heard the noise of the plane, he looked up without fear, almost challengingly. The plane passed the peak of the mountain and flew on over the ranges toward the place Paiwo had heard of but never seen, Goroka: the place where the white man was coming in numbers to take the black man's land.

Paiwo spat out a glob of betel juice. It landed on the path and glistened for a moment like blood before it sank into the yellow clay.

2

Figgins leaned forward in his seat and tapped the shoulder of the man seated beside the pilot. "That is Kundavi over there. The place I was telling you about."

The man in front peered out of the window of the plane. He was a tall thin man whose khaki shirt and trousers still showed their newness; his feet ached in the new yellow boots tucked under the instrument panel in front of him. His gray felt hat, settled precisely on his head, had done nothing to protect him from the rays of the sun; his thin bony face was lobster red and his long nose had begun to peel. He had not wanted to make this trip, since he hated discomfort of any sort, but he had kept his complaints to himself. He had been warned before he had left the mainland that the Territory hands had little time for men from Canberra, especially those who complained about conditions in the Territory. He was not a man given to forthright opinions, which perhaps, he mused, was why he had been chosen to write the government report, and he always played safe: "Looks a nice layout. Mr. Narvo must be very comfortable over there."

Figgins raised his eyebrows at Maugham sitting beside him. "If he is comfortable it is all due to his own efforts. He built that post out of virgin country."

The man from Canberra realized his mistake. "Oh, I'm sure, I'm sure." Why hadn't they sent someone else to do this survey, someone who was really interested in New Guinea? He had been in the public service twenty-six years and he had always done a conscientious job; his very conscientiousness had raised him to a position of seniority in a department in which he had very little interest. He knew his attitude was wrong, but he just could not get excited about the future of a million natives who were not even Australian natives. He had been brought up to hate colonialism, and now here he was acting the part of a colonial official: it didn't help him at all to think that he was acting for the United Nations. Now if he had stayed in Treasury instead of transferring to Territories after the war . . . "He has done a magnificent job, one can see that."

The poor bastard, Figgins thought. *He's well-meaning but so ignorant.*

"Does Mr. Narvo have much trouble in his area?" The plane banked and the man from Canberra, fighting the sickness in his stomach, looked down and saw the line of natives like ants on the mountain path below.

"More than most," said Figgins, all at once deciding there was little to be gained by taking this man too much into confidence: the Benamaua business might be solved before it got to the Canberra level. "Kundavi has only recently been classified as a restricted area. And that classification doesn't apply to all of it."

Maugham, sitting beside Figgins, shifted his bulk in his seat. "That line of kanakas down there—they seemed to be carrying a litter with someone on it." He leaned forward and the young Polish pilot removed the radio headpiece from his ear. "Can you turn back and go down lower?"

The pilot shook his head and pointed ahead to where clouds were banking up above the ranges. "It's closing in over Goroka. I can't afford to take the risk."

"It'll have to wait. We'll hear about it if anything is wrong," Figgins said to Maugham. He looked out at the mountains below, then straight ahead at the back of the neck of the man from Canberra. "We always do."

The man from Canberra stirred uneasily in his seat, and wondered why the clock of history had moved so fast. The British, going against tradition, were giving away their colonies; the Americans, sticking to tradition, were not taking any on. The Australians, without the experience, the power or the wealth of either, were stuck with this most backward colony in all the world. It was enough to make a man write a report recommending that the country be given up to whoever wanted it. It was a report which, of course, the government wouldn't accept; and which he, not being a man of strong conviction, would not write, anyway. He valued his pension more than his politics.

9

WITHIN HALF AN HOUR news of the attack on Benamaua had reached the patrol post at Kundavi. No one from Benamaua crossed the bridge, for the Benamaua men knew that the Kiap still wanted them for the massacre of the women at the salt spring; but the word traveled, like a secret wind, down the mountain, along the ridges, across the gorge, and up to Kundavi. It was one of the police boys who finally brought the word to Sergeant Beraki.

Beraki took the news to Narvo. "*Tru*, Kiap. They say the bodies are still warm."

Narvo let out a curse that was like a grunt of pain. "They must have attacked while we were still on our way back from Vaikaka. You are sure, Beraki, that the attack was made by Vaikaka men?"

"The word says so, Kiap."

Narvo turned to Rossi. "I'll go back to Vaikaka, Frank, with a dozen of the boys. You take Beraki and the rest and go over to Benamaua."

"Do I bring anyone in?" Rossi took the rifle the police boy handed him, and worked the bolt. He had only one rifle, all he could afford; Administration funds did not run to well-stocked arsenals, and a patrol officer bought his own extra weapons. Narvo had four, all beautiful guns; and Rossi aspired to the same number. In this country, as in every backward country and even some not-so-backward ones, guns were a symbol of power. *Boong,* the sound of a gun being fired, had been the natives' first name for a white man. Years after the name had first been coined by the natives, Allied soldiers in the Pacific, proud of their own word coinage, drunk on inventions such as *doover, snafu, drongo,* had, as they thought, invented the word *boong* to describe the natives. The word was rarely heard now in New Guinea, but down on the coast some of the older, more sophisticated natives still smiled to themselves at the conceited self-delusion of those now-departed white soldiers. Rossi, who had never used the term *boong,* who never called a native even kanaka, patted the rifle almost affectionately and handed it back to the police boy to hold for him.

"Do I bring anyone in?" he said. "That is, if I find anyone alive."

"Bring in any buck who's still alive and was in that business down at the bridge," Narvo said. "They may think that now the Vaikaka have been at them, we've forgotten the massacre. Well, we haven't and I want them to know it!"

Then Jack Bermingham, one eye squinted against the sun, came up the parade ground with Father Shawn. "Roy, I got bad news for you," Bermingham said.

"Pile it on," said Narvo. "I'm punch-drunk with it."

"Paiwo led that attack on the Benamaua."

Narvo looked at Father Shawn, then back at Bermingham; for a moment he really did look punch-drunk. "Where did you get that? Wangamunggu is the Vaikaka fight-leader."

"He *was,*" said Bermingham, and hitched up his red lap-lap; one-eyed and scarred, he could have been an old fight-leader himself. "He got done over early in the piece, and Paiwo took over. The wife's old man just came in with the news, Roy. You can take it for gospel. I'm sorry, Roy," he said, and his voice softened. He recognized the beginning of defeat when he saw it: he had seen it so often in this country. "My word, I am."

Narvo said nothing. He felt sick, a sickness that was almost like a grief. Paiwo had somehow become a symbol to him, an example of what education and respect and, yes, affection could do for a primitive native. Paiwo was to have joined the police boys in a few months, and it had been part of Narvo's dream for the quiet native that he should someday take over from Sergeant Beraki. And that had not been the end of the dream: Paiwo, sometime in the distant future, was to have taken his place in the native parliament that was sure to come. But it was not just the disappointment of the broken dream that sickened Narvo. He had looked on himself as Paiwo's friend, and Paiwo had betrayed him. It was an old-timer's maxim that you could never trust a kanaka, and back in the bars of Goroka and Lae and Moresby there would be a sage nodding of heads when they heard of this. Narvo still did not believe the maxim, but that did not lessen the sickness he felt. The sense of personal disappointment was so great that for the moment he did not see the wider implications of Paiwo's act. He forgot completely the coming visit of the UN party.

The parade ground now was in commotion; people seemed to be coming from all directions. Beraki had lined up the full squad of police boys and was handing out ammunition to them, five rounds apiece; the boys took them and slipped them into the clips, the small drill done as slickly as could be done by any white man. The other natives, the houseboys and gardeners and hospital orderlies, stood around and admired and envied. They, too, would have given anything for a gun. The fact that the guns, in the hands of the police boys, were being taken out possibly to kill some of their relatives meant nothing to the envious onlookers.

Elisabeth, Traxal and the Macys had come down to join the

group of white men; they were followed a moment later by Joan Duggan, immaculate in white, like a prim starched angel.

"We have only four beds vacant," she said to Narvo. "I hope we aren't going to be swamped with casualties."

"So do I," said Narvo, too dispirited to argue with her. "And not just because of the lack of beds. Peter, would you go over to Benamaua with Frank? Just in case——"

Traxal nodded. "Shall I need to take a gun?" It was the first time in all his stay here that he had been involved in such an explosive situation. There had been several skirmishes between villages, and Narvo had been attacked half a dozen times out on patrol; but up till now Traxal had managed to avoid any real danger, and was glad of it. He was not afraid, but he was congenitally opposed to any violence; it was that part of his make-up that had, long ago as a schoolboy, made him argue with his father about Munich. It sickened him to see Narvo, or any of the natives, use violence; and he doubted, even if he did take a gun with him, that he could bring himself to use it on the Benamaua. He was relieved when Narvo shook his head.

"You'll have enough protection. I don't want them to look on you as part of punitive authority—we'll bear that label. You're supposed to be the Good Samaritan."

"A character they have no doubt heard of," said Duggan, her veil crackling softly.

Father Shawn looked at her and smiled, removing her barb from Narvo: he knew how sick the man was at Paiwo's betrayal. "I'm glad you think so, Sister Duggan. It means my sermons must be getting through to someone."

Duggan, a good Presbyterian, sniffed; but her sniff was aimed at Narvo, not at Father Shawn. She liked the little priest, even if he had none of the antiseptic holiness she expected in a good cleric. What he wanted, of course, was a good woman to manage him; but his benighted church didn't allow such a thing. She smiled belatedly at him, to show him the sniff hadn't been meant for him.

Rossi and Traxal left five minutes later in one of the Land-rovers, with four police boys in the back. The clouds had come in over the ranges and the valley was dull green, impassive as marble; the shadows had gone, drained from the contours, and the mountains presented the same dull bland face. It began to rain as the Landrover went out of sight down the road, and most of the natives turned and scattered for shelter. A native girl came running across from the hospital with an umbrella, and Duggan, looking like a young Queen Victoria, stood under it while the girl, holding the umbrella at arm's length, missed its shelter and quickly became drenched. *Shades of the British Raj,* Father Shawn thought: *some of these Australians were born in the wrong country and the wrong time.*

Bernice seemed oblivious of the rain. "Roy, are you taking the rest of the police boys over to Vaikaka with you?" He nodded. "Who's going to look after us?"

He turned away impatiently. "Oh, stop playing the fool, Bernice! I'm busy——"

"No, I'm serious!" She grabbed his arm. She was wet through, her hair hanging down in rats' tails over her forehead and her thin dress clinging to her body. Water streamed down her cheeks, but it was impossible to tell whether it was tears or rain. "They could come over here while you're gone——!"

"Bernice!" Narvo spoke sharply to her, as he might to a way-ward child. He suddenly recognized that she was really afraid, and he was sorry for her. The near loss of Harry in the massacre down at the bridge had had its effect on her, and now she was looking for dangers that had never previously troubled her. "If there was going to be any trouble—and I'm dead sure there won't be—I know Eric could cope with it." He looked over her head at Macy, staring unhappily at his wife. "Take her up to the house, Eric."

Macy went to put his arms about Bernice's shoulder, but she turned quickly away from him and went running up through the rain to their house. Halfway she stopped and turned round. "Harry! Harry, come here!"

The boy hesitated, looking up at his father. Macy, without any weakness, feeling more confident of the boy than he had felt in a long time, said, "You better go, Harry. I'll be up in a minute."

"Righto, Dad," Harry said, and turned away. "Good luck, Roy."

He walked slowly at first, and then, because of the rain, perhaps because Bernice called to him again, he suddenly began to run. He ran right past his mother and on up into the house, blundering a little as he went up the steps, as if tears, or a flurry of rain, had momentarily blinded him. Bernice stared after him, then abruptly she, too, began to run and in a moment had also disappeared into the house. The kapok trees on either side of the steps stood like skeletal sentries guaranteeing the privacy of the misery that had just entered the house.

Macy looked about at the others. "I'm sorry. She's been a bit off-color——"

The others gracefully fell in with his lie. "Sure," said Father Shawn. "It's the weather. I feel that way myself when the wet's coming on——"

"The wet's here," said Duggan, looking down at the mud freckling her white shoes. "Or anyway, it's having a practice run. I can't stand out here waving farewell to you, Narvo—" Narvo grinned, and lifted his dripping hat. "There's plenty of work to be done."

"Perhaps I could help you?" Elisabeth had been standing in the background. She had felt useless, not able to contribute anything to the discussion by the group; yet she had been reluctant to turn away, afraid that her uselessness would have been more pointed if she had shown a dislike of merely getting wet.

Duggan looked at her, face blank with surprise. Rain smeared the thick-lensed glasses, and Duggan bent forward myopically: it lent an unfortunate look of disbelief to her, as if she were peering at Elisabeth to see if the latter were joking with her. Her relations with Elisabeth up till now had been cool, almost frigid: she was just another part of Peter Traxal's baggage, and she had always avoided being intimate (she shuddered at the word) with Traxal. "Why, yes. Yes, Miss—" Her forgetting Elisabeth's name was genuine. She had never been able to retain names in her memory: it was another brick in the defenses.

"Call me Elisabeth," said Elisabeth, feeling sorry for this ugly, unsympathetic woman, who made everything so difficult for herself.

"Why, yes, Elisabeth. Would you care to share my umbrella?" Duggan was as formal as if she were welcoming the administrator's wife come to open a new hospital. Elisabeth recognized the effort behind the gesture; drenched, she moved in beneath the umbrella. "My name is Joan. But call me Matron in front of the kanakas——"

Narvo watched the two women move off across the parade ground, walking close together with Duggan holding the umbrella, and the native girl trailing behind. "Sisters under the skin—you think there's any truth in that, Mike?" The priest shrugged, and Narvo turned to Bermingham. He had a job to do, and now was as good a time as any to forget Paiwo's treachery. Nothing would be gained by crying over spilt blood. "Righto, Jack. Let's go and bring in some of your brothers-in-law."

"That's what I like about you," said Bermingham, his good eye gleaming. "You never play any favorites. You insult *everyone*."

2

Through the accident of other people's misfortunes, Elisabeth found herself fitting into the life of the patrol post. She helped Joan Duggan prepare the wards for the expected casualties, she saw that Bandi had his proper lunch instead of the bowl of *kaukau* that Narvo's new houseboy would have fed him, and in the late afternoon she went up to have tea with Bernice.

"I'm going out to Goroka on next week's plane." Bernice still hadn't quite recovered from her outburst of the morning, but the thought of escape, even if only to Goroka, was having a quick curative effect on her. Her vivacity was her built-in protection against moroseness: moods passed over her as quickly as rain clouds across the valley. Beyond the mountain the sun was shining brightly now, and here on the veranda she was already thinking of the parties she would be attending in Goroka.

"How long will you stay there?" Elisabeth wondered if this had been Bernice's own idea or had been suggested by Macy. It would be ironic if she and Bernice went out on the plane together on Monday, both going in the same direction but for entirely opposite reasons: one to get away from her husband, the other sent out by the man she had hoped would be her husband. She looked across the cane table at Bernice, not wanting to become involved in the latter's domestic troubles, but feeling that, as a woman, Bernice was looking to her for comfort. She asked what she hoped was an innocent question. "You will come back soon, won't you?"

But it wasn't an innocent question: to Bernice it contained all the seeds of her discontent. "That depends on Eric. It'll give him time to come to his senses——"

Elisabeth looked around desperately for escape, afraid that Bernice was going to drag her into the Macys' quarrel. She had already learned over the tea and scones what the trouble was, and she had no desire to learn more. She was saved by the arrival of Harry from somewhere at the back of the house.

"What do you want?" He was no longer Bernice's favorite: she knew now that he was on his father's side.

"I was looking for my camera, Mum." Harry spoke cautiously. He had taken sides, something he had never done before, and he knew how his mother felt. He had for the first time caught sight of the darkness that was part of adulthood and he was frightened by it. Perhaps there was not much in growing up, after all. "Have you seen it?"

"What do you want it for?" Bernice wanted to sweep him into her arms, but she knew that might be the last straw that would estrange him from her completely: he was no longer her baby, and she was realizing the sadness of a woman who had turned a corner for the last time.

"Roy might be bringing in some prisoners. I wanted to take some pictures for him."

"It's in the—you wanted to *what?*" He was no longer a baby, nor even a child: he was a man, with all a man's callousness, with all Roy Narvo's callousness. "Let him do his own dirty work! The idea of it, getting a boy to take pictures of murderers—!"

"Gee, Mum, you got it all wrong. Roy didn't ask me to take the pictures. I just like to help him—it's training for me to be a patrol officer—"

Bernice's make-up threatened to crack under her surprise. "And when did you decide upon that career?" She could become stiffly formal at times, looking and sounding slightly ridiculous.

Harry lowered his head; he knew he had gone too far. "Forget it, Mum. I won't take any pictures."

"And you won't be a patrol officer, either. Not if I have anything to do with it."

Harry stood irresolute for a moment. He suffered from the

curse of the young, the inability to make an exit. He edged
toward the door, like a prisoner trying to escape, stood there
for a moment, then turned abruptly and was gone. Bernice
stood up, the teapot in her hand. She wanted to weep, but she
had enough respect for Elisabeth's feelings not to weep in front
of her. She had felt no embarrassment at telling Elisabeth her
troubles, but to weep her misery in front of this warmhearted
Czech girl was another matter altogether. Bernice, despite her
occasional selfishness, was not lacking in consideration for others.

"I'll get some more tea," she said, holding back the tears, and
disappeared into the house.

Elisabeth lit a cigarette and sat looking out across the post and
the gorges to the mountain opposite. The rain clouds had gone
now, but long white clouds stretched at intervals across the blue;
the sky looked like an inverted sea down which the cloud break-
ers rolled to the rocky coast that was the distant ranges. The
shadows had come up from the gorges and climbed the eastern
side of the mountain; the sun was a dying strip of yellow fire
on the very peak itself. The valley, blue with mist now, was a
steep-walled bowl of silence; even the roar of the river far below
in the gorges was more like a throbbing of the silence than a
sound in itself. Elisabeth, a city girl, was discovering the silence
of mountains: the stillness of air that is like the stillness of death.
And the thought of death reminded her again how much the
country itself was a part of one's life here in New Guinea. Older,
more civilized countries somehow dropped hazily into the background of their inhabitants; men's lives in those countries turned
on events that arose out of the men's own actions. She began
to realize for the first time that this continual awareness of the
country, its mystery and its savagery, must condition the lives of
all men who moved into new lands. She began to realize, too,
the pressures that were threatening to crumble Bernice's life,
and all at once she felt sorry for the woman. Wrapped in the

silence, her gaze lost in the climbing shadows, she did not know Bernice had returned to the veranda till the latter spoke.

"Where are you and Peter going to live in Australia?"

Startled as much by the sound of Bernice's voice as by the question, Elisabeth had no answer for a moment. To cover her confusion she held out her cup for a second cup of tea she did not want. "I—we haven't really discussed it yet."

"Have you noticed any change in Peter?" Bernice had made up her mind, while in the house, to forget her own troubles by trying to show an interest in Elisabeth. She had had her weep, and repaired her make-up: she had put on a new face, she had told herself, and been pleased at her own small joke. She had always longed to be witty, but her tongue ran too fast; she thought of witty sayings long after everyone had gone home, but she had never had the talent to be able to introduce them into future conversations. "Since you saw him last. I mean, it's five years, isn't it?"

"If he has changed, I have not yet had time to notice it." Elisabeth was not going to commit herself; *she* was not one to spill out her troubles to another woman. "One needs more than a few days."

"Yes, I suppose so," said Bernice, wondering how long it had taken her to notice that Eric had changed. Or had she changed herself, and had he always been dull and ambitionless? *Poor Eric,* she thought, and through her anger at him a spark of love glimmered once again. "I don't suppose you ever really know men, do you?"

You poor creature, Elisabeth thought, *you could not have a simpler man than Eric, yet even he has you baffled.* "No, I suppose not," she said, and tried to tell herself she had always known Peter.

"I mean, they're like children in lots of ways. And who understands children?" Bernice glanced toward the inside of the house, where she could hear Harry talking to the houseboy in pidgin, speaking the bastard language like an old New Guinea hand.

Please don't prattle, Elisabeth thought. *I have tried not to think about Peter and me, because I can't think of any alternative to the two of us being together.* An unbeliever in miracles, she was hoping for one: something would happen, something would turn up that would solve everything for her. It was the blind, stupid, almost animal faith that, she knew, had kept her mother alive in the concentration camp.

"Having children of one's own may be different," she said. "I often found it difficult to understand other people's."

"It's just as difficult to understand your own, believe me," said Bernice, and wanted to weep again: inside the house, Harry laughed aloud with the houseboy at some secret joke.

Then a Landrover came up the road from the gorge and pulled up outside the hospital. Rossi and Traxal got out, and Elisabeth, as much to escape Bernice's confidences as anything else, stood up. "Let us go down and see what has happened."

"There don't appear to be any casualties," said Bernice; and there weren't. Rossi and Traxal stood outside the hospital hut and told Macy, Duggan, Bernice and Elisabeth of what they had found at Benamaua.

"Six men dead," said Rossi. "But no wounded."

Father Shawn came hurrying down the road and walked into the group to hear Traxal say, "There had been a bit of cannibalism, too. One of the Benamaua had had his buttock sliced off."

The women wrinkled their mouths, and Father Shawn said, "That's going to be a shock to Roy. He thought he'd stamped out that sort of thing."

"You can't stamp anything out of these natives," said Duggan. "When people have an ingrained habit, you can't stamp it out of them. Could you get Australians to give up gambling or beer-drinking?"

"There's a slight difference between beer-drinking and cannibalism," Traxal said, smiling gently at her: she was an intelligent woman, the most skillful nurse he had ever met, and yet her sour disposition at times made her utter childish remarks. "But I agree with you that it looks an impossible task to convert these kanakas. And I don't mean in your use of the term, Mike."

"I don't agree with you, whatever way we use the term," said Father Shawn, looking down the road. "And I'm sure Roy, despite his disappointment, will disagree with you, too."

The second Landrover came up the road, and Narvo and Bermingham got out. Narvo looked across at Harry, who had come down and stood slightly apart from the group of adults. "No prisoners, Harry."

"It don't matter," said Harry, avoiding his mother's gaze. "I couldn't find my camera, anyway."

Narvo looked at the boy a moment longer, sensing something was wrong, then he turned to the group by the hospital steps. "How'd it go, Frank?"

"Six dead, no wounded."

"We found nobody at Vaikaka but women, kids and old men. I'm afraid we're in for a long hunt."

"Paiwo has turned cannibal again," said Traxal, and told what they had found.

Narvo swallowed a curse. Father Shawn saw the look of pain cross his face, as if he had been hit physically. "You sure? It wasn't a wound——?"

"Too neat," said Traxal. "In any case, the flesh was missing."

Narvo shook his head, looking at Father Shawn. "You can't win, can you, Mike? I thought I'd done a good job on Paiwo."

"You had done a good job," said Father Shawn emphatically. "He'll come back, Roy, I know it."

"The faith of the faithful," Narvo said, grinning, putting his hand on the priest's shoulder. He showed little of the intense, sickening disappointment he felt. The cannibalism was the last straw: man could go no further down the pad of atavism than to eating his own kind. Murder and killing in battle were still civilized habits, or at least habits found among the civilized: cannibalism was the one distinguishing mark of the real savage. "Or the faith of the innocent. Take your pick."

"I'm not the only one around here with faith," said Father Shawn doggedly, lying for the sake of this big man whom he loved. "You had it—up till a day or two ago. Jack, you've been up here longer than any of us. Do the kanakas go back to cannibalism once they've been weaned away from it?"

Bermingham shrugged. "I guess a man will go back to anything once he's tried it and liked it. Or if he's starving. Some of the Nips went in for cannibalism during the war up here."

"I just can't see how anyone could stomach human flesh!" Bernice looked green.

"I've tried it," said Bermingham. "Didn't know it was a piece of man till afterwards, when the kanakas told me. I've tasted worse. It's just like sweet pork."

"You disgusting old man," said Duggan, almost spitting. "There doesn't appear to be anything you haven't done!"

He winked at her with his good eye. "I'm a reformed character now, Duggie, old girl. But I was just trying to point out that none of us is sure of being able to swear off his habits forever. The alcoholic can always go back to his grog, the pervert to his perving—" He looked at Traxal. "You're the doc around here, Peter. You know how hard it is for a man to turn his back on the things he was brought up on."

Traxal nodded, but said nothing. He was aware of Elisabeth watching him, aware that she had caught the unconscious irony of Bermingham's words. Prague was a habit on which he could not turn his back.

"Well, it settles one thing," said Narvo. "I'm going after Paiwo and I'm going to get him. If I have to spend the rest of my life in these hills!"

3

"I'm going prospecting," Bermingham said. "I need some more money in the kick."

"You're not going fossicking in these hills while this trouble is on," said Narvo. "I don't want them carving steaks off you."

"Please," said Father Shawn. "Human flesh as food revolts me anyway. But a cut off him—" He drew on his cigarette, as if to get the imagined taste of Bermingham out of his mouth.

"I'd taste as good as some people around here——"

"Righto, righto," said Narvo, and stood up, kicking off the Chinese sandals he wore and yelling for the houseboy to bring him boots and socks. Father Shawn had been cutting his hair, and now as the priest put away his clippers and scissors, Narvo brushed the thick black hair from the towel around his shoulders. He felt his chin and decided to shave after he had held the morning parade. Father Shawn had stayed with him last night rather than walk home in the sudden downpour that had come on; and Jack Bermingham had come up and joined them this morning on the veranda as breakfast had ended and the hair-cutting had begun. "You're not going to be eaten, Jack, and you're not going fossicking. Not till I give the word, anyway."

"I'd be all right," Bermingham protested. He was wearing a bright green lap-lap this morning; he had more lap-laps than any native on the post, and was the envy of them all. His wife Mary washed them every day and was proud of the fact that she had a husband whom even the vain men of her own race admired. Only the unlaced, unpolished army boots spoiled the effect of Bermingham's simple elegance. "These kanakas know I'm on their side. I married one of them, didn't I?"

"You married a Vaikaka woman. Do you think the Benamaua would reckon you were on their side?" The houseboy brought Narvo his boots and socks and he was putting them on. "You stay here, Jack, that's all there is to it. If you're short of anything, see this bloke." He jerked a thumb at the houseboy.

"I don't want your charity," Bermingham said.

"It's not charity. It's just insurance on my part. Because if you got done over in these hills, I'd have every bastard in Canberra on my neck. A murdered white man in this Territory right now would be like a bomb in a diplomatic pouch. I'll see you later." He stood up. "I've got to go up and stand in for Queen Bess. How do I look—vice-regal?"

Bermingham told him what he looked like. Narvo bowed in acknowledgment, put on his hat, and went across to where Rossi and Sergeant Beraki were assembling the police boys before the flagpole. "Sometimes I think Roy wears a bit too much red tape," Bermingham said, looking after the tall straight figure that had now all at once assumed a military bearing.

"You're talking through your neck," said Father Shawn. "You know what he is suggesting is for your own good as much as anything else."

"Thirty years I been up here. Never had to ask anyone where I could go. Just went, my word, I did. Never had to ask anyone for a penny or a feed, either." He shook his head. "All my life I been free to come and go like I please. That was what I liked about this country. The world's getting too bloody civilized."

"You're forgetting Mary and the kids, Jack. It's not just that the world is getting too civilized. You're married now."

"It's them I'm thinking of. I mean, in the long run. Mike, I know where there is gold! I got a little bit out there last year. Not much, just stuff I panned in a creek. But there's more farther up this creek, my word there is, and I wanna get it. I ain't greedy to be rich or anything like that. You asked me the other day what future my kids had. I can give 'em a future, Mike, if I get that gold. Send 'em South to school—" He looked down at the green lap-lap stretched across his flat stomach. "Their old man's gone kanaka, but there's no need for them to grow up the same way."

Father Shawn, choked by emotion, had nothing to say. The only two friends he had in the world were this old sinner and the agnostic now taking the salute beneath the flagpole across the parade ground; but he loved them both as if they were saints, and he was burdened by the sadness of the knowledge that he seemed unable to help either of them. All he could do was pray for them, and because his prayers for himself had never been answered, he was beginning to doubt the efficacy of such help.

He mumbled an excuse about work to be done, patted Bermingham's shoulder awkwardly, then left and walked up the road to the mission. The heavy rain during the night had turned the road into a strip of red mud. He had just begun to tread his way carefully along the side of it when he heard his name called.

"May I walk up with you, Father?" Elisabeth said, and came up to join him. She was wearing stout walking shoes and he noted that her steps in the mud were less finicky than his own. He put his foot down firmly, even a little recklessly, and almost slipped on his backside. He went back to stepping carefully.

"You wanted to see the mission?"

"Yes. But there was something else, Father—" She walked a few yards in silence. There was the embarrassment of putting her proposition to a man she hardly knew; and there was the tongue-tying difficulty of giving to a man a title she hadn't used since she was a child. There were still priests in Czechoslovakia, but she had had no contact with them.

Father Shawn saw her hesitation, and mistook the reason for it. "Are you a Catholic, Miss Palyardi?"

"No." She was further embarrassed by her lack of religion, of belief of any kind; she lacked even the will to be an atheist. She had lacked the faith to be a Communist, or even an anti-Communist; she knew the world was full of people like her, apathetic neutralists in the matter of belief. It made her no less ashamed to know there were so many others like her, but she had never done anything about it. "My mother was, but I wasn't brought up a Catholic. My mother died in a concentration camp during the war, and I was brought up by an aunt. No, it has nothing to do with religion, Father."

Father Shawn felt the hope die in his breast. It had seemed for a moment that he was to have the opportunity to be a real priest, to bring back into the Church someone who had strayed. But as hope died, relief flooded in; and he was ashamed. He was too deep in the rut of failure: he did not have even the faith to test himself. "What is it then, Miss Palyardi?"

Did one ask a priest to call one by one's first name? Miss Palyardi: it was another sign that she was still an outsider, the very situation that she was now trying to remedy by approaching Father Shawn. "Peter—Dr. Traxal, mentioned that you have been trying to run a school up at the mission."

"Trying is the word," said Father Shawn, smiling ruefully. "I haven't got very far. I don't seem cut out to be a teacher."

"I was a governess in Prague. You see, Father, I want to do something useful here!" She hurried on, turning to talk directly to him as she walked beside him, occasionally missing her footing in the mud, but never missing a word, selling herself, an old capitalist custom that she had never before had to use. "I am university trained. I know English very well. I can teach arts and crafts—my father was a potter, one of the best men in ceramics in Czechoslovakia. I like to think I have inherited a little of his talent—it was all he had left to leave me." She missed her footing, and Father Shawn put out his hand to steady her. "He—he died when I was quite young, but his friends taught me. I could help you, Father, I know I could. Please allow me!"

Father Shawn stopped. The mission lay up ahead of them, at the bend in the road: a *kunai*-thatched chapel, his own hut, and half a dozen native huts, all on a small escarpment that jutted out like the prow of a ship above the gorge. It was not much, God knew; and he hated to think what God thought of it. He had seen other missions in New Guinea, Catholic, Lutheran, Seventh Day Adventist; and he knew what could be done by an efficient, hard-working missionary. A school, a going concern instead of the spasmodic confusions he had been holding, would give some dignity, some solidity to the Kundavi mission. He knew that the bishop did not think much of him nor of what he had done here, and he suspected that he would have been recalled long ago if there had been a replacement for him. And there was nothing he feared more than recall: eternal damnation would be no worse.

"I think that would be a fine idea, Miss Palyardi."

"Could—could you call me Elisabeth, Father? I mean, every-one here is called by their first name. Miss Palyardi sounds so formal."

Father Shawn recognized the desire to belong. He had seen it when he had last been home, his family members of almost every group in town, and, for all their Catholicism, looking on him, the first priest among the Shawns, as a nonconformist. His gentle contempt for his family did not lessen his sympathy for Elisabeth. It was so obvious that she belonged to nothing right now but the human race: she had no club nor church nor even country.

"Would you care to call me Mike?" He smiled, his thin face wrinkling with humor, the scar down the cheek looking like another laugh line. "When I first came here Roy told me a joke. He said a missionary was a man who was called Father by other men's children, and Uncle by his own. He started in calling me Mike right off. I've been rather wary of the title Father ever since." Then he looked at her without smiling and said, "Elisa-beth, I think we may be able to do a good job together. I hope so—for both our sakes."

She looked at him at that, but said nothing more than, "Thank you, Mike."

Then he took her on up the road and, with no pride and some embarrassment, showed her the mission. If she was surprised at the meanness of the place compared to the patrol post, she did not show it. They had just come out of the chapel when Frank Rossi drove up in one of the Landrovers.

"I've brought some flowers for the altar." Rossi was a Catholic, the only white member of Father Shawn's congregation. "It seemed a pity to watch them just die in the garden."

This was the first time Rossi had ever brought flowers for the altar, but Father Shawn felt it was not a time for comment. He saw Rossi looking at Elisabeth, and he knew at once that the flowers were only an excuse: the young patrol officer's thoughts were anything but spiritual. The priest was troubled, but he knew there was nothing he could do at this stage. He was worldly enough, despite his long exile from the world, to know that a beautiful woman could not be set down amongst a group of lonely men without having some effect on them. Among these sensual mountain savages, he had been made well aware of the devil in the flesh; he knew it was a devil that never cared about the color of the skin of the flesh. It was a devil that Kundavi, with the trouble brewing now in the surrounding mountains, could well do without.

"Miss Palyardi," he said, using her formal name, as if by doing so he could discourage Rossi, "is going to help me with the school."

Rossi nodded seriously, acting the role of junior government representative. "Excellent. That means you will be staying with us, Miss Palyardi?"

"For a little while, at least," Elisabeth said. "Peter and I have still not made plans——"

"Are you going back to the post now?" Rossi said abruptly, and bit his bottom lip. "I can give you a lift."

He opened the door of the Landrover and helped Elisabeth in.

He did it with a solemn gallantry that Elisabeth, still thinking of him only as a boy, found touching.

"The flowers, Frank," said Father Shawn dryly. "Or have you changed your mind about putting them on the altar?"

"Oh, no! No." For a moment Rossi lost his stern composure; he floundered like a schoolboy ticked off for some social error. He reached into the back of the Landrover and brought out a small bunch of dahlias.

Father Shawn had trouble in keeping a straight face. "You shouldn't have gone to the trouble, Frank. I mean, picking them and driving all the way up here—" He took the flowers and, still straight-faced, looked at Elisabeth. "He may be bringing you flowers next, Elisabeth."

Elisabeth caught the warning behind the words. She had attached no significance to Rossi's sudden arrival at the mission; burdened with one problem, she was not looking for others. But now she was all at once alert. She looked at Rossi, who was staring directly at her as if waiting on her reaction to Father Shawn's remark, then she looked back at the priest.

"I shall see he does not neglect the altar," she said, then relented and smiled to take the sting out of the remark: she had seen the sudden hurt look in Rossi's eyes, as if she had shut a door in his face.

Rossi climbed in beside her and they drove slowly down the greasy road. He said nothing till he had pulled the Landrover to a halt at the bottom of the path that led up to the guest hut. He pulled on the brake, put the vehicle in first gear and switched off the engine with a deliberateness that both amused and annoyed Elisabeth. It was so obvious that he was going to say something of importance, to him if not to her: she would not have been surprised if he had produced a written, prepared speech.

"Elisabeth—may I call you Elisabeth?" She nodded, and he went on in his deep grave voice: "Elisabeth, are you and Peter going to marry before you leave Kundavi?"

"I do not know, Mr. Rossi——"

"Call me Frank, please."

"Frank. Whatever it is we do, it is really only the concern of Peter and myself, isn't it?"

He colored, and at once she felt sorry. She did not like hurting anyone, least of all someone who so obviously had only goodwill toward her. If the boy had fallen in love with her, he had done no crime by doing so, nor done her any harm. At least, not yet.

"I didn't mean to interfere," he said stiffly. He was out of his depth, and he wondered why he had allowed himself to blunder on into this situation. Back home in Melbourne, among the young girls of Brighton, their heads full of parties and clothes and dates in sports cars, he had also been out of his depth; but at least with the girls back home he had not felt like a schoolboy, and one or two of them had even thought he was interesting and, as a patrol officer, romantic and adventurous. All his life he had been cursed by his inability to take life any way but seriously; his years were signposted by crises, all of his own deliberate making. He was not helped by the knowledge that he would go on forever taking life just as seriously.

"I didn't mean to interfere," he repeated. "I only thought that if there was anything I could do——"

Elisabeth, feeling a rush of sympathy for the boy, put her hand on his arm. "Frank, if I do want anything, you will be the first I shall call upon. That is a promise. The other men are too busy"—out of the corner of her eye she saw Narvo standing down on the parade ground looking up toward her—"that is, if they want me here at all."

Rossi was gazing straight at her. He could not see Narvo, nor indeed anything but this beautiful woman beside him with her hand on his arm. He was not naïve enough to read more into the gesture than Elisabeth meant; he was romantic, but he was also intelligent and practical. She was promising him nothing really, he knew that; but quite suddenly he was genuinely and deeply in love with her. Something warned him he might be making another crisis for himself, but he ignored it.

"You won't have to call," he said, and smiled; but he was no good at flattery: his dark, serious eyes, declared his love: "You can depend on me, Elisabeth."

4

That night the patrol post was shaken by a violent earth tremor. Elisabeth awoke, not sure that she wasn't in the middle of a nightmare. The bed beneath her slid across the floor; the hut shook as if hit by a swift succession of furious wind blasts. She heard a glass tumbler crash to the floor; and immediately after it, one sound merging into the other, there was the scream of a child down in the native quarters.

She scrambled out of bed, feeling the floor moving beneath her. She glanced up quickly, but there was only darkness above her: the roof still held. She groped for her coat on the end of the bed, flung it around herself and stumbled toward the door. She pulled on the door, but it wouldn't budge. She had a moment of hysterical panic, and she cried out without realizing it. She pulled again on the door, tugging desperately on it while the floor still shook beneath her and the hut creaked and rustled about her. Then abruptly the door swung open and she staggered out onto the veranda.

The shuddering of the earth abruptly subsided. Somewhere down the gorge there was a loud rumble, as if a landslide had occurred; then there was silence but for the crying of children and the shouts of men down in the police boys' quarters. There were no lights in any of the huts nor down in the hospital; then she was aware of the fact that the humming of the generator had stopped. A moment later she saw the flash of a torch on the veranda of Narvo's hut, and he was yelling for Sergeant Beraki. Then there was the quick rush of boots on the gravel path and

Traxal was coming up the steps of the hut and gathering her in his arms.

"Oh, Peter, I was so frightened! Was it an earthquake?"

"Just a tremor. We get them occasionally here in the mountains. That was a bad one." They were speaking in Czech. She would remark later that each of them, in moments of stress, of love and anger and fear, had dropped back into their native tongue. "It has gone now. There should not be another—at least, not tonight."

"Has anyone been hurt?"

"I do not know. I came straight up here." He kissed her on the cheek. Even if she no longer loved him, she welcomed the comfort of his arms. "I must go down now——"

"I shall come with you. Perhaps I can help if someone *has* been hurt."

But there were no casualties; only a few frightened children. Elisabeth looked about at the faces of the adult natives, the light from the flashlights of the white men and their own fire-sticks reflected in the dark gems of their eyes; one or two of them smiled at her, their smiles laid across their black faces like bone exposed. A few of the small children were still whimpering, but there was no fear on the faces of any of the adult natives. Earth tremors were part of the climate to them, as snow and ice had been to her in Prague. When she looked at the whites she saw there was the same look of acceptance on their faces, even on Peter's. Once more she felt the outsider, and she did her best to hide the fear that still trembled inside her, like an echoing vibration of the earth tremor itself.

"You all right, Elisabeth?" Narvo said, and when she nodded, he turned away immediately and spoke to Macy and Duggan. The abruptness of his turning away pleased, rather than annoyed, Elisabeth: it meant that he was making no special case of her, that he was accepting her as just another member of the Kundavi community.

Then Jack Bermingham said, "Looks like there's a fire over the other side."

On the mountain on the other side of the gorge a fire blazed fiercely; even as everyone turned to look, the fire seemed to increase its area and intensity. Nothing could be distinguished but the red glow of the flames; it bloomed on the black wall of the night like a luminous rose. "It looks like Vaikaka," Rossi said.

"Probably a hut has collapsed on their night fire," Macy said.

"It looks as if the whole village has gone up." Father Shawn had come down from the mission. He had wrapped a blanket around himself for warmth, and beside the tall figure of Narvo he looked like a gray-haired waif.

"That means more burn cases," said Duggan. "I wish these people could find some other way of keeping warm at night. We are never without a burn case."

Elisabeth looked at the nurse to see if she was complaining. But Duggan was staring across the valley with the pain of compassion somehow softening her ugly features; she was just unfortunate that on her lips even mercy had the sour sound of complaint. Elisabeth was glad when Narvo recognized the true note in Duggan's voice.

"I wish we could find another way," he said sadly. "Frank, you and Eric had better go over there in the morning. In the meantime, there's no point in our standing here in the cold. Let's get back to bed."

"Were you frightened, Elisabeth?" Bernice had been the last to arrive. She hadn't been able to find her shoes at first, and she hadn't wanted to spoil her mules by coming down in the mud in them. At last, groping in the dark, cursing Eric for having already rushed out of the house, she had found her shoes well back beneath the bed, sent there by the heaving of the floor. When she had at last arrived down at the group it was preparing to break up.

"I was a little frightened," Elisabeth said, hoping her real fear had not shown when she had first come down here. "It was so strange. I didn't know what was happening——"

"Ah, you'll get used to these little shakes," said Bermingham. "Wait till we have a real one, or have a volcano blow."

"That's right," said Narvo. "Try and keep her awake for the rest of the night."

"I was only telling her," Bermingham said. "You can never know too much about this country."

"That is what I was telling you this morning," said Narvo, grinning. "When you wanted to go out into the hills."

"That was different," Bermingham said. "I trust the kanakas more than I do the earthquakes."

Then the group broke up and Traxal took Elisabeth back up to the guest hut. At the door he kissed her goodnight, but made no attempt to come inside the hut. Beyond his shoulder she saw the fire still burning on the other side of the valley; it flared for an instant, then suddenly seemed to die away to just a pale glow. Peter's kiss had the same pale warmth, the flickering flame of a love that was dying or had perhaps already died. But now was not the time to ask if her guess, and hope, was true.

"You will be all right?" he said, speaking in English.

"Yes," she said. "I think I shall be all right now."

5

Sometime in the early morning Jack Bermingham left the patrol post and went looking for gold. It was ten o'clock before Narvo learned the news. Sergeant Beraki came to the House Paper, where Narvo was writing his report on the Vaikaka attack on Benamaua, and said that Mary Bermingham was outside and wanted to see the Kiap. He did not call her Mary nor Mrs. Bermingham: he called her Mr. Bermingham's woman. He was not in favor of native women who slept with white men, even if legally married to them.

"What's the trouble, Beraki?" Narvo was in no mood for interruptions. He was finding the report difficult to write and had already torn up four sheets of paper. It was proving difficult because he knew that with every word he could be sealing his own transfer; and it was proving doubly difficult because, for the first time in his life, he was writing a report that would be incomplete. In the past it had been the detail, plus the uncompromising opinion, that had offended certain people at headquarters; in this report he was striving carefully to make no opinion, and he was leaving out the cannibalism by the Vaikaka men. He was a man of strong conscience in certain matters, and doing his job honestly was one of those matters.

"She would not say, Kiap. She has the children with her."

"Bring her in," said Narvo, and sat back resignedly in his chair. The House Paper had just the one big room, with a table in the center, at which Narvo sat, another table to one side, which was Rossi's, and two steel filing cabinets against the back wall. A picture of the Queen, in coronation robes, hung on the back wall, and underneath it were three flags, the Australian flag, the Union Jack and the United Nations flag. Below the flags was a calendar carrying a picture of a redhead wearing less than many of the natives who came into the room. The redhead had no attraction for the natives, who, when they were not looking at Narvo, focused their gaze raptly on the splendor of the Queen. It amused Narvo to compare their loyalty with that of the white males who came in occasionally from Goroka.

Mary Bermingham, whose native name was Giamin, was a small woman, jet black and good-looking; she had not yet begun to fade and crinkle, like yesterday's flower, into the husk of the usual native mother. She had been only eighteen when Bermingham had married her, and now she was in the bloom of full-blown womanhood; the bloom was enhanced by the new child she carried in her belly, the one whose coming had been the final persuasion for Bermingham to go off into the hills. She wore a cheap cotton dress, long blue glass earrings, and no shoes: she had dressed in her best to come and see the Kiap. Two small children clung to her skirt and edged behind her, their eyes standing out like marbles in the coffee-colored plates of their faces.

"What is it, Mary?" Narvo spoke in the local dialect, the woman's only tongue. "Where is Jack?"

"He has gone, Kiap. He told me not to tell you till I heard the bugle blow for the police boys to stop for their first rest. He has gone looking for the stuff he calls gold."

Narvo's first reaction was one of black anger. He thumped his fist on the table and the bottle of ink bounced and spilled over. The ink ran off the table, away from the papers on which he had been working; but even if it had run the other way, spoiled his morning's work, he would hardly have noticed. He could not abide anyone, white or black, disobeying his orders; and though he had been jovial with Bermingham yesterday, what he had told the one-eyed man had been nothing less than an order to stay on the post. And he knew that Bermingham had understood it as such.

He controlled himself, but his voice was still a harsh growl. "Where has he gone?"

With Narvo's outburst, the children had disappeared completely behind their mother. She herself was almost paralyzed with fear; she stared at Narvo as if she expected him to strike her next. When Beraki jogged her elbow she almost jumped in the air. "Answer the Kiap, woman!"

Her throat quivered as she sought her voice. "Out toward Wabut, Kiap. Not so far, but in that direction. He said he would be gone perhaps four weeks."

"Or maybe forever," said Narvo in English, then dropped back into dialect. "All right, Mary. You and the children will be looked after. You are not to leave the post, you understand? You are not to go back to Vaikaka, not even for a short visit."

Mary Bermingham nodded, then turned and ushered the children out ahead of her. Narvo stared at her, not seeing her but seeing Bermingham going down into the swamp country around Wabut, passing through territory where natives might already be preparing for battle. He understood, better than the man himself realized, why Bermingham had gone out prospecting; but he could not place the welfare of one man's family above that of an entire people's. And right now he felt that he was battling for the welfare of all the people in these mountains, battling even some of the people themselves for something that he believed in the long run would be their salvation.

Narvo looked at the upset ink bottle, threw down his pen and stood up. It was time for morning tea; although he felt more like getting drunk. He went out of the House Paper, and saw Elisabeth crossing the parade ground toward the hospital. On the spur of the moment he headed in the same direction.

Duggan was pouring tea for Traxal and Elisabeth on the veranda of the hospital hut. "Well, aren't we honored! The Kiap comes to tea!"

"Black, with two lumps of arsenic," said Narvo, and sat down on the veranda rail. "Jack has gone out fossicking."

There was silence for a moment. Duggan sat with the teapot poised above a cup, then she said, "The damned fool! Is he trying to commit suicide?"

"Not intentionally." Father Shawn came out from a ward onto the veranda. He looked a little disappointed: he had been looking for mission natives among the sick and dying and had found none. "I know how you feel, Roy."

"I feel like killing him myself," said Narvo, taking the cup Elisabeth handed him.

"He's worried about those kids of his." Father Shawn leaned beside Narvo on the veranda rail. "If things change after the UN party comes in here——"

"Change? How?" Narvo asked.

Father Shawn shrugged: it wasn't his place to broadcast that Narvo's future depended on the reaction of the coming committee. "Well, there could be changes. You know. This area could be reclassified as uncontrolled, and we'd all be kicked out. That would be the end of Jack's prospecting. And he needs the gold—that is, if he finds it—to give his kids an education and get them started in life. He doesn't want them to live in a grass hut all their lives."

"He shouldn't have had them in the first place," said Duggan, little finger crooked daintily beside her cup; her glasses flashed and the end of her long nose twitched.

"He's been a good father to them," Narvo said.

"Now you're defending him!" Duggan was exasperated. "A moment ago you wanted to kill him."

"That was because he disobeyed my orders." Narvo put down his cup. A *prunus* tree grew beside the veranda, and he plucked one of the leaves and idly began to pick at it. He was more disturbed by Bermingham's departure than by any other event of the past week. He no more cared to see a dead native than a dead white man; but a dead friend was a different thing altogether. He had had so few friends in his life, mainly because of his uncompromising approach on matters that were important to him, and those that he did have he loved. And now he feared that he would never see Bermingham alive again. Lonely prospectors had been dying in the New Guinea mountains for years; their own murder was the possible price for the gold they found. Fifty miles in certain directions from the post were natives who had never seen any white man but Narvo; they had attacked him, even with his twelve police boys and sixty carriers; a single white prospector would be easy meat. It was a further sickening thought that Bermingham could be easy meat in the literal meaning of the term. "It's my job to look after the whites in this area as much as the kanakas. I can't do that if a man won't take any notice of me."

"Will you be blamed if anything happens to Mr. Bermingham?" Elisabeth asked.

"He'll be blamed," said Father Shawn, looking sadly at the tall figure beside him. "Because he'll take the blame in his report."

Traxal spoke for the first time. "I don't think you should, Roy. I'm sure we'll all back you up that Jack went against your orders."

"Thanks, Peter," Narvo had reduced the *prunus* leaf to pulp; his fingers shone with its juice. "It wouldn't do any good. Not the way things stand now." He made no attempt to explain to Traxal and the others how things did stand. He was agreeably surprised by Traxal's offer of support, but he did not feel he had to take the doctor completely into his confidence.

"Why don't you go after Mr. Bermingham?" Elisabeth asked.

Narvo shook his head. "I can't afford to, not just yet. Not with this other trouble brewing. All we can do is hope."

"And pray," said Father Shawn.

"The stupid and the sinners," said Duggan. "Wouldn't it be a nice change to pray for the wise and the good?"

"You'll never need anyone's prayers," said Narvo straightening up and putting on his hat. "The Lord has a place right beside Him dusted off for you."

"And the devil has the same for you," said Duggan.

Narvo lifted his hat, bowed and left the veranda. Father Shawn looked after him. "You may be wrong, you know, Joan. He might sneak into heaven by the back door."

"Heaven forbid," said Duggan. "If he does, I'm not going."

Father Shawn smiled, shaking his head; then he looked over at Elisabeth. "There are a few things I'd like to talk over with you before we start school this afternoon."

"School?" Traxal was puzzled.

"Yes." Elisabeth had not yet told Traxal of her decision. She was not a moral heroine, and facing up to people whom she might hurt, even if she felt she was right, had never come easy to her. "I'll come up to the mission in a little while, Mike. I want to see Peter first."

Traxal followed her off the veranda and they walked down to the top of the path that led down into the gorge. Elisabeth sat down on a rock and Traxal stood beside her. A little way along from the path a houseboy was hanging out some washing behind Rossi's house, but he appeared disinterested in the two white people. He sang a song that could have been cheerful or sad, a black man not yet civilized enough to have the blues.

Elisabeth said, "Peter, I am not going out on the plane on Monday. I am going to help Father Shawn with his school."

Traxal stared out over the valley for a moment. Far below them, above the chasms of the gorge, a hawk floated: it passed through a rainbow in the gorge mist and for a moment became a brightly plumaged parrot. It reminded Traxal of what lay eternally in these mountains, the death behind the beauty: it was another of the things he hated. "Darling, please don't get yourself too settled here. It will be harder for you to break away when you have to."

"Shall I have to go at all, Peter?"

"You won't be able to stay on—I mean, if you don't come with me when I go."

"I was not planning to," she said evenly.

He hesitated, still looking down into the gorge. The hawk had come out into the sunlight again, death looking for a victim; he wished suddenly for a gun, although he knew it was too far away for him to hit it. He had shot for sport in the fields around Olomouc, bringing home the ducks for his mother to cook; here, one shot purely for the pleasure of killing, out of a stupid animal hatred. This country did that to one: made one live on its own terms of savagery and vengeance. "I am going home, darling. To Czechoslovakia."

She felt no surprise, she had been half-expecting it; but she still felt suddenly sick and empty. Loneliness came back as a chill; and she felt again the fear she had thought was past. She looked up at him, unconsciously looking for a revival of her love for him; but he was just a man whose face and body she knew, and that was all. Her nails scratched against the rock on which she sat, but she was not aware of their doing so. "I think you are making a mistake, Peter."

"It couldn't be a bigger one than the one I made by leaving there." He picked up some pebbles and began to throw them; they went skidding down the path to plunge off into the shining mist of the gorge. "I'm not politically minded, darling. I'm no Communist, but I think I could learn to live with them. I can't live with the Australians."

"What makes Australians so incompatible?"

"I don't know. Perhaps it is my fault—" He had tried to be fair-minded, but it hadn't helped: being objective carried its own curse, the truth: "We educated Europeans feel superior. Perhaps the feeling is bred into us through centuries, but it's there. A stronger man would fight, would adapt himself—I am sure there are many better educated Europeans than I who are quite happy in Australia. I tried and I failed and I was terribly unhappy. It may sound cowardly, snobbish, even childish, but all I want to do is go home."

"How do you know you will be welcome? After all, you did escape——"

He tossed a pebble in his hand, then he threw it far out into the glittering air. "My father has been writing me. He has seen certain people—he says it is all right for me to come home if I prove myself."

"So that is why your father came to see me." She thought of the tall thin man in the steel-rimmed spectacles and the black suit who laughed with too much determination, as if to convince himself that he was happy. He had come to her just before she had left, although she hadn't seen him for three years, and, laughing as if she had made a joke, asked her why she was leaving Czechoslovakia. Then, still laughing, he had told her to tell Peter that they had not given up hope of ever seeing him again. What had seemed then a conventional greeting to bring to Peter, now took on significance. Then something Peter had just said clicked in her mind: it too became significant. "What do you mean, if you prove yourself?"

"I have to prove I am not anti-Communist." He had no more pebbles left; he stood gazing out across the valley. A breeze came up from the gorge, bringing the sound of the river with it and a sweet dank scent, and his long fair hair blew across his forehead.

"How do you do that? By being a Communist?"

"No." He sat down on the rock beside her. "Elisabeth, come back with me. We both love Prague—we can start all over again there. I can get a job—Father tells me they need doctors, that in some hospitals the doctors are working sixty hours a week because there aren't enough. I don't mind the work—I work as long as that here—" He took her hand. He was not sure that he still loved her, but he knew that he could live with her and not be unhappy. If he went home, he would be compromising with the principles that had driven him to escape five years before; in those years he had learned that compromise was a way of living to a great majority of the world's population. To live with a woman whom he respected and physically desired but no longer loved would not be a difficult compromise. "I should have written you, darling, told you not to come out. But I didn't know—you were on your way before I knew I could come home. Come home with me."

"But how are you going to prove you are not anti-Communist?" she persisted.

He looked down at their locked hands. "The Czech member of the UN committee has asked that I be attached to the party as its medical guide."

Her face was stiff: she felt afraid, sicker even than before.

"You mean that if you show this committee what it wants to see, you'll have proved yourself? Is that what you mean? What about Roy Narvo? What about the Australians? There must be a lot wrong here—Roy has told me there is, that it will take time—but do you have to go out of your way to point it out, just because you want to go home?"

"I've examined my conscience," said Traxal, and removed his hand from hers. He knew now that they could never live together in happiness: in marriage it took two to make a success of compromise. "All I can say is that one can't betray something one doesn't believe in. I don't believe in the future that has been planned for these savages in this country."

6

"I don't care what you say," Bernice said. "I am going out to Goroka till this trouble blows over. And Harry is going with me."

"You're being bloody ridiculous." Macy had often felt angry with Bernice, but never as explosively so as now. He had never hit her, but now he wanted to do so as he might a spoiled child. Only the thought that he might then lose her forever prevented him from taking his belt to her. Some women, he had been told, reacted meekly, even admiringly, to such treatment; but he did not think Bernice would be one of them. In any case, he doubted his own ability to play the role of wife-beater. He had been the weak partner in the marriage for too long.

"Don't start swearing at me!"

"You make a man swear. You're lucky you're not hearing worse."

"Words like Roy uses?" She used an expression that seemed to bubble on her lips: it popped out of her mouth before she could stop it.

His hand came up almost of its own volition: the smack of his palm against her cheek shocked him as much as it did her.

She stared at him for a moment, then she spun away to run out of the room, but he grabbed her by the shoulders. She struggled, but he had more than enough strength to hold her. "I'm sorry, darl. Really. I was afraid Harry would hear you—" He searched for excuses: even now he couldn't tell her the truth, that he had been wanting to hit her because she deserved it.

"What would it matter?" Her head was turned away; she mumbled into the hand clutching her shoulder. "He's on your side——"

"Darl, there are no sides in this! Can't you understand that? I'd leave here, go with you, if we had something to go to. But there's nothing!"

She wasn't listening to him; she was beyond argument. She had reached that point before this row today, when she had realized that whatever argument she herself had had was hopeless. She had relied on Traxal to help her, and he had let her down. She had asked him not to recommend Eric to take charge of the hospital when he himself left; but he bluntly, and without telling her why, had refused to commit himself.

She had ranted at that, brought up the weekend at Moresby, accused him of thinking her good enough to sleep with but not good enough to grant a favor. She had had her face slapped then for the first time; Traxal had done it coldly and calmly, then walked away and left her standing on the path above the cliff that fell sheer into the gorge. For one awful moment, which made her shudder when she thought of it later, she had thought of flinging herself over the cliff. But she was neither desperate enough nor courageous enough; with Traxal's slap on her cheek, hysteria had drained out of her and cold realization had crept in. And now her face had been slapped for the second time, this time by her husband; later, her novelettish mind would see the irony of it, slapped by both lover and husband, and in her self-sympathetic moments she would wallow in the humiliation of it. But right now the hysteria had fled again, and she was once more aware of the hopelessness of her position. But she couldn't surrender: pride was always the last to drown under hopelessness.

Then Harry came into the room. He stopped short, embarrassed, seeing his parents in what he at first thought was an embrace: parents loving or parents fighting were an equal embarrassment, grownups doing things he would rather not see. He turned to go, but his mother said, "Harry, would you like to come out to Goroka with me?"

He hesitated. "How long for, Mum? Just for the day, like?"

Bernice had broken away from Macy. She was glad she had not begun to cry; she knew that nothing scared off a boy so much as a weeping mother did. "No. Till—" She stopped then. She knew that "till this trouble blows over" would be no more of an argument with Harry than it had been with his father: they stood together in masculine territory there. "Oh, for a while. You could go to school there, meet other boys. You could go riding—and they have pictures twice a week——"

Harry shook his head. "No, I don't think so, Mum. I ain't a city kid."

Macy wanted to laugh, but he kept control of himself. Bernice was not so successful: she almost took Harry by the shoulders and shook him. "City kid! Goroka's got only five hundred people——!"

Harry stared at her. "I'm sorry, Mum. I still don't wanna go. I like it here—" He looked up at his father. "And so does Dad. I think I—we oughta stay with him."

Bernice had never known she had such control. Her voice was thin, but it was quiet: "I'm going out on the plane on Monday. I'll radio in tonight that they are to pick me up."

She left the room, her high heels clicking like bones on the floor, and Harry looked up at his father. "Are we gonna let her go on her own, Dad? Or are we gonna go with her?"

Macy looked out through the open door down toward the hospital. He pushed his hat back on his head and ran a weary hand across his brow. At daylight he and Frank Rossi had gone in one of the Landrovers over to Vaikaka. Six of the huts had been burnt down, and there had been four natives to treat for second-degree burns. One of them, an old woman, had been brought back to the hospital, and it looked as if she might lose an arm. The others had refused to come, and Rossi and he had argued and cajoled and threatened to no avail; something was brewing in Vaikaka, and the clanfolk were sticking together for security. The earth tremor, besides causing the fire, had demolished the picket fence of the stockade; when Rossi and he had arrived, the natives were already repairing it, as if attack were imminent. When he and Rossi had returned at last to Kundavi, the last thing he had wanted was an argument with Bernice.

He stood there, listening to Bernice opening and slamming drawers in their bedroom. He knew the risk he was taking in letting her go alone to Goroka: the Cessna that would take her in to the town connected with the Quantas airliners that went South. And if she went South he knew, with a sad sickening certainty, that he would never see her again. Then he turned and looked at Harry, his son, who had said he was not a city kid.

"No, Harry," he said. "We stay here."

10

Narvo had raised no objection to Elisabeth's helping Father Shawn with the school at the mission. Although he had never raised the point directly with the priest, he had often hinted that a good school would be an asset to the patrol post. He had not insisted, because he had his doubts, which he had never expressed for fear of hurting the priest, that Father Shawn could provide a good school. Although he was not aware of the full extent of the priest's failure but had only his suspicions, he did know Father Shawn's shortcomings, one of which was his almost total inability to organize anything that depended upon discipline. He knew that the bishop had little time for the priest, and several times had wanted to replace him. Narvo had got wind of what was in the bishop's mind before the word had got to Father Shawn; and he had told the bishop, in terms verging on blasphemy, that while he ran the post at Kundavi no other priest but Father Shawn would be allowed in here. He had managed to get Neil Figgins at Goroka to back him up, and in the end the bishop had given way. The bishop, smiling, had threatened Narvo with excommunication; and Narvo, smiling in return, had asked how could one banish a man who was already living in the wilderness. Father Shawn had never known of the fight that had gone on for him, but now and again Narvo had felt like dropping a hint, just to see if the priest would pull up his socks. That he had decided to let Elisabeth help him in the school might mean he at last was going to make an effort to be a successful missionary.

"You won't find much trouble with the youngsters themselves," Narvo told Elisabeth. "They're pretty keen to learn. Especially to speak English. You'll have to apply discipline to the old folks, make them see that the kids aren't to be kept away from school— call on me if you want any help that way. The old people don't want the kids educated—it means eventually they're going to lose control of them. It's just one of the unrewarding steps in educating the backward races. The elders resent you because you're taking the youngsters out from under their authority. Then the youngsters, educated to our ways, grow up and accuse you of exploiting them, no matter how benevolent you've been."

"Why do you go on, then?" Elisabeth asked.

"I've asked Mike Shawn the same question. Maybe it's for the same reason he and other missionaries try to Christianize the heathens, why the Communists battle on in Australia even though most people are against them—a question of faith, I suppose you call it. I guess mine boils down to a faith in civilization. I just don't see why these kanakas, in time, shouldn't have everything we've got." He looked across the parade ground at an old woman squatting on the sward, cutting the grass. Her thoughts were hidden behind the hideously carved mask of her face: the wrinkled elephant-skin of her empty breasts made her a mockery of womanhood. But she had once been a young and beautiful girl, and she had borne men and other women to follow her; she was one link in a long chain of primitiveness that was out of place in today's world. He did not want to change the way of living of this old woman for the mere sake of change; it was a matter of conscience with him that she, and her children and her children's children, should share the good things of life that the rest of the world had discovered and developed. He knew it was also a matter of conscience with governments and with organizations such as the United Nations; but the conscience of a corporate body and that of a single man were never the same thing. A man, working alone, carried the extra burden of having to be practical.

"And you are going to give it to them whether they want it or not?"

"Oh, they want it, all right," he said. "Or anyway, they want the material things. Someday I'll tell you about the cargo cults among these kanakas. Whether they want the moral values of civilization is another thing. You can form your own opinion when you get among the natives up at the mission. Myself, I think the converted ones put on all the trappings of Christianity, but underneath they still have the same old values and ethics. You can teach a kanaka who Jesus was, but you can never teach him how Jesus thought. Holiness, as we understand it, is beyond his comprehension."

"Aren't there a lot of white people like that?"

He grinned. "*Tru*, as they say in pidgin. But white people, because of their skin, are accepted without question as being civilized. No one queries whether they have ethics, or even understand what they are—being civilized, to a lot of self-styled civilized people, means knowing the right wines, recognizing Bach from Beethoven——"

"I've met them in Prague," she smiled. "Even among the party members."

"This mere fact of a white skin being accepted as a sign of being civilized is another of the things educated blacks hold against us. We had a fellow from one of the new African States through here last year. He was intelligent, university educated, and he knew I was on his side—but he couldn't stand me. He went home and told his black brothers we were doing out here exactly what the old colonial powers did to his ancestors a hundred years ago. Some of the biggest obstacles to helping these people here are put up by people of their own color, the so-called enlightened ones who have gained what they call their independence." He looked down at her. "If you find things up at the school tougher than you expected, don't give in. You have to learn to live with your disappointment if you want to go on."

"As with your disappointment over Paiwo?"

He nodded slowly, then took the conversation off on another tack. "But why are you going to help in the school? Peter told me you would probably be going out on Monday's plane, down to Moresby."

"Oh, he did?" All at once she wanted to tell Narvo that everything was over between her and Peter; but she still did not know him well enough to trust his reaction. He might put her on the plane on Monday, anyway, glad to be rid of her. And as yet she did not have the confidence to face the outside world alone. Last night, in the darkness of the guest hut, with the gecko lizard click-clicking in the roof, reminding her of the rat in the ceiling of the house in Prague, reminding her of home, she had cried herself to sleep for the first time in weeks. "No, I am not going. Do you mind, Roy?"

He looked down at her, his face sober and, she thought, a little stern; then abruptly he smiled, the gold tooth flashing. "Hell, no!" he cried, and she almost expected him to thump her on the shoulders as she had seen him do to Father Shawn. "I hate to admit this, but I like having you around. You're a change after—" Then he stopped. "No, I shouldn't say that. It's not a real compliment to you. And the others can't help how they are."

"Roy," she said, smiling gently up at him, "you are nicer than you want people to believe."

They were standing outside the House Paper and he turned and plucked a hibiscus from the bush that grew beside the steps. "Wear that in your hair. It's my thanks for your compliment. I get so few of them."

Then he turned and went up into the House Paper, shouting for Sergeant Beraki, yelling for the store clerk, stamping in his boots across the bare floor, being the assistant district officer that everyone knew, the character he presented to the world. He had long ago realized that the natives were always on the watch for any sort of weakness, and his gesture toward Elisabeth, a woman, might be interpreted by them as a weakness. The face he presented to the natives was the important one, and those whites who came in contact with him had to accept it. A few white men had seen behind it: Mike Shawn, Neil Figgins, Eric Macy, Jack Bermingham. And now he had shown part of his true face to a woman. Elisabeth was not to know she was the first, nor was he going to tell her. That would be showing real weakness.

As for Elisabeth herself, the fact that he had shown a part of his real self to her had brought a sudden glow to her, a dispelling of the sense of loneliness with which she had woken that morning. She no longer felt an outsider in the Kundavi community.

2

The Cessna came in on Monday morning out of a sky that blazed with heat. It appeared out of the haze over the distant mountains, glittering like a translucent insect; its humming grew louder, it came in a low bank over the patrol post, then headed across the gorges to the airstrip. Even from the ground one could see the plane bouncing on the air pockets, and Bernice, standing on the airstrip in her best clothes, suddenly felt sick and wished now that she weren't going. She was not sick only because of the thought of the rough ride in the plane; the beginning of the sickness had been with her all through the long sleepless night she had just spent. She knew she had taken a step over a cliff back up which she might never be able to climb. But she could not turn back now: pride was as much part of her luggage as the two suitcases that stood beside her. If she gave in now, having come this far, she knew she would never get Eric out of these mountains.

"I think you're making a mistake, darl," Macy said, watching the plane come in, bouncing occasionally as if to jump invisible obstacles: he shut his mind to the thought of what could happen to the plane if it met an air pocket just as it took off.

Bernice knew that her dark glasses hid her own doubt from him: the opticians had become merchants of deceit. "That remains to be seen. I've got to get away from this place. I'd be a nervous wreck if I stayed."

"Whoops!" said Harry. "That was a beaut! See him bounce then! Geez, Mum, you're gonna have a rough ride." He looked up at her, his young eyes frank with misery. "You reckon you oughta go, Mum?"

She nodded, afraid to let herself speak. The plane had landed now and was running up the strip. The moment of departure loomed over them, like a sudden cloud in the burning sky; the increasing roar of the rapidly approaching plane seemed to increase the pressure of the moment. Then the motor cut out and the natives who had gathered on the strip rushed forward. Macy bent and picked up the suitcases.

The three of them moved down through the throng of natives. Bernice was wearing a bright yellow cotton dress, a brown straw picture hat and white stilt-heel shoes; the natives, men and women alike, looked at her with admiration and envy. A native woman put out a greasy hand to finger the dress; but it was Harry, and not Bernice, who knocked the hand away. He shook his head at the native woman and she smiled shyly at him; but he had no smile to give her in return nor even a word of rebuke. He had nothing but tears inside him, and he was determined that they would not break out. He knew that if he broke into tears his mother would probably stay; but something, perhaps wisdom borrowed from the future, an instinct of things to come, told him such a reconciliation would solve nothing. The gap between his mother and father was not because of him. It was because of a lot of things, none of which he was entirely sure of, but which, and this he was sure of, could be lumped together under the heading of *New Guinea.* He would not be aware of it till years later, but it was an argument that had been going on for centuries among families where one or other of the parents had had the pioneer spirit. The spirit itself had several manifestations, not all of them commendable: a lust for gold or some other riches, an urge to escape from a crushed city existence, a desire for a healthier life for one's children: it was doubtful if more than one in a thousand pioneers consciously thought of himself as a builder of a nation's future. That Macy's determination to stay at Kundavi stemmed from his ambition to dispense medical care, did not lessen him as a pioneer. Australia itself had been built by many men who, having been convicts, only remained because they did not have the money to return to their homeland.

But Harry knew none of this, nor would he have thought of it if he had. His only thought was that his mother was leaving them, and though she was only going to Goroka, something told him she might continue farther South, never to come back. He would write a long letter to his brother Rob tonight, telling him what had happened and asking him, if their mother did go South, to persuade her to come back to Kundavi. Rob, from his letters, preferred the mainland to New Guinea, but Harry knew he wouldn't be such a stinker as to try to keep their mother down there. A woman's place was with her husband: why, come to think of it, he had heard his mother say exactly the same about some of the women down South who wouldn't come up to join their husbands in Goroka.

Macy handed the suitcases up to the pilot, and turned to Bernice. "I'll write to you tonight, darl. There's a lot I want to say. I think I can say it better on paper——"

"There's not much to say. We know where we stand—" But Bernice couldn't trust herself to say more. She turned quickly, hugged Harry to her, the tears already in her eyes behind the dark glasses, then let him go and clambered up into the plane.

"It's going to be a rough trip, Mrs. Macy," the pilot said. "You sure you want to risk it?"

"You're going to go out anyway, aren't you?"

"It's different with me," the young Pole said. "They need the plane back in Goroka. I've got to go."

"So have I," said Bernice, and turned to wave good-by to Macy and Harry, unable to see them for the tears that were blinding her.

The pilot started up the plane and turned it around; dust blew back in a thick yellow cloud over Macy and Harry. The Cessna went down the strip, waddling on the uneven ground surface, then it was airborne. It climbed flatly, heading down the gorge; it went smoothly, its passage unmarked by air pockets, and disappeared into the haze.

"When will Mum be back, Dad?"

"I dunno." Macy looked down at his son. He ran his tongue around his mouth: farewell was grit on his lips. "But we're here at Kundavi for good."

"I don't mind, Dad," Harry said, not looking at his father, staring away into the haze into which his mother had gone. "I wouldn't wanna live anywhere else."

Macy almost choked with emotion. He wanted to hug the boy to him as Bernice had done, but he knew that eleven-year-old boys hated that. They were surrounded by the natives, all of them grinning widely at the white man and the boy; Macy knew that he and Harry were well liked, and he knew more than ever that this was where he belonged. He put his hand on the back of Harry's neck and tilted the boy's straw hat, with its band of possum fur, forward over his eyes.

"Come on, mate," he said, and turned to walk across to the Landrover.

3

Paiwo, sitting in his hut in the village of Vaikaka, heard the plane come in over the mountains. He and the other warriors had come back into the village yesterday morning. Guards, women and old men, were posted down the track to warn if the Kiap approached. Kundavi could be clearly seen from Vaikaka, and as soon as the Kiap left the patrol post a mirror would blink a warning: the mountain men had learned the many uses of the sun. Paiwo, as the new fight-leader, the man who had distinguished himself so much in the fight against the Benamaua, had gone alone into his hut, as custom said he must, and there he had remained all day. He was a hero, but he was also the symbol and source of his village's strength.

He had not eaten all day yesterday. Last night a pig had been roasted and a feast held in his honor, but no one had brought him food nor disturbed him. The villagers had gathered outside his hut, stamping their feet and chanting his praises; but no one had come in through the low narrow door of the hut to honor him. He was a hero, and a hero deserved to be left alone that he might ponder on the strength and courage and sacrifice that put him apart from ordinary men. He was not left alone to feed on vanity, but on pride, which is a different quality altogether, the pride that is not diluted when it is mixed with humility. He was the strength of Vaikaka, but from now on he had more than himself to consider.

There was a rustling at the door, and a man came crawling into the hut. He carried some cinnamon bark and some salt, and Paiwo took them and began to chew them. Bowls of *kau-kau* were passed in from outside, and into each Paiwo spat some of the bark and salt.

"This is for my son," said the man, and Paiwo spat an extra large mouthful of the bark into the bowl held out to him. He spat into more than two dozen bowls, the bowls of the children and the sick, those who needed the strength of the new fight-leader, the hero Paiwo. He looked in vain for the bowl of his own son Bandi.

Paiwo came out of his hut late in the afternoon, and all the young boys, the ones with their noses just pierced and the older ones who had been through the *marita* ceremony, the coming to manhood, crowded around him, touching him shyly, shouting aloud their praise of him. Paiwo stood for a moment, blinking in the glare of the sun after the gloom of his hut. He smiled, looking around at the villagers, feeling the glory of his new title, then he moved slowly through the crowd and down toward the open-sided hut where the body of Kabu was still being smoked. Kabu's mother and sister sat beside the fire, tending the corpse that was now beginning to look wasted, the skin brittle as crackling on it. The mother and sister now wore the gray mud and the strings of beads of mourning. Paiwo said nothing, and the crowd fell back from him.

He stood there for almost five minutes, staring at the shrunken body that had once been Kabu. He had loved Kabu and he would miss her; she had been more than just someone to cook for him, to share his bed. It hurt him even more that she had had to die to bring about the circumstances that had made him fight-leader. She would have enjoyed being the wife of the fight-leader, he knew that, thinking kindly of the harmless vanity that had been hers, and she would have been a worthy wife for such a man.

Then he turned away from the corpse, and the *luluai* came toward him. "We hold another sing-sing for you tonight, Paiwo."

Paiwo shook his head. "I do not think it is wise. The Kiap would know of last night's feast—he must know that I and the others are back in Vaikaka. We must go back to the mountains again."

"You cannot be running forever," said the *luluai*, secretly glad that Paiwo would have to leave the village, jealous, as only an old man with his wife behind him can be, of the new fight-leader's status.

Paiwo shrugged. "It is the way things are, Angitape. The Kiap has his law—he must abide by it."

"Is that the way a fight-leader should talk?" said Angitape, although he did not speak loudly enough for the others to hear him: Paiwo's position was too new and too strong for the *luluai* to begin undermining it just yet.

Paiwo smiled: he recognized the jealousy in the old man. "Is that the way a *luluai* should think? After all, Angitape, you are supposed to represent the Kiap's authority."

Angitape dodged that question. "But what sort of fight-leader will Vaikaka have if he spends all his time away from the village?"

"I shall not spend all my time away from Vaikaka," Paiwo replied, realizing that this man would waste no time in sowing the seeds of rebellion against him. "I shall keep coming back, Angitape. And it would be well for you to remember where your duty lies—with Vaikaka or with the Kiap."

The *luluai* could not resist one last jibe: "Where does your own lie, Paiwo?"

"That is something I have also thought about while I have been in my hut," said Paiwo. "You do not need to worry, Angitape. I have been a Vaikaka man all my life, and in my veins is the blood of countless Vaikaka men. The Kiap was my master only while I remained at Kundavi. I have left Kundavi forever."

Then Kasin, the young buck who had cut the flesh from the dead Benamaua fight-leader, came forward. He had waited till Paiwo had been leading the Vaikaka party out of Benamaua, then he had run back and picked up the piece of meat he had cut and hidden it among the leaves in his *bilum* bag. One or two of the other young bucks had seen him, but under pain of injury or even death, he had sworn them to secrecy. He had been determined to eat the flesh of the Benamaua fight-leader, to inherit the latter's courage and strength and prowess. It was his consuming ambition that he, too, should someday be a fight-leader. He envied Paiwo, and he saw no reason why he should not someday succeed him.

"Paiwo, the white man called One-Eye, the husband of Giamin, has left Kundavi and come into the mountains. He has gone up toward Wabut looking for the yellow stuff he calls gold."

"What is that to us?" asked Paiwo.

The young buck looked cunning. "He carries the weapon he calls a gun. And he has other things—dishes, cans, a canvas bag for carrying things, the shelter he calls a tent."

"He is married to one of our women," said Paiwo, seeing more trouble; he was beginning to realize that the position of fight-leader had its problems.

"He is a white man," said Kasin. "If we do not take the things from him, there are others who surely will. Why should they have them? They belong to us, since he is our cousin by marriage."

"So we kill him to make certain his belongings stay in our family?" Paiwo smiled sarcastically, then shook his head. He could see the way things were going. In these mountains killing for the sake of killing could spread like a virus, and the poison was already in Kasin. To kill a white prospector, with his tools, his gun, his knife, even his mirror, was much more profitable and exalting than killing a black man. "Perhaps we may head in his direction, to make sure others do not kill him, but we do not kill him ourselves."

Kasin looked at the *luluai*, and recognized the support in the old man's eyes. Ordinarily, a young buck would never question the fight-leader's authority without openly challenging him to a duel: but Kasin was no ordinary young buck. He suspected that

Paiwo could beat him in a hand-to-hand fight, and so he had to think of other, if slower means, of deposing him. He had been too young to remember Wangamunggu's installation as fight-leader; and it had been Paiwo's installation that had all at once fired his latent ambition. He wanted the acclamation and the praise and the honor for himself, and he was determined to get it.

"Why do the white men have these things and we do not?" he asked. "Perhaps our ancestors sent us these things from the other world and the white men intercepted them before they reached us here in the mountains. We have heard stories from the police boys of great canoes spouting smoke that come in over a vast river bringing goods to the white men——"

Paiwo could see what Kasin was leading up to. It was what he had heard the Kiap call the Cargo Cult, although the natives themselves had many names for it. It had happened once before in these mountains, just after the Kiap had arrived here, and Paiwo remembered how angry the Kiap had been. The cult had started in the village of Kagata, prompted by a renegade carrier who had come back from the patrol post to promise his clan a wealth of goods such as the white Kiap had. The Kagata people, certain that their ancestors were going to provide them with everything for a new life, had begun to burn their houses, dig up their gardens and slaughter their last pigs for the huge farewell to the life they had been living and soon would be leaving behind them forever. When the goods had not arrived, the cult leader had blamed the Kiap, and parties had gone out from Kagata to kill him. The Kiap had met them halfway, killed the cult leader instead, and ordered the Kagata men back to re-build their village. The cult had died as quickly as it had been born, but Paiwo remembered the effect it had had on the other villages in the mountains.

Paiwo looked around his own village, then back at Kasin. "Perhaps we, too, shall have all those things someday."

"But why not now?" said Kasin, and the *luluai* murmured his agreement.

"Because we should have to kill the white men to get them," said Paiwo, and stared both men down. "And I am not going to lead the men of Vaikaka into fights against the Kiap, to kill him and take his goods from him."

"What if the Kiap comes looking for you, to kill you?" said the *luluai*.

"That would be a different matter," said Paiwo, and hoped it would not happen.

He turned and left Kasin and the *luluai*, walking up through the admiring throng of young boys to his own hut. He stood outside his hut and looked around the village. Women were working out in the gardens, turning over the *kau-kau* domes, digging up the sweet potato for tonight's feast; other women were coming up from the lower slopes, clumps of green bananas supported on their heads like huge fantastic hats. In the stockade itself women were slicing up two pigs, and young girls were cutting wild sugar cane into short lengths. Men were still re-building the huts that had been burnt down in the fire on the night of the earth tremor, and beyond the new huts other men were building the fire pit for tonight's feast. They had dug a large pit and were throwing firewood into it. Young boys were bringing up large stones, and Paiwo knew there were others farther down the mountain gathering banana fronds. The wood would be lit and when it was a glowing fire the stones would be thrown in on it. Banana fronds would then cover the stones and the meat to be cooked, the pigs, and fowls, and rats and pos-sums, put on top of the fronds. The meat, in turn, would be covered with more banana fronds, and on top of the fronds would be thrown more stones, heated in another fire. The whole pit would be sealed with earth, then a length of bamboo would be driven down through the earth and cold water poured down it on to the hot stones beneath. The resultant steam, trapped by the lid of earth, would cook the meat in quick time. Paiwo, without understanding the term, had once heard the Kiap call it the original pressure cooker.

Paiwo, after eighteen months on the patrol post, knew there was a better life than that lived here in Vaikaka. What the white men had was better: the houses that were large and comfortable; the clothes that kept them warm; the metal pots in which their food was cooked; the vehicles that carried them quickly over the roads and saved one's legs; the guns that were so much more effective than the spear and the bow and arrow. The black men deserved these things, too, but Paiwo could not bring himself to the thought of killing the Kiap to get them.

4

There was a loud hiss, and almost immediately the Landrover began to bump on one of the rear wheels. Narvo swore, and signaled to the native driver to halt the vehicle. He climbed out and inspected the rear offside wheel. The tire was flat, punctured by the branch of thorn-bush that still clung to it.

He took his rifle from the seat of the Landrover, told the driver to change the tire, and began to walk up the road toward the patrol post. He had come down to the bottom of the gorge by vehicle, then walked along the bank of the river to the salt spring to see how work on the new footbridge was progressing. The surviving women of Vaikaka had not yet come back to the salt spring to work, but Narvo had posted two police boys on daylight guard to warn off any other village clans who coveted the spring. Prisoners had been brought down from the stockade, and under the stern and contemptuous eye of Sergeant Beraki were now working on the new bridge. Narvo, satisfied with what he had seen, had then gone farther down the river to inspect the landslide that had occurred on the night of the earth tremor. Thousands of tons of rock had crashed down, but the river was at its widest here and the slide had barely impeded the rush of water. Narvo had looked up at the great new gash in the mountainside, shrugged, and returned to the Landrover. Slides like this were commonplace in these mountains, and one only reported them if they blocked a road or killed someone.

He walked slowly, the rifle slung from his shoulder, the sweat beginning to break from him as the heat bore down on him. This was the hottest day for months; summer was on its way and soon the rains would begin. He passed a clump of crotons, and their scent was heavy on the still air; farther up the bank a tree blossomed with a flock of green parakeets. From below the roar of the river came up, like deep music to his ears; and farther up the valley a waterfall glittered like a long column of crystallized air. He loved this country, he had become part of it and it part of him, and if he ever had to leave it he would have the greatest difficulty in starting over again.

He had had the greatest difficulty in starting his life at all: *his* life as distinct from the life planned for him by his parents. All through his boyhood they had taken it for granted that he would become a dentist, or better still, a doctor. His mother was a snob who looked down her nose at the mouths of the patients who gave her husband his living: a doctor had more social standing than a dentist. The war, which had killed and wrecked so many others, had saved him: he had escaped into battle, as it were. New Guinea, a death-hole for many and an ugly memory for others, had been a fortunate accident for him; he had fallen in love with it as he might have with a woman, from the moment he had stepped ashore as an infantry reinforcement at Lae. If he had stayed in the air force he might have been sent to Britain or the Middle East; and though he had seen neither of those places, he had known they were not for him. It had been New Guinea all along, almost as if it had been waiting there in the tropical sea for him to grow up and come to it. And he would never be able to leave it—or if he did, he would leave the best part of himself behind.

Three natives came down the road, the two women bent forward under the weight of firewood each carried, the wood resting on the back of their necks and held by a fiber rope around their foreheads, and the man striding along with a long spear clutched in one hand and a small *bilum* bag of *kau-kau* slung under his arm. The man advanced on Narvo, offered a hand in greeting, Narvo took it and said, "Greetings, you lazy unchivalrous bastard," the man smiled and went striding on down the road, his head-dress a blaze of color in the bright sun, and his women bent to the Siamese twin of their black shadows. *Poor devils,* Narvo thought, and included the man in his sympathy.

He had not had much love nor sympathy for the natives when he had first come here to New Guinea during the war; nor in 1946 when he had returned as a patrol officer. His interest in them had stemmed mainly from his job: they *were* his job and therefore he had to look after them. Privately his attitude toward them had been that of most whites thrown as masters into a black uncivilized country: sympathetic but distant, genuinely trying to think of them as human beings but unable completely to stifle the feeling of superiority, trying hard not to be arrogant but unable to squash the occasional contempt in an order given. Because of his size and his uninhibited manner he had, at first, been feared more than respected. Respect had come later, and then loyalty; he did not allow himself the ultimate conceit of wondering if any of the natives loved him. He loved no particular one native, as he loved Mike Shawn, and he was honest enough to admit that it was probably impossible for him ever to have such deep affection for one of these New Guinea natives. Love between men was based on a mutual understanding, a common appreciation of certain aspects of life and thought; it was inevitable that two men so close together in affection had to come from the same civilization. The most he, or any other officer in the Administration, could hope for was respect and loyalty. He had been sure he had had both from Paiwo, and it had been almost like a physical blow when Paiwo had deserted and gone back down the trail of savagery.

He heard the sound of an engine down the road behind him, and turned to see Macy and Harry coming up in the second Landrover. "Bernice get away okay?" he said as he got into the cabin beside them.

Macy nodded. "She's gone."

Narvo looked at the trouble in the other man's face; then he looked down at Harry squashed between them. "How's it, chum? Miss Palyardi tells me you're starting school with her up at the mission."

"Four hours a day," said Harry, grimacing. "Make you sick, wouldn't it? A bloke might just as well be down South."

"You reckon?" Narvo said.

Harry looked sideways at his father, then back at Narvo. "No, not really. I'm not gonna like it, though. Not at first."

"Oh, I don't know," said Narvo. "I wouldn't mind having a teacher like Miss Palyardi."

"Yeah, she is a good sort, isn't she?" said Harry, man of the world and connoisseur of women. "Waddya reckon, Dad?"

But Macy's mind was full of another woman, the one he might have just lost forever. "Yeah, I suppose so." Then it suddenly struck him who had made the first favorable remark about Elisabeth, and he looked at Narvo. He grinned, joining in the fellowship that existed between his son and Narvo. "Roy, don't tell me you're gonna become a ladies' man?"

"Geez, I hope not," said Harry fervently, suddenly a man's man again.

Narvo grinned easily. "She's Peter's girl. I'm not a kanaka who goes around stealing other fellers' women."

Then the Landrover had pulled up before the hospital and they all got out. Harry went on up toward the Macy house, and

Narvo looked at Macy. "How did it go, Eric? Was she still browned off when she left?"

"I dunno. I suppose so." Macy put some fresh gum into his mouth and began to chew. "I just hope she comes back, that's all."

"And if she doesn't?"

Macy shrugged. "Then I'll come up and join you and Mike at night, be in the bachelors' club." He looked down toward the end of the hospital where the native outpatients were queued up. Traxal and Duggan were on the veranda there, working from a table as the patients filed by them: treating a burn, giving medicine for a sick baby, using a needle on natives who shut their eyes and turned their faces away from the devil in the hypodermic syringe. "There'll be no one else to talk to."

Narvo followed the direction of Macy's gaze. "I've never asked you before—why don't you like Peter?"

Macy was silent for a while, then he said, "When we first came up here, I couldn't get near him. He's a superior bastard."

"I know what you mean."

"Then—" Again he hesitated. "Then, I dunno when it was, but I began to think there was something between him and Bernice."

Narvo was both puzzled and surprised. "They couldn't have got away with anything here. We'd have known about it."

"Not here. But they were down in Moresby at the same time last year. Oh, I dunno, maybe I'm imagining it, you know how you build things up. I'd catch her smiling at him sometimes—"

"Did you ever tackle her about it."

Macy shook his head, chewing slowly on his gum. "I wasn't game. I've never liked the truth, Roy. You're all right, you can take it. But I can't. And I know I'm not the only one—though that's not much compensation. Half the people I know, yeah, even some of them here at Kundavi, they look on the truth as something like cancer. We can't stand up to the thought of it."

Narvo was angry and upset by the other man's trouble: it had been bad enough to begin with, but now it had suddenly become sordid and much more complicated. "Do you think that's what all of a sudden has made her put on an act—the fact that Peter brought Elisabeth in here?"

Again Macy shrugged. "I've thought about it, though I've tried not to. A man doesn't like to think his missus is jealous of another man's girl friend. I mean, thinking like that is like putting the boot into yourself."

"If that's the way it is," Narvo said, "then it looks as if Elisabeth has to go before Bernice will come back."

"Elisabeth or Peter. Or both."

"I'll have a talk with Elisabeth. Oh, don't worry. I shan't mention you or Bernice. For my own reasons I'm entitled to know how long she's staying and what she plans to do. This is no place for a single woman."

Macy saw Duggan come out into the sunlight and take a baby from the arms of its mother. "What about Joan? She's single."

"Poor old Duggan," said Narvo, looking down toward the spotlessly white figure of the nurse. "Nothing would please me more than to see the men hanging around her, single or otherwise. But Duggan isn't Elisabeth. Sour ugly spinsters don't get men into trouble."

"I didn't think you would have noticed what sort of woman Elisabeth was."

Narvo shook his head. "Everyone has the idea that because I'm not in favor of women here on the post, I'm a pansy or misogynist or something. Who wouldn't have noticed what she's like? Even young Harry did."

"I noticed it myself," said Macy. "And so has Frank."

11

ROSSI THREW down the leaking fountain pen, and wondered what the tempers had been of men who had used quills. All his life he had been plagued by leaking fountain pens: some men had acne, some had sinus trouble, he had leaking fountain pens. The stores list before him was blotched with ink: blot dozen electric globes, blot shovels, blot pounds of blot. He looked at his ink-stained fingers and decided that he had had enough. He carefully picked up the pen and made an entry in the Goods Required column: 12 pens with nibs. Then he got up, went out of the House Paper and across to his own house. He washed his hands, brushed his hair, cleaned his teeth, put on his hat with its black and gold puggaree, a relic of his days in the school cadet corps, and walked up the road to the mission.

He was on his way to what he felt was the most important decision of his life. All morning he had been thinking about it, and all morning he had been putting it off; if the fountain pen had not begun to leak so badly, he might still be sitting at his desk. Then he would have missed her coming down to the patrol post for lunch, and he would have spent an afternoon as disturbing as the morning had been. A proposal of marriage was not something you could put away in a drawer in the Pending file.

It stayed with you like—well, like acne or sinus trouble. Or, as in his case, like leaking fountain pens.

Elisabeth had already left the school hut and was walking down the path to the road. He was glad of that: he had everything prepared to say to Elisabeth, and he had no words left for Father Shawn. He saw the priest in the door of the school hut, and he waved; then he turned quickly to Elisabeth, before Father Shawn could catch his eye and call him up for a drink.

"I thought I'd stretch my legs," he said. "I've been at my desk all morning."

"I thought you would get enough leg-stretching in these mountains." Elisabeth smiled at him and stepped on to the road beside him. She was finding it tiring teaching at the school, and she was always glad of the midday break. Though English was not a difficult language for her, it was not easy for her to communicate in it to children whose own grasp of it was tenuous and limited.

"I do, I suppose. And leg-pulling, too," he said, thinking of Jack Bermingham's rough chi-acking of him.

"You are not going to pull my leg?" Elisabeth said.

He lost his composure for a moment. His carefully prepared speech was like a train on the wrong track: the wrong switches had been pulled. "Oh, gosh, no! Why should I want to do that?" He walked beside her in silence for a moment, then he said, "Elisabeth, I came up here with a purpose this morning."

Oh, Frank, she thought, *so stern, so proper and so young.* He tried to cloak his youth and only made it more apparent. Half a dozen children suddenly rushed past them, arms and legs flickering in the air, the leaves over their buttocks bouncing like the beards of ancestors; they went down the road at speed, their thin laughter and screeching scratching on the noon stillness. One child looked back at them as he ran, lost his footing and went over in a cloud of dust and a yell, rolled back on his feet and kept running. Elisabeth laughed and looked at Rossi to share the laugh with him, but he hadn't even seen the child tumble.

"Elisabeth, I heard you and Peter talking the other morning. Oh, I didn't mean to eavesdrop, but I was in my house—your voices carried—" He looked at her, his face turned squarely toward her; even though he was walking, he gave the impression he was about to bow from the waist, he looked so stiff and formal. "Please believe me when I say I am sorry it hasn't worked out for you and Peter."

"How much did you hear?" Elisabeth said quietly.

"Enough. I tried at times not to listen—I got up and went to the other side of the house——"

"But you kept coming back?" It was a question: there was no accusation in her voice.

He nodded and bit his lip, looking more tentative than ever. "Elisabeth, you have nowhere to go, have you? I mean, you don't want to go back to Czechoslovakia, do you?"

Elisabeth was aware of the heat: beating down from the sky, reflected from the road, it even came out of the bush by the roadside as a dank warmth, the green heat of decay. She had forgotten her hat, left it in the school hut, and the sun seemed to be laying hot knives across her scalp. The skin on her face and arms was tightening, and she could feel the sweat starting on her body beneath the thin dress. But there was a chill in her, too: the returning cold dull fever that was loneliness.

"No, I have nowhere to go. But please do not worry, Frank. It is not your problem."

"Elisabeth, I am only twenty."

"It is no disgrace. Why do you say it like that? Everyone was twenty once."

Why was she being so stupidly blind? Who was it had said women were intuitive about a man's love for them? He wanted to go on, to say the words that lay like pebbles on his tongue, but all at once he saw the ridiculousness of his asking her to marry him. She would laugh at him; and he would not be able to blame her. He had thought seriously of his proposal, had weighed all the pros and cons; he had even broken down his income to see if it would be sufficient to keep two people. He was passionately, romantically in love with her; if he had had cause to write to her, there would have been poems included in his letters. Yet for all his romanticism, he was also cautious and levelheaded; and now he saw clearly and all at once that if he proposed to her, she might not only not believe him but might also laugh at him. And he had been laughed at too often.

"Elisabeth, why don't you stay here and let me look after you?" He put a hand on her arm, and she could feel the sweat in his palm. "Please listen to me——"

She had been about to ask if this was his idea of leg-pulling. Then she saw the strain in his face, and she was glad she had not joked. But he could not be serious: did he realize that he was suggesting he should keep her? "Frank, are you asking me to be your mistress?"

He bit his lip and shook his head. "No. No, that wasn't what I meant."

"I am sorry, then, if I misunderstood you. But do you mean that all you want to do is take responsibility for me if I stay on here? Frank, that couldn't be! How could I ever repay you?" She was striving to be, to sound, kind. Kindness never really became difficult till it, in itself, was the gift; then one tried too hard. "Thank you for asking me——"

"Thank you for asking—!" The words burst out of him; he was younger than ever. "You make me sound as if I'm just trying to be kind to you! I love you, Elisabeth! I'm in love with you, don't you understand? I don't want you to leave here——"

They had reached the edge of the patrol post: she passed through the picket gateway as if into safety. She saw Joan Duggan sitting on the veranda of the hospital, like a great white bird sheltering from the sun. Peter came out of the hospital, saw her and waved to her, and crossed to the pharmacy hut. Roy

Narvo came out and stood on the veranda of his hut, yelling for Sergeant Beraki. She could turn to any one of them for escape from this hurt, bewildered boy beside her; and she chose Narvo. It was a reflex action, one she would ponder on later.

"Frank, please, I do understand. Oh, I do not want to hurt you—" She could feel the tears at the corners of her eyes; there was a taste of salt on her lips, but it could have been sweat. "It would not work out, do you not see?" Whenever she became agitated, her English became as stiff and formal as the books from which she had learned it: grammar made no allowance for emotions. This was even more difficult than trying to talk to young native children who hardly understood the language. "You have so much to look after now. There is this trouble with the natives, the UN party coming in here, Mr. Bermingham going out into the mountains—don't you see, you have enough problems without worrying about me. I shall find somewhere to go. I must find somewhere to go, now——"

She turned quickly and headed down the parade ground toward Narvo's house. Behind her she heard Rossi say, "You don't have to leave here because of me——"

2

Narvo saw Elisabeth hurrying down the parade ground toward him. Behind her he could see Rossi standing stiffly with one hand upraised, as if trying to give Elisabeth something she had refused. Even at the distance Narvo could see that Elisabeth was agitated, and he moved down one step off the veranda to go and meet her. Then he stepped back up onto the deep shade of the veranda. If she was really upset about something, she might prefer that as few people as possible should know about it. The open parade ground, with the inquisitive natives ready to appear at any moment like an audience on twenty-four-hour call, was no place for a meeting.

Elisabeth came up onto the veranda almost in a rush. Narvo saw the tears in her eyes and immediately turned and led her into the house. He motioned her into a chair, got her a drink, then sat down opposite her.

"You wouldn't have come down here if you didn't want to tell me about it. What's the trouble?"

She sipped the gin and tonic, part of her mind remarking that he had remembered what she preferred. She had wiped her eyes and while he had been getting the drink she had regained her composure. "I should not have come, Roy. You have enough trouble."

He did not deny it: he was not a man who wasted time on flattering pleasantries. "What's the trouble, Elisabeth?"

Then she told him, about Traxal, about Rossi, all the time looking down at the glass cupped in her two hands. Only when she had finished did she look up. He had not spoken while she had recited her trouble, and now he sat in silence with a black look on his face that frightened her. She put down her glass and made to rise.

"Where are you going?" he barked.

"I—I don't know——"

"Sit down! That's just it—you don't know where you're going. Where have you got to go to?" He stood up and began to wander about the room. There was gravel on the soles of his boots and when he walked on the floor where there were no mats there was a rough grating sound that seemed to fit his mood. "Why the hell did you come here, Elisabeth?"

"To marry Peter. I—I thought I still loved him."

"Maybe I shouldn't have asked that. Maybe it's enough reason for a woman—tearing off to the ends of the earth because of a man. Everyone else is here for a good and solid reason. Except perhaps Bernice——"

"Being with one's husband is a good and solid reason," Elisabeth said. "I had hoped to be with my husband, too."

He stared at her for a moment, then he nodded. "I admit the point." Then he turned away and walked to the window, gazing out. He was more disturbed by Elisabeth's dilemma than he cared to show. Against his will and the frame of outlook in which he had trained himself, he liked the girl; not just physically, although he had to admit to that, too, but for her personality and warmth of character. She was a troubled girl, despite her outward composure, and if she wasn't already grievously hurt, she was going to finish up that way. "It's no use my saying that you shouldn't have come here—and I don't mean because I object to your coming. I mean because of Peter—and what's going to happen to you from now on." He turned around. "What *is* going to happen to you?"

She shrugged, feeling helpless. She had had this feeling of helplessness before, but she had managed to survive those occasions because they had taken place in surroundings that were familiar to her, that in themselves were of some help: there had always been the chance of a friend turning a corner when she needed him most. There were no familiar corners here, no friends to appear suddenly. None, that is, but this big dark man; and she wasn't sure of him. She tried desperately to remain calm, not to give way to tears: all at once it seemed to her that he *had* to be the one on whom she could depend.

"I do not know. Perhaps I shall go down to Australia. I should be able to get a job." She looked up at him. "I am sorry, Roy. Especially now with this problem of Mr. Rossi."

Narvo waved a hand of dismissal. "He'll have to get over it. At twenty most men are pretty resilient. It will be difficult for him for a while——"

"You will not do anything to him, please? Do not discipline him."

He gave a short laugh, shaking his head in wonder. He had built up a reputation for firm discipline, but he was amused that anyone should think he would only operate within the limits of

it. "Look, this isn't a monastery. I'm not some martinet abbé
dedicated to wiping out sins of the flesh. I can't blame a man for
falling in love. I'd kick him in the behind if I caught him muck-
ing around with the kanaka women. But it's no crime to fall
in love." He stood over her, looking down at her with a direct-
ness that, despite her upset, moved the blood in her. "I can't
blame him at all for that."

"I am glad of that," she said, lowering her eyes, afraid of
further complications. She liked this man, but it would not help
her to like him too much. He would only finish up resenting her
for having complicated his own life. "Mr. Rossi is a nice boy.
I should not want to see him hurt."

"Oh, he's been hurt, all right. But he'll get over it. He'd bloody
well better," he said, sounding more like the Narvo she had first
met. He turned away from her and went to stand against a
wall, leaning on the bookshelves. Out at the back of the house
the houseboy and his assistant, the house-monkey, laughed aloud
in their high girlish giggle: someone was happy. "Elisabeth, is
it definitely all off between you and Peter? You're not going to
marry him?"

"Not if he persists in wanting to go back to Czechoslovakia."

"And if he changes his mind about that?"

She hesitated. "No," she said at last, and wondered why she
should choose Narvo as her father-confessor. "I no longer love
him."

"What about him? How does he feel?"

"I don't know." She was on the verge of tears again. "It was
such a long time, five years—one almost forgets what love was
like."

"I didn't think you could ever forget that," he said; then added
defensively: "I've only read about it. I wouldn't know."

She wanted to ask him did he mean he had never been in love,
something she found incredible. But she hadn't come down
here to ask him his troubles; nor, she knew, would he welcome

her question. "I did not mean being in love myself. I meant having someone in love with me. That was how it was with Peter and myself five years ago—we were *both* in love."

Narvo stood beside a bowl of scarlet hibiscus on the bookshelves. There were no roses in these mountains; other flowers were the flowers of love. Vivid flowers like the hibiscus, redolent of passion more than of love; but their petals did not fall as easily as those of the rose, passion was not as fragile as love. All he had ever known was passion, or its socially inferior twin, lust: hibiscus, and not roses, were for him. He wondered what flowers Traxal liked: what was the flower of self-interest? The narcissus didn't exactly suit him: self-love was a different thing from self-interest. Narvo knew that in the last twenty-five years, from the days of Hitler on, there had been countless Europeans whose only means of survival had been self-interest. He did not think that Traxal's case was quite so desperate, but he could understand, even if he could not forgive, the Czech doctor's preoccupation with his own future. He could not forgive Traxal because of the latter's seemingly callous disregard of Elisabeth's future.

"You can't stay here, Elisabeth. But where else have you to go?" He looked out the window, saw Macy walking slowly up the path to his house, head bent, hat tilted back over his neck. Bernice would have landed in Goroka now, would be sitting on the hotel lawn under the umbrella, drinking her rum and lemonade, looking across at the airdrome and the planes taking off for Moresby and Australia. She was another who had nowhere to go; and Narvo wondered if she now realized it. "I can't kick you out, put you on a plane and tell you to get lost."

"Why can't you, Roy? I am not your responsibility. I am really sorry I have been such a nuisance. You were right in the first place. I should never have come here."

He said nothing, leaning back on the bookshelves with both elbows. He had had to make decisions before about women; but with one exception, they had always been native women. The one exception had been the blonde whom he had almost married on his leave five years ago; it disturbed his conscience that, though not nameless, she was now almost faceless to him. Hibiscus had been the flower in the buttonhole on that leave; passion had been the substitute for loneliness. It was in the cold light of morning after the hot passion of night that he had decided not to ask her to marry him; and the decision had not been so difficult after all, because he had never hinted to the girl that he was even considering marriage. She was married now, had two children, and, he guessed, was far happier and contented than she would have been with him. He would be a difficult man to live with, he knew, and she had not been a girl of much patience. Given the same circumstances, she might have been another Bernice. He looked down at Elisabeth and wondered how much patience she had. She would need a great deal of patience—and courage—in the next few months. She would be starting a new life—a prospect that could face him very soon, and which increased his sympathy for her.

"Elisabeth, if I let you stay here—not permanently, but for a while, till you're more settled in your mind and, maybe, have had a chance to get a job down South, or even in Moresby or Goroka—if I let you stay here, how will you handle Peter and Frank?"

She said nothing for a moment, surprised that he should want to help her: she appreciated that what he was suggesting was going against the grain of his whole attitude to life here at Kundavi. "I can work harder up at the school. If I occupy myself with something, they should be no problem."

"It won't be as easy as that. You've been around, Elisabeth—" She looked vague, and he smiled. "I mean you must know how men think. I don't reckon the men in Prague were any different from those in Sydney or Melbourne. And up here it's worse. The farther men get away from civilization, it seems the more they're concerned with one thing. Am I embarrassing you?"

"You are not making me feel comfortable," she said, and took another sip of her drink. "But if this is the price of my being allowed to stay here——"

"It's not the price of anything," he said equably. "I am just trying to explain to you the facts of life—of life up here. A woman's attraction—that is, if she's attractive at all—becomes pretty basic. A man up here, if he is to succeed in his job, has to live a pretty monastic life—and it is tougher for us than it is for Father Shawn, because we haven't taken any vows of celibacy. He has the thought of sin to hold him back—a condition of mind which I'm afraid isn't too prevalent among men in these islands. I've known patrol officers to break under the strain and start sleeping with kanaka women—and that's the end of them as patrol officers, even if the Administration never finds out. I mean their end as efficient officers."

"I shan't allow Peter or Mr. Rossi to sleep with me," she said coldly, putting down her glass and rising from her chair. "If that is what you mean."

"It wasn't what I meant at all," said Narvo unflustered.

Elisabeth had the feeling all at once that he wasn't speaking to her as man to woman, but as the assistant district officer to someone on his staff. She felt a sudden flash of resentment, then just as quickly was ashamed. She knew that his attitude was right and there was nothing she could do about it.

"What I meant," he said, "was that you are not to give them any encouragement even to *think* such a thing. If it is all over between you and Peter, then that is the way it must be—utterly and completely over. If you change your mind about him, then I ask your promise that you'll let me know immediately. So that I can put you on the first plane out of here."

"I give you my promise," she said, confident that she would not change her mind about Peter. "But it seems so contradictory —if I make up with Peter, why will you send me out of here?"

"Because I don't trust him. Because I think that after a few weeks you might be back exactly where you are now. It would be better for all concerned if you became a sour spinster." Then he grinned, the gold tooth flashing, the assistant district officer abruptly gone and the man himself returned. "But only while you're here."

She walked to the door, then turned, grateful to him but unable to restrain herself from being a woman. "And how do I act toward you?"

"You won't trouble me that way," he said, still smiling; but she couldn't remember a man who had been less flattering in his truthfulness. "I've got too many other things on my mind."

"Someday, Roy, I should like to meet you somewhere away from Kundavi," she said, and went out of the house before he could reply.

12

LATE THAT afternoon Narvo was working on the generator when Sergeant Beraki came up to tell him that Mr. Bermingham's woman wanted to see him again. Since the night of the earth tremor the generator had been functioning at less than its best, showing its age and promising to expire at any moment. Narvo, beset by other worries, had ignored it as long as he could; but this afternoon he had decided that the job of repairing it, of trying to coax a few more months of life out of it, could be put off no longer. Next time he went down to the coast he would have to see if there were any more second- or third-hand generators going cheaply. He ruminated ruefully on the fact that the government was most conscientious about improving the lot of the natives, but left its patrol officers to their own devices when it came to keeping up their own standard of living. The cost of the generator would come out of his own pocket.

He was dressed only in a pair of shorts and sneakers, his hands, face and body streaked with grease, when Sergeant Beraki, immaculate as a palace guard, came up the hill to him. "What does she want, Beraki?"

"She would not say, Kiap. The woman does not confide in me."

Narvo remarked the sour note in Beraki's voice, but said nothing. "All right, bring her up here."

A few minutes later Beraki returned with Mary Bermingham, marching her and the two children up the hill as if they were a party of prisoners to be charged. Narvo, wrench in hand, straightened up from the generator. "What is wrong, Mary?"

"It is my husband, Kiap." Mary Bermingham held the children behind her, like a living bustle: fear bound the little group, common in the bloodstream. She looked down at the grease-stained sandshoes of the Kiap and spoke without lifting her head. "My father brought me word that the men have gone out from Vaikaka to hunt him."

"To hunt him? What do you mean by that?"

"I do not know, Kiap. Perhaps they mean to kill him."

Narvo swore and looked at Beraki. "Have you heard anything?"

The sergeant shook his head. "No, Kiap. I can send one of the boys over to Vaikaka to make certain. Perhaps this is only woman's talk—" He did not even glance toward Mary Bermingham, but the little native woman shifted nervously.

"No, this is more than woman's talk." Narvo stood for a moment, bouncing the wrench up and down in his hand; if Bermingham were here now, he would lay it across the back of the one-eyed man's skull. Friends could sometimes be bigger burdens than enemies; at least you did not have responsibilities toward enemies. "All right, Mary. I shall see that Jack is not harmed. Let your father take the word back to Vaikaka that if any harm comes to your husband, the government will hold the whole village responsible." He did not think the threat would mean much to a hunting party that was already on its way after the game; but he had to make some show of authority. "And remember—you are not to leave Kundavi!"

Mary Bermingham mumbled in reply, then turned and hurried the children ahead of her down the hill. Beraki did not look after her, ignoring her as if she had not even been here on the hill. But Narvo stared after the little native woman, wondering how much she would miss her husband if he were killed. These people, he knew, had the same emotions as whites and the same depth of feeling; but they also had a stoicism and a fatalism that made it hard for an outsider to guess at the true depth of their love or grief. Mary Bermingham loved her children, but Narvo doubted if he would ever know if she truly loved her husband.

"Do we leave this evening, Kiap?" said Beraki, thirsting for action: he was really just a fight-leader in uniform.

"It is too late, Beraki." Narvo had gone back to work on the generator. Steel banged against steel, and his voice had the same hard ring. "We shall leave at first light in the morning. Six boys and enough carriers to carry supplies for ten days."

Beraki could see the anger rustling within the white man, but it was not his place to say anything nor even to show that he saw anything amiss. He often overstepped himself when it came to dealing with the police boys and the local natives, but he knew his place with the Kiap: he had learned his lesson the hard way early in their relationship, and it was not a lesson he would forget. He saluted, his feet thudding into the dirt as he about-turned and went down the hill, and Narvo straightened up to look after him. *What a pity,* he thought, *that my friends don't respect my orders like that man does.*

Half an hour later Narvo had finished work on the generator. He started it up and felt his first pleasure of the day when it ran smoothly; like any man good with his hands, he got a genuine if small sense of achievement out of making something work. He stood for a moment, shaking his head with satisfaction. He left the generator running; it was almost dark and the lights would soon be switched on. The evening fires were already being lit in the native quarters; smoke columns stood like a conclave of ghosts above the row of huts. Narvo looked out over the post, savoring the deep blue hush of the valley; even the throb of the generator right beside him did not seem to disturb it. This was his favorite time of day, always had been, even as a boy: it was the time when dreams began to move in the mind not yet sunk into night. But he had no dreams now, only a gathering harvest of regrets. This time of day, he realized, must be a time of sadness for old men; and today he felt old. In another three months he was due for leave again, but the thought did not lessen his depression. Furlough would not give any solution to the problems that burdened him.

He came down the hill and across the parade ground to his house, scratching his bare chest where something had bitten him, marking himself with more grease, and Traxal was waiting for him on the veranda. Narvo shouted at the houseboy to bring drinks, pulled on an old shirt over his sweat and grease, and dropped into the chair opposite Traxal.

"What's wrong, Peter?"

Traxal looked at the man across from him, aware at once that Narvo was troubled. "Do you expect something to be wrong, Roy, when I come to see you?"

"Today, I do." Narvo punctured two of the cans of beer the house-monkey had brought, poured them out and offered one of the glasses to Traxal. "I'm sorry, Peter. But if someone came to me with a piece of good news right now, I think I'd keel over with the shock."

Traxal sipped his beer. He liked this Australian brew: it had a body to it he couldn't remember in Czech beer. But he wouldn't miss it once he was back home: even nectar couldn't take away the taste of homesickness. "A *kuru* patient died this afternoon. And we have two more who I don't think will last the night."

"What did I tell you?" Narvo sipped his own beer as if it were poison. He laughed, but without humor. "Why couldn't you come and tell me that the department down in Canberra was dying of *kuru?*"

"Would that solve anything for you?"

"Probably not. The one thing about public servants, and I appreciate that I'm one myself, is that they multiply like weeds, replacing each other just as quickly when the old ones die off. And in the big departments, you'd never get a hint that there'd been an interruption in the thought. No, it would solve nothing. Just give me some satisfaction, let them see that government policies can't always run exactly to theory and blueprint." He took another drink, still getting no taste from it. "Have you sent word over to the relatives at Benamaua?"

"Not yet. But I don't think we shall have to—the word will soon get over there without our having to send it."

Narvo swore, stood up and paced up and down the veranda. Worry was like an itch in the seat of his pants; he could never sit still when troubled. Traxal, glass poised in his hand, sat calm and relaxed in his chair. With his impending resignation this problem was almost over for him; but even if it had not been, he would still have had the same cool air of detachment. He was not a cold nor an unemotional man, but like so many selfish people he had learned to control himself when it meant getting what he wanted. And right now he wanted out, as he had heard Father Shawn describe it.

"The Benamaua are quiet enough now, after the doing-over they got from the Vaikaka," Narvo said. "But if three of their people die from *kuru* in a couple of days, they're going to start thinking about evil spirits again. And that means *tukavu.*" He swore again. "Why couldn't I have stayed home and spent a nice easy time trying to civilize Australians?"

Traxal smiled. "Am I meant to take that as a joke or am I expected to endorse your remark?"

"Don't be too bloody superior," Narvo said without rancor. Then he grinned and opened another can of beer. "You and I might have had some stimulating arguments if we'd got off on the right foot at first."

"Perhaps," said Traxal, unsmiling: he was not going to start the complications of a friendship this late in the piece. When he left here he wanted to leave nothing behind.

Narvo recognized the rebuff, but it didn't worry him. He was willing to meet Traxal halfway, but that was all; he was not hungry for the other man's friendship. He was already burdened enough with friendship; then he chided himself for the sourness of his thought. He looked at Traxal, wondering what Elisabeth had seen in the man: cold, selfish, yes, even a little callous. He supposed Traxal would be good-looking to some women, maybe to a lot of women; if what Macy suspected was true, then Bernice must have found him attractive. Perhaps Traxal was good in bed, but Narvo thought that Elisabeth, even at twenty-one or however old she had been, would not have fallen in love with him for that alone. He guessed she was a passionate woman who would find great pleasure in loving, but she was too intelligent to believe that love was just a pulse in the blood. Traxal had a certain charm, even toward men, but he could turn it on and off at will; and it did not take long for any perceptive person to discover it. Whatever it was that Elisabeth had fallen in love with was well hidden in Traxal now, perhaps forever. Looking at the man Elisabeth had once loved, Narvo suddenly felt a surge of sympathy for the girl: she deserved better than the promises this man had given her and broken, and the empty life that now faced her. He made up his mind then that he would let Elisabeth remain at Kundavi as long as she cared to stay. At the same time he realized, with a cynicism he could not deny, that he was adding another link to the chain of friendship that might in the end strangle him.

But Elisabeth was the most minor of his problems right now. He told Traxal of Jack Bermingham's danger from the Vaikaka men. "I'm leaving first thing in the morning. I'll send two police boys over to Benamaua till I come back. Their presence may restrain the locals from any thought of *tukavu*."

"What if the Benamaua decide the government is the evil spirit and commit *tukavu* on the police boys?"

"You have a fiendish mind, Peter," Narvo said, and grinned again. "Do you think you'll be safe back in Czechoslovakia?"

"Who said I was going back to Czechoslovakia?" Traxal had been about to sip his drink, but he brought the glass sharply away from his mouth.

Narvo saw that he had made a slip; with less on his mind he would have been more careful of Elisabeth's confidence. He hesitated, trying to think of an answer that would not implicate Elisabeth; but his mind was not quick enough this evening for plausible lies. Then he heard the footsteps on the gravel and he turned. Elisabeth stood at the bottom of the steps, holding Paiwo's son Bandi by the hand.

"He wanted to see the Kiap," she said, smiling up at both men. "He has a devotion to you, Roy, that makes me think you should be a father."

"I'll think about remedying the oversight," said Narvo, glad of the interruption and yet upset that it had been Elisabeth herself who had provided it. "If ever I can find the time."

Elisabeth looked at Traxal and only then saw the tight look of anger on his face. At once she sensed the tension between the two men and wondered what had caused it. She had come upon them at the wrong moment, and she did her best to retreat in good order and without embarrassment.

"I'll take Bandi over to Mary," she said.

Since Paiwo's departure from the post, Bandi had been sleeping with the Bermingham children. Mary Bermingham was his closest sub-clan relative on the post and by clan law she was morally responsible for him. She was glad to let Elisabeth look after him during the day and she had no objection to his sharing a room with her own children at night. If she gave the small boy no love, she was no worse than a lot of aunts and cousins of another color.

Elisabeth took the boy's hand and led him across the parade ground. Traxal, who hadn't spoken while she had been present, looked after her, suddenly hating her. "Was it Elisabeth who told you?"

"No," said Narvo, hoping the lie wouldn't show. He was surprised at the intensity of feeling showing in Traxal's face as the latter looked after the retreating figure of Elisabeth. He would have to get to Elisabeth before Traxal did, apologize for breaking her confidence and ask her to back him up in the lie. The web of his relationship with her, too, was already beginning to become complicated. "I was just making a guess. You haven't made any secret of the fact that you don't like Australia."

"That doesn't necessarily mean I intend returning to Czechoslovakia." Traxal stood up. He put down his glass, the beer only half drunk.

"No," said Narvo, and decided his only defense was attack. "But you'd go back if you had the chance, wouldn't you?"

"That depends," Traxal said, careful with his words as a gem dealer with his diamonds. "I learned a long time ago the disappointments that lie in hypotheses."

Narvo relaxed a little, shaking his head in mild wonder at Traxal. "You should have been a lawyer, Peter. I've read legal tomes that had more hope and heart in them than you have."

"In the right place and time," Traxal said, not admitting that he wanted to go back to Prague, but unable to let Narvo have the final word, "you might find I also had the right outlook on life. You are fortunate, Roy, more fortunate than I think you appreciate. You *are* in the right time and place. In this particular moment in history there would be no other place in the world for you but these mountains, no other place where you could be as happy."

"You think I'm happy right now?" said Narvo, and grinned sourly. "You're right about one thing, Peter. This is the place for me. But it isn't the time. I'm a hundred years too late."

Traxal looked puzzled. "Things would have been more difficult for you a hundred years ago."

"I doubt it. I'm a bloke, a do-gooder if you like, whose conscience is out of step with the world's conscience. A hundred years ago the world had less, if any conscience. I could have gone my own way about helping these kanakas."

"You are very certain that your way is the right way."

"If I wasn't so certain, I should have packed it in years ago. You'll see what I mean if and when you ever go back to Czechoslovakia. The Communists can't have everyone backing them, yet they keep going because they are convinced they're right. Such conviction is the mark of evangelists and fools. I haven't yet made up my mind what category I come in." He had been looking out over the dark parade ground; now he turned back to Traxal. "I shan't ask you for your opinion, Peter. Don't let any more *kuru* patients die on us. I'll see you in a week when I come back with Jack."

When Traxal had gone, Narvo debated whether to have a shower or go across at once to see Elisabeth. He decided on the latter course. Still in his dirty shirt, shorts and sandshoes, still grease-stained, he headed across the parade ground. Two police boys, going on night picket, threw smart salutes as they passed, and he returned the salutes without really noticing who the boys were. He heard the boys giggle behind him, and he slowed his pace for an instant, thinking to turn and berate them. Then he shrugged and hurried on. It was more important that he get to Elisabeth before Traxal did. But he was sharply aware that the official side of him was suffering because of obligations assumed by his personal side. His behavior had always been uninhibited, but he could never remember that any of the police boys had laughed at him within his hearing. Perhaps he had even slipped in what he had considered the simplest of his duties, the maintenance of discipline among the police boys.

Elisabeth was coming out from the Bermingham hut when he

reached her. She said something to Mary Bermingham and hurried across to Narvo as soon as she saw him. "Something is wrong, Roy?"

He told her at once of his slip of the tongue with Traxal, making no excuses nor attempting to minimize what he had done. "I put my foot in my open mouth and that's all there is to it. I'm sorry, Elisabeth."

"I know it wasn't deliberate, Roy, and I know that you are not one to knowingly break a confidence. If you did, it is because you must have something else on your mind."

He was amazed at her insight into him. None of the other women he knew or had known had ever been understanding of the mistakes he had made; and he was honest enough to admit there had been many, at least in his relationship with them. For a moment, suspicious as always of women, he wondered if she were buttering him up, trying to sound understanding only so that he would tolerate her continued presence on the post. But there was a sincerity in her face that at once dispelled his doubt.

He nodded. "There is something else, Elisabeth. The Vaikaka men are out hunting Jack."

Elisabeth looked back at the hut she had just left. "Mary said nothing," she said, puzzled. "And I can't read the faces of the natives—one never knows how they feel——"

"You're not the only one who finds them unreadable. I've been up here long enough and sometimes even I find them as inscrutable as a stone Chinese. Look, Elisabeth," he said, putting Bermingham out of his mind for the moment. "I'll be gone from here maybe a week. Will you be all right on your own?"

She looked up at him, amazed in her turn. "Roy, I was all right for five years on my own in Prague."

"That was different."

"Not so different as you think," she said, then she smiled and put a hand on his arm. It was an impulsive gesture, something she was not normally given to, but it embarrassed neither of them. "I shall be careful, Roy. I shall stick closely to Father Shawn and Joan Duggan. And there are always young Harry and Bandi. I shall be all right. Trust me."

"I do trust you," he said, staring down at her for a moment before replying. "My circle of trustworthy friends seems to be rapidly diminishing, but you I do trust, Elisabeth."

And instantly she was sorry he had said it. Ever since Peter had told her how he intended buying his right to return to Czechoslovakia, she had been troubled whether to tell Narvo or not that he was the one to be sacrificed. She could not bring herself really to believe that Peter could be so callous; yet at the same time she had the sickening feeling that Peter was certain to do what he had threatened. Narvo had just said he trusted her; yet Peter, too, trusted her, otherwise he would not have told her of his plan. Though their love was finished, there was something that still bound her to Peter: the love they had once had, the five years of waiting, perhaps even just the fact that they were Czechs together in a strange land. Narvo had accepted her, but he had said nothing yet that bound her to him. Nothing but that he trusted her, and she could not convince herself that that was enough. Trust, she had learned, could be both a bribe and a gift. Though she respected Narvo, admired him and liked him, she still did not know the man well. And because of her own disillusionment over the years and especially the past two weeks, she hesitated to make a gift of her own trust.

"I hope you find Jack alive," was all she said, and she turned and walked quickly away into the gathering darkness.

2

The sun was not yet down in the gorges when Narvo and the police boys and carriers crossed the river on the way out toward Wabut. The crossing was made at a ford above a barrier of large rocks; the water tore through here at a great rate but was no more than three feet deep. Narvo went into the middle of the stream and stood there, propped against one of the boulders, while the police boys and carriers passed slowly across. The mountain natives were poor swimmers, if they could swim at all, and if any one of them was swept past the boulders it would be the end of him.

The last police boy crossed, and Narvo, wet through to the neck from the river and its spray, followed him. The whole party waited while Narvo went to its head, then it began to climb slowly out of the gorge. They climbed up into the sun, out of the mist and the dripping vegetation, away from the strangling vines and the tripping roots, and came out on to a long ridge where only *kunai* grass grew. Here the party had its first rest and in the hot sun Narvo's clothes dried on him in a few minutes.

Narvo offered Beraki one of his cigarettes, and the sergeant took it ostentatiously, keenly aware of the envy of the other police boys and the carriers. All the other police boys had at some time or other had a cigarette from Narvo, but he never made a practice of wholesale handouts. He had learned very early in his stay in New Guinea that large-scale benevolence gained one no respect among these natives; one was more likely to be marked down as a soft touch or, worse by far, be looked upon as a white who had intercepted goods sent by their ancestors to the black people themselves.

Beraki lit the cigarette with great deliberateness, then blew out smoke as if he were performing some ritual. *You show-off bastard,* Narvo thought, amused but not annoyed. "Do you expect a fight?" Beraki said at last.

Narvo noticed at once the lapse. "Sir!" he snapped.

Beraki coughed on his cigarette. He had been squatting on his haunches, but now he stood up, almost at attention. "I am sorry, sir. I did not mean—" Then when Narvo nodded and waved a hand of dismissal, he squatted down again. "Do you expect a fight, sir?"

Narvo shrugged, more concerned with Beraki's lapse than with any impending fight: he *must* be slipping if even Beraki were taking him for granted. "I hope not," he said, and saw the disappointment pass like smoke over Beraki's black face. "Our job is to bring in Mr. Bermingham without any trouble."

Beraki said nothing, but continued to smoke his cigarette, looking back down the line of carriers sprawled along the spine of the ridge. He was an intelligent man and he made a fine sergeant of police; but he was not the sort of man who would ultimately contribute much to the future of this country. Narvo was convinced that the future of New Guinea lay in an amalgam, on equal terms, of black and white. He was convinced also, against the policy of Canberra, that that amalgam could be more quickly and best achieved by the development of a black elite who would help in the development of their own backward majority. There was the risk, he knew, that the elite, in time, might demand the right to rule autocratically the primitive majority; experience in other lands had proved that independence for the black race did not necessarily mean independence for all black men. All imperialists were not white, as the Chinese and certain new African rulers had proved. If such an autocratic elite did emerge, it would contain men like Beraki. Narvo smiled wryly at the thought that his own best candidate for native representation should be the leader of the party now out hunting a white man. It did not presage a peaceful parliament of the two races.

The party moved on, heading west. The trail, along which Narvo had trekked on his patrol some weeks before, ran along the tops of ridges for most of the first day. They stayed that night in a village perched on the end of a spur; a wind hurled cold daggers down from a col opposite, but the villagers preferred those to the spears of enemies. A 360-degree lookout could be maintained from any spot within the village stockade, and the villagers took their chances on pleurisy and pneumonia against the certain death of spears and arrows.

When he had passed through here on patrol Narvo had ordered a resthouse to be built, and since then the villagers had erected a solid if primitive hut for the Kiap's needs. They had overlooked the difference between their own and the Kiap's height, and Narvo had to get down on his knees to enter the low door. But the hut afforded him protection against the night winds now skiing down the col opposite and it would keep him dry against the rain that was sure to come in the night. The carriers crowded into the stockade and set up their palm shelters, three or four men sleeping together for warmth, and the police boys made their beds against the lee of Narvo's hut.

During the night a thunderstorm broke. Through the open door Narvo, lying on his stretcher, saw the mountains across the valley come and go like rearing horses in the blazing blue light. Thunder tore the world apart and put it together again; the bottom fell out of the heavens right above the village and the spur seemed to tremble in the vibrating air. Narvo lay in his blankets and sweated a little. He did not believe that any man with imagination could not be afraid; and he himself had been afraid often. But he usually managed to conquer his fear of the dangers that periodically confronted him in this job; he had, however, never managed to conquer the fear, that had been with him since childhood, of lightning. It was an ancestral fear, something that bound him to these primitives in whose village he slept tonight. He knew that they too would be awake in their huts, muttering incantations against the devil-men who had brought the lightning; and he took his own hand from beneath the blankets and blessed himself. It was something he did every time he saw lightning, something he would never confess to Mike Shawn; both the fear of lightning and the invocation against it were a weakness, something of which he was ashamed. He was an agnostic who would not admit there was hope for him.

In a momentary silence he heard a rustling in the hut. He sat up, switching on the flashlight that, with his pistol, he always kept beneath his pillow when out on patrol. The bright beam showed at least a dozen large rats scurrying about the earth floor of the hut; as soon as the beam hit them they went in a rush out of the door into the rain. Narvo cursed them and lay back, switching off the flashlight. After a long time he dropped off to sleep again, but it was a restless sleep, a nightmare in which rats gnawed at his lightning-burned corpse.

When he woke at dawn he felt as if he had been through a bout of fever. His eyes burned, his tongue tasted as if it were coated with rat's fur and his whole body felt as if it were carrying invisible weights. He had felt like this once before, after his first night in action during the war. It had been a violent battle in a coconut plantation north of Sio, much more violent than the company had expected. They had gone in to do some cleaning up, as they thought; but the surviving Japanese, desperate with the desperation of little hope, had had other ideas. The battle had gone on all through the night. Narvo, when his platoon had been relieved, had retired to a foxhole, still within mortar range, and tried to sleep. Two men had died within six feet of him during the night, and when dawn came he had found himself wondering if they had not been the fortunate ones. He woke this morning with the same feeling of utter despondency.

The rains had gone again during the night and the day was another blazing one. Narvo's despondency lifted as the day wore on, but his general mood didn't improve. In the early afternoon they went down off the ridges into swamp country; and here Narvo cursed Bermingham for the specific discomforts he was undergoing. He forgot the wider and deeper possibilities that could arise from Bermingham's foolish intransigence, and cursed the one-eyed man for each individual leech he had to burn off his legs and the lower part of his body. The carriers, who had been singing all the way along the tops of the ridges, were now silent. The swamp steamed in the heat, and the stench of it was almost a tangible thing that clogged the nostrils. A line of logs, laid by local natives, ran through it, but Narvo was never less than shin-deep in mud and twice slipped off the logs and went in up to his waist.

The sun came through the tangle of greenery in pale, green tinted shafts of light. Dead palms stood in the swamp like ruined headstones of men who had died here. The party came to a slight rise in the middle of the swamp, a tiny island in the sea of mud, and Narvo called a halt. Narvo and the police boys and the carriers, the latter now sullen and unhappy, huddled together on the tiny rise, picking the leeches from themselves while the birds that had been disturbed from the island swooped and fluttered above in a deafening screeching blast of protest.

Beraki pushed his way through the throng to Narvo. "The carriers complain, Kiap. They wish to return to Kundavi."

"So do I," said Narvo wearily, burning five leeches off his thigh. A scorpion had got up into his shorts and bitten him on the belly and he had had to treat the bite before he could remove the leeches. The bite would get worse before it got better, and he would probably feel some effect from its poison. But a slight case of poisoning was the least of his problems now. If the carriers deserted, he could not go on to bring back Bermingham. It would be practically impossible to recruit new carriers in this hostile area.

He stood up and looked about at the crowd of sullen, silent natives, grouped about him. If he had not been so much taller than they, he would not have been able to see more than the men pushing against him, so tightly was everyone packed together. He stood there like the white crest of a small black mountain that rose out of the dark green swamp. He turned slowly full circle, staring down the slope as if looking at each man individually. Then he spoke and his voice was so loud that it could be heard even above the screeching of the birds. Beraki had never seen the Kiap so angry. His voice thundered and threatened, and the hill of men quaked with fear. With his bare hands, Narvo swore, he would snap the neck of any man he caught trying to desert; if any carrier did get away, he would hunt him down and kill him as they killed the wallaby. They were going on till they found Giamin's husband, Bermingham of the one eye, and there would be no more talk, not even a murmur, of going back to Kundavi till Giamin's husband was found.

"All right, Beraki." Narvo was still keeping up the pretense of anger. His whole speech had been full of a false anger: he was too weary and depressed for real wrath. He had begun to believe that Bermingham was already dead, that there was no chance of finding him alive, and he could not really blame the carriers for wanting to get out of this soul-destroying country. But even if Bermingham were already dead, he had to go on till he found the body, or what was left of it, and give it decent burial. It was part of his duty as patrol officer, but more important to him it was part of his duty as friend. You did not desert your friends, not even when they were beyond your help. It was an old-fashioned and possibly out-of-date ethic, but lately he had begun to feel that his whole life was in the same anachronistic mold. "Beraki, we move on at once. I'll take the head of the line and you go to the rear. Crack anyone who looks like wanting to drop out."

"Yes, sir!" Beraki somehow found room to salute in the crush, then turned to bellow orders. Two minutes later the carriers, still sullen, had picked up their loads and were following Narvo down into the swamp again.

In the late afternoon, when the sun had gone down behind the steep escarpment that rose suddenly from the end of the swamp, the party came to the village at which Narvo intended staying the night. The natives here were even smaller than the mountain men, and there was a fierce meanness to their faces that they made no attempt to hide behind the hypocrisy of a smile. Narvo had been through here before and had a brush with these men. The police boys had had to fire their rifles into the air above the menacing natives, and Narvo had forcibly taken a knife from a young buck who had tried to carve him up. He had spent three days in this village, hating the stench and heat from the nearby swamp, going to bed at sundown to escape the mosquitoes that came up out of the swamp like a dark miasma. He had spent the three days trying to impress on the obstinately silent headman that the white man's government was the new authority in this area, that its primary aim was the welfare of the people themselves but that it had to enforce the law, and the law said that killing, of white or black men, was now a crime. He had left orders that a resthouse was to be built for him and that when he came through here next time he was not to be greeted by a shower of arrows. When he had returned to Kundavi he had written in his report that, though there had been difficulties, he thought he had impressed upon these villagers of Wanagl that the government's word was law.

He was wrong. As the party came up the slopes from the swamps toward the ridge on which the village was built, it was met by another shower of arrows. The Wanagl men stood along the top of their ridge and hurled insults and threats as well as arrows and spears. They must have known Narvo's party was coming, for they were dressed in war dress. Red and yellow mud streaked their faces and bodies; they wore their second-best headdresses; and bright feathers were stuck in the bracelets of possum fur on their arms and legs. Each of them wore a gaily decorated belt in which a stone knife or a stone ax was held by a loop, and several of them wore necklaces of pigs' tusks. Except for their war paint, which was only a camouflage and not a covering, they were as naked as new babies and twice as primitive.

"Over their heads!" Narvo ordered, and the police boys, standing in line as if firing a salute, fired a rapid volley up the ridge. Instantly the clamor ceased, and Narvo, covered by Beraki and the other police boys, walked slowly and deliberately up the hill to the village.

The headman, his face as belligerent-looking as the stone ax he held in his hand, stood at the top of the path. Behind him the men of the village, thirty or forty of them, were arrayed in a solid phalanx, their gaily patterned cane shields forming a shifting but solid-looking wall. They had been frightened by the volley of shots. They still did not understand this weapon they had never seen till this white man had come through here weeks before. But they remembered the effect of the weapon on one of the village pigs. The white man had raised the weapon to his shoulder, there had been a loud noise and the pig had fallen over dead. No spear or arrow had ever been so effective, and if the weapon could kill a pig so easily, it could also kill a man. They were frightened; nonetheless they would not flee. The nature of their existence had bred in these men a stoicism toward death that verged on contempt for it.

Narvo walked right up to the headman and halted only a pace from him. The native's headdress came only to Narvo's chin; with Narvo standing so close to him the headman had to tilt his head right back to look up at the white man. The native went to step back, but Narvo put out his foot and lodged a heavy boot on the headman's toes. The headman winced, but did not attempt to prise loose his foot. There was an angry mutter from the tribesmen, but none of them moved forward. Narvo stared down at the headman.

"I told you to build me a rest hut and I see it is not built." He had discovered that these natives spoke a dialect related to that of the natives closer to Kundavi; they might miss a few of his words, but they would get his general meaning. "You are fined two pigs, which will be killed now and cooked at once for the supper of my men."

Again there was an angry mutter from the villagers. They moved closer and several of them raised their stone axes. Down the slope behind him, Narvo was aware of a stirring among the carriers. If they broke and ran, the Wanagl men would instantly spring into action, determined to kill at least a few of the patrol party before they themselves died. The first one they would kill would be the white man. Narvo, still standing close to the headman, felt the constriction in his stomach and the breaking of sweat on him that always hit him when he was afraid. He had been depressed enough this morning not to care much about living, but now, with death so close that he could smell its breath and the stink of the grease and dirt that covered it, he wanted passionately to stay alive.

Without turning his head he shouted to Beraki in police Motu. "Beraki! Turn round and cover the carriers with your gun. If any one of them goes to run, shoot him!"

"Yes, sir!" Beraki shouted, and without looking around Narvo knew that Beraki had already turned around and his rifle was at the ready. He knew Beraki would get a certain sadistic satisfaction from shooting one of these mountain carriers, for whom he had only contempt. But that did not matter: the point was that Beraki was a police boy who did what he was told and could be relied upon.

The headman rumbled something in his throat, staring up at Narvo with a hatred that was more than just that of one man, but of a whole race, the hatred of one world for another. Narvo, gazing down into the paint-daubed face, into the black fire-flecked eyes, felt the fear he had experienced once or twice before in this country, the fear that was as old as the fear of lightning. He looked into the eyes of the devil himself.

He pressed his boot harder into the foot of the man before him. "Because there is no rest hut built for me, I shall share your hut tonight. Now order the men to kill the pigs!"

There was silence on the ridge and slope. Far away in the middle of the swamp birds screeched and somewhere in the village itself a child whimpered. But here on the ridge the silence was so acute that Narvo could hear the breeze rustling through the headdress of the headman. The man said nothing. He continued to stare back at Narvo, his face impassive as a wooden mask, not even his eyes moving; and yet his face, black and Semitic, the face perhaps of a man from the Lost Tribes, was alive with hate. The men behind him now slowly raised their axes and there was a current of movement behind the wall of shields. Without taking his eyes from the headman's face, Narvo was conscious of bows being raised at the rear of the mob of natives: a dozen arrows were aimed at his head, the strings taut in the bows. Narvo leaned forward, putting his full weight on the boot that pressed into the headman's foot. The headman showed no sign of the pain he must have felt. Then all at once Narvo saw the shine of sweat on the black face, glistening even through the paint.

"Kill the pigs!" he repeated, and his voice was a bellow that stilled the movement in the war party.

Then the headman's gaze broke. He turned his head and spoke over his shoulder, his voice thin with the pain he could no longer hide. The tribesmen hesitated, muttering, then they broke up and moved away. Narvo lifted his foot and stepped back.

"You black bastard," he said in English, breathing deeply, feeling the sweat running on him in rivulets, feeling again the pain of the scorpion bite. "You're enough to shrivel the guts of any man's goodwill." Then in dialect, because he couldn't help admiring the little man's courage, he said, "You are a brave man, but you are foolish and wrong."

"No one is to be trusted," said the headman, limping as he led Narvo up to the village. Beraki and the police boys, the carriers strung out behind them, were now coming up the slope. "It is the only way to live in this country."

Narvo could not blame the man for his outlook, but neither could he condone it. Trust, of both the white man and of each other, was the whole basis on which the civilization of this country must progress. It had been taught to the natives down on the coast and they had learned to accept it; the natives in the Eastern and Central Highlands were coming to appreciate the advantages of it. But to these men in these mountains and farther west, trust was not a philosophy but a disease of the mind that must be avoided. It was like asking the possum to bed down with the crocodile.

The village itself showed how little the men of Wanagl relied upon trust. The stockade wall was composed of stone-hewn tree trunks shaped into spiked stakes thirty feet high. The gate was a hole only three feet high, and Narvo had to get down on his hands and knees to enter it. Inside was a second stockade of stakes about ten feet high with a slightly larger gate hole. Narvo went through this, straightened up and stood in the village proper. It was little different from a hundred other villages he had been in, except that Wanagl had its gardens within its stockade. The men of Wanagl obviously trusted no one.

"There are other ways to live," said Narvo, and wondered if his next words sounded as hollow to the headman as they did to himself: "It is the reason the government has sent me into this country, to teach you."

The headman grunted skeptically and led the way to his hut. Two women stood by the entrance and four small children peered out from the inside of the hut. The headman spoke to the women and they gathered the children and moved off at once. Narvo was disturbed to see them go, knowing he was evicting them from their home, but he could not afford to show weakness and invite them back. In the small low hut there would not be room for all of them, particularly in view of his own size; yet, having stated his demand that he should share the headman's hut, he had to carry it through. As soon as he got down on his hands and knees and crawled into the hut, he further regretted his demand. The hut, dark as a tomb, smelled of smoke and bodies and urine and filth; Narvo's nose wrinkled and his stomach fluttered, but there was no backing out. If for no other reason than safety's sake, he had to sleep with the headman; with the headman, disarmed, in the hut beside him, the villagers would not attempt any night massacre. But Narvo made a mental note that for future emergencies he would carry a bottle of deodorizer with him. If he had to bring civilization to these people, he would enlist all the aids of civilization.

The pigs were killed and eaten, a night picket was rostered among the police boys, Narvo crawled under his net and slept, and the night in the Wanagl passed without further incident. Before he dropped off to sleep Narvo lay listening to the soft breathing of the wide-awake headman in the darkness on the other side of the small hut.

Where had this man come from and where would he go? Was he really a descendant of the Lost Tribes? Had his ancestors come down over the land bridge that had once linked New Guinea to Asia, and settled in these mountains, gradually growing more primitive and savage as the country never relaxed its assault on them? The headman, washed of his paint, had sat across from Narvo tonight at the meal, and Narvo had not been able to stop staring at him. The Semitic cast of features had been amazing; except for his color, the headman could have come from any ghetto in the world. What fate had placed him in these remote mountains and what fate was his future? Did anyone on the outside really care? Narvo wondered.

He himself had never been out of Australia other than to these islands, but he had read and seen newsreels and listened to travelers' stories of the poverty in other lands. He knew how the peasants of India lived on the border of mere existence, how the fellahin of Egypt were only now looking toward a better life, how, even in southern Europe, there were people who still lived in medieval squalor and on the thin degrading edge of starvation. When these things were brought to the notice of the fortunate ones of the world, there was sympathy and often an effort to do something about it; but the sympathy and the effort more often than not petered out, because conscience was a plant that did not grow well in a world of comfort and well-being. What the outside world would think or feel toward this man sharing the hut with him, Narvo could not even surmise. How could you convince a man in his centrally heated flat in Sydney, with a full table before him and no stockade outside his front door, that he owed the right to a better life to this savage about whom he had never heard and whose struggle to survive he could not even comprehend? The Bill of Human Rights was a wonderful document, but like all documents it depended for full realization on the perception, understanding and compassion of the man who read it. There was nothing, Narvo mused sadly, that said that any man, in the pursuit of happiness, had to guarantee the means of happiness for any other man.

In the morning Narvo repeated his order that a rest hut should be built, saying that he would be back this way in a few days' time, and the patrol party moved on. That day, trekking up and down razor-backed ridges, they covered five miles as the goura pigeons flew, yet they walked for ten hours. They came to no village, and that night they camped on a ridge that hung like a green stick across a cauldron of winds. The carriers huddled together in groups, back to back and with their arms crossed on their chests and their hands locked behind their necks: a position that Narvo knew was warming, despite its contorting discomfort. Narvo saw that everyone got a hot meal, then he retired to his pup tent. The rains came again during the night and again he shared his shelter with large rats that came scurrying in out of the wet. When he woke in the morning there was a nine-inch spider resting on his mosquito net; and still only half-awake, with the net resembling a green web and the huge spider only a few inches from his face, he screamed aloud.

Beraki came running, lifting the tent off Narvo with one sweep of his thick arm. The net fell in on Narvo and he felt the spider run across his face. He lay paralyzed, sweat popping from him, and through the tangle of net saw Beraki kill the spider with the butt of his rifle. When he at last stood up, throwing off the net, he was shivering. He could feel Beraki looking at him and as he looked along the ridge he saw every eye in the party was staring at him. *I'm cracking up,* he thought, and struggled to regain control of himself.

He stooped and picked up the great hairy body of the spider. He had heard that there were strange and frightening creatures in this part of the country, and he had seen some of them on his previous trip through here: a day-flying moth with transparent wings, millipedes nearly a foot long; but he had not been prepared to meet one of the most frightening of them so close to him so early in the morning, and he knew the seed had been planted for future nightmares. He laid the crushed spider on his palm and, somehow managing a grin, turned and offered it to Beraki. The black sergeant backed hurriedly away, shaking his head. And slowly a murmur of laughter ran down the line of police boys and carriers and in a moment the top of the ridge was a shaking line of merriment. Instantly Narvo was sorry. To save himself he had sacrificed Beraki. He stood for a moment not knowing what to do, staring at the consternation and slowly growing look of disbelief and disillusion on Beraki's face. Then he did something he had never done before: he stepped forward and threw his arm about Beraki's shoulder. He held up the spider, then threw it high out and down the slope of the ridge. He stood with his arm about Beraki's shoulder and waited for the laughter to subside. Then he let his arm drop and stepped back.

"I am sorry, Beraki," he said softly. "I should not have tried to frighten you like that. Thank you for killing the spider."

"It is all right, Kiap," said Beraki, but his face was still cracked with consternation and it would take him a long time to get over the shock the Kiap had given him. He had already forgotten the spider, but he would not soon forget that the Kiap had made fun of him in front of the police boys and the carriers. And Narvo, seeing the look on the black sergeant's face, knew too that it would not soon be forgotten. From now on he knew that he could not depend on Beraki—and it had been entirely his own fault. What was it he had tried yesterday to tell the Wanagl headman about trust? Beraki had trusted him, and he had let him down.

The party moved on and in the middle of the afternoon they came upon Jack Bermingham. They were traversing a bare ridge that stuck up above the jungle bordering a mountain stream. Ahead of them and to the west a steep escarpment of limestone rose, a gray wall of rock that occasionally showed brilliant patches of white, like ancient snow that had defied time and the tropical sun. Narvo saw the hornbill rise slowly from the trees below and go in heavy-winged flight, so slowly that one wondered how it stayed in the air, down the stream. He stopped, his gaze following the lazy white slash of its wings against the still blue air; then he saw it wheel sharply to the right, as if it had come up against an invisible wall, and fly off to be lost in the trees that hugged the foot of the escarpment to the west. But Narvo had not followed the flight of the hornbill to the trees. His gaze had remained riveted on the silver jagged dagger of the stream. A man, bare to the waist, in old dungarees and a battered straw hat, sat on his haunches beside the stream, a dish in his hands, panning for gold.

Even as he saw Bermingham, Narvo also saw the Vaikaka men moving down through the trees from the base of the tall limestone cliff. He raised his arm, still keeping his eye on the Vaikaka men, and the police boys, led by Beraki, came quietly up beside him.

"We are just in time," Narvo said to Beraki. "There isn't time to get down to the river, so we shall have to shoot from here. Shoot *at* them. It is no use shooting to warn them. They could kill Mr. Bermingham and be gone again before we could cross the river. I'll hail them, and then if they don't halt, we shoot!"

The police boys raised their rifles to their shoulders. The distance was a good two hundred yards and Narvo had no confidence that the police boys could hit any of the targets; but the shots would go close enough to show the Vaikaka that the patrol party meant business.

"Paiwo!" Narvo suddenly yelled, and his voice almost at once came echoing back from the limestone cliff. It went on echoing, dying away at last like a soft sigh of appeal. Down on the dry wide bed of the river the Vaikaka men abruptly stopped. Jack Bermingham stood up, the dish dropping from his hand, and for a moment the hunters and hunted were tiny frozen figures in the great white bed of the river. "Paiwo, I shall shoot you and your men if you harm the husband of Giamin! Lay down your spears and bows and arrows or you die!"

Then he raised his own rifle, sure of his own ability to hit his target, and looked down the sights at the chest of Paiwo.

3

The Vaikaka men had been watching Bermingham for two hours. And with the exception of Paiwo, the Vaikaka men believed that Bermingham, through the magic that was only his, had been watching them ever since they had come upon him here at the river. He had gone about his work as if guarded by a hundred men, working along the edge of the stream, stooping to scoop sand and gravel into his dish, then squatting down to swirl the dish while he peered into it with the fierce concentration of a man calling on some devil spirit to help him. He had put down his dish once and walked back to his small tent and made himself some tea and sat there on a rock, staring across the river and its wide dry bed, his back to the hidden Vaikaka men, and yet his eye always watching them. For his eye, catching the light like a blue and white gem, sat on a small square of red cloth on top of a large smooth rock.

Paiwo, more sophisticated than the other Vaikaka men, knew the fun Bermingham used to have with the native children on the patrol post at Kundavi. He would take out his glass eye, show it to the children and tell them he was leaving it to watch them and report on them while he went up to see the Kiap. He would then leave the eye on top of a post and go away, and the children would stand transfixed, never moving, staring at the staring eye, till he returned and put the eye back in its socket. It had taken Paiwo himself a long time to accept this display of magic, but after several months and some stern lecturing from Kiap Narvo, he had come to realize that Bermingham's trick was no more than a trick, and no more magical than a lot of other things white men had achieved. He had sat here in the bushes all afternoon with the other Vaikaka men, smiling inwardly at their foolishness but never saying anything, glad of the harmless eye yet hoping it could somehow conjure up magic to prevent the attack that had to come.

For now the Vaikaka men were becoming restive. Kasin squatted beside Paiwo and said, "We must risk the white man's magic and attack him. His eye is watching us, but it can do no harm."

"We cannot be sure of that," said Paiwo, and one or two of the bucks nodded.

"We have not come all this way just to sit in the bushes," Kasin said, and Paiwo, sensitive to even the slightest degree of antagonism, was aware that in the murmur of the rest of the men there was growing support for Kasin's point of view. Kasin himself was aware of it, and he stood up. "If you are the fight-leader, Paiwo, you should lead us in now to kill the white man."

Paiwo rose slowly. He was a good half a head taller than any other man in the party and he straightened up to his full height. "I am the fight-leader, Kasin, let there be no doubt of that. Or do you challenge me?"

Paiwo would have welcomed a challenge. It would have meant either the death of Kasin, the troublemaker, or his own death; and he was depressed enough not to care very much which of them should die. He was still sorrowing for the death of his wife and he missed the company of his son; and he had found that he hated the problems and responsibilities of a fight-leader. In the time he had spent here in the bushes watching the white man down by the river, he had begun to think again of life on the patrol post at Kundavi. He had liked most of the white people there, especially the Kiap and the priest, and he had come to enjoy the comforts to which he had been introduced. The Kiap, over a long period, had slowly conditioned him to the idea that this sort of life was possible for the black man but that the black man would have to work for it and would above all have to be patient. He had heard tales of black men down on the coast whose way of living had reached almost to that of the white man; there were only a few who had reached this level, but he believed that what was possible for the few would eventually be possible for all. He was not optimistic enough to believe that he himself might someday live as the Kiap did; but the Kiap had promised him that Bandi would someday live as the white men lived. Then the hates, the beliefs and the customs of his own people had come bursting back into his life, like the fever that used to take hold of him in the days before the white man had brought him medicine. What the Kiap had taught him and promised him had not proved sufficiently strong as a medicine; what his fathers had taught him and expected of him had been too strong a fever. He had been drawn back till now here he was about to lead an attack on a white man who was married to his own cousin and who had never done him any harm.

Kasin stared back at Paiwo. The men stood among the bushes like blackened tree stumps, not moving, all their attention on the fight-leader and his antagonist. Above them the limestone cliff, catching the last of the sun, threw a blaze of lemon light down through the trees; the Vaikaka men stood in a small pale green world in which the only movement was the occasional shiver of a hanging vine. They were standing beside a huge orchid bush, one such as Paiwo had never before seen; its stems were taller than a man, and it was covered with flowers larger than a man's hand. Kasin had picked one of the orchids and stuck it in his hair; it lay on his head like a golden plate. A python slithered down into a large clump of bamboo, saw the men and lay still, a long patterned log among the yellow stalks of the bamboo. A large hornbill flew downstream, suddenly turned, its wings making a white sail against the sky, and rustled its way overhead to settle somewhere in the trees behind them. Kasin heard the bird pass over, but he did not look up. He knew that the Vaikaka men were waiting on him for a decision. If he challenged Paiwo, none of them would interfere; but neither would they help him, and the fight would be all his own. He knew, too, that Paiwo could probably kill him; and his desire to go on living was greater than his ambition to be fight-leader. He reasoned that he had enough support to make Paiwo lead them in an attack on the white man, without having to risk his own life to prove the point.

"I do not challenge you, Paiwo," he said. "You are our fight-leader and we respect you. But our respect will be greater if you lead us against the white man and allow us to take his things." And he looked around at the other men as if to ask them wasn't he speaking for them as well as for himself.

Paiwo knew he had lost the fight without its ever having taken place. This man Kasin was too cunning; Paiwo could never allow the young buck to succeed him. Kasin would lead the Vaikaka into nothing but war and a quest for white man's goods; and Paiwo knew that in the end it would be only the Vaikaka who would suffer. He had to remain as fight-leader, if only to keep his people out of fights that they could never win. He looked down through the orchid bush at the white man, the husband of Giamin, and sadly condemned him to death. Better that Bermingham should die and not his own people.

"We shall kill him," he said. "Approach him quickly, so that he may not use the noise-making weapon he carries in his belt. Get close to him before you fire your arrows."

The Vaikaka men split up and began to move silently down through the bushes. The forest thinned out abruptly above a bank that dropped sharply to the river bed. In the wet season this would be a wide tumbling river, but now it was just a shallow stream that glittered its way down through a broad expanse of sun-bleached rocks. Even as the Vaikaka men began to move down through the forest, Bermingham, as if the eye had warned him, had picked up his dish and crossed to the other side of the stream. He was now separated from the Vaikaka men by about fifty paces of water and bare rocky ground, a distance too great for the arrows to land where they would be aimed.

The Vaikaka men were ten paces across the rocky ground, running swiftly with bows already raised and strings drawn taut, when the voice boomed out in the narrow high-walled valley. Paiwo, shocked, pulled up sharply; the other Vaikaka men stopped with the same suddenness. For a moment, as the sound of his own name bounced from cliff to cliff, Paiwo thought that Bermingham had worked some magic, that perhaps the glass eye was indeed a devil's charm. Then on the ridge on the other side of the river he saw the long line of carriers and at their head the police boys and the Kiap. He flung up an arm and pointed.

There were yells of alarm from the Vaikaka men. They hesitated, looking toward Paiwo for a lead. Again the Kiap's voice rang out, threatening to shoot them if they did not lay down their arms, and again the valley boomed with what sounded like a hundred voices. In one swift wide glance Paiwo saw that the police boys had their rifles raised to fire, that Bermingham had drawn his pistol from his belt, that Kasin had already half-turned to flee, and that the Kiap had his rifle pointed right at his, Paiwo's, own chest.

Paiwo hesitated, staring up at the distant figure of the Kiap, seeing only him and none of the other figures on the ridge. He knew in his heart that if he gave the order for the Vaikaka men to flee, the Kiap would surely shoot him. The valley was silent now but for the whisper of water over the rocks. Behind him Paiwo heard Kasin suddenly whisper his name: it was a frightened plea and he knew that Kasin was beaten, that he would never be fight-leader. Abruptly he nodded. The Vaikaka men, led by Kasin, turned and fled back toward the forest.

There was a volley of shots and the valley clanged and crashed and whined with echoes. Chips flew off the rocks and bullets went away like angry bees. Kasin threw up his arms, stumbled on a rock and plunged headlong, to lie still and twisted, the orchid covering his face like a golden wreath. Paiwo still stood, waiting for death, gazing up at the tall figure of the Kiap on the ridge, seeing the gleam of sunlight on the barrel of the gun aimed right at him. Bullets were still hitting the rocks about him and the valley still thundered with the shooting; but no bullet came for Paiwo and the Kiap's rifle still remained steady. Then he saw the light go from the barrel and slowly the gun was lowered.

Paiwo stood for a moment more, unable to comprehend why the Kiap had not shot at him, then he turned and went swiftly across the rocks and up into the green and silent haven of the forest.

Behind him he heard the Kiap calling his name, heard it come back from the cliff ahead of him, heard it dying away like the cry of a drowning man, but he did not turn back.

4

"I hope they find Mr. Bermingham alive," said Elisabeth, and made a check mark on the page of the book open before her. She had found there was little time for correcting her pupils' work during school hours: the native children, though eager to learn, would stop work at once as soon as she took her eyes from them. Even Harry, given the slightest opportunity, would relax and find something else to do. So she now brought home the children's lessons and sat on the veranda of the guest hut and corrected them while she drank afternoon tea with Joan Duggan.

"Oh, he'll be alive, you can be sure," said Duggan, adding lemon to her tea. "I just hope no one else gets hurt, bringing him in."

Elisabeth corrected the spelling in the book before her: *The Prime Ministr of Astralia is like the luluai ony more big.* It was still hard work trying to communicate fully with the children, but she was compensated by the fact that all her pupils appeared to give her their complete trust and respect. She had taken on the job only as some sort of payment for being allowed to remain at Kundavi. But even in the short time she had been at the school something had taken hold of her that had raised the task above being just a mere job, a way of repaying a debt. She had spent her life in an atmosphere of dedication: that of her father, dedicated to fighting the tyranny of nazism, and that of the Communists, dedicated to a way of life that was not for her. Yet there had been nothing to inspire her to dedication: she had been too young to inherit her father's spirit and carry on his fight, and she had been a victim of the general apathy and disillusionment with the Western powers that had resulted in so little opposition to the Communists. She had lived surrounded by causes and had had no cause of her own. Then in this past week, in the rough sacsac hut up on the mission hill, something had happened to her. Something in the faces, the voices, the very existence of the small dark savages had reached out and touched her.

"How long will it take before life becomes peaceful in these mountains?"

Duggan shrugged. "Years, I'd say. I don't think I'll live to see it."

"If you are so pessimistic, Joan, why do you stay up here?"

Duggan did not answer at once. The cup and saucer were held just before her face and she was looking down into the dark liquid in the cup, as if into the bowl of the past. "I was a missionary of sorts when I first came here to the islands. I suppose that is what we all are, in a way—those of us here at Kundavi, I mean. Most of the people back in the towns and down on the coast are only up here to make a living now. But here—" She looked out over the patrol post. She loved Kundavi, although she had never admitted it to anyone: sentiment had become bracketed with all the other diseases she knew. "Perhaps Peter and Bernice are not missionaries, but the rest of us are. Or were."

"You are not any longer?" Elisabeth closed the last book: another day nearer civilization for the class.

Duggan sipped her tea, smiling; then shook her head. "I can no longer afford the sympathy. I need it for myself." She saw the look of surprise on Elisabeth's face. "Don't be shocked, my dear. When you reach my age—and I'm not telling how old I am, not even to another woman—when you reach my age, you have to begin keeping a little of yourself for yourself. It's the only way to survive. For a woman, anyway."

"Have you always been a nurse?"

"Always."

There was silence for a moment, the conversation lapsing for want of some rope of intimacy between these two women. Neither of them had ever had any close confidences with another woman; it was their unrealized common bond. Both of them at that moment were full of regrets for moments of friendship passed and not grasped; the regrets were there even if they were not immediately conscious of them. One of them had lived in this isolation because of the tragic events that had, all her life, hounded her like wolves besieging the stockade of herself: invasion, war and revolution, coming in rapid succession, made strangers of one's neighbors. The other's isolation had been caused by the tragedy of herself, by the ugliness and abrasiveness of personality that had been her birthmark: she carried *her* war within herself. Yet both of them, because they were human and man was born to be gregarious, wanted, despite their fear, to touch and know the world around them. Elisabeth, being the younger, had more hope and therefore less fear. Duggan, despite the barricades she had thrown up, stacking them one on another till her real self was hidden, was still able to dream. They sat at opposite ends of a corridor of loneliness.

At last Duggan said, hiding her face behind her cup and saucer, "Nobody wanted me as a child. Even my mother was disappointed in me. There's more truth than people realize in the saying that charity begins at home. It often does—because nobody at home wanted people like myself. We go out and become nuns and nurses and welfare workers. If I had been beautiful and easy to get on with and my father and mother had loved me, New Guinea would never have seen me." She blinked behind the thick-lensed glasses and showed her big teeth in a smile that cracked her face. "I'm indulging in self-sympathy. Charity is really at home now."

Elisabeth said nothing, having nothing to say; all she could do was smile back at the other woman, trying not to make her own sympathy too obvious. Secure in her own beauty, it had never crossed her mind that ugly women had no security; never having had any women friends, she had never learned at close hand the fears and troubles of a plain woman. Looking covertly at Duggan she knew there had never been any hope: the other woman had not *grown* ugly, but had been born ugly: her future had been written on her face at birth. The harsh grating personality had come later and Elisabeth thought it was a pity that it should have: behind the sour wit and the misanthropy was love, shriveled but still alive. She carried love for a man as she might carry a blanket to cover a patient, but no man had ever asked her and none ever would. Elisabeth sipped her tea, tasting the salt of another's tragedy.

"Don't ever tell this to anyone," Duggan said, putting down her cup, putting on her old face. "It would ruin my reputation."

"You like the reputation you have?"

"No," said Duggan. "But it's the only one I have. At least I am not a nonentity."

She stood up and at that moment the teapot jumped from the tray on the table and smashed to pieces, like an exploding white hand grenade, on the veranda floor. The table itself leapt crazily, then fell against Elisabeth's chair, sending books and cups and saucers and plates and cakes spilling into the hibiscus bush beside the veranda rail. The veranda floor heaved, there was a splintering of wood and the thatched roof of the whole hut slid forward slowly like a hat being tilted over a sleepy man's face.

Elisabeth sat in her chair, gripping its arms with both hands, holding to it as if it were the only stable thing in a crazy, tumbling world. The veranda floor heaved and creaked beneath her feet like a living beast, and behind her the hut rustled and groaned as if in agony. Joan Duggan stood holding to a leaning post of the veranda, swaying drunkenly, her mouth open in a strangled shout of terror and her glasses hanging from one ear like a madwoman's ornament. Elisabeth, her eyes registering everything with startling clarity, as if this were her last look at life and she had to store memories for eternity, saw the lizards come out of the walls of the hut in a burst, like long green splashes of oil, and slide away across the veranda into the bushes. There was a smell of burning in the air, thick and sulphuric, but no smoke nor fire.

Elisabeth watched the earth bounce down the length of the parade ground, a liquid roll of motion that seemed to take all solidity from the earth. Down at the end of the parade ground the flagpole had teetered sideways; the flag had somehow slipped down to half-mast. A group of native children stood together in the center of the ground, holding tightly to each other, swaying on the trembling earth in an involuntary dance of terror. Harry's cassowary was running around in circles, lurching crazily like a drunken woman as it tried to keep its feet on the ground that seemed continually to be slipping away from it. An old native woman lay flat on her back in the middle of a path, screaming at the top of her voice; in one hand she held a string at the end of which a small pig danced like a rubber toy. Beyond her some of the men had been building a new hut; the outline of its framework lay like a yellow sketch against the dark wall of the mountain opposite. A man sat on the ridgepole holding tight with arms and legs, like a man riding the skeleton of a bucking horse. Across the valley, beyond the ludicrous figure of the ridgepole rider, an exclamation of smoke appeared on the mountain, then was gone.

Elisabeth watched the tremor run down to the very end of the parade ground. On the flat stretch where Narvo's and Rossi's huts stood above the gorge, the ground suddenly gave a convulsive heave and a great red gash appeared in it. Even as Elisabeth watched Narvo's hut split down the middle, as if carved by a giant knife, and slowly, almost with dignity, slid over the edge of the cliff and disappeared.

Then, as quickly as it had come, the tremor had gone. The veranda stopped rocking, and gingerly, suspiciously, Elisabeth put her feet down on the floor. She stood up, feeling the trembling, of herself or of the earth, she was not sure which, still in her. She looked at Duggan, who, still with her glasses hanging ridiculously from one ear, peered at her as if uncertain that Elisabeth was still alive.

"Oh, my God!" Duggan suddenly and shockingly burst into tears; the ugly face crumpled as if it had been hit by an invisible fist. "I thought that was the end! It's never been like that before!"

Elisabeth put out a hand and Duggan clutched it. The two women stood together like friends, as indeed they were now. The mental pain and shock of the moment they had just lived through bound them together; they had looked into the face of the common enemy, death, and become intimates. With her free hand Duggan fumbled for her glasses and put them back on. But she still was a stranger, one whom Elisabeth liked; or perhaps she was not a stranger but the real Duggan, the one Elisabeth wanted to know. The hand holding Elisabeth's had a sincere and warming clasp to it.

Duggan laughed, without the usual harshness, almost like a girl. "We must have all looked funny!" The memory of what she had seen from the veranda was coming back; it was as if everything that had happened on the post had been impressed on her myopic eyes and was only now reaching her brain. "That man, trying to stay up on the ridgepole of that new hut–!" She laughed again. There was no hysteria and the old cold calm Duggan was reappearing out of the wreckage of the woman who had been frightened almost to death. Yet Elisabeth felt that the old Duggan would never be completely seen around here again: the chilling flood of terror had swept part of her away, gone completely like Narvo's hut over the edge of the cliff——

"Bandi!" Elisabeth suddenly screamed aloud. She tore her hand from Duggan's, jumped down the twisted steps from the veranda and ran on wobbling legs down across the parade ground. There were cracks in the grass of the parade ground, but she didn't see them. She ran right to the edge of the gaping slice in the cliff where Narvo's house had stood. She pulled up sharply and looked down, her whole body shaking as if the tremor were still going on. Far below, like a brown withered wreath that had broken apart, was the wreckage of Narvo's hut. A small patch of red—a bunch of flowers, a curtain, a dead boy's lap-lap?—lay among the wreckage.

Elisabeth retched violently, but nothing came. Then she heard people running down toward her and then Traxal was putting his arm around her shivering body. "It's Bandi! He was in Roy's hut!"

"Elisabeth, it wasn't your fault!" Traxal shook her, trying to stop the hysteria before it began.

"What will Roy say? I should have been looking after the boy—" She knew Peter was trying to help her, to calm her down, and she struggled to retain control of herself. Then down at the bottom of the gorge she saw the long line of ants that were men moving along the trail beside the river, approaching the shattered remains of the hut, and she knew that Narvo would learn for himself what had happened to Bandi.

Half an hour later the police party came up the path from the gorge. The carriers carried two rough litters on which were two bodies covered by blankets. The carriers went on across the parade ground to the natives' quarters, carrying the bodies with them. The police boys lined up, Beraki collected the ammunition they hadn't used, they saluted Narvo and then they were dismissed. Narvo and Bermingham walked across toward the hospital.

Elisabeth had now regained her composure, although she was still white and shaken. Traxal was in the hospital helping Macy and Duggan with some of the patients who had been hurled out of their beds by the earth tremor. Father Shawn was up at the mission and Rossi was still down in the gorge with a working party. Elisabeth was alone when Narvo and Bermingham approached her.

"I'm sorry, Roy." She nodded toward the gap in the cliff where Narvo's house had stood. "There was no warning—we could do nothing——"

"Poor little beggars. Bandi and the house-monkey—the good

thing was they both must have died instantly." There was no condemnation of Elisabeth in his voice, and she felt a flood of relief. Peter had tried to tell her that Narvo knew this country better than she did, that he knew how it could throw tragedy into a person's lap without warning and without the person's being able to do anything about it. Narvo had learned to live with this country as the natives had. "Poor Paiwo, too. First his wife and now his boy. He'll never come back now."

"He might have welcomed that bullet," Bermingham said.

"I couldn't pull the trigger," Narvo said, and Elisabeth looked in puzzlement at both men, but they didn't enlighten her.

Then up in the hospital there was suddenly the sound of a loud mad laugh; it had an ironic ring to it, as if one of the *kuru* patients were playing the part of fate. Traxal came out of the hospital and a moment later was followed by Macy and Duggan. Father Shawn came running down the road and Rossi came up the path from the gorge.

"I'm home again," said Bermingham, and winked his good eye. "Anyone glad to see me?"

"No," said Duggan. "Except Mary and your children."

Bermingham looked across the parade ground to where Mary Bermingham stood with her children. He was her husband, but she would not have dared to come and greet him while the whites surrounded him; none of them, with the exception perhaps of Duggan, would have snubbed her, but she was still afraid of them. Bermingham turned back to Narvo.

"Thanks, Roy," he said quietly. "I'm in your debt, my word I am."

Then he turned quickly away and went across to Mary and the children. He put his arm about her, kissed her on the cheek, picked up both children and the family moved across to its hut. The whites stood looking after them, not saying anything till the group had disappeared into its hut.

Then Narvo said, "We got to him just in time. He has learned his lesson."

"Anyone hurt?" Rossi asked.

Narvo hesitated. "We shot one of the Vaikaka men. But that is unofficial. Officially this patrol never went out. You didn't report anything on the radio, did you, Frank?"

"You told me not to," said Rossi, and bit his lip. "You're boss."

"What's all the conniving about?" Duggan asked.

"I should report Jack for disobeying a direct order," Narvo said. "And that means Neil Figgins would have to banish him from this area. He doesn't want to leave here and neither does Mary. I don't know that I want him to leave here, myself. I like having him around. He's a help, too—with Mary as his wife, he can pick up bits of news I'd never otherwise get." He looked around at all of them. "So officially I've been on the post all this past week. Right?"

"If you say so," said Father Shawn. "In any case you'll have enough to fill a good-sized report with this latest tremor."

"Has there been much damage, any casualties?" Narvo said to Traxal. "Besides young Bandi and my house-monkey?"

"No deaths, at least not on the post. We haven't heard from the villages yet. We've had a few burns, where women fell into their cooking fires. And a *kuru* patient broke her leg when she was flung out of bed. But she will be dead by tonight anyway."

"Any more *kuru* deaths while I've been away?"

"Two," said Traxal; then was interrupted by a gasp from Macy. He turned around. "What's the matter, Eric?"

"Harry! Where's Harry?"

Elisabeth felt the trembling start again in her legs. She looked at Narvo and he had gone pale under his tan. "Was he in my hut? All we found were Bandi and the house-monkey."

"No, no, I don't think so!" Duggan took off her glasses and wiped them and put them back on; her hand shook so much she bumped her nose as she replaced her glasses. "He was up on the road, I remember seeing him——"

They all turned to look up toward the road that led up to the mission. And at that moment a small figure came out of the bush, leading the cassowary on a rope. Harry waved and his shout came down to them as a thin treble.

"Hey, Roy! Roy! We bloody near lost him that time!"

It was hard to tell which was the father, Narvo or Macy. A wide smile broke on the face of each and they looked at each other, their eyes shining a little.

"His language is terrible," said Narvo, grinning.

"He learned it from you," Macy said, grinning still wider. "We better not tell Bernice he went chasing off into the bush after the bird."

"She hit the roof when I first brought it home for him," Narvo said.

"I'll have to talk to him," said Macy. "About his language."

He left them quickly and almost ran up the parade ground and up the road to Harry. Narvo and the others saw him tilt Harry's hat forward over his eyes, saw him rest his hand for a moment on his son's shoulder; then he and the boy and the cassowary walked down the road to the Macy house, which leaned drunkenly on its foundations like a Disney drawing.

"The two of them need Bernice," said Duggan, then abruptly she was her brisk self again, throwing up the defenses again. "Well, there's a lot to be done. We can't stand around gabbing——"

The party broke up and Elisabeth was left with Narvo and Father Shawn. "This was a bad tremor," Father Shawn said. "The worst I've known in years."

"I know," Narvo nodded, staring across the valley toward the mountain. "We were down in the gorge. We had a few bad moments. There was a cliff fall a couple of hundred yards behind us. I thought for a moment the whole mountain was going to come down on top of us."

"I was watching the mountain," Father Shawn said, looking across at it. "There was smoke coming out of it that didn't come from any fire. It's gone now, but it was there, I'll swear to it."

"I'll go across first thing in the morning," Narvo said. "I wonder if they'd think I was panicking if I asked for the vulcanologist to come in here?"

Elisabeth did not know the word. "Vulcanologist? What does he do?"

"If he knows his job, he can tell you when a volcano is going to blow its top." Narvo nodded across the valley to the mountain, dark, silent, majestic and all at once threatening. "Any mountain in this range could be a volcano. Including that one."

13

"Roy Narvo has asked for a vulcanologist," Neil Figgins said, and moved his chair farther back under the umbrella, away from the sting of the morning sun.

Bernice fanned herself and looked across at the Cessna as it took off from the airstrip. It turned west and headed up the valley toward Mount Hagen; she knew it would pass within fifty miles of Kundavi. She would have to make up her mind soon what she was going to do; she had been nearly two weeks here at the hotel and her money was running out. She had been to the pictures or a party or to a friend's house for dinner every night since she had arrived in Goroka; and each night she had come back to the hotel and cried herself to sleep. Figgins was still talking, but she had lost track of what he was saying. This had always been a bad habit with her, caused by her impatience to have the other person finish talking so that she could say what was bubbling inside her; but she had little to say this morning and her lack of concentration was caused by her inability to forget her worry and unhappiness. She took a biscuit from the plate on the table and bit into it: it was chocolate, but for all the taste there was in her mouth it could have been cardboard.

"Do you think I should go back, Neil?"

Figgins tried to hide his exasperation. He had his own worries and he had taken time out from his office to come down here and impress upon Bernice just what was happening out at Kundavi.

"I try not to interfere in the domestic affairs of people in my district, Bernice. You know that. I'm your friend and I'm Eric's friend. You can't expect me to take sides."

She had not wanted him to take sides, she had wanted his advice; had, she admitted to herself, wanted him to make up her mind for her. "I didn't mean that. I meant, is there likely to be any danger out at Kundavi?"

Figgins looked away, angry with her. He watched the native prisoners working on the road that bordered the hotel lawn. They were building a curb of rough stones, working lazily but happily, lawbreakers without a care in the world. A car went past them, covering them with dust, but they heeded it no more than they would have a passing breeze; the dust settled on them but they were unaware of it, it was part of the things they took for granted, like flies and the sores on their legs and yesterday's earth tremor. Only the two police boys, half-civilized, vain about their blue tunics and lap-laps, brushed the dust from themselves. *Sometimes,* Figgins thought, *it is easier to talk to a half-civilized savage than it is to talk to a woman.* Then he smiled to himself: he was beginning to think like Roy Narvo; and the thought put him in a better humor, gave him more patience, and he turned back to Bernice.

"I don't know till we get a report from the vulcanologist. He's over in Rabaul—the volcanoes there have started smoking in this past week. It may be two or three days before we can get him over here. But from what Roy said on the radio last night, it must have been worse out there than it was here. He went over to the mountain across from Kundavi, and the water in the springs is warm. That's a bad sign."

Something of Figgins' concern began to seep through to Bernice. "We couldn't have another Mount Lamington up here, could we, Neil?"

"I don't know. This western region of the Highlands is supposed to be dead volcanically. But I never believe in dead volcanoes, just as the natives don't. I don't *think* we'll have anything like Lamington. I hope not, anyway." He had been in one of the rescue parties that had gone down into the Mount Lamington area in Papua after the mountain had blown up in 1951. It was an experience he would never forget, even though he had not reached the area till two days after the major eruption. Four thousand natives and forty whites had died and a county-sized area had been completely devastated. He looked across the table at Bernice, knowing now that she wanted him to tell her to go back to Kundavi. "I'd go back, Bernice. I don't think any mountains will blow up, but I think you'll be easier in your own mind being back there with Eric and young Harry."

"You could get us out quickly, couldn't you, if anything did happen?"

Again he was exasperated. "Bernice, are you thinking about yourself or Eric and Harry? Do you want to go back to Kundavi or not?"

She nodded, suddenly unable to speak, afraid of breaking into tears. Figgins rubbed his mustache with his knuckle and stood up. "Do you want me to arrange for the Cessna to take you in? And I'll call Eric, shall I?"

She swallowed. "Please, Neil." Then she looked up at him. "Do you think I have been a fool?"

He smiled kindly at her. He put his hat carefully and neatly on his head. He ran his hand around the brim, then straightened his bush jacket. He did it all as if he were standing in front of a mirror, his vanity plain to see; yet the effect was also that of a government officer who set an example of neatness and efficiency to those under him. Across the lawn, even as he stood up, he saw the police boys straighten up and adjust their berets.

"Bernice, I don't tolerate fools working for me—I can't afford to, with the job we have. But anyone who did not tolerate a person's foolish mistake in their personal relations would be a fool himself. Yes," he said bluntly, "you've been a fool. But you'll get over it and so will Eric. Shall I tell them you'll be going in on the Cessna tomorrow?"

She nodded. "I'm sorry, Neil. Women up here are a problem, aren't they?"

"Don't let Roy Narvo hear you say that," Figgins said with a smile.

Bernice had been smiling, but her face suddenly sobered. "It's going to be harder to go back to him than it will be to Eric."

"I should come in with you, only I haven't the time. The tremor caused some landslides down in the Chimbu area—I have to go down there. I just wonder what's going on out at Kundavi, though. Roy hadn't been on the air for over a week till last night. I just hope things haven't got him down and he's gone on the grog."

"He never has before," Bernice said flatly but without defending Narvo.

They had been walking across the lawn toward Figgins' Land-rover parked in the roadway. Figgins stopped now and looked hard at Bernice. "I don't know how to say this to you, Bernice—whether to say it as your friend or as the district commissioner. Both sides of me come into it."

Bernice waited a little impatiently: now she had decided to go back to Kundavi she was more her old self, touchy to criticism. "What are you trying to say, Neil?"

"About Roy. I spoke about tolerance a minute ago—I think you could use some toward Roy. Not just because of his job and the worries he has. But because up here in this country we are pretty close to being a microcosm of the world in general. Blacks living with whites; Australians with Europeans, or the

New with the Old, if you like; officialdom with ordinary people —yes, and men with women. This is a UN Trust Territory. If anywhere, this is where people really should be united. Give Roy a go, Bernice."

"Has he ever given me, or any woman for that matter, a go?"

"Perhaps I'm risking our friendship, Bernice, but I have to say this. Roy, because of his job, is more important than you are. There should be tolerance on both sides and Roy doesn't have much of it, I'll admit that. But in this particular case I think it's up to you to show the more tolerance. It's as I said, men living with women. And I seem to remember that women boast it's always they who have to be more tolerant. At least that's what my wife tells me."

"You're asking a lot, Neil."

"It's all one can do, Bernice. Ask and hope." His smile had gone and he looked all at once tired. He knew he was not being fair with her. The UN Committee was due here in another week and on its report would depend the fate of Roy Narvo. And all he, Figgins, had been able to do was to warn Narvo of his fate. He would not do any more because, he told himself, he would only be jeopardizing his own job in a hopeless cause. Yet he had called himself Bernice's friend and he knew in his heart he was not really her friend, but Roy Narvo's friend; and weren't friends supposed to rally round in all causes, hopeless or otherwise? He was asking Bernice to be tolerant of Narvo, to go against the whole grain of her character; and all he had offered Narvo was a few words of warning. He hurried away before his shame at himself showed. "I'll see you over at the airstrip in the morning."

He walked across to the Landrover and she stood there without a hat in the blinding glare of the day and looked after him. She did not see the man but the officer; and again she felt her resentment at Eric for his failure. She knew that she did not really want to go back to the mainland; down South even Neil

Figgins would be a nobody. But here in Goroka he was some-
body, he was *the* man; even the whites, some of whom disliked
his ideas of discipline and behavior, had to bow to his authority.
Perhaps if Eric had left the medical service, in which he would
never get anywhere, and had joined the Administration, he might
now be a district commissioner or have hopes of being one. She
knew that she could be completely happy as the wife of a district
commissioner. She looked across to the veranda of the hotel where
the coffee planters and the airline pilots and the trading store
managers sat with their wives and women over drinks, and
imagined how they would treat her if Eric was the D.C. Social
ambition was her affliction, like the sinus that occasionally
troubled her in the wet; there was no cure for it but the promotion
of her husband to the position of which she dreamed. And she
knew that was impossible, and once again was angry with him.

But she would go back to Kundavi. She was not really afraid
that the mountain would blow up; she had spent time in other
areas where volcanoes were continually smoking. But the continuing earth tremors were unusual and worrying; and, she told
herself, a woman's place was with her husband and family in
such times. She could not desert Harry; and there was still some
love left for Eric. She had tried to tell herself that it was all
over between her and Eric; but in the lonely hours on the tear-
wet pillow in the hotel room she had known that was not true.

She was foolish, she knew, but she was not a fool. She had
seen what had happened to Joan Duggan, a woman who had
tried to be independent of love.

2

There had now been five *kuru* deaths in the past month, the
highest death rate since Traxal had first come in here and en-
countered the disease. There were still seven cases left in the
ward and two of them seemed certain to die.

"God's mercy, as you call it, Mike, is impossible to understand when it comes to something like this," Traxal said. "A killing disease visited only on one tribe, no clues as to what causes it, nothing we can do to cure it. And why should it happen only to these people? I have looked into their history. They are no worse, morally, than any other tribe in New Guinea."

"You think the Lord visits afflictions only on the Sodoms and Gomorrahs? I'll tell you something, Peter. These people, in the moral sense as we generally understand it, that is, sexual morals, are a damn sight better than most whites. But don't quote me." Father Shawn smiled and puffed on the butt of his cigarette. His stocks were running low and he was now smoking every cigarette down to his fingers. His family back home kept him supplied, but they must have missed the mails this time. He knew that he could borrow the money from Roy to have a carton or two sent in from Goroka, but he did not believe in borrowing to finance his vices: you had to have some moral sense, he told himself now and smiled wintrily. "If I understood the ways of the Lord, Peter, I shouldn't be out here in these hills. I'd be at least a cardinal."

"Why do you go on believing then?" Traxal was smoking, but he smoked filter tips, something Mike Shawn wouldn't touch. He knew when Mike was getting low on stocks: as Mike's stocks went down, so did the length of the butt before he threw it away. Traxal smiled to himself, wondering if Mike would eventually be reduced to smoking the *South Pacific Post* rolled around wild or trade tobacco, as the natives did. "I can never understand you Catholics. And especially you priests—the more you study and learn, the more skeptical you should become."

"The deeper you dug into cadavers in anatomy class, did you think less and less of man?"

Traxal smiled. "That is the answer of a man who has no answer to his own doubts. When in doubt, answer a question with a question. You're not a real priest, Mike. You're a fake."

"And that may be the truth," said Father Shawn, looking up the road toward the shabby mission.

Traxal had meant his remark as a joke, but he saw at once that it had hit home. He was sorry: he liked Mike Shawn and might have made a friend of him if the little priest had not been so close to Roy Narvo.

Then Eric and Harry Macy came down the path to the hospital veranda where the two men sat. "We're going over to pick up Bernice. Any message for the pilot?" Macy looked as happy as a man about to go South on leave; he was just a large reflection of his son beside him. "Will I ask him to check at the post office for your smokes, Mike?"

Father Shawn looked wryly at the tiny butt in his fingers. "Is it becoming that obvious?"

"We've had the Merthiolate ready for a week just in case you burned your fingers." Macy grinned hugely; and beside him Harry mirrored the grin. *It's wonderful,* Traxal thought, *what even a silly woman like Bernice can mean to a man and a boy.* He looked up the hill and saw Elisabeth playing ball with a group of native children. When he went back to Prague would he miss her as much as Eric had missed Bernice? It was a question that had nagged him ever since he had told Elisabeth he was going back and she had refused to go with him; and it was a question to which he would have no answer till he was settled in Prague. He had been without her for five years, but always there had been the hope that they would be rejoined someday, either in Australia or, as he had come to think over the past six months, even back in Prague. But if he went home, he knew that it would be good-by forever to Elisabeth. She had changed from the girl he had left behind five years ago; he didn't know whether it had been gradual or suddenly over the past three weeks, but she had changed. She had determination now, a fixity of decision that she had never had before.

"I hope Mum brings me back something," Harry said. "I'd

like an air gun. If I get one, will you come shooting with me,
Father Shawn?"

"If she brings one for me, too," said Father Shawn. "The
bishop doesn't supply us missionaries with guns. And though
I've tried occasionally, I've never yet been able to bring a bird
down just with prayer alone."

"Perhaps the bishop knows what he is doing, not issuing you
with a gun," said Traxal. "He could be afraid that you would
take pot shots at him while his plane is coming in."

Oh, this is the day for home truths in the dark, thought Father
Shawn, and turned the conversation: "Bernice isn't afraid of the
mountain going up, Eric?"

"I haven't spoken to her on the radio," Macy said, "but
evidently she isn't."

"Do you think it will go up, Father Shawn?" Harry said, and
turned a half-anxious, half-expectant eye on the mountain across
the valley.

Father Shawn shrugged. "I don't know, Harry. All we can
do is wait on the vulcanologist."

"That's what I say," Macy said: erupting volcanoes were nothing, his wife was coming back. "We'd all look goats if we packed
up and got out of here, then he came in and said there was
nothing going to happen."

Traxal smiled. "I wonder how many tragedies have occurred
because people were afraid of looking goats?"

Macy laughed: he was irrepressible this morning. "You'll
never look a goat, Peter. Even without your pants you'd look
the picture of poised dignity, a real man of distinction."

"Thank you," said Traxal, smiling faintly but not unkindly:
you could not be annoyed by Eric this morning, his happiness
was so contagious.

The Macys went off down the path to the Landrover that was
waiting for them. Father Shawn looked sideways at Traxal.
"Don't you wish you had what Eric has?"

"What is that?" asked Traxal, surprised.

"The capacity to feel both the pain and joy of love."

"That sounds like an unfriendly question," said Traxal, sparring for time, suddenly on the defensive.

"It was meant to be a charitable question." Father Shawn had at last thrown away his butt. He clasped his nicotine-stained hands, making a yellow steeple of his fingers. "You aren't happy, Peter, haven't been for a long time. And I've often wished I could help you."

"I am not happy," Traxal admitted. "But not in the way you think. I am homesick, that is all. Whatever it is that Eric has, I don't think I should gain much by borrowing some of it."

Father Shawn nodded up the hill to where Elisabeth spun a dark Catherine wheel of children about her. "It is none of my business, I know, but I feel sorry for her."

"Has she been talking to you about me?" There was no mistaking the cold anger in Traxal's voice.

"I am not her confessor, Peter. But I'm not blind, either. She is very unhappy."

"Why don't you mind your own business, Mike?" said Traxal, glad now that he had never made a close friend of the priest. "You have managed to do so up till now."

Father Shawn ran his finger pensively down the scar on his cheek. The scar was the result of an encounter with one of his mission natives who, drunk on betel juice, had gone back to the devil. Father Shawn, on the point of being murdered, had grabbed the first thing that had come to hand and knocked the crazed man down with a plaster statue of the Virgin Mary. He had never been able to make up his mind whether the statue had come into his hand as an act of God, a practical illustration of the title Our Lady Help of Christians; or whether he had committed sacrilege, forgotten to pray and grabbed the first weapon at hand, sacred though it was. In the end he had decided against himself, a man who wanted to be a saint but had no desire to be a martyr. It had been Traxal who had treated and stitched up the *sarif* wound in his cheek, and he remembered now that Traxal had made no comment on the shattered statue that had lain about the head of the unconscious native. It had been Roy Narvo, the lapsed Catholic, who had made the mild blasphemy with the joke about Our Lady Help of Christians. Traxal, the atheist, had minded his own business, and perhaps he owed Traxal the same compliment. But he knew he was failing again in his duty by backing down.

"I accept the rebuke," he said, and stood up. "But we might all have got on better here at Kundavi if we hadn't minded our own business quite so much. God knows we, all of us, need each other too much."

Then he put on his old straw hat and left the hospital veranda and walked up past Elisabeth and the laughing native children toward the mission. Traxal looked after him, suddenly afraid for the first time in years. Was this shabby wreck of a priest right in saying that they did all need each other?

Locked away in a drawer in his hut, Traxal now had all the notes for the report he would write for the UN committee. Not all the notes could be incorporated in the report; they were too self-evidently malicious and accusing. But not too obviously he would be able to bring them to the notice of the committee members; that is, to the notice of the members who stood to help him personally. There was not one false point, not one untruth, in what he would tell the committee members: cautious and calculating as always, he knew his own case with the Czech member would be strengthened if everything he pointed out could be proved. There would of course be arguments by the Australians against the accusations against them; but the arguments, honest though they would be, would come long after the damage was done. The committee's report would be published and public opinion always tended to believe what it first read, especially if there was truth to it, and to suspect arguments and excuses against it.

There could be no argument at all against the shooting of the Vaikaka native by the patrol that had gone out to look for Jack Bermingham, the man who had been expressly forbidden to go into the uncontrolled territory. Traxal knew that in the end only one man, Roy Narvo, would suffer; that though Australia's name might be besmirched in the Trusteeship Council, New Guinea would not be taken away from it. Indonesia had claims on Dutch New Guinea to the west, but it did not want this main part of New Guinea; no country wanted it because of its problems, but it made a good subject for an ideological battle. So in the end the committee's visit would really only decide the fate of two men: it would send Traxal home to Prague, where he wanted to go; and it would send Narvo away from Kundavi, which he did not want to leave. He was sacrificing Narvo, a man who, he had to admit, had never done him any harm; but it had to be done if he was to get what he so passionately wanted, return to Prague. He had steeled himself to have no feelings about the matter, but now, suddenly and inexplicably, Father Shawn had got under his skin and frightened him. Did they all really need each other? When he left here would he, after all, really leave something of himself behind? He looked up the hill toward Elisabeth, remembering her story of the years of aching loneliness in Prague, and all at once Prague was no longer home but a city that he would have to learn to know again, that he might never know again.

He stood up, staring out across the valley and the gorges to the mountain opposite, hating it all yet seeing it really only for the first time. He had been lonely here, but at least he had been secure; it was the sort of security that had kept Mike Shawn and Joan Duggan and Eric Macy here. He would write his report and he would go home to Prague but he might never know security such as this again.

He turned and went into the ward to look at the *kuru* patients. Death was the one thing of which he had never been afraid.

3

Bernice came back to the patrol post with a gay front, all laughter, gossip, new resolutions and a new dress. She swept into their house and within the hour had the houseboys spring-cleaning the place, as if she had been away for months; or, as Eric Macy saw it, as if she had come back determined to clean the house of old arguments, to sweep out everything of the past and make a new start.

She went around the post and said hello to everyone, even to Narvo and Jack Bermingham, came back to the house, kissed Macy on the front steps in view of everyone, laughed till the tears came at Harry's story of chasing the cassowary through the bush during the earth tremor, then went into her bedroom, closed the door and had a good cry. She was back and she knew there was no escape, ever.

In the evening, putting off the moment of being alone again with Eric, she had everyone up for drinks. Even Bermingham was asked, and he came, although he was well aware that the invitation, brought down by the houseboy, had pointedly omitted Mary, his wife.

"I realize it's gotta come gradually, this being taken into society," he said to Narvo as the two of them walked up the path in the blue evening hush. He was wearing trousers and shirt, the only ones he had, and had even polished his old army boots with polish borrowed from Narvo. Only when he would sit down and his trousers would creep up would it be noticed that he wore no socks. His thick gray hair was wet with water and slicked down, and traces of his early handsomeness showed through the wreckage of him. Mary, watching him from the door of their hut, unperturbed by the fact that she had not been invited to Mrs. Macy's house with him, admired him and preened herself under the envious stares of the other women at the doors of their huts.

"I dunno that I wanna go all the way back, tell you the truth," Bermingham said. "But if I live long enough and my kids ever get to the Administrator's house down in Moresby, maybe they'd like to know their old man hadn't forgotten how to wear trousers and boots." Then he looked directly at Narvo, throwing away the small talk. "Did you mention me in your report? I mean about me going out when you told me not to?"

"What report?" The last thing Narvo wanted right now was to go to a cocktail party, but as soon as Bernice had asked him, he had known it was necessary that he should go. She had offered him an olive branch, he realized, and he had to accept it. No matter what other problems he had, he had to keep working at keeping relations here on the post as smooth and amicable as possible.

"Well, if you haven't written one, you're a bloody fool, my word you are. Shoving your neck out for me. . . . What will happen if word gets back to Moresby about the kanaka you bowled over?"

"Who's going to tell them? Paiwo?"

Bermingham shook his head and the neatly combed hair came unstuck; a silver fringe fell down over his forehead. "Righto, righto. You win. I shouldn't abuse you, not after what you done for me. But when you get it in the neck, how am I gonna help you?"

"How do you know I'm going to get it in the neck?"

"The writing's on the wall, mate. This UN party isn't coming in here looking for the good you've done—it'll be looking for things to find fault with. And it'll find plenty, you know that."

Narvo didn't argue with that. The UN party would spend two days here at the post and in that time not even the most perceptive and unprejudiced member of it could understand the problems there were. The prejudiced members would find everything they were looking for. They would see the shabby little priest and his mission that had achieved nothing; the white supremacy attitude of the matron of the hospital and the wife of the medical assistant; the renegade white man who lived with a native woman; and the white woman who seemed to belong to no one but was allowed to stay on the post. They would hear from the Vaikaka *luluai* of how the white officers on the post had failed to prevent the massacre of the Vaikaka women by the men of Benamaua; and they would hear from the Benamaua *luluai* how the same white officers had failed to prevent the pay-back on the Benamaua by the Vaikaka men. They would hear of the cannibalism that the Administration claimed had been stamped out in this area, and eventually they might hear of the Vaikaka native who had been shot on the recent unreported patrol. They would see the mission school that so obviously had been so belatedly started, but they would turn a blind eye to the opposition of the native elders to having their children schooled in the white man's ways. They would turn the same blind eye to the well-kept patrol post itself, to the disciplined and contented police boys, to the statistics in the hospital book showing the prodigious drop in infant mortality. The committee would write its report and far away in a hall in New York, only a block away from murder and rape and thuggery and racial prejudice, a vote of censure would be passed by delegates from countries where starvation was part of the standard of living, where a man was shot for his beliefs and not for his crimes, where nationalism excused any outrage against the outsider, no matter how innocent. A vote of censure would be passed on Australia, to whose trust this Territory had been given; but in the end only one man, excepting perhaps the natives themselves, would suffer. And Narvo knew it would be himself, who had tried to be friend to black man and white man both, and had been betrayed by friendship.

"I'm past caring, Jack." He had had no depth of affection for young Bandi such as he had for Harry Macy; nevertheless the death of the small native boy had been a shock to him. He had hoped that Bandi, somehow, might have been the means of bringing Paiwo back to the post and the road to civilization. The boy had been too young to capture his immediate interest; despite Elisabeth's comment, he was not by nature a father type. Harry Macy was old enough to talk to and show interest in the things that interested himself; he did not have the time nor the patience to wait till Bandi grew up to the same age. Still he would never have abandoned the boy, and there had always been the hope that someday he would see Bandi and Paiwo, the latter with his crimes expunged, working with him here on the post. But Bandi was gone forever now and so was Paiwo. "If I get kicked out, I'll join you on the beach. There's a good one north of Madang. Just the place for a couple of down-and-outs."

"Speak for yourself, mate. I've never considered myself a down-and-out."

Narvo grinned, looking at Bermingham and admiring him. Then they walked up the steps into the Macys' and Bernice, bosom displayed in the new dress, came to greet them. "Roy, I'm under strict instructions from Neil Figgins to be more tolerant toward you! Don't make it hard for me!"

Narvo, on the spur of the moment, with the rather desperate gaiety that sometimes comes with depression, did something he had never done before: he leaned down and kissed Bernice on the cheek. "How's that?"

Bernice's bosom almost jumped out of her dress in her surprise. "Roy, you're sick!" She took his hand and squeezed it: perhaps she had misjudged him after all. "If you kiss me every time we meet, it's not going to be hard to be tolerant toward you at all! It's more than Eric does."

Macy came across the room, grinning like a middle-aged bridegroom who had not only at last got to the altar but had married the beautiful daughter of the boss. There was a slightly incredulous look on his face, as if he couldn't quite believe Bernice had returned. He kissed her on the ear and was relieved when she did not shrink away. She had kissed him when she had got out of the plane over on the airstrip and again on the steps of the house, but he had been able to feel the constraint in her and had wondered if it was just a front she was putting up, a front that she would take down as soon as they were alone.

"Not any more. I'm gonna be the kissingest husband you ever saw."

"How disgusting," Duggan said to Elisabeth and Traxal. "What will the kanakas think of all this kissing in public?"

"They may go in for it themselves," said Traxal. "Wouldn't you like to be greeted by a kiss from the *luluai* every time you went out to a village?"

"Now *you're* being disgusting," said Duggan.

She walked off to speak to Father Shawn, who never made insulting remarks to a woman, even if he was a priest; and Traxal and Elisabeth were left alone in their corner by the window. Elisabeth looked out the window and saw the party of natives coming up from the gorge and making their way across to the native quarters. She knew at once who they were, even though the women in the party were not wearing the mourning mud and the Job's tears: it was the party come from Vaikaka to collect the bodies of Bandi and the house-monkey and take them back to their village. The children's bodies would not be smoked, Narvo had told her, and she was glad of that. She had come to have real affection for the shy little Bandi and she did not want to think of his shrunken smoked tiny corpse sitting high on the mountain opposite staring out across the valley to the patrol post where he had been happy and where, unhappily and shockingly, he had died.

"The UN party is due in here next week," Traxal said, keeping his voice low and speaking in Czech. Elisabeth had been avoid-

ing him for the past week and he had found it difficult to be
alone with her. "Are you still sure you do not want to come back
to Prague?"

"Quite sure." Elisabeth deliberately replied in English. She
looked up at Traxal over the top of her glass. "I am sorry, Peter,
but it is all over. I thought you would know that."

"One hopes," he said, still speaking in Czech. Now that he
was on the verge of losing her, he wanted her; something told
him he *would* miss her if she did not return to Prague with him.
"We met again in the wrong place, darling. It would have been
different—still could be—if we had met in London or Paris or
New York."

"It is too late, Peter," she said, still speaking in English, still
keeping the barrier between them: Czech was a reminder of
the past, the old intimacy. "You will never go to those places
now. And in any case——"

"Yes?" he said in English when she hesitated.

"I do not love you any more, Peter. It is not just the returning
to Prague. Something died while we were separated. I had to
come all this way to find out—" She looked out the window: the
funeral party had disappeared, but now there was wailing down
in the native quarters. The Vaikaka party had been expected
for the past twenty-four hours, but something had kept them.
Now they had arrived late in the evening and they would stay
the night on the post and all through the night there would be
the wailing and the mournful tuneless singing. *Who will wail
for me*, Elisabeth wondered, *when I send Peter away?* She
looked about the room at the people who in the past few weeks
had become her friends; but who among them would really miss
her if, by chance, she died?

Then she saw Rossi staring at her across the room, his love,
or what he felt was love, plain on his face. She turned away
from him, afraid that he might mistake the look on her own
face, the loneliness she all at once felt again, as encouragement

for him to come and speak to her. She turned away and Narvo was standing immediately before her, a full glass of beer in his hand and the gold tooth showing in a smile of secret amusement. But there was a tired beaten look to his eyes, and all at once she knew that he was as lonely as herself. And the discovery shocked her: she had taken him to be self-contained and self-sufficient, and to find now that he wasn't made him somehow a different man. He had faults, he had admitted those himself, but she had suspected no weaknesses. Now, to find that there were weaknesses in him completed the humanness of the man.

"Is the UN committee still coming, Roy?" Traxal said, more by way of conversation than by query: he had not considered the possibility of the committee's not coming.

"Depends," said Narvo. "The vulcanologist gets in here first thing tomorrow morning. If he says the mountain is dangerous, then I guess we shan't see them." He looked at Elisabeth seriously but without alarm. "Could you leave here in a hurry if you had to?"

"I left Prague in a hurry," she said, surprised.

"This will be quicker. If he gives the word, I'll have all you women over on the strip within an hour."

"Is it as bad as that?" Traxal said, and looked out the window at the distant mountain: up till now the earth tremors had worried him but hadn't actually frightened him.

"Some of the kanakas are already moving off the mountain. They've never done that before. The water in their springs is really hot now, hotter than it was yesterday."

Against the clink of glasses and the chatter of the others in the room, watching the houseboy moving around with a plate of savories and seeing Harry sitting out on the steps of the house gently stroking the head of the cassowary, Elisabeth found it hard to believe that Narvo was talking seriously about possible disaster. Yet she knew that this was the way it could happen. She had been too young to remember, but her mother had told her they had been at a children's party when the Nazis had marched into Prague. It had been snowing and they had all gone out into the garden to watch the tanks and trucks roll almost silently past on the snow-covered road, and she had caught a cold: she could not remember it, but that was how the first major disaster of her life had occurred. It had been snowing on the day the mobs marched on Prague in 1948 and she had had a cold then, too. She had been sitting in a coffee shop with her mother when they had heard the chanting as the mob turned into the street. The owner of the shop, a small woman with a cast in one eye, had blessed herself and gone out through a curtained doorway in the rear. Elisabeth had gone back to the shop many times after that, but she had never seen the owner again. It was not snowing now and never would on this post, but suddenly she had the feeling she had lived through all this before.

"If this is so serious," she said, "why didn't the vulcanologist come in earlier?"

"Vulcanologists are not a plentiful breed," Narvo explained. "Men don't go in for it like they do for other professions. It doesn't pay well and it has its dangers. And even if they were plentiful, would it be economical to have a big staff of them? Sometimes they might be sitting on their behinds for a couple of years doing nothing. We have two of them up here and generally that should be enough. But right now there is evidently a lot of activity going on, and the two of them have been working round the clock checking on possible eruptions. And naturally they've gone first to the areas where there are the most people. We're well down the list."

"Why don't we move out, then, till we get some sort of reassurance?" Traxal said, and made no attempt to hide his concern. Something was happening to him, he knew; he was becoming nervous, even frightened. Was it because he was now so close to leaving here, to going home; was he suddenly afraid of death or was he afraid that he might lose the chance of returning home? "We could all go out to Goroka——"

"And whom would we leave to look after the post? Move all the whites out, you mean, and leave the police boys? And if we took them, there'd be no post left in a week, assuming the mountain didn't go up. The kanakas would come down and clean it out like a plague of locusts. And we'd come back and have to start all over again, and down in Canberra someone would ask why we had run out just because of an earth tremor. If we have to go, Peter, I'll see you get out in time," he said, and did not try to keep the irony from his voice. "But the last ones to leave will be you, Eric, Frank and myself. Right?" The gold tooth showed, but the smile meant nothing: it was an order and Traxal knew it was such.

And right then he wished that the mountain would not blow up, that he would have the chance to write his report and finish off Narvo: all at once that desire was as strong as the desire to go home.

"I shan't go out ahead of you, Roy," he said coldly. "I shall wait to share your last look at Kundavi."

Only Elisabeth was aware of the threat behind the words, and again she had a twinge of conscience: should she tell Narvo what Traxal intended to do? But Narvo had already turned away, gone across to talk with Harry who now stood at the doorway, a small boy with his nose pressed against the window of adulthood. She saw the look of delight on Harry's face as Narvo spoke to him. The man put his arm about the boy's shoulder and they went out on to the veranda together. If she was going to tell Narvo of Traxal's treachery, it would have to be later.

"Would you be falling in love with Narvo?" Traxal said quietly behind her.

"If I were, Peter, I should not tell you," she said, and wondered if falling in love with Narvo could be another disaster in her life.

4

That night Narvo was on the air to Goroka. He was surprised when the operator told him the district commissioner wanted to speak to him. He had spoken to Figgins only that morning and tonight's call to Goroka was the usual routine one. For a moment he feared that Figgins was coming on to tell him that the vulcanologist had been delayed. He sat before the trans-ceiver in Rossi's hut, where he had been sleeping since his return from the patrol, and looked out through the window across the valley to the mountain dark against the death's-head moon. If the vulcanologist was delayed, what decision would he himself have to make about the people in the valley?

Then Figgins' voice, crisp even above the faint static, was saying, "Roy, this is Neil Figgins. Stan Hlasko, the Cessna pilot, was in to see me this evening." He paused, and Narvo, sensitive at once to nuances, a habit he had acquired dealing with in-transigent natives, knew that Figgins wanted to say something that he would rather not have said over the radio. "He said the *luluai* from Vaikaka came to see him on the strip. Do you know anything about that? Over."

The word *that* was emphasized: Narvo was expected to know what it covered. And he knew at once: the Vaikaka *luluai* had got the word to Figgins about the man who had been shot by the patrol that had gone out after Bermingham.

"Are you there, Roy? Did you hear me? Over."

"Yes, Neil. I heard you. I—I have a report to write. It may take a few days, because of this business with the mountain. That's got me worried at present."

"The vulcanologist will be in tomorrow," Figgins said. "But get me the report written as soon as you can—before the UN party comes in here. And don't leave anything out."

"It will be a full report."

Then Figgins said casually, "How is everyone out there? The women all right?"

"They're fine," said Narvo, wondering if Figgins was leading up to anything else.

Figgins was: "The men okay, too? How's Jack Bermingham—is he on the post with you?"

"Everyone is here," said Narvo, and knew that Figgins knew the whole story now, that the report would be complete and damning. Questions would be asked in Canberra and New York, where friendship was just a word found in treaties, and the dead native would begin to assume the halo of a martyr.

Narvo switched off the transceiver and turned around. Rossi, sitting on the other side of the room cleaning his pistol, said "That makes a mess of things, doesn't it?"

"Roy, it makes a mess of it for both you and Jack." Father Shawn was down to his last cigarette; he smoked it with the elaborate care of a condemned man. "Jack will be moved out of the area and God knows what will happen to you."

"It was a risk and it didn't come off," Narvo said dully. Then he smacked the table with his fist and stood up, swearing violently. "That bloody sneaking little *luluai!* I'll wring his neck when I catch him!"

"Do you blame him, really?" Father Shawn said. "You killed one of his sub-clan. Do you expect him to be on your side?"

"Why didn't he come and see me first? He's responsible to me, not to Neil Figgins!"

"Wake up, Roy. Your anger is making you naïve. You know these natives better than anyone in these mountains, and yet you ask a question like that. Simmer down, Roy. If you wring the *luluai's* neck, you'll have to wring Jack's, too. He deserves it more."

But Narvo was still cloudy-minded with anger: not only at the *luluai* but at the whole sequence of events that had brought about this situation. "It's all so bloody unfair! *I* didn't shoot the kanaka! I had Paiwo in my sights, I could have bowled him over like a rabbit, and God knows why, I put my gun down and let him get away. I didn't even fire a shot!"

Father Shawn put down the ash and the tiny stub that was his last cigarette: from now on till the mails arrived he'd have to steady his nerves with prayer. He stood up and moved to the door. "Walk up to the mission with me. You need some night air to clear your brain. Good night, Frank. When you become an A.D.O., make up your mind not to make a fool of yourself over your friends."

Rossi was on his feet, biting his bottom lip, the pistol hanging from a limp hand. His dark, serious face looked all at once young and uncertain: he was seeing a future that had more complications than he had expected. "Roy, if it is any help, I'll back you up. I——"

"Thanks, Frank." The two men, the veteran and the novice, had never really come close to each other; but now Narvo looked at Rossi and saw a recognizable image of himself years ago. It was suddenly a little frightening to think he had come so far; he not only felt lonely and angry but all of a sudden old. "Don't shove your neck out for me. In the long run it won't help either of us. You'll have enough troubles of your own in time."

Rossi hesitated: perhaps Narvo was right, perhaps he should not borrow trouble when he had an inheritance of it coming to him some time in the future. But he had his code and he could not stand by while injustice was done: it was the same old-fashioned code of conduct that had made the girls back home think him dull. "No, Roy. You can count on me. And Mike, too, I'm sure."

Narvo said nothing, afraid to speak. He was not an emotional man but he could be moved by emotion. For a while in his bitter, more cynical moments on the trek out to pick up Berming-ham, he had begun to look upon friendship as an insidious form of treachery. He knew that judgment was wrong now: these two men here would never betray him, not even by accident. He nodded to Rossi, and went ahead of Father Shawn out of the hut.

Father Shawn didn't speak till they were halfway up the road to the mission. "If anything happens to the mountain, I mean if it blows its top and we have to get out of here, it will be the end of me as a missionary." He looked across at the mountain, a black broken-topped wall against the cold blossom of stars. "It could blow me right back to Cape Cod."

"And you wouldn't like that?" Narvo had got his emotions under control again.

"Do you want to go back to Sydney?"

Narvo grinned, seeing the priest's point. Then, suddenly, as a release from the tension that had held him all day, he laughed aloud. The laugh rang down the road, could be heard in every hut on the post: it sounded like the old Kiap. "You can join Jack and me on the beach! We'll live like bums for six days of the week and go to church on Sundays!"

"I don't live much differently now," said Father Shawn quietly, having no laughter in himself.

Narvo sobered at once. He stopped, taking Father Shawn by the arm and turning him round to face him squarely. "Mike, you'd better pull up your socks. You're starting to weep into your beer now, feel sorry for yourself——"

"You're wrong there, Roy," Father Shawn said without heat.

"All right. Then you're taking pride in what you've done—or what you haven't done, if you like. And that's worse for a priest, isn't it?" He had never argued religion with Father Shawn, nor discussed the needs of a vocation: as it was impossible for some people to understand why he should exile himself in these mountains as a patrol officer, so it had been impossible for him to understand how a man could give himself up to the sacrifices and limitations of the priesthood. But now, with his own career doomed, he could not see the other man condemning himself because he had failed to be perfect. Even if the mountain blew up, if he lost his own job, something had to be saved: his was not the nature to accept complete calamity. He shook the little priest as if he were talking to a recalcitrant native. "You gave me a pep talk a few weeks back. Now I'm giving you one! You told me you had ambitions to be a saint, and I think that's your bloody trouble. When you found out you couldn't be one, you didn't want to be anything less. I've never yet met a saintly priest who was any good in country like this. It's the practical priests who make the best missionaries—the ones who can build a chapel with their own hands, nurse a sick kanaka, teach a kid to read and write. Yes, and be able to recognize that sin is a human condition and not a rare disease—which is about the only attribute you've got!"

"Thank you," said Father Shawn. "I was beginning to despair."

"None of your bloody priestly humor! I'm telling you, wake up to yourself, Mike. Good missionaries get into heaven by the same door as the saints go in. Don't spend your time being sorry for me. I've been wanting to say this for a long time, but I've held off—mainly, I think, because I needed you around, because I couldn't have stuck this past six months without you to argue with and to give me sympathy when I thought I needed it. But I'll be gone from here soon—whether the mountain goes up or the UN committee comes in, I'm on my way out, there's nothing more certain. I'll find a job somewhere, either still in the Administration or out of it. But you won't! There's never any job for a sacked priest, Mike, in the Church or out of it. Get cracking before it's too late. Don't spend your time arguing for me. Start arguing and working for yourself. You're the one person on this post that none of us can help!"

He slapped the priest on the back and turned on his heel and went walking swiftly down the road. Father Shawn stood in the middle of the road staring after the huge figure that went away from him into the night without a backward glance. Perhaps Roy was right: perhaps he had come to the wrong country to be a saint. But he knew at the back of his mind that he was never meant to be a saint: even if his parish had been the door-step of heaven, he would have failed. Perhaps there was time to change his ambition; but even as the thought came to him, he knew that it was too late. He lacked faith in himself, and that was as necessary as faith in God.

He turned and walked up the road to the mission. He stopped at the gate and looked up as he heard the stiff rustle of wings. He saw the flying-foxes come out of the trees in a black cloud, and, his mind on other things, he wondered for a moment what had frightened them. Then he felt the earth begin to tremble beneath his feet, and he looked up and imagined he saw the mountain shiver against the stars. And all at once he committed the final sinful surrender and prayed for death, like a suicide.

5

Paiwo, lying in his hut in Vaikaka, felt the mountain shudder beneath him. He heard women and children cry out in the other huts in the village, and there were one or two shouts from men; but he remained lying on his bamboo mat, not even turning his head but just staring at the roof of the hut. A small night fire glowed in the center of the hut and as the earth trembled the flames leapt up. Shadows danced on the *kunai* roof, and the roof itself rustled as it shook. The walls of the hut leaned in, then settled back; and a large crack appeared in the smooth earth of the floor. There was a sharp click-click and a gecko lizard dropped with a soft plop to the floor and scurried away, but Paiwo neither heard it nor saw it. All he could see were the faces of his wife and son, and behind them the face of the Kiap.

The corpse of Kabu was still being smoked in the village, but soon it would be taken higher up the mountain to the ledge where the smoked dead sat and stared at the valley and moun-

tains which had been their past and of which they had no
memories. Bandi would be brought back from Kundavi tomorrow and he, too, would be taken up the mountain. He would
not be smoked because children, the old people who had died
because their time had come, and the evil ones, the sorcerers,
were never smoked. Bandi would be taken up to the caves
higher up the mountain and left there with all the other dead of
Vaikaka. He would be left there and Paiwo would never go near
his son again. But Paiwo knew he would never forget Bandi,
and it was that knowledge that burned in him now, like a pain
he knew would be with him till he died.

In the morning he would go down and kill the Kiap. He had
not blamed the Kiap for Kabu's death; the Benamaua had done
that and they had been paid back. But the Kiap had told him,
when he had first left Kundavi to bring Kabu's body back to
Vaikaka, that Bandi would be looked after. Paiwo had been told
by the *luluai* that the Kiap had brought Bandi back to the village
and when he did not find Paiwo there, had not left Bandi with
his sub-clan, as he should have, but had taken the boy back to
Kundavi. The Kiap had failed to look after Bandi, had let the
boy go to his death while he had come to hunt his father, and
for that the Kiap would have to be paid back. It was the law of
these mountains and Paiwo knew now that he was committed
forever to live by those laws. He would never again have the
chance to live by the laws of the white man.

People were moving about the village, stirred by the earth
tremor which had now passed on and had not been severe.
Someone came to the outside of Paiwo's hut and called to him,
but he answered only with a grunt, to let them know he was all
right, and did not get up from his bed. The villagers soon
settled down again and the night moved on, while the fire in
Paiwo's hut died down and finally was just cold ash. Paiwo lay
there, not feeling the cold, feeling only his grief which was

colder than any wind, and at last saw daylight come in like golden lizards through the cracks in the walls of the hut.

He got up and ate a breakfast of *kau-kau* and some pandanus nuts. Last night he had taken some water from the spring that was now hot and had left it to cool overnight; he drank some of it now and hardly noticed the new taste it had. He put some pandanus nuts, a few bananas and a cooked rat into his *bilum* bag; then collected the weapons he would need to kill the Kiap and to protect himself if he should be attacked by the police boys. He took his blackpalm bow and the new arrows that he had cut and shaped yesterday, his stone ax and bamboo knife, and his fighting spear; then he was ready for his journey, to kill or be killed. And in his heart he hoped that both events might come to pass.

He crawled out through the narrow door of his hut and walked down to where the corpse of Kabu, now hairless and shrunken and leathern-looking, sat above the smoldering fire. He stood there, no particular thought in his mind, just grieving. A breeze came up the side of the mountain and a puff of smoke rose from the fire; an ember glowed for a moment, like life in a dark eye, and a twig snapped like a creaking joint. The breeze increased and the platform on which the corpse sat swayed a little; Kabu seemed to lean forward, as if trying to come back to join him. Paiwo swallowed, feeling his sorrow dry in his throat, then he turned and hurried out of the stockade, leaving Kabu and Vaikaka perhaps forever.

He went quickly down the trail that led down the mountain to the gorge. A white cloud rose out of the gorges and covered the western side of the mountain; the rising sun touched it with color and made it sparkle. But Paiwo saw nothing of the morning; he was running too swiftly. He had to cross the river before the workers from Kundavi came down to the new bridge, and climb up out of the gorge to find a hiding place in the forest that bordered the post. He would wait all day in the bushes there and then that night would come down into the post and kill the Kiap while he slept. He would have to hurry because the day was already bright and some people would already have begun their day over at Kundavi.

He came to a spot where the trail crossed a small rivulet that ran down from the spring above the village. He had stepped into the water before he noticed the steam rising from it. The water was hot, almost scalding, and he cried out with the shock of it. He stopped, feeling the skin on his foot shrink from the burn of the water, and looked back up the mountain. There was no smoke coming from its peak, but even as he stood there he felt the shuddering beneath his feet. A crack appeared in the trail ahead of him and two bushes on a ledge suddenly plunged away like birds and fell down the mountainside. The rivulet seemed to boil and the water all at once changed its course; Paiwo watched with fear and amazement as it abruptly turned and went *across* the mountainside instead of *down* it. A big rock eased itself out of the earth, like an animal stirring from sleep, and went rolling down the slope, gathering speed and other rocks with it as it went. The shuddering went on and the mountain seemed to grunt with pain. Then abruptly it subsided and in the silence immediately afterwards Paiwo heard the cries in the village. There was no need to go back to warn his clanfolk; it sounded as if the whole village was awake. He turned and went running on down the mountain, desperate now, knowing that everyone over at Kundavi would be awake now.

He reached the bottom of the gorge and ran along the trail to the new bridge that spanned the river. He was halfway across the bridge, making it sway dangerously as he ran, when the side of the mountain blew out an immense eruption of smoke and fire and rocks and dust.

14

NARVO, STANDING on the veranda of Rossi's hut, saw the mountain erupt. The tremor had woken him and he had known at once that this was the worst yet. Still in his pajamas he had gone out on to the veranda and with sleep still in his eyes saw what looked to be the end of the world.

The whole eastern side of the mountain, at right angles to the patrol post, blew out in a giant black, red and gray storm. The sound of the explosion was more than just noise: it was a smashing blow against the ear. The whole of the valley shuddered, seemed to constrict, as if it were going to close up. The ranges danced against the sky, at war with each other. Narvo saw a bird flying up the gorge, moving with panic-stricken haste: one moment it was there, alive and brilliant with color, the next moment it had gone, disintegrated into nothing. Smoke streaked with flame came out of the side of the mountain and at once, so quickly it was incredible, a yellow dusk came down on the patrol post. The white cloud that had been on the western slope of the mountain peeled back like fur being stripped from an animal. The sky and the valley and the mountains to the east were suddenly gone and the world in that direction had turned to seething dark smoke.

The sound of the explosion rolled away down the valley and over the ranges. It was heard in Goroka and the explosion itself was felt in Moresby three hundred and fifty miles to the southeast. The smoke and dust rose in a towering column that spread to form an immense furiously boiling cloud; it was seen by aircraft pilots flying up the coast a hundred miles away. The blast and heat of the explosion went away from Kundavi and down the valley and gorges and over the eastern ranges; people, animals, birds and earth died in an instant of hell that they did not have time to comprehend. Nature had laughed again at man who had boasted he had tamed it.

Narvo, standing in his pajamas, felt the backward blast of heat from the explosion. For an instant after the explosion there was a vast vacuum in the valley; Narvo gasped for air and found none. Then the air came rushing back in as a wind, sweeping up from the gorges, flattening bushes, hurling birds before it, carrying dust and heat and the smell of hell. Narvo, about to take a deep breath, waited till the wind had gone past. Then he gulped, feeling the raw thick air rush into his lungs, and his nostrils rebelled against the coarse sulphuric smell that assailed them. His eyes hurt, smarting and watering, and his ears were dead.

Rossi came out on to the veranda and he saw Rossi turn to him and his mouth open. But no words came; then he was aware of the awful silence. It was not the silence of the mountains; it was the terrible utter absence of sound of death. *Oh Christ,* he thought, *I'm deaf!* Panic rushed through him: he shook his head as a swimmer does, hit his ears with his palms, put his fingers in his ears and poked frantically. Then a long way off he heard a sound, a scream that grew and grew till it was like another wind coming up from the gorges. He turned his head and saw the natives coming out of their huts, spilling out like black lava to cover the parade ground and stand there staring across at the mountain and shrieking in the one continuous pitch that was like the sound of a human siren. Then he heard Rossi say, "We've got to do something about the natives," and he almost wept with relief: he was not deaf after all.

"Come on!" he snapped, and turned and went into the hut. He pulled on his boots and a sweater over his pajamas and went at once out of the hut and up toward the parade ground. The natives came down on him in a black bobbing wave, their voices still shrieking but now with some words coming through the shrieks, calling *Kiap, Kiap!* as if he were some deity come to save them from death. He pushed his way through them, smelling the fear coming out of them, and followed by Rossi went up the small slope in front of Macy's house. All the whites except Father Shawn and Bermingham were already there, but he ignored them to turn and face the crowd of fear-stricken natives.

The mountain was still rumbling, with intermittent loud cracks, like the sound of howitzers, as there were new explosions. Dust and smoke now obscured the sky and the sun was just an angry radiance, like the reflection of a distant fire. Narvo gazed out over the restless crowd, then he spoke. His voice was even louder than usual, as if he were trying to convince himself that he was not deaf: "Do not be afraid! Be brave, as mountain people should be! The danger is past and now we have to prepare to move out of Kundavi. Go back to your huts and prepare for a journey. Bring food, water and cloaks. Go quickly but quietly. Remember—do not be afraid! None of you, not even the smallest child nor the oldest woman, will die. I promise you that!"

The shrieking had subsided. Some children still cried and a few old women murmured; but the crowd was now comparatively silent. The natives stared up at the giant figure of the Kiap, his face dark with stubble, his hair unkempt, dressed in pajamas that gaped immodestly and a sweater out at the elbows; they stared at him and saw something reassuring, and they turned quietly, all panic gone for the moment, and went back to their huts. Rossi, standing behind Narvo, was aware of the power of the command, of the ability to inspire faith, of the quality that distinguished a leader from the ordinary run of men.

"Do you really think the worst is over?" Bernice was shaking violently. Macy, standing with his arm about her, could have been comforting his mother: she looked all at once old and sick and ready to die of fright. Harry stood on the other side of her, but Bernice didn't have the strength to lift an arm to draw him to her. She leaned against Macy, letting him hold her up, and when she spoke to Narvo her voice was a mere whisper.

"We'll be all right," Narvo said gently, and tried to sound confident. He had no more idea of what the mountain would do than did any of the natives who, accepting his reassurance, had gone back to their huts. "It's a bit early in the day, Bernice, but maybe a drink would help you. Duggan will give you a brandy."

"I could do with some myself," said Duggan. "Any other starters?"

"I should like one," Elisabeth said, and suddenly there was an outbreak of weak smiles, as if everyone found it shameful but amusing to be drinking so early in the morning.

Then Father Shawn came running down the road, an old woolen dressing gown flapping about his bare legs, looking for all the world like some queer large bird that had forgotten how to use its wings. He arrived gasping for breath, drawing the dressing gown modestly about him; he tried to say something, but he had no breath and all he did was nod weakly to everyone. Then Jack Bermingham, in lap-lap and sweater and unlaced boots, came up the slope; and Narvo noted that even in this moment of crisis Mary and the children had not come to join the whites. The others, who had been about to move off, stopped and turned back as Father Shawn and Bermingham arrived. Then as one they all looked at Narvo.

"You're the boss, Roy," Bermingham said. "What do we do?"

"Nothing just yet—there's nothing we can do." Narvo looked at Traxal. "You'd better be the first to be prepared, Peter. We may get a lot of casualties in—or we may not get any at all."

They all looked down the valley, still obscured by dust and smoke. The cloud from the eruption was gradually spreading and they stood in a pale orange light that was unreal and as frightening as any further threat from the mountain itself. On the mountain, under the smoke boiling out of its eastern side, they could now see the crater, etched by the flames that fluttered violently in it, as if it were a pit of captive bright yellow and red birds beating their wings against the invisible bars that held them. Lava had begun to flow, red and frightening and yet at the same time beautiful; it spread down the mountainside like a rapidly growing giant octopus. Seeing it, Narvo realized for the first time that Vaikaka and Benamaua were doomed, if not already gone. He saw Father Shawn bless himself and knew the priest had realized the same awful thing.

"There's no point in going over to the mountain," Narvo said. "What we have to worry about now are the kanakas on this side of the valley."

"What about us?" Duggan said, peering at Narvo. She had rushed out without her glasses, only stopping to pull on a dressing gown over her nightgown. She was barefooted and she had stubbed her toe on the gravel path as she had run up here. Ash was now drifting across the valley, coming down to settle on them in a fine creamy-gray dust, and for some reason there appeared to be more of it on Duggan than on any of the others. With her hair uncombed, her eyes almost shut as she tried to see, and gray with ash, she looked even more ugly than before. "The whites, I mean."

Narvo was surprised at his own lack of temper: a question like this a week ago would have brought on an eruption of his own. But the fact had to be faced: there were people on this post who, because of their color, felt they had a prior right to survival. He had always tried not to lose his temper in the face of facts, although he had not always been successful. The attitude of the people was despicable and enough to make him justifiably angry; but what had to be faced now was not the attitude but the fact that the attitude existed. A display of temper, of the old Narvo, would solve nothing.

"If we go out, Duggie, we'll all go out together. But it is a bit early to talk about that yet. We don't know how we are going to get out. Being white or black right now doesn't count for anything. The color of our prayers is the same."

"Look!" Elisabeth said suddenly, and pointed across the valley. "The airstrip!"

The smoke lifted for a moment, driven up by a blast of air from the crater, and they saw the ridge where the airstrip had been. A huge crack ran right across it; below the crack the ridge had dropped away to an even greater angle than before. The steep-sided ridge looked like a great broken-backed monster that had crawled up out of the gorges and found it could go no farther, it lay against the slope of the ranges, smoke and steam coming out of the wound in its back and lava flowing like gray-red blood. No plane would ever land on it again.

"That puts the kybosh on that," Narvo said, and tried to sound calm and matter-of-fact, as if the airstrip had been only one of many ways of getting out of here. But he was worried and he knew that all the others were worried. Bernice was on the verge of hysteria, and her hysteria could soon communicate itself to the natives. There was trouble enough now, but three or four hundred panicking natives would reduce any attempt at evacuation to a horrible farce. He was the leader of this community and he had to be the last to show any weakness. It suddenly seemed to him that, in one way or another, he had been fighting weakness ever since he had landed here in New Guinea, and the effort was beginning to tell. He ran a tired hand over his face, streaking the ash that covered it, and said, "I'll get on the radio to Goroka. We'll need their help whatever happens."

"Ask them if they have any supplies available for burn cases," Traxal said. He had been severely shaken by the eruption and he had to struggle to remain and sound calm. He was not concerned with impressing any of the others with his composure. His calculating brain was already at work and he reasoned that if he remained calm the others would take less notice of him. And that was what he wanted, to be taken for granted and remain unwatched. If Narvo was going to insist that the whites should take their chances with the hundreds of natives, then he for one was going to rebel against the order. He would quietly plan his own escape and when the time came he would leave without being noticed by the others. How he would go and in what direction, he did not know as yet. But he had escaped from Czechoslovakia, which had been no less difficult than this, and he would escape from here. In the meantime he had to go on playing the doctor, the man of mercy. "They had better send in some serum in case typhoid breaks out. We shan't be able to touch the drinking water."

Narvo slapped his hand angrily against his hip. "Of course, I forgot! Frank, you'd better go down there quick and tell them to lay off the water. Tell them to use only what they had in the bowls in their huts." He looked back at Traxal. "How much have you down at the hospital?"

"Not much. Four or five waterbags—perhaps twenty gallons," said Traxal, and determined to get some for himself before it was all gone.

"Righto. I'll give you two police boys to guard it," Narvo said, and turning away missed the expression that crossed Traxal's face.

But Elisabeth, now tuned to watching closely any exchange between the two men, had seen the mixture of anger and frustration that Traxal had not been able to conceal. As the group broke up she hesitated, wondering whether to go back into the guest hut and begin packing or to follow either Traxal or Narvo. Then Duggan said, "That brandy is on for those who want it. Only a medicinal nip, though."

"That cuts me out, then," said Bermingham, and with a wink turned away and went down toward his own hut.

Elisabeth, because she still could not bring herself to carry tales to Narvo, because she still felt the shreds of some loyalty to Traxal, followed the group that went down toward the hospital. Duggan led the Macys up into her own hut, but Traxal went on down to the hospital itself. In the confusion of natives coming and going across the parade ground, in the dim light and with his own attention held by the belching mountain across the valley, Traxal did not see Elisabeth following him. He stood for a moment at the bottom of the steps looking across at the mountain, then without a backward glance he hurried up into the hospital.

Elisabeth also hesitated at the bottom of the steps. She did not like spying. All her life she had rigorously restrained her curiosity in the affairs of other people. Growing up in a time when spying and informing had been second nature to many people, a way of earning a living, she had rebelled by going to the other extreme: rejecting even voluntary confidences she had found herself without friends, and because of her isolation had even been suspected by some of being an informer herself. Peter had been the first person in whom she had ever confided, of whom she had ever been curious; and now he was the first one on whom she was going to spy, was if necessary going to betray. There was a loud crack from across the valley and the crater of the mountain looked for a moment like a bright pink brush as molten rock blew out of it. There was no time for hesitation, she told herself.

She went up into the hospital and found herself in an empty ward. She looked about but could see no sign of Traxal. She heard a moan, and she went through a door and down some steps into another ward. This ward had an earth floor and she did not recognize it at first. Then there was another moan from one of the beds, followed by a hiccupping giggle. Now accustomed to the gloom of the ward she saw the wasted face staring at her, the eyes blank as bubbles and the mouth a gaping wound from which issued the horrifying giggle. It was the first time she had been in the *kuru* ward since her first day on the post, when Traxal had shown her around, and now she shivered and turned quickly away. Almost as if pursued, she stumbled through the bead curtain that hung across the doorway at the end of the ward and came into the dispensary. Four canvas water-bags hung by wires from the roof joists, and Traxal stood at one of them filling a smaller, portable bag.

"Peter!"

He turned, startled, spilling water from the bag he held in his hand and letting water run from the wooden tap in the large bag. Elisabeth brushed past him and turned off the tap. Now that she had actually discovered his treachery she felt no shame at her spying. She was trembling with fury and disgust, and when she spoke she was almost incoherent.

"Control yourself, Elisabeth!" She had been speaking in Czech, unable in her anger to remember any English; and Traxal snapped at her in the same tongue. "Why aren't you packing to leave?"

"Because I suspected you were going to do this! Peter, what's got into you? You're a doctor! You're supposed to look after your patients—not after yourself!"

"I don't know what you're talking about." Traxal had regained his composure. He looked at Elisabeth with such calm objectivity that an outsider coming in might have thought he was diagnosing the cause of a woman patient's outburst of hysteria. He methodically screwed the cap on the waterbag he held in his hand. "You had better watch yourself in front of the natives. If they felt that any of us whites were going to show panic, it would soon spread to them. And that would be disastrous."

Elisabeth turned away, unable to say anything in the face of his brazen if unspoken denial that he was doing anything wrong. His startled look as she had come through the door had been enough admission of his guilt; yet now he had turned the whole situation against herself. She moved toward the door of the dispensary, lost for words and unable to determine what to do next. And then Narvo appeared in the doorway.

"Roy!"

Narvo took in the situation at a glance, but he was still puzzled. These two had obviously had another argument, but what about? With the threat of the volcano over them, had Elisabeth decided to go back to Traxal? He felt a stab of jealously, the first he could remember, and sarcasm was on the end of his tongue as he looked at Elisabeth. Then he saw the waterbag still in Traxal's hand. "Where are you going with that?"

"Nowhere." Traxal was the calmest of the three of them. "Is there something wrong with filling a waterbag?"

"He was filling it for himself, Roy!" Even Narvo was surprised at the high pitch of Elisabeth's voice. He had never seen her as excited as this, and it was a shock. Was she going to be another Bernice, had the volcano wreaked its effect on her, too?

Traxal shook his head at Narvo: they were men together, one knew what to expect from women in moments of crisis. "I don't do those sort of things, Roy. Have I fallen down on my job as a doctor before?"

From across the valley there was a crack, then another loud rumble. The earth floor of the hospital moved as if a wave had passed under it, and the walls and roof of the dispensary rustled and shook. The waterbags swayed violently on their wires, like punching-bags hit by invisible boxers, and some water splashed from the top of one of them. There were shouts and screams from the natives now regathering on the parade ground; and from the *kuru* ward, as if one of the patients there was enjoying the fear of the healthy and the undying, there came a giggling laugh. The light outside deepened and here in the dispensary there was only gloom.

Elisabeth was still nervous and excited, but now she had control of her voice. "Roy, he is thinking only of himself! That is the way it has been ever since I came here. This UN committee——"

Traxal started forward angrily; for a moment it looked as if he were going to hit her with the waterbag. Narvo stepped in front of him. "Hold it, Peter! What about the UN committee, Elisabeth?"

"She is hysterical, Roy. Don't take any notice of her. I'll give her a sedative——"

"Shut up! What about this committee, Elisabeth?"

"He is going to tell them everything they want to know! He is buying his way back to Czechoslovakia——"

Narvo felt the rage fly through him; he was amazed that he was able to stop himself from leaping on Traxal. "You miserable crawling bastard! I never liked you, but I trusted you!" He stepped forward, taking Traxal by the front of his pajamas. The two men stood inches from each other, but Traxal didn't flinch. And Narvo, even in the heat of anger, noted that and admired Traxal for it. Traxal had been about to do a cowardly thing, but he was not a coward. Narvo, too long in these mountains perhaps, thinking *kanaka*, still found he could give the man credit for not backing down. "I should break your neck!"

"You wouldn't gain anything by that," Traxal said, and across the valley there was another loud rumble. Out on the parade ground there were more shouts and screams, and the light deepened still farther. Here in the dispensary it was almost like night now; and above the smell of the drugs and medicines there was now the smell of the volcano. "You need me, Narvo—at least till we get out of this. *If* we get out."

He was not afraid, neither of the volcano nor of Narvo. All at once Prague had become remote again; he would never go home now. The UN committee would not come in here, and the Czech member would forget all about him. He was gripped by a resignation that allowed him to stand his ground and talk to Narvo as if he were the one who held all the cards.

He didn't hold all the cards, and Narvo knew it. He let Traxal go and stepped back. "If we get out of here, it will be either Jack Bermingham or myself who'll get you out. None of the others will be able to do it. We need you—but you need me more!"

"I don't need you at all," Traxal said, and his utter resignation was suddenly apparent to the others: they were the ones with hope and they were the ones to be afraid. "It is Elisabeth and the others who need you." He looked at Elisabeth, hardly able to see her in the gloom. "I told you you had made a mistake coming here to Kundavi, Elisabeth."

"I made my mistake five years ago," she said bitterly. "When I said good-by to you in Prague and believed your promises."

She turned and went out of the dispensary. Narvo remained staring at Traxal. "You've come down to the level of the kanakas you despise, Peter. With them it's every man for himself—and I don't blame them. It's their only way of surviving most of the time. But part of being a white is that we should all help each other. Isn't that supposed to be part of being a Christian?"

"You had better ask Mike Shawn. He is the representative of Christianity on this post."

"You blow with the wind, don't you? If the UN party were to come in here tomorrow with that Czech in it, you'd suddenly be a Communist."

Traxal shook his head, looking almost amused. He unscrewed the cap of the waterbag he held and reached up and began to pour the water back into the larger bag. The surrender was as insolent as if he had poured it on the ground; he was pouring it back because he wanted to, not because Narvo had ordered him to. "I am an egoist, Roy. It is my way of surviving. There are more of us in the world than you would suppose. You have been too long in these mountains. Your ideals are out of date."

Narvo clenched his fist, but he kept it at his side. "Touch that water other than to give it to your patients, and I'll kill you! A lot of people must have died this morning and one more won't be noticed."

"Patrol officer kills medical officer—that would look good in a UN report."

"The UN will never know of it," said Narvo. "You're the only informer on this post and you'll be dead." He turned on his heel and went out onto the veranda. He yelled for police boys and a moment later returned with two of them. He gave them orders in police Motu, then looked at Traxal. "I haven't told them about you—I don't want us whites to lose face. But I've told them to bayonet anyone who tries to take water from the bags without my express permission. And they understand that means every-one. Including you."

2

"What do they say?" Father Shawn had gone back to the mission, dressed and had returned to the post. He had packed his few belongings into two old suitcases and two mission boys had brought them down to the parade ground for him. His altar stone, chalice, paten and pyx were in the small canvas bag slung over his shoulder. He had debated whether to pack his altar garments and in the end decided against it; they were so old and worn that if he escaped to the outside world he would be ashamed to appear at Mass in them. A ragamuffin priest would not be tolerated in Goroka or Moresby: the blacks up at the mission had not been so fastidious. If he could not come back to Kundavi and he were sent elsewhere, the missions' home office would have to supply him with new garments. *Oh Lord, forgive my chicanery,* he prayed, and felt like a defrauder of divine social welfare.

"Did you get on to Goroka?" he said.

He met Narvo and Rossi as they came out of the latter's hut. Both officers were now fully dressed and Father Shawn noticed that both of them had strapped on holster belts and carried pistols.

"Neil Figgins is coming in in the Cessna to see how much country has gone under," Narvo said. "They took off twenty minutes ago. We can't do much till we hear again from him."

"The vulcanologist is in the plane, too," said Rossi. "He'll give us word if there's likely to be another eruption."

Father Shawn cocked an eyebrow at the mountain. "And if there is, what do we do?"

Narvo grinned, feeling far from happy. "Then we'd better wait on word from your Bloke. We'll probably need Him."

The parade ground was now full of natives. They were sitting or standing quietly, but there was an undercurrent of fear that one could feel; they were on the crumbling edge of panic and it would take very little to send them tumbling over. The smoke from the volcano had lifted now, swung away to the east by a wind; the morning light was still yellow and dull, but there was now no dusk. With the coming of the wind from the west, ash had stopped falling on Kundavi; nevertheless a thin covering of it lay all over the post. The ash was lighter in color than Narvo had expected; it had seemed gray in the first gloomy light, but now it looked almost creamy. No rocks or embers had been flung to this side of the valley, and the ash lay on everything like a deadly snow. Despite the wind the stench of the volcano came across the valley: it was frightening as well as sickening, the smell of hell itself. There was a continuous rumbling and cracking from the mountain, but it seemed now to have settled down to a steady, if sinister, boiling over.

Then they saw the plane. It was coming in from the north-east, skirting the boiling cloud of smoke and dust, a tiny thing that seemed to be flying to its doom, a moth unable to resist the biggest flame it had ever seen. The entire population of the post stood up and watched silently and tensely as the Cessna, bucking fiercely, again and again swept off its course by the drafts coming up from the crater, edged its way in over the mountain. It seemed to be exactly over the crater when suddenly it plummeted down. Up on the slope outside her house Bernice screamed, and Narvo turned quickly, not looking at her but at the crowd of natives, searching for the panic and hysteria he feared so much. But the crowd of natives remained transfixed, still staring across the valley, and when he turned back he saw that the plane had climbed again and was once more circling the mountain. It made one more run in over the crater, then it climbed, turned and came across the valley toward the post. It flew low over the parade ground and the natives let out a yell, a cry that was a mixture of admiration, relief and a plea for help. It turned as it climbed the slope of the mountain behind the post, then came back in another low run. A cabin window opened, an arm appeared and a small bag was hurled out. The plane went on down the valley and a moment later one of the police boys brought the small mailbag to Narvo.

It contained a note written with a ballpoint pen. The writing was almost illegible, as if the writer had had difficulty in keeping the sheet of paper steady while he wrote: *We don't think the mountain will blow up again. At least it won't blow another crater. This is an unusual type of eruption—it has erupted horizontally, just like the Mt. Lamington show. The country for more than fifty miles to the east is completely wiped out. I think you are safe if you stay where you are. Stand by your radio. Good luck. Figgins.*

"Good luck," said Bermingham, reading over Narvo's shoulder. "That's a bloody lotta help."

Narvo was now surrounded by all the whites, and the natives had pressed in behind. He read the note aloud in English, then in dialect. Continuing in dialect he told the natives to settle down and wait. There were murmurs from the crowd and no one moved. Narvo gazed out over them, then he stepped through the ring of whites, moving Duggan aside without apology, and the nearest natives pressed back away from him.

"Mountain people!" he roared. "Where is your courage? No one here has died yet—why do you wait for death with so little hope of living? Are you afflicted with *kuru?*" There was another murmur from the crowd: it was impossible to tell whether it was fear or anger. But Narvo had gone too far now: he could not back down. He had to shame these people into being patient, he had to make them utterly dependent on him. If the mountain did erupt again, it would not matter. There would be no pay-back on himself, because they would all be dead. "I promise you again—no mountain man, woman or child shall die ahead of myself! Sit down, be patient and wait. We shall all get out of here alive!"

For a moment he thought he had lost the battle. He saw two of the old men say something to those about them, and for a moment that segment of the crowd hesitated. But the majority of the crowd had broken up, turning away to go back up the parade ground and sit down, and slowly the whole throng turned away. The two old men were last to go, but Narvo, without moving toward them, stared at them and their gaze broke under his. Without a word to each other they moved off and were lost in the crowd.

"They're going to be hard to hold," Narvo said, his back still to the whites. "They're on the point of running now."

"So am I," said Bernice, disregarding Macy's waving of his hand for her to be quiet. She had control of herself now but she was still frightened and she wanted to be gone from here as soon as possible. She had packed their things and six suitcases stood up on the veranda of their house; it was typical of her that she had not given a thought as to how so much luggage would be taken out from here. When the plane had flown so low over the post she had almost cried out in furious frustration at seeing a means of salvation so close and yet so unattainable. For a moment she had hated Neil Figgins for his safety. "Roy, you've got to do something!"

"He will do something, darling." Macy was torn between the gladness that she had come back, and the wish that she had stayed in Goroka, where at least she would have been safe. He was not frightened for himself and he was surprised at that: he had never imagined himself a hero nor had much confidence in his courage. But he was frightened for Bernice and Harry, and he knew that if it came to it, he would sacrifice everyone else to save the two of them.

"I can't do anything till we hear from Goroka," Narvo said.

"What help do you think they will be?" Bermingham said. "He's just wished us good luck. That doesn't sound very bloody helpful."

"You said that," said Duggan tartly. "There's no need to keep repeating yourself. Especially your swearing."

"You'll be swearing yourself if we're stuck here too long," said Bermingham, and for once also sounded tart and worried.

"Righto, break it up," Narvo said, irritably but with authority. "If we start bickering with each other, that, too, will soon get through to the kanakas." He looked out over the crowd, now filling the parade ground, then across the valley at the volcano. "We can't stay here indefinitely. The vulcanologist may be right about the mountain not going up again, but I doubt if I'll be able to convince the kanakas of that. We can't get planes in, now the strip has gone——"

"What about helicopters?" Elisabeth said.

"No helicopters could get into this valley even before the mountain blew up. The winds are too strong, there are too many up

and down drafts. We'll wait on word from Neil Figgins. But . . ."
He turned away from the volcano and looked at all of them.
"Whatever they say in Goroka, I think it'll be up to ourselves
to get us out of here. And I don't see any other way but to
walk."

Then there was a disturbance in the crowd on the parade
ground. Narvo, sensitive to any change in the mood of the hundreds of natives, turned quickly. Sergeant Beraki and a police
boy were coming through the crowd, all of whom were on their
feet now. The two police boys were leading a native, but in
the crush of the curious crowd it was impossible for Narvo to
see who the third man was. Even when Beraki came through
the last line of natives and pushed the man up to Narvo, the
latter did not recognize him. He was coated in thick ash, but
even beneath the ash it was possible to see that his face and
shoulders and arms had been badly burned. He carried a blackpalm bow, but it was useless: the string hung as gray wisps of
ash from either end of it. He had lost his arrows and spear, and
the belt that carried his stone ax hung only by a thread. The
bamboo knife in the belt was just a charred piece of wood; and
Narvo wondered how it could have been burnt as it was and
yet the man himself survive. The cassowary bone in the man's
nose, turned upwards in the sign of war, was coated with pieces
of skin from his burned face.

"It's Paiwo!" Harry said, and the women gasped. Bernice and
Elisabeth turned away, sickened by the man's appearance, but
Duggan moved forward.

Beraki spoke sharply in police Motu. "Careful, Sister Duggan!
He was coming here to kill the Kiap."

"Who told you that?" Narvo said.

"He told us himself, Kiap. He was crazy when we found him
down on the path above the bridge. He had dropped his knife
and he was looking for it under a red-hot rock." Only then did
Narvo notice that Paiwo's hands, too, were badly burned. The

man must have been in intense pain, yet there was no murmur from him. "He has quietened down now, but he was crazy then. I should be careful, Kiap."

Narvo put out a gentle hand and took the bow and the ax from Paiwo. The Vaikaka stood as if dazed, his head bent, shivering a little but with no sound coming from him. "You'd better look after him, Peter."

Traxal looked at Paiwo, then at Narvo. But he said nothing: he would never understand this man Narvo. He was neither a sadistic man or, when it came to treating patients, a completely callous one; but all his life he had made decisions only after weighing one thing against another. In this situation the life of a native murdered did not, he thought, add up to much. He nodded to Duggan and each of them took Paiwo by the arm and led him away.

"You're gonna have to watch him, Roy, my word you are," said Bermingham.

"No more than I'm going to have to watch the others," Narvo said. "There's four hundred kanakas there, every one of whom will kill me—and you, too—if we put a foot wrong. They are depending on me to get them out of here. And they're not going to make any allowances for mistakes. There are one or two old blokes in there who might try blaming me for the mountain going up. No," he said, "Paiwo is the least of my troubles right now."

Rossi had gone back to the hut and now he came to the door and called to Narvo. "I've got Goroka on the air, Roy! Neil Figgins should be back any minute now."

All the whites followed Narvo down to the hut. The natives, knowing that something was happening, began to move down again from the parade ground. They came down in a solid black mass and for a moment it looked as if they might push Rossi's hut and the House Paper right off the end of the plateau into the gorge. But Beraki yelled an order and the police boys formed a line to hold back the crowd with drawn bayonets. Over in the stockade the prisoners had begun to yell and scream, but no one took any notice of them. All eyes were on Narvo, seen through the open door of Rossi's hut sitting at the transceiver.

It was ten minutes before Figgins came on the air. The static was bad, but the gist of his message was clear: the situation was bad and Kundavi was still in real danger.

"If it's up to me, Neil," Narvo said, "I want to bring everyone out. The kanakas are scared stiff—the situation on this side of the valley is just as explosive as over on the mountain. If they panic, we'll all be goners—themselves as well as us whites. Over."

Figgins's voice came into the room, faint and broken with static, like a man choking: "Which way will you come out? The straightest route, the usual patrol track, lies right through the country that got the worst of the blast. And you'll be in direct line if there should be another eruption out of the same crater. Over."

"That's the way we'll have to come," Narvo said, and behind him he heard Bernice gasp and Macy say something to her. He looked up at Bermingham and the latter nodded. As if reassured by the opinion of the only other man on the post with his experience, he leaned back toward the microphone: "There are only two other ways out, Neil. One is out through the swamp country up around Wabut and the other is straight over the mountains to the south. Both trips would take weeks and I wouldn't guarantee to get even half this mob out. I've got a lot of old people and kids on this post. And I don't know that the women here, the white ones, could stand up to the hike. I've been over both tracks and they're pretty bloody. Over."

There was only static for a few moments, as if Figgins was thinking. At last his voice came through: "I can't make the decision for you, Roy. It is no use sending anyone in from here—it wouldn't help much and it only means endangering more lives. We'll come out to meet you, but that's the best we can do. Can we have anything dropped to you? Over."

Narvo told Figgins what they would need. "And Neil . . ." He hesitated, looking around at the others: the room was silent but for the crackle of static and the rumbling across the valley. "Neil, don't send anyone in to meet us. We're all right and we can make it on our own. The mountain *could* go up again. What are the casualties so far? Over."

"We can only guess," Figgins said. "So far we think anything up to a thousand people could have died. Even if you wanted it, Roy, we couldn't send in more than a small party. As we flew back to Goroka, we could see the first of the survivors beginning to come out. We're going to be swamped here. Come on the air again just before you move out. Carry the transceiver with you, and we'll be listening right round the clock. Good luck, Roy—and the same to the others. Over and out."

"Good luck," said Bernice. "That seems to be about the extent of his help!"

Narvo switched off the transceiver and stood up. "He's well aware that he can be of little bloody help to us, Bernice! I know Neil too well—he won't sleep till we're out of here. And if we don't get out of here, he'll blame himself, whether it's his fault or not, but just because we happen to be in his district and he feels we are his responsibility. Don't start picking on Neil. Get out of that whining frame of mind and those bloody silly high-heeled shoes and start standing on your own two feet!" Then he abruptly slumped, leaning against the table. He was silent for a moment, head bent, then he looked up. "I'm sorry, Bernice. Tell her I didn't mean it, Eric."

Macy stood with his arm about Bernice's shoulders. "I think she knows that, Roy. Like Jack said a while ago, you're the boss. That goes for Harry, me and Bernice. Don't it, darl?"

She looked up at him, biting her lips, tears at the corners of her eyes, then she looked across at Narvo and nodded. "I'm sorry, Roy. And I promised to be tolerant, didn't I?"

Narvo's face was wooden, as if his thoughts were a long way

off; then abruptly he grinned and straightened up. "All right, we start moving out right away. You'd all better get ready. Just the clothes you stand up in and a sweater or something to put on at night. Leave everything behind that isn't absolutely necessary."

"Roy," Harry said, then hesitated for a moment: "Roy, can I bring the cassowary?"

Narvo looked at Macy, then he grinned at Harry. "He'll have to share your rations."

"I won't mind. He don't eat much anyway."

Elisabeth was the last to leave the hut. She waited at the door till the others had gone, then she said, "Roy, perhaps I should have told you about Peter earlier. I mean about what he was going to tell the UN committee. I've known for some days now."

He put his hand on her elbow and smiled down at her, wearily but with affection and kindness. "It doesn't matter now, Elisabeth, one way or the other. I don't blame you. You owed me nothing——"

"I owe you a lot," she said.

There was another loud crack from across the valley, and a gasp of fear from the natives out on the parade ground. "For letting you stay here perhaps to be incinerated?" he said.

"No," she said. "For reminding me that decency still exists in the world. You are a decent man, Roy."

"That's all I ever wanted to be," he said. "It wasn't much of an ambition."

"It was a good ambition," she said. "And a more difficult one than you make it sound."

There was another crack, followed by a loud rumble. Narvo pressed her elbow. "We'd better chuff off out of this."

"Do you think we shall get through safely, Roy?"

"I shan't lie, Elisabeth—I really don't know. I'm just hoping, that's all. Are you frightened?"

She nodded. "Very. But I am like you—I still hope."

He bent and kissed her cheek, and when she looked surprised, he said, "That's the second time in two days I've kissed a woman. Only this time I'm not being tolerant."

"Why did you kiss me, Roy?"

"Because I'm just glad I met you. Remember that, if anything happens. I'm glad you left Prague and came all the way out here so that I could know you in Kundavi. I would not have wanted to meet you anywhere else."

Then before she could reply, he took her arm and they went out of the hut together. As he left her and walked through the crowd of natives toward the hospital, Narvo felt a sympathy for and a bond with her that he had never felt for any other woman. *It is just my luck*, he thought, *to find the right woman at the wrong time.* He looked across the valley at the mountain still belching smoke and fire and molten rock, and cursed it aloud. Some of the natives looked at him inquiringly, but he shook his head at them and went up the steps into the hospital. He was the Kiap and he was not supposed to have troubles.

Duggan was finishing dressing Paiwo's face, and Traxal was washing his hands in a small basin. He gestured at the basin and said coolly, almost insolently, "It is not drinking water."

Narvo ignored him and looked at Duggan. "How's Paiwo?"

"A very sick man," she said, and it was impossible to tell whether she felt sympathy for the native or not. "He will need careful nursing."

Paiwo lay without moving on the bed. His eyes, skinned and without lashes, stared out at Narvo from a slit in the dressing that covered his face; his gaze was so rigid he could have been blind or even dead. The cassowary bone had been taken from his nose and now lay on the small table beside the bed, beside the stone ax and the charred bamboo knife. Somehow the removal of the bone from his nose had disarmed him more than the taking away of his bow and ax and knife: it was as if a knight had been stripped of his armor. He was defenseless, at the Kiap's mercy, and the thought hurt more than his burns.

"How many patients have you, counting him?" Narvo said.

"Twenty-two," Duggan said, without having to stop to check: she knew every fact, every figure in the register of her hospital. "Why?"

"I'll get you carriers. We move out of here on our way to Goroka within the next half hour."

Both Traxal and Duggan straightened up. The cake of soap shot from Traxal's hands and landed with a thud on the floor; he did not seem to notice that he had dropped it. "There are people here who can't be moved! The *kuru* patients, for instance——"

"So long as they're still alive, they'll have to be moved," Narvo said. "I'm taking everyone out of here. Every one."

"But the *kuru* patients—four of them are certain to die, anyway." Traxal was drying his hands now. It was an unfortunate thing for him to be doing at that moment; Narvo, watching him, had the feeling he was washing his hands of the *kuru* patients. "Duggan and Eric and I will have our hands full looking after the others. Some of them may not last the journey. This man, for instance—" He nodded at Paiwo.

"Are you suggesting we should leave some behind, those that are bound to die anyway?" Narvo turned to Duggan. "What do you reckon, Duggan? If there were no doctor here, would you leave them behind?"

Duggan had methodically begun to clean up after her. If she was going to leave here, she was going to leave a clean hospital behind her: one never knew, she might be coming back here in a month or two. A native nurse had come into the room to help her, but with an abrupt gesture Duggan dismissed her. She had her back to both men; her face was hidden by the angular white blankness of her veil. *This is where she has her pay-back,* Narvo thought; *all her time here she has hated me and now she is going to side with him.* Yet he knew he couldn't abandon the dying *kuru* patients in the ward next door. Even while he waited for Duggan to make her decision, there was a pitiful giggle from behind the cane wall, a sound that was like a despairing and hopeless appeal for help.

Then Duggan, her hands full of dressings and instruments, turned around. "I've never yet given up on a patient who still had breath in him. Even if these ones are going to die, I don't think they should be buried under ashes." And avoiding the eyes of both men, she went out of the room, leaving a silence behind her that was broken only by another giggle from behind the cane wall and the vicious threatening sounds from across the valley.

"She is not in charge of this hospital," Traxal said.

"The hospital is part of the post, and I'm in charge of the post," said Narvo. "Just as I said, we take *everyone.*"

He went out of the room, aware of Traxal staring with hatred after him, aware too of the eyes of Paiwo that had suddenly come alive behind the mask of gauze.

15

THE VOLCANO was still cracking and rumbling, blowing out smoke, dust and rocks, when the trek began half an hour later. Lava was now welling out of the crater in a great creeping wave; where Vaikaka had stood there was now only a red-gray mass of smoking living earth. The wind still came from the west, blowing the smoke and dust away in a cloud that went diagonally up the sky. The sun had now climbed till it was above the cloud, a sullen red eye that added to the threat of further disaster. Kundavi was in bright sunshine, beyond the angle of the shadow cast by the cloud, but the country through which the party had to pass was darkened as by a storm. The stench of the crater still hung over the valley, and occasionally as the wind lapsed for a moment there would be a light rain of ashes falling on Kundavi.

Bermingham and Rossi led the way down into the gorges. With them went Mary Bermingham and the children, the Macys, with Harry leading the cassowary, and Traxal. Narvo brought up the rear and with him were Elisabeth, Father Shawn, Duggan and Sergeant Beraki. Immediately in front of them were the prisoners from the stockade carrying the patients from the hospital, among whom were the *kuru* patients and Paiwo. Between

306

the whites at the rear and those in front stretched a long line of frightened natives, over four hundred of them.

Narvo stopped at the top of the path that led down into the gorge and looked back at the patrol post. In the bright sunlight it looked as spick and span as ever, except for the snow of ash that lay over everything. But no one moved across the parade ground nor between the lines of huts; there was no singing from houseboys hanging out the washing nor from old women chopping the grass; no police boys stood beneath the flagpole nor did the pole carry a flag. No one might move nor sing nor chop the grass nor raise the flag ever again in Kundavi. He had built it out of the wilderness and the wilderness might take it back. Three years of his life had gone into this post and all he had to show for it were the lines on his face and the brittle respect and loyalty of the natives now filing ahead of him down into the gorges and their possible death.

"Breaks your heart, doesn't it?" said Father Shawn.

"It may survive, Roy," said Elisabeth. "You may come back here."

He shook his head. "Kundavi is finished. The airstrip gone, the land route in here—God knows what's happened to that. We'll find out soon enough. No, if they ever open up another post in this area, it won't be at Kundavi. We'll have to find another spot where they can put a plane down. You'd better say good-by to Kundavi, Mike."

Father Shawn nodded, took one last long look around the post, looked up the road toward the mission, blessed himself and turned quickly and went down the path into the gorge.

"He's just said good-by to his last chance of being a saint," said Narvo, and didn't attempt to explain to Elisabeth what he knew of Father Shawn's ambition.

They began to walk down the path together. Below them the natives had begun to sing, a soft mournful chant that came up out of the gorge like a lament from the grave. The words, unintelligible to Elisabeth, floated up past them, up over the silent and deserted post and the mission, to die against the tangled slope of the mountain against which Kundavi was built. It was singing that had no echoes.

"At least the UN committee won't come in here now," Elisabeth said.

That was true, but he felt no comfort in the thought. He was still sickened by the knowledge of Traxal's intended betrayal of him; that affected him more than the thought of the report that would have finished him. He was not naïvely idealistic, despite Traxal's sarcastic reference to his being out of date, and he knew that treachery could sometimes be as common as loyalty. He had read enough of history to know that treachery was one of the gears that kept it moving; he had seen enough of it here in these mountains to know that it could also be a means of survival. Self-interest, which could be another manifestation of treachery, had been claimed by Traxal as his means of survival. But like all men to whom loyalty was a habit, a way of thought as ineradicable as belief in birth and death, he could not accept the ultimate cowardice, the sacrifice of others by a man to save himself. He was not afraid of Traxal, but sickened by him. And he had forgotten the UN committee.

Because now the United Nations and its policies, its Trustee Council and its committees, meant nothing in the disaster that had overwhelmed Kundavi. He believed in the idea of the United Nations, but he had long ago become pessimistic that it could ever achieve its aim. It suffered from the handicap that saddled all idealistic aims when two or more people subscribed to that aim: the clash of human natures. Perfection was not possible in one man because of his nature. When man met with man, the defects multiplied: nations and organizations of nations stood even less chance of perfection. But whatever he thought of the United Nations or whatever its Trustee Committee had intended to do, none of it mattered now.

All the ideals, the arguments, the words of the delegates in New York, the ones who depended upon men like himself to carry out their policies but ruthlessly got rid of those same men if practical considerations proved those policies unworkable, all the ideals and arguments meant nothing now to the natives singing their way down into the gorges and the dead country beyond. There was only one man who counted now and that was the Kiap, Roy Narvo. He felt no honor but only a great burden of responsibility.

"It's a pity," he said. "Perhaps those committee members would learn a thing or two on the walk out from here with us."

The long line of refugees stretched down the twisting path into the gorge. They were walking in single file and the line was long enough; but it seemed to grow longer the farther it went down into the gorge. Then Narvo saw the other lines of natives coming down the steep slopes to join the Kundavi line halfway down the gorge.

"Oh, Christ," Narvo said, and Father Shawn stopped and looked back. "I'm not swearing, Mike. Maybe I'm asking for help. Look!"

Father Shawn looked down the gorge, then along it where it cut below the slope of the southern ranges. For perhaps two or three miles on this side of the river the ranges were covered only with a fine ash: then they turned sharply northeast and that was where they showed the full effect of the blast. The northern side of the river had got the full force of the eruption, and it would be a miracle if anyone had survived there. But here on the southern side of the river, east of Kundavi, people were still alive and now they were coming down to join the march out to safety.

"There must be a couple of thousand of them!" Father Shawn exclaimed, and looked back up the path at Narvo. "What are you going to do, Roy? How are you going to feed them? How are you going to stop them from drinking the water on the way out?"

"Here's your chance to be a saint, Mike," said Narvo, not unkindly, still staring down along the gorge. "If your prayers are answered—just ask Him for help of any sort—I'll personally recommend you for canonization."

"If He answers my prayers on this one, I shan't worry about sainthood. Seeing those people get out alive will be enough reward."

And that's the remark of a true saint, thought Narvo; and knew that Father Shawn didn't realize it. "Chuff off ahead, will you, Mike, and see they get the word they're not to touch the river or any springs for drinking water. Tell Frank he'd better drop halfway back along the line just to keep an eye on them. Jack can continue leading the way."

The natives from the mountain villages were still coming down into the gorge as Narvo and Elisabeth reached the spot where the newcomers were joining the trek. Duggan was waiting there with the hospital patients and their prisoner carriers.

"Any burn cases among this new lot?" Narvo asked.

"None that I can see." Duggan had posted herself where she could inspect every newcomer as he went past her. Each of the natives smiled at her as he passed by, but Duggan was not wearing out her face muscles in reply: she had never learned the trick of the official smile that could be worn without effort. Occasionally she nodded to a native she recognized, but she could have been the stern matron of a large school inspecting her pupils for measles. "They haven't brought much food with them, Roy. And no water at all."

"Then that's what Goroka has got to send us right away."

Narvo turned to call Beraki. But the sergeant was already standing right beside him; and Narvo felt a glow of affection for the proud smug police boy. *I don't have to worry about you, son,* he thought; and knew that if they had to die, Beraki would die right beside him. This man's loyalty was not brittle, nor was there any treachery in him. He was arrogant and vain, but he was loyal. "Beraki, get up to Mr. Rossi and tell him to radio in to Goroka. We want water dropped from the airplane to us. As much as they can send. Quick!"

Beraki stepped back, snapped a salute and was gone at a swift run down the path, yelling at the natives to make way for him, that he was carrying a message for the Kiap and he would hurl anyone into the river who did not let him past.

"He would have made a wonderful storm trooper," Duggan said.

"Don't talk like that about him!" Narvo's anger was so evident that Duggan at once backed down.

"I'm sorry, Roy. I apologize."

It was the first time she had ever apologized to him for anything, and later the irony of it struck him, that she should have to apologize for a remark she had made about a black.

"I wish there were more like him, because we are going to need him on the way out of here." The anger had gone out of his voice: he recognized the surrender of Duggan's apology. Then, to let her know the matter was already forgotten, he said in as gentle a manner as he could, "I don't know how much water we'll get. They'll have to parachute it down, otherwise the containers will burst. And I don't know how many containers they'll have."

"Perhaps we could ask Mike Shawn to pray for a miracle with a waterbag."

"We don't want to wear out our welcome," Narvo said. "We may need Him more desperately later on."

The natives were still coming down the steep slope into the gorge. Narvo turned and looked back up at the volcano. It was still coughing up molten rock, and the lava flow was well down the mountainside now. Ash and pumice dust were floating down into the gorge, coating everyone thickly. As the natives filed farther down into the gorge, into the mist above the river, the ash and dust turned to a fine gray mud: to Elisabeth they looked like a long line of people wearing mourning mud for themselves as they walked into death. The wind had dropped and the smoke and dust from the crater was spreading, turning the gorge into a chasm of gloom. The roar of the river now drowned out the crack and rumble of the volcano, but occasionally the earth would shudder. The long line of natives would suddenly break up and scatter as rocks and slices of earth slid down across the path. Miraculously no one had yet been hit or swept away by the plunging rocks.

"You'd better go on ahead," Narvo said to Elisabeth. "I'll stay here with Duggan till the last of these kanakas come down."

"No," she said, and like so many Europeans, with none of the closed-faced embarrassment of Australians, looked up at him with frank regard and affection. If she was in love with him at that moment, she did not query it: now was not the time for giving her heart but only her loyalty. She had begun to recognize how much this man depended upon and was sustained by loyalty. "I'd rather stay with you."

Even though he knew Duggan was watching them closely, he put out his hand and took Elisabeth's. "You're going to stay with me till the end of this trek." Then he looked at Duggan and grinned. "I'm no longer against women, Duggan."

"Did it take a volcano to bring that about?" said Duggan, then smiled at Elisabeth, the dust coating her teeth but not diminishing the warmth of her smile. "You could do worse, Elisabeth. I've never admitted it before, but he's not a bad bloke."

Then at last no more natives were coming down from the slopes into the gorge. The prisoners picked up the patients and began to move on. Narvo stood beside the stretcher on which Paiwo lay. He looked like a mummified corpse; as the carriers lifted him, the ash cracked and slid off him like a shroud of dust. He was lying with his eyes closed, but he opened them as Narvo stood over him. Narvo leaned down and gently brushed the ash away, but there was no spark from the dark eyes.

The burial party that had come to pick up Bandi and Narvo's house-monkey was somewhere farther along the gorge, but it had not brought the bodies with it. The corpses had been left in a hut in the native quarters; they would rot there or be buried beneath ash, but they would never go back to the mountain across the valley. They would forever be separated from their ancestors by the gorges where the winds blew like souls writhing at the gates of eternity, caught between time and no-time. Bandi had suffered the ultimate abandonment, but Narvo could not bring himself to tell Paiwo. He could only hope that Paiwo would never learn of it.

"I am glad that you came back, Paiwo," he said in dialect. "Perhaps we can still live together in peace."

Paiwo closed his eyes again and there was no sign that he had even heard Narvo.

2

Up at the head of the long column, now almost two miles ahead of Narvo, Bermingham said, "I don't like the look of that up there."

Traxal, who had been walking with his head bent, looked up. Ahead of them the gorge widened out slightly. The trail, hidden beneath ash and pumice dust but marked by the ash-blooming bushes that grew alongside it, ran along the southern side of the river. Two hundred yards ahead the river turned sharply north, and on the opposite side of the river from the trail a sheer cliff rose hundreds of feet up the side of the mountain. The top of the cliff seemed to be smoking and, even as Traxal watched, what looked like a section of it fell off. It dropped like a meteor, smoke streaming behind it, and hit the river in a fountain of steam.

"It's lava!" Macy exclaimed, horrified. "How the hell did that get so far so quickly?"

"I dunno." Bermingham had stopped, and gradually the long line behind him slowed, then came to a halt. The natives had been singing softly, the sound only a faint murmur against the roar of the river, but now the singing died away. The long dark file, strung along the bottom of the gorge like an immense snake, stood and watched the lava come over the edge of the cliff, a border of red bushes whose flowers fell even as they bloomed. "Unless there is another crater in the mountain farther down. Neil might have missed it because of the smoke. Anyhow, I don't like the look of it, my word I don't."

The lava now rimmed the entire top of the cliff. It glowed against the dark cloud that covered the sky, an aurora of death. Sections of it were falling off and coming down in plumes of smoke to hit the river and disappear in explosions of steam.

"What are we going to do?" Bernice almost screamed. "We can't stay here!"

"We can't turn back, either," said Macy, and looked at Bermingham. "We can get through, Jack, but what about the others at the back?"

The natives were moving restlessly, edging forward along the trail, then pulling back, wanting to go on but afraid to. Harry had buried the cassowary's head against his chest and was stroking it and talking to it, but the bird was trembling and would have fled if Harry had not been holding it so tightly. Mary Bermingham had the younger child in a net bag slung from her head and carried on her back; the trek, the baby in her belly and fear had taken their toll of her and she looked on the point of collapse. Bermingham was carrying the older child on his shoulders, and for some time he had been looking anxiously at his wife. He had waited for one of the whites to offer to take the younger child from Mary, but none of them had and he was burning with anger at them.

"I think you all better go on," he said. "I'll stay here with Mary and we'll hurry the kanakas along. We gotta keep in mind that Roy and the others are right at the end of this string."

"I'll stay," Traxal said suddenly. "They need you to show them the way, Jack."

Bermingham was surprised, but he did not argue. The lava was now falling steadily over the cliff. Steam was rising from the river, thickening the mist till the cliff itself was slowly being obscured. It would not be long before the river was boiling, before it overflowed as it was dammed up by the falling lava. There was no time to argue with Traxal, nor to ponder his reason for volunteering. Bermingham, after a life of danger, misfortune and sometimes miraculous good luck, took things as they came. It was his means of survival, although it was a question he had never discussed with Traxal. Come to think of it now, he had never discussed anything with Traxal. If Traxal stayed here and were to die, Bermingham knew he would have trouble later in remembering the man. He felt a spasm of loss, of something not achieved: men were meant to remember each other. But this was not the time to seek a memento of Traxal. A large chunk of lava fell with a loud hiss into the river.

"Righto," Bermingham said. "Keep 'em moving quick. Don't forget that Roy's the last man in this line."

"I shan't forget," said Traxal, flat-voiced.

Then Macy all at once let go of Bernice, whom he had been helping along the rougher sections of the trail, and stepped up to Mary and took the child from the net bag on her back. Then he looked at Bernice. "I think Mary could do with some help, darl. She's just about done in."

Bernice hesitated, and Bermingham waited for her to refuse. Then she moved forward and took Mary by the arm. The little native woman leaned shyly away, looking at her husband for reassurance. Bermingham made no attempt to blink away the moisture he felt in his one good eye. He just nodded at both women, reassuring one and thanking the other, then he turned and led the way along the trail past the thickening cauldron of steam.

Traxal watched them go, wondering why he had volunteered to stay here. It had been an involuntary gesture, the words out of his mouth before he had realized what he was saying. Was it an unconscious desire to expiate his intended treachery on these people? Or was he waiting to see the death of Narvo, even if he died himself in the act of watching? But there was no time to wonder about it now. The natives were going by him at a steady shambling run, old people helped by the young, children caught up and carried like so many black sacks. He yelled at them to hurry, his voice only a thin bleat against the roar of the river and the hiss of the lava as it plunged into the water.

The cliff now was hidden as if behind a red smoking waterfall. Lava fell steadily and the gorge was just a deep basin of whirling clouds of steam through which the falling lava glowed. The natives went stumbling past, some of them muttering but most of them in silence, and disappeared into the steam that enveloped them like a giant swirling curtain. The mist of steam spread slowly along the gorge, and with it came the smell of the lava, pungent and sickening and frightening. The steam came creeping up on Traxal, warm and clammy, and moved on past him. All he could see now were the natives who passed immediately in front of him. They were holding hands, each man following the man in front of him, running blindly into the mist: they went past like dark figures in a dream, suspended between living and dying, unable to know what lay ahead of them but afraid to turn back. The mist of steam glowed pinkly as the lava continued to fall: it came down like falling strips of fire behind a window of frosted glass. And the hissing now seemed almost as loud as the roar of the tumbling water.

Traxal stood there, the ash and dust on him turning to watery mud and his clothes becoming drenched, and lost all sense of time. There was something Walpurgian about the scene: he would not have been startled if witches had appeared. The natives came and went in the mist of the stream, none distinguishable from another, dark, faceless wraiths running, for all he knew, in a circle; and gradually the steam itself grew warmer, thickening till it was almost like spray, and the gorge filled with heat. There was a scream from somewhere up ahead and the line of running natives faltered momentarily; then the running line went on and Traxal stayed where he was, knowing there was nothing he could do. If someone had missed his step and plunged into the river, he was already dead, boiled alive.

Then Rossi and Father Shawn and Sergeant Beraki came up, and a moment later the first of the patients was carried by. The two white men and the police sergeant stepped off the path and stood by Traxal. No one said a word till the last of the patients had disappeared into the mist, and Narvo, Elisabeth and Duggan had come up.

The heat in the gorge now was intense. The cliff beyond the swirl of steam was just a red glow; it was as if they stood across the river from the open doors of a huge furnace. The very air, thick with steam, seemed to be boiling; as they breathed, it scalded their lungs and made them gasp. The roar of the river had disappeared now; there was only the hissing, and a crackling and popping sound as the lava fell. The burning smell was almost as overpowering as a gas.

Narvo took Elisabeth's hand, and the others fell into place behind. Traxal found himself at the rear, but there was no resentment: he was resigned to dying now and it did not matter whether one died first or last in the line. Then he saw Sergeant Beraki fall in behind him. Without hesitation he put out his hand, the first he had ever offered to a black man, and Beraki took it. Then the human chain began to move forward.

It moved slowly because the trail had now disappeared. They

walked into the steam, Narvo feeling his way with the long stick he carried. Traxal had once seen children from an orphanage for the blind walking in the same shuffling crocodile; but they had been chattering and laughing, walking with blind confidence in their leader. There was no chattering or laughing here in this white-filled gorge; the Kundavi crocodile edged its way along in a silence of fear. The river at times sounded right below their feet, as if they were walking along the very edge of the bank; once Traxal flinched as hot water splashed on him, and behind him Beraki uttered a short gasp of pain. Then Traxal felt the hot water seeping into his boots and for a moment he thought he had stepped off into the river. He cried out in Czech, but he would never know whether he had cursed or prayed or shouted just an animal cry of despair.

Then he felt Father Shawn in front of him jerk him abruptly to the right. He slipped in the mud of ash and pumice dust; and his wet and slippery hand almost lost its hold on the priest's. Behind him Beraki, barefooted in the hot, watery mud, was making no sound; but his big hand had tightened till it was a vise on Traxal's. *I am going to lose my grip on the whites and die with this kanaka,* Traxal thought, and had enough bitter humor left within him to appreciate the irony.

Then Father Shawn's grip tightened, and Traxal was pulled away from the creeping scalding water of the overflowing river. The mist of steam suddenly thinned, and the world was created all over again. Shapes pressed against the gaze like sweet pains; and the light, gloomy though it was, was almost like a benediction. A burned and shattered tree had a beauty that was spurious but no less valuable to those that saw it; the gorge under its crust of ash and pumice dust could not have been more luxuriant. Father Shawn turned and looked back over his shoulder, his thin scarred face ugly with sweat and mud; but to Traxal it was almost the face of a stranger, a stranger he could love. In turn he looked back at Beraki, and when he dropped the black man's hand he did so reluctantly, as if he were saying good-by to a friend. The chain of people had been bound by something stronger than friendship, by the primitive urge to survive.

Narvo said something to Elisabeth, and the talk ran down the line. Someone laughed, not with humor but with relief; and they hurried on and soon caught up with the last of the natives. They did not look back at the cliff and the lava that fell from it in a firey cascade.

Then the gorge widened out. The mist and steam and the hissing of the lava were behind them, and even the acrid smell of burning had faded till it was more just a memory in the nostrils than an irritation and a threat. They were in a shallow valley now that ran down gently to a distant spur of the ranges; a valley that Traxal, with a shock, remembered as being lush and green. There had been native gardens here, and villages on the ridges that ran out from the slopes on either side. Clumps of trees had grown along the banks of the river, and bamboo had waved like the pennants of an invisible army in the lee of the ridges. Now there was only a dead world and a world of the dead.

The long dark line of refugees stretched down the floor of the gray devastated valley, the only moving living thing in the whole awful landscape. Ash and pumice dust and rocks of solidified lava had turned the valley into a crater of the moon; one looked up toward the smoking sky and expected to see the earth. The gardens were a desert of gray dust: they grew only patches of black rock. The villages on the ridges had been flattened; in one or two places a stake in a fence remained standing, like the futilely defiant spear of a dead native. Trees had been stripped of leaves and branches; some trunks still stood, like remnants of a petrified forest. Rocks were embedded in the tree trunks; a possum, devoid of flesh and fur, was a dark pattern against a boulder. Dust rose from the feet of the trampling line of refugees and caught by the wind rose in spiraling ghosts to add to the unearthly impression of the desolate scene.

Traxal, staring ahead, saw the curve in the line and wondered what caused it. It took him twenty minutes to reach the spot. Narvo, who had gone ahead, was waiting for him. They stood on the edge of a native garden, around which the natives walked in a wide loop as if devils grew there.

"You'd better see if they are alive or dead," Narvo said, and pointed across to the cluster of gray figures that seemed to be asleep among the domes of *kau-kau*.

3

There were ten of them, four men and six women, and they were all dead. Elisabeth, standing outside the flattened picket fence with Father Shawn, could not tell whether they were blacks or whites. The blast had burned them so badly it had obliterated not only their color but their features; later Narvo was to tell her that he knew they were natives only by the shape of their feet. The coating of ash and dust concealed the extent of their burns at first; there was a decency about their death. Then Elisabeth saw Traxal bend down and turn one of the figures over; its arm fell off at the shoulder and lay beside the body. Elisabeth stared at the arm lying in the dust, unable to believe that it had once been part of a human; it lay there like something obscene, the hand open in a gesture of appeal, a silent blackmail. Sickness came up in a sour wave from her stomach and she turned away.

"I'm afraid we're going to see worse," said Duggan beside her, and put a comforting hand on Elisabeth's arm. "The only consolation is that the poor devils must have died at once."

Elisabeth nodded dumbly, unable to speak. In a country that had experienced relatively little bombing during the war and where nature was mild and predictable, she had seen nothing of the degradation to which death could sometimes reduce the human person. Even though her father had died violently, she had not seen his corpse: death, on the rare occasions when she had seen it, had looked to her to have no more effect than a deep and blanching sleep. To die as these natives had, as in a horrible nightmare, was more than man should have to endure. As all ten bodies crumbled and fell apart under Traxal's hands it was as if the dignity they had borne all through their lives was being reduced to nothing, not even a memory.

"Are you going to bury them, Roy?" Father Shawn said.

Narvo looked up from where he stood surrounded by the ash-covered shambles. "I've got all those to think about," he said, and nodded down along the valley, where the natives had halted and waited impatiently and fearfully. "If we stop to bury these, we'll owe the same to all the other dead we'll meet. And there may be thousands of them."

Rossi was staring back the way they had come, to the volcano crouched like a red-jawed beast behind its cover of smoke. From here they could plainly see the crater. They were in direct line from it; the middle of the blast must have passed right over where they stood. The crater was still spewing lava, and occasionally there would be a flare-up of flame; the lava would glow fiercely and the smoke would darken and thicken. The whole of the sky now was stained by the smoke and dust. The valley was bathed in a light that had the softness and the tint of eternity that Rossi had seen in cathedrals when the sun struck through the windows from the west. *We are not going to make this,* he thought, and looked down upon the dead in the desolate garden and envied them their release. At least for them it was over.

"Frank!" Rossi started, realizing that Narvo had been calling to him for some moments. "Frank, did you get through to Goroka about the water?"

"They were going out to collect the containers right away,"

Rossi said, recovering himself, throwing off his despair and trying to think of survival. "They weren't sure, either, about how many parachutes they had."

"We'll move on to the end of the valley and wait there," Narvo said. "It will be easier for dropping."

"What if the mountain blows again?" Rossi said, unable to forget it. "We're right in its path."

"Then we shan't need the water," said Narvo, and Elisabeth wondered if he spoke with bravado or was indeed so in control of himself and his fears that he could make a statement that was a fact and not a macabre joke.

They moved on through the valley, leaving the burned dead in their shallow graves of ash. Dust rose from the thousands of tramping feet, and Elisabeth felt thirst beginning as a small torture in her throat. Dust was still falling from the sky, and blacks and whites were now gray brothers. The day was warm and Elisabeth could feel the dust turning to mud beneath her eyes and in the hollow of her throat where the perspiration ran. Her lips were closed tight against the insidious dust that was trying to find its way into her body, but her nose was slowly becoming blocked and breathing was difficult. Her hands and arms wore long gloves of fine ash, and the legs that had been bare when she had begun the march were now covered to the tops of her thighs, even beneath her skirt, with stockings of gray dust. She could feel the dust finding its way all over her, like the soft touch of a seducer who would eventually smother her. She could bear the intrusion of the dust into her person, she knew, if only her thirst did not become worse.

But it did, and so did that of the natives. Three times Narvo had to fire his pistol as men broke from the long file and ran across to the river; the natives hesitated and finally turned back and rejoined the long trudging line. On the third occasion of this attempted break to drink from the river, Narvo waited for Traxal to come up to him.

"What about the river?" he asked. "Do you think it would be dangerous for them to drink from it?"

"I have no way of telling," Traxal said. "Unless you want to delegate a guinea pig. But I should not like to risk it myself. The water is running swiftly enough, but I don't think it has come far enough to clear itself. It must contain a lot of ash and pumice dust, and less than a mile back it has come over all that lava. I'd rather go thirsty for a while."

"You'd better dole some of that water in the bags out to the patients," Narvo said. "And you and Duggan can have a mouthful each."

"Why the favoritism?"

"You're a doctor. I may have to keep you alive longer than anyone else, just to save myself."

"You have a pragmatic mind. Perhaps if we are the only survivors, you had better come back to Prague with me. The Communists could use someone like you."

"Thanks," said Narvo dryly, and wiped the dust from his lips. "The thought spurs me on."

Narvo halted two of the carriers who were carrying one of the waterbags on a pole between them. The patients were put down in the dust, and Duggan went along them, giving each half a cup of water. Some of the patients smiled gratefully; the *kuru* patients were not aware of what was being forced between their lips; Paiwo's expression was hidden by the dressing on his face. The carriers stood by, sullen and envious, but Narvo ignored them.

Then Duggan stood up at the end of the line of patients. "That's the lot."

"Now it's your turn," Narvo said. "Half a cup."

Duggan hesitated, then she wiped out the cup, ran water into it from the bag and drank. Then she turned and offered the cup to Elisabeth.

"No," Narvo said, and both Duggan and Elisabeth looked at

him in surprise: his voice was impersonal but authoritative. "Peter has half a cup. But that's all. No one else drinks till the plane comes."

Traxal took the cup, raised it in salute to Narvo and drank. The carriers watched in silence the pantomime between the whites: they did not understand a word that had been spoken, but every gesture had been intelligible. Narvo made no attempt to apologize or explain to Elisabeth why he had refused her a drink, and she felt resentful. Then she found herself watching the carriers. The sullenness died out of their faces; enlightenment relaxed their expressions. They watched Traxal hand the cup back to Duggan, who wiped it and put it away. The carriers looked at Narvo and Elisabeth, the two whites who hadn't drunk, then without a word they bent and picked up their burdens and moved on, still envious but no longer sullen and angry.

Then Elisabeth felt her own resentment at Narvo disappear. And found herself admiring him. By the single gesture of refusing her the drink, he had killed at birth any rebellion the natives might have felt. She looked along the seemingly interminable line of natives stretching down to the end of the valley, and tried to imagine what would have happened if they had known that at the rear of the procession the whites were drinking what water was available. And knew that at this moment she might already have been dead.

"Roy," she said through a throat dry and swollen with thirst, "I am glad you stopped me from taking that drink."

"You'll all get a drink in good time," he said, and there was still no apology. She was coming to learn that he made no apologies in his job, for it or because of it: she was at last beginning to understand the sense of dedication he had to it.

The plane came over an hour later. They heard it long before they saw it, flying somewhere above the pall of smoke, going round and round in circles it seemed while it sought them. Down in the valley two thousand faces were turned upwards, and at last a concentration of will brought the plane down out of the dark cloud. It was an old Junkers, and Jack Bermingham looked up at it with the affection of an old friend.

"I first started flying them back in '33," he said, and even the dust on his face couldn't cloud the nostalgia there. There was only one thing that blighted his simple happiness, and that was that he would never fly again. Some men regretted their lost youth, some their lost loves; till he died he would regret the lost thrill of flying. "But my word, that one sounds sick."

"Just let it stay up there long enough to drop us the water," said Macy. "After that, I don't care what happens to it."

"I hope they've brought enough water," Bernice said. "I can't go on much longer." Then she looked at Mary Bermingham. "And Mary is worse than I am."

Macy did not look at his wife, still keeping his eyes on the circling plane. But he felt a weakness within him that was almost like a desire to weep. Bernice was learning the meaning of charity, something that had escaped her up till now, that he had thought would never come to her. There was hope that she yet might come to understand why he wanted to stay on here in these outposts. All he had ever wanted to do was practice charity, the charity he knew was in his hands. He was not religious, but he knew that to heal was as blessed as to help or give. With Bernice beside him, there was nothing more in life that he would ask than to stay on in these mountains to act as doctor to natives who needed his care and never asked to see his degree. He looked across at Harry, standing in the dust and ashes with the cassowary beside him, and the boy smiled back at him out of a face that cracked like that of an ancient *luluai*.

"Gee, Dad, I could do with a drink, all right!"

Macy looked up at the plane, unaware that he stood in an attitude of prayer. "It's like being in a drought. The farmers must always be looking at the sky like this."

"Yeah," said Harry, careless of drought-stricken farmers, wanting a drink more than he had ever wanted anything in his whole life. He looked up at the plane and out of a throat dry as that of an old man, croaked, "Drop that bloody water!"

The plane made a run along the valley, then turned back. The natives had started to chant and yell, stamping their feet, and dust rose up till the long file of people seemed to turn to just a gray bank of mist laid along the floor of the valley. Narvo and Rossi moved out to one side, into another flattened native garden, and stood there among the stubble that had been a corn patch and the domes of *kau-kau* that now looked like children's graves. The plane came in over them and the red parachute blossomed from its side. It swung out and away from the plane, carrying the water container with it. But the plane had been too low. The parachute dropped away behind the plane, a red streak against the amber sky, and fell with awful sickening suddenness. The container hit the ground, raising an explosion of dust that turned almost instantly to mud as the water burst from the container. There was something between a moan and a scream from the natives and they plunged forward. The long file suddenly congealed, so quickly it was almost incredible; the farthest natives came in with the speed of running birds. The dust rose in another explosion, went up in a storm so that the crew of the plane could have thought there had been another eruption down in the valley.

Narvo, running awkwardly through the dust and ashes, stumbling on hidden rocks and bushes, beat the natives to the container. One look told him it held no more water. He stood in the mud it had created and raised his pistol and fired it. The sharp report brought the front runners of the stampede to a halt. But they were hurled forward, falling headlong into the dust, by the impetus of those behind them; and for a moment Narvo thought that he and Rossi, now beside him, were going to be overwhelmed by the gray avalanche of thirst-crazed men, women and children. He raised his pistol and fired again, and movement slowly died. The front ranks of the huge throng were no more than ten feet from Narvo and Rossi; coated with dust and ash, they looked like creatures of the dead. But their eyes were alive. They glared with angry frustration at the container, lying beside Narvo like the fleshless carcass of an angular beast, and at the water disappearing quickly into the dust and ash.

The two white men stood facing the thousands of natives; and Narvo wondered where Elisabeth and the other whites were. Had they been trampled underfoot in the wild stampede to get to the water? But there was no time to look for them now. The natives had to be held in check till the plane came back with another container.

He opened his mouth to shout at them, but only a croak came out of his dry and aching throat. Desperately he sought his voice and at last found it; but it was agony to shout as loud as he had to. In dialect he yelled at them to retreat, to stand back till the plane returned. There would be water for everyone, he told them; but he, the Kiap, would hand it out to them. None would get more than others, and any man who attempted to take more than his share would be shot. He stepped forward, still shouting, his voice only a ragged echo of the stentorian roar that had once been his; but there was still authority in his bearing, he still had the power to turn back a tide of men. Slowly the dark throng retreated and a wide flat space was opened up between the natives and the river.

Then the plane was heard coming back, higher this time, flying just below the ceiling of dark smoke and dust. Again the parachute was seen at the side of the plane. It swung out and for a moment Narvo thought it had caught on the tail assembly of the plane; there was a gasp from the crowd of natives, then everyone seemed to hold his breath. Then suddenly the parachute filled with air; it swung across the smoke-tangled sky like a giant and beautiful flower. It came floating down, the container swinging beneath it, and hit the ground with a soft thud only yards from Narvo and Rossi. The dust rose up in another cloud, but when it cleared the container was seen to be intact. There was a roar from the natives and once more they surged forward. And once more Narvo raised his pistol and fired. The crowd moved back while the plane came in again.

Four more water containers were dropped and all of them landed undamaged. There would be no more than half a cup of water for each person; and Narvo knew there would be many who would be thirsty, even desperate for more. But the plane kept making more runs, dropping food containers; Figgins had done a wonderful job of supply at such short notice. No one was going to get much of anything, food or water, but no one was going to die of thirst or starve to death. Death from the volcano was still their greatest threat.

Elisabeth and the other whites had now appeared out of the crowd. All the women had been knocked headlong by the rush of natives; and Father Shawn, trying to protect Elisabeth and Duggan, had had his glasses broken. But they were all safe and comparatively unscathed, and now they came forward to help Narvo and Rossi dole out the food and water. Narvo had called up the police boys and they formed a guard at either end of the serving line.

There was fighting and scrambling to head the line that was to file past the food and water containers; but Narvo, with a hoarse shout and another pistol shot, soon fixed that. Women and children went by first, amazement as well as gratitude on their faces. The men stood back, muttering at this stupid custom of the white men; what was the point of feeding the women and children if the men were not going to be alive and strong to protect them? Then Narvo gave the word for the men to come past and there was another wild scramble. Four or five men were fighting to see who would lead the line, when Narvo stepped up to them. He swung his fist, and one of the men shot out from the struggling group as if he had been fired from a cannon. The others stopped fighting at once.

Narvo swore at them in dialect, telling them to stand back or he would break their jaws so that they could neither eat nor drink, then returned to stand beside Father Shawn. "The last shall be first and the first shall be last, eh, Mike?"

"I don't remember the Lord putting the example in the same primitive way," Father Shawn said. "But I'm sure He wouldn't disapprove of the way you handled that."

"Sometimes it pays not to be a perfect Christian," said Narvo, teasing the priest but looking at him with concern. "How are you holding up, sport?"

Narvo had seen the little priest moving up and down the line all morning, ever since they had left Kundavi. He had been helping old people over difficult stretches of the trail, taking babies from their mothers and carrying them for a while, walking farther and using more of his meager strength than any two other people in the long procession. Without his glasses, the scar showing even through the dust on his cheek, his straw hat gone and his hair matted with dried mud, he looked old and on the point of collapse. But when he smiled up at Narvo there was evidence that the spirit that had kept him going all these years was still very much alive.

"I'm going to make it, Roy. I've been thinking while we've been on this walk. I might even go home and try to start all over again."

"Start trying to be a saint?"

Father Shawn shook his head, disturbing the dust on his face. He dropped a spoonful of wet rice into the dusty bowl a native held out to him. "No, start trying to be a priest."

"You wouldn't be happy back there, Mike," Narvo said quietly.

Half a dozen more natives went by and got their share of rice, before Father Shawn replied. He did not look up and all at once the spirit had gone out of him. "No, I wouldn't, Roy.

And that's the sad bloody truth, if I may borrow some of your language."

"You may borrow anything of mine you want," said Narvo, and restrained himself from putting his arm about the priest's shoulders: the latter didn't look as if he could support the weight of even a friendly arm. "If I had any piety, which I haven't, you could have borrowed that if it would have got you where you want to go."

"Thanks, Roy," said Father Shawn, and grinned sadly: the one sustaining thing in his time here in the mountains had been his friendship with this man whom the bishop called an agnostic and others called a misanthrope and still others called a kanaka-lover. His thanks to God for Narvo's presence and friendship would always be his own secret.

Then the last of the natives had filed by and got his food. The whites doled out shares to the police boys, Beraki, always the correct sergeant, stationing himself at the end of the line; then they began to dole out their own portions, careful to take no more than they had given the natives. But Father Shawn turned away first to help Duggan and Macy feed the patients, and knelt in the dust beside the still figure of Paiwo. Narvo watched him anxiously, afraid that the little man was going to work himself into the ground. He was still looking at Father Shawn when Bermingham and Rossi came up to him.

"That volcano is spitting again," Bermingham said. "I don't reckon we oughta stop tonight, not till we're over that range up ahead."

Narvo looked back at the volcano, now shooting molten rock and steam a hundred feet or more into the air. The sound of it carried down across the slopes and down into the valley; it was almost continuous now, like the barrage before an attack. The lava spread right down the mountainside now in a brilliant fan that, at this distance, held little threat or even hint of the death it contained. Yet somewhere under its smoking mass were

Vaikaka and Benamaua and the people who had lived there. Then Narvo turned and looked up ahead, to the range that rose like a gray scarred wall at the end of the valley.

"It's a bloody long way. At least another eight hours' walking. The kanakas can probably do it, but what about the white women?"

"I'm buggered meself," said Bermingham, "but I'll walk from here to Moresby if it means I'm gonna miss being buried alive by whatever that volcano spews out. That's all you gotta tell the women. Walk or be buried alive."

"As simple as that," said Narvo with a dry grin; but that was exactly what he told the women.

"I know I'll never make it," Bernice said, "but I'll try."

"Me and Dad'll carry you if we have to, Mum," Harry said. "The thing is to walk nice and easy, like, and not think about it."

"Where did you learn that?" Bernice said.

"Roy taught me."

"I might have known it," said Bernice, but she spoke without malice. She looked a wreck, she knew, but she did not care. All she wanted was to survive, no matter how scarred it left her for the rest of her life. And she wanted to survive with Eric and Harry; without them she did not want to survive at all. She was afraid of dying and always would be; but she was afraid of living, if she had to live alone. She had unaccountably and all at once forgotten all about her other boy, Rob, down on the mainland: it was as if he were someone else's child, a boy who had written her and told her (something she had never told to Eric) that he never wanted to come back to New Guinea. When the mountain had blown up she had started another life with Eric and Harry. She could only hope that it would not be a short life.

"I am certainly not going to be buried alive," said Duggan, cleaning her glasses of dust, peering back at the volcano that was too distant for her to see. "It's not a decent Christian burial."

"Hooray for the Presbyterians!" said Narvo. "There's a certain Knoxian stubbornness to you, Duggan old girl, that I'm coming to admire."

"Thank you," said Duggan with a touch of her old tartness. "At one time you used to call it my feminine pigheadedness."

Narvo looked at Elisabeth. "Can you make it, Elisabeth? Do you have enough feminine pigheadedness to get over that range?"

"I'll help her," said Duggan, who had now fully accepted Elisabeth as a friend, even if she had not and never would admit it to the Czech girl.

"So shall I," said Father Shawn.

"There you are," said Narvo. "What more help could you want? A representative of the Pope and one from John Knox."

"She could be split down the middle," said Traxal, and at that moment there was a loud explosion back on the mountain and the floor of the valley began to shudder. There was a roaring seemingly right beneath their feet, and the core of the earth seemed to be trying to hammer its way out of the thin crust that was the floor of the valley. Dust rose up, though the air was absolutely still; and Narvo, watching the river, saw it suddenly change course. The water rose up above the banks and went in a gray flood across the valley, away from the line of refugees. The ranges were trembling against the sky, their outline turned fuzzy, as if viewed through astigmatic eyes. Cracks appeared in the floor of the valley, the dust and ash sliding into it like gray snow into crevasses in a glacier, and away up on a slope Narvo saw a slice of earth peel off and slide down in a landslide a quarter of a mile wide. Looking back he saw the volcano shooting flame and rock and steam hundreds of feet into the air. Then he saw the first of the cinders and rocks falling four or five hundred yards behind them and he knew they were safe, at least from the threat of the volcano. The trembling of the earth suddenly subsided, there was a loud crack that seemed to come from the sky itself, and a wind blew down the valley and lifted the dust and ash in a blinding storm.

No one moved while the dust swirled about them. They stood there with their eyes and mouths tightly shut and with their hands over their noses, trying to remain conscious on the breath they still held in their lungs. Elisabeth felt the dust raping her, burying her even as she stood, and suddenly she wanted to scream. Her mind seemed to go black with the effort of holding in the scream; she trembled as much as she had when the earth had rocked beneath her. But she held the scream in and didn't open her mouth. She knew that she would have choked to death on dust and ash if she had.

Then all of a sudden the wind stopped. She felt the dust stop biting at her; it began to settle softly. Slowly, cautiously, she opened her eyes, blinking away the dust that coated them, and looked out on a nightmare land. Parts of the valley had been exposed by the scouring effect of the wind. The villages on the ridges were now stripped of the decency of their death shrouds that had been dust; they were now exposed in all their ugly and pathetic tragedy. Bodies lay about the hillsides and the gardens in the attitudes of people sleeping in the noon heat; but the dust had been blown from them and they no longer had the faces of humans. The river, diverted from its bed, was now rushing across the valley floor, picking up other dead: limbless bodies, pigs, fowls, even a cassowary went floating by, flotsam that no one would ever salvage. The valley was just one vast graveyard.

Then Elisabeth turned her head and saw the strangest sight of all. The long line of natives, as soon as the earth tremor had begun, had dropped flat to the ground, as if the Kiap or some fight-leader had shouted a command. They had lain there while the dust boiled above them, and quickly and completely it had covered them. When the wind had dropped they had remained lying there beneath their dune of dust and ashes, a small ridge that stretched like a low rampart for over a mile along the valley.

And as Elisabeth watched the natives slowly began to stand up. The dust broke, the rampart fell apart and the gray deathly-looking figures stood up: a row of ghosts over a mile long. To Elisabeth it seemed at that moment the most remarkable thing she had seen in this remarkable land; and yet she was neither alarmed nor even surprised. And she knew then that, even in a few short weeks, she had come to accept New Guinea. It was a measure of her rootlessness, of her irrevocable farewell to her own land.

She looked at Narvo, wanting to tell him that, but he was looking back at the volcano. "I think that was its last kick," he was saying. "Look, it's dying down."

"I still don't trust it," Bernice said. "I'd rather walk over those mountains up ahead."

"Me, too," said Harry, brushing dust from the cassowary as if he were preparing it for some bird show. "Let's go on, Roy. I'm getting the creeps."

Father Shawn was carefully scraping the dust from the half a cup of rice he held in his hand. He had held the cup under his tattered shirt while the dust storm had raged; it had seemed to him the final punishment the Lord had visited on him, and he had been passionately angry. He had shouted aloud in the wind, swallowing dust as the curse burst from him; then he had buried his head in his arms, afraid of God's wrath and the curiosity of the others. Now he was making a great pretense of scraping the dust from his rice, afraid to look at Narvo and the others.

Then Narvo said, "Mike, while we're on the move this time, you're not to go running up and down the line looking for some-one to help. The kanakas will be all right, and if they're not, it's my job to look after them. All you have to do is get yourself over that range."

"Roy, it's my job as well——"

"You'll do what you're told, Mike," Narvo said evenly, and Father Shawn knew then that Narvo at least had heard the curse in the howling storm of dust. "I don't want you cracking up. When the bishop meets you at Goroka, I want you to be standing on your feet."

"I didn't think appearance meant so much to you," Duggan said, suddenly wanting to defend Father Shawn: she was knitting a web of friendship, something she would never admit to those she caught in it.

"It depends what you mean by appearance," said Narvo, oblivious of his torn and dirty clothes. "I've always believed in the appearance of dignity."

"You have your own ideas of it," said Duggan.

"Haven't we all?" said Father Shawn, who had recognized Duggan's offer to help. He wanted to stop the argument before it began: he did not have so many friends that he could afford to lose any. "You're the boss, Roy."

"That's what I keep telling everyone," said Narvo, and managed a smile, although he felt no humor nor happiness. He had enough vanity to welcome the opportunity to lead when it came; he had enough humility to know that if this flight should fail it would be largely his fault. Big and powerful though he was, he carried the weight of over two thousand lives on his shoulders. He was well aware of the frightening fact that it could cripple greater and better men than himself.

4

It took them six hours to reach the top of the range at the end of the valley. Three of the *kuru* patients died on the way and were left where they died, their graves a covering of ash and dust: Narvo, regretfully but firmly, decided there was nothing more that could be done for them. Another corpse or two in the four or five hundred they had already passed did not seem to matter. Elisabeth remembered what Traxal had written her: death was part of the climate of New Guinea.

The long procession climbed slowly up the slopes that had once been green and soft with *kunai* grass, on which the breezes had appeared as dark moving shadows; now they were gray desert hills and the breezes stirred up only ghosts of dust. They came to the beginning of the road that led on to Goroka, and passed the ruins of a Lutheran mission. The two missionaries and their wives and children were dead; they had died on their knees at morning prayer in their *kunai*-thatched chapel. There were almost a hundred dead natives in the gardens and huts of the mission; pigs and fowls and dogs lay about like burned rubber toys. The blackened carcass of a goat hung in a tree, its horns hanging down like the double beak of some strange bird. The long file of refugees sat down in the road that skirted the mission, looking at the multiple tragedy without curiosity, and waited till Narvo and Elisabeth had come up from the rear to join the other whites.

"They were dead unlucky," said Bermingham, oblivious of his macabre pun, and nodded up to the top of the range, no more than two hundred yards above them. "If they had been on the other side of that ridge, they'd've missed the worst of it."

"I can't believe the blast came this far," said Macy, staring back over the valley at the distant volcano, now looking no more threatening than a faraway fire. "The crater must have been aimed right at this range."

"It only makes me realize how lucky we were to be round the corner from it," Bernice said, and shuddered so that dust shook on her like gray fringes on her dress.

The cross had been blown from the roof of the flattened chapel and had landed upside down in a thick mound of ash. Father Shawn walked across, picked up the cross and, without thinking why he should leave it where it was, shoved it right way up back into the ashes. Then he returned to Narvo and the others. He stopped for a moment beside the twisted frame of a child's bicycle, then he came on. "Are you going to bury the Vocklers and the Underwoods, Roy?"

"I can't, Mike." Narvo had known these people and respected them. He knew they had considered him too uninhibited in many ways for their tastes and beliefs, but they had always made him welcome. It had been their creed never to turn anyone away from their door, least of all a sinner like himself. But now he had to refuse them burial. "I can't bury them and not bury all those kanakas. And we haven't got time to do that. I'll come back later with someone from Goroka."

"I can't understand why someone from Goroka hasn't come in here," Rossi said. "It's only four or five hours' drive."

Narvo, too, was puzzled. He had hoped to find a truck or two waiting for them here at the mission with food and water. He looked up at the top of the range immediately above them, expecting to see a truck appear against the sulphur-colored sky; there was nothing but the long line of natives, waiting on him to lead them to safety. They squatted without moving, like a long wooden python nailed against the wall of the slope. All their faces were turned back toward him, waiting patiently on him; but their demand on him plain even through the dust that masked their faces. *Neil, you bastard, you've let me down,* he thought; and for the first time felt the beginning of a breakup within himself. Why couldn't the bloody trucks have been here? What had held them up?

He must have shaken with anger, because the dust moved on him and fell off, so that in the fading saffron light he looked like a man falling apart. He grunted, a curse that was unintelligible, and his hand came up in an involuntary gesture of anger and despair. His hand brushed against Elisabeth, who had come up silently in the thick dust of the road, and at once he felt his wrist gripped. He turned, startled, and looked at her.

"Roy," she said softly, "is something wrong?"

He could feel the pressure of her fingers, soft yet strong. They could only encompass half of his massive wrist, but there was something about their touch that held him. She was coated with dust and it was impossible to think of her as beautiful. She had taken off her hat as the afternoon heat had worn off and now she wore a wig of thick gray dust. Her face was cracked and lined as those of the old crones in the procession of natives stretching up and down the road; even her eyes seemed faded, as if the dust had aged and taken the life from them. The dust on the inner edges of her lips was a thin line of mud, and her teeth were dark with the dust so that they looked decayed. The thin dress she wore, once yellow, was now a grayish-brown; it clung to her body in parts, where she had sweated in the climb up from the valley, but sex was dead under the dust. Yet he knew now that she was important to him, as no other woman had ever been. For the first time in his life he placed reliance on a woman, depended upon her for comfort and strength. And in Elisabeth's gaze he found it.

"No," he said, and turned his hand over and took hers. He put pressure into his own fingers, awkwardly as he tried to be gentle, and he felt a rush of pleasure at the answer in her soft touch. "No, nothing is wrong. I just want to get to the end of this trek."

"So do I," said Elisabeth, and all at once the end of the journey had become a very personal thing for both of them, more than just the attainment of safety.

"Do you think the road has been washed out or something?" Macy said.

"The river doesn't go anywhere near it," Bermingham said. "Well, come on, we can't stand around here magging like a lotta old hens. Let's get over the other side of that ridge. You gonna call a halt then, Roy?"

"I think we might as well," Narvo said, "and go on first thing in the morning. Maybe they'll have got the trucks through to us by then. I'll radio in as soon as we stop."

Bermingham went back to the head of the procession and the long file slowly and painfully came to life. The natives stood up, the men helping the women gather up the children, and they began to trudge up the long steep curling road. They walked in silence, their throats too dry and their bodies too weary for singing, and slowly the procession climbed out of the dead valley, over the topmost ridge and down a long col through which the road ran, then fell like a twisted rope to the far bottom of another gorge.

Here there was ash and dust, but only a faint coating of it, and this side of the range showed no effect of the blast. Trees still had their leaves, even if with the dust they all looked the same silver-gray color, and the *kunai* grass rolled like a dull sea under the evening breeze that blew in from the east. But people, animals and birds had fled, and this side of the range was just as still and dead as the valley they had just left. Then there was a harsh mournful cry and a solitary crow, gray as a ghost bird, flew down the slope of the mountain, its cry and its single lonely presence only accentuating the desolation of the ranges.

Half a mile below the top of the range, in a fold between two ridges, Narvo called a halt. He stood at the top of the range and shouted down to Bermingham. His voice echoed and re-echoed in the silent empty valleys and gorges, and far below him he saw Bermingham raise an acknowledging arm. He waited on the top of the pass, with Elisabeth beside him, till the last of the natives had filed past. Traxal, walking with Duggan and the patients, went by and looked at them with a closed face that could have hidden bitterness or jealousy or just sardonic amusement.

"I'm still worried about him," Narvo said as he and Elisabeth began to walk down. They were fifty or more yards behind Traxal and Duggan, and they were able to talk without having to whisper. "I'm sorry, Elisabeth, but I can't bring myself to trust him. Not after this morning."

"Was it only this morning? I had forgotten what happened. I had even forgotten him."

"Were you ever really in love with him?" he asked, beginning to act like all men in love, anxious for the pain as well as the pleasure.

"Yes," she said honestly. She had lied to Traxal about knowing any men in Prague, but somehow she knew Narvo would prefer the truth. "Don't be stupid, Roy, and ask me how I could be. Just accept it that I was."

"I wasn't going to be stupid," he said, not hurt. "I just wanted to know, that was all. I wanted to know if you would tell me the truth. A silly woman wouldn't have."

"You don't know women," she said, smiling up at him with dust-dimmed teeth. "Even silly women know when it is wise to tell the truth to a man."

"I've got a lot to learn," he said, and lifted her hand to his mouth and kissed the dust from it. It was so unexpected, so unlike him, so European almost, that she looked at him, frightened for a moment that he was deceiving her. But the look in his weary grimed face was enough: he loved her and she knew he would never deceive her. "You'll stay on in New Guinea?"

"Yes," she said, and looked down the road at the head-bent figure of Traxal, now shadowy and remote in the evening gloom. "If you want me to."

Then they had caught up with the end of the procession, now lying in the *kunai* beside the road, exhausted and thirsty and hungry, every native and white hoping that sleep would come without effort and wipe out for a few hours memory and thirst and hunger and fear. Narvo and Elisabeth went on down to where Rossi had set up the portable transceiver and was trying to contact Goroka.

Maugham, the district officer, answered from Goroka. "Neil Figgins is out with four trucks waiting for you, Roy. He says he is on the road about eight miles south of the Lutheran mission at Bingam. Have you passed there? Over."

"We've just passed Bingam," said Narvo, and gave the news of the tragedy that had overwhelmed the mission. "What's holding up Neil? Over."

"The road has fallen off the side of the mountain," Maugham said. "From what he says, you are going to run into the chances of landslides from now on. You'd better watch your step."

"Yeah, we'll do that," said Narvo, hoping his sarcasm wouldn't show too plainly over the air. "All right. We're going to bed down now for the night. I'll check in at six o'clock tomorrow morning, just before we start walking again. Good night. Over and out."

"Ask him what's on at the pictures this week," Harry said, and ducked and grinned as Narvo cuffed a playful hand at him.

Narvo stood up. "Righto, you'd all better get some sleep. We move out at five-past six in the morning. I'll have you all eating and drinking like hogs by lunchtime."

He turned away and Father Shawn said, "Where are you going?"

"I'm going to have a word with the kanakas," Narvo said. "Put them in the picture."

"I'll come with you." Father Shawn tried to hide his pain and exhaustion as he rose. His eyes were sore from dust and the strain of trying to see without his glasses, and each of his heels was covered by a large blister where his sock had worn away. Several times he had ruminated ruefully on what he would have done if the devil had appeared and offered him a cigarette. He managed to grin at Narvo and said, "I'd like to stretch my legs."

Narvo hesitated, about to tell the little priest to lie down and rest, but all at once he relented. "Come on, you skinny little bastard. Anyone ever tell you you look like an underfed altar boy?"

"I can't say the same for you," said Father Shawn, "either as to the physical or spiritual look."

Narvo laughed, and the two men, so incongruous beside each other, went down the road toward the head of the procession. The other whites, now all grouped together, lying in the great dusty bed of the *kunai*, looked after them.

"Mike never lets him have the last word," said Duggan, polishing her glasses, putting them away carefully in their case before she went to sleep.

"I think Roy lets Mike have the last word," Macy said. "Mike could be his son."

"I always thought it was the other way round," Bernice said, wiping the dust and grime from her face as last night she had wiped off her make-up. She loosened her brassière beneath her dress and lay back in the grass exhausted. Her feet were blistered and burning, and she was chafed and sore where the dust had got into the crevices of her body. She cleaned her teeth with her tongue and was ready for sleep.

"Good night, darl," Macy said, and leaned across and kissed her. With his lips close against her cheek, he whispered, "I love you, hon."

She raised a hand and lifted back the long strand of hair that had fallen down over his face. He looked gray and aged, his plump face slack with weariness, and his shirt and trousers were torn and dirty. All afternoon he had carried the younger Bermingham child on top of the pack on his back; the straps of the pack had worn holes in his shirt and a dark weal showed on either side of his collarbone. He looked so exhausted and worn that all at once Bernice was afraid that she might not see him alive in the morning. She lifted her face and kissed him fiercely on the lips, feeling the dust turn to mud between them.

Harry, lying a few yards along in the *kunai* from his parents, turned his head away in embarrassment. But he was full of a happiness that made him forget the soreness of his feet and the dryness of his throat and the aching emptiness in his belly. After the initial eruption of the volcano he had not been frightened by anything that had happened since. To him it had been a great adventure, the sort of thing he had read about, and throughout the day he had modeled his behavior on that of Narvo. He had been disappointed he had not been able to walk at the rear of the procession all the time with Roy. But in the last week he had grown up enough to know that his presence meant something to his father. If he had gone to join Roy, his father would have been hurt, and he did not want that. As the day had gone on he had noticed the change in his mother, that she had trudged on through the heat and dust without complaining, that when she spoke to his father there had been none of the old bickering in her voice. And all afternoon she had walked with Mary Bermingham, helping her almost as if they were sisters, as if Mary were not black but white. When he had seen his mother kiss his father good night in the way that she had, even though he knew nothing of passion, it had seemed almost like the end of a perfect day.

He patted the head of the cassowary lying in the grass beside him. "Good night, Wally. Don't bite me, you bastard."

"Talking to me, Harry?" said Traxal.

"Gee, no, Dr. Traxal!"

"A small joke, Harry. I think I must be lightheaded with hunger. I feel I should like to tell a thousand jokes—if I could remember them. I suppose one must hear a thousand jokes in one's lifetime."

"I wouldn't know, Dr. Traxal. You hear some pretty crook jokes around our house, though. Dad ain't much of a joke teller."

"I used to know some very good ones," Traxal said, and for the life of him couldn't remember one that he could tell to a small boy. Jokes among medical men were often too ghoulish, even sometimes cruel; the best jokes were always told by lawyers.

But he was no lawyer and he had no jokes for Harry; and he wanted to go on talking to the boy. All of a sudden he had become very lonely.

"I dunno any jokes at all," said Harry sleepily. "Good night, Dr. Traxal."

And Traxal saw the boy stretch out in the long grass beside the cassowary and appear almost instantly to drop off to sleep. A spasm of ridiculous anger gripped Traxal and he sat up straight, halfway to leaning across and telling Harry to wake up and listen to him tell a thousand jokes. Then reason and control came back, and he smiled and shook his head at himself. He lay back, his head propped on his small pack, and tried to see the stars through the dust that clouded the sky. But there was none bright enough to shine through, only the moon glowing like a brazier, a yellow reflection of the crater now miles behind them. He turned his head and looked up over the top of the range and saw the glow on the sky behind the ridges. Other refugees during the war in Europe, he mused, must have looked back like this and seen the glow of burning cities. He would never want that to happen to Prague.

Then he heard a movement and turning his head still farther saw Rossi moving up through the grass toward Elisabeth. The young patrol officer was moving cautiously, bent over like a soldier sneaking in for an attack; and without surprise, suddenly too exhausted and alone to care, Traxal thought, *he's going to rape her.*

He watched as if this were something he was seeing in a film, something that was only supposed to resemble life but which wasn't life: for five shillings, he could buy identification, put himself in place of the hero or the villain. But Rossi was neither hero nor villain. Traxal saw him draw something from behind him—a bag with which to smother her cries?—and lean down and touch Elisabeth's shoulder. She sat up, and the bag turned into a jacket that Rossi was offering her. *You poor fool,* Traxal thought, *you are in love with her, too.*

He turned his head away. He was still in love with her himself, but he had lost her. Yet there was no regret, that was the strange thing. He had lost everything, and he had slipped into a sea of resignation that had swamped regret, recrimination, jealousy, even something of memory. He had said good-by to life, but life was still with him, like a relative to whom he owed a debt and who would not leave him till it was paid. But he could think of nothing that he owed life: he had paid in full and with interest for everything it had given him. He and life were square; but how to get rid of it? He could not commit suicide; he did not have the courage for that. He had heard of the contagion of courage and he had seen evidence of it today. But it was not contagious when it came to taking one's own life.

He looked down the slope, now copper-colored under the light of the yellow moon, and saw Narvo and Father Shawn slowly working their way back up the long line of natives. *Who does he think he is?* Traxal sneered. *Some general looking after his troops?* That would be one way to get rid of life: shoot the general. He would be dead within moments of Narvo's dying, killed by Narvo's police boys. He shuddered at the thought: not just at the thought of his own horrible death, but at the thought of killing Narvo. Violence was still a sickening anathema to him. He had no more courage to commit murder than he had to commit suicide.

From down the slope there came a burst of laughter from Narvo, echoed by the lighter laughter of Father Shawn. Out of the sea of resignation there rose a sudden spurt of hate. Why had he been denied companionship? Life owed *him* something. Why had it given him the personality it had, the character that had made him an island in the ocean of men?

It was too late now. He could never change. He would die as he had lived, a lonely man who had only just recognized

loneliness. He knew now that he would have been lonely even
in Prague. He saw Rossi stand up, say something to Elisabeth,
then turn and go quietly back down the slope. Traxal half-raised
his head, wanting to go to Elisabeth; but exhaustion and resignation were too much of a burden. He lay back, hoping that
Elisabeth might come to him, but knowing, with something like
bitter masochism, that she was now as remote from him and
unattainable as Prague.

Elisabeth herself lay hoping that Narvo, when he returned up
the slope, would make his bed, for what it was worth, beside
her. It amused her to think that if they should lie together for
the first time, it would be in a rough, dusty bed of *kunai* grass;
but she was also struck by the thought that it would somehow
be symbolic and appropriate. She had met Narvo in New Guinea,
had in a way been drawn to him because of New Guinea, and
New Guinea should be their bed.

Down the slope, where Duggan had now gone down with the
native nurses to sleep beside the hospital patients, she heard a
giggle. In the high stillness of the mountains, where sound
traveled as if on invisible wires, the giggle seemed disembodied,
the sad empty echo of the laughter of the thousands who had
died this morning. There was a stir right down the line of
natives. In the moonlight Elisabeth saw the dark line tremble;
it was as if another crack were opening in the earth. Then she
heard Narvo's voice, soothing as a lover's, and slowly the line
stilled.

Elisabeth had not been able to accustom herself to the *kuru*
patients, nor to accept the fact of their mysterious illness. There
was a nightmare quality about both the patients and their illness
that put them in a world of devilish fantasy; they could have been
creatures who had come out of the bowels of the mountain back
at Kundavi. They were more unreal and incredible to her than
the volcano: one could comprehend death that came in the form
of lava and ash, but not death that came as a laugh. She won-

dered if things would have been different at Kundavi if the *kuru* patients had not been there. All the native trouble had grown from the murder of the woman *kuru* patient by the man from Vaikaka: the massacre at the bridge, Paiwo's desertion of Narvo, the pay-back on the Benamaua by the Vaikaka, the cannibalism, the hunting down and attempted killing of Bermingham.

Yet the native trouble had been only part of the trouble at Kundavi. The *kuru* patients could not be blamed for the treachery of Traxal, the discontent of Bernice, the pathetic attempt at religious living by Father Shawn, the precipitant and unhappy love of Rossi for herself. In the end there was only one answer: New Guinea. That, and the twisted and interminable strings of human nature that knew no geography and about which one could do nothing.

Then she looked up and saw Narvo was standing over her. "Where did you get the jacket?"

"Frank gave it to me. It's all right—it was just a friendly gesture. I couldn't say no to that."

"No," Narvo said, and looked down at the hill at the still figure of Rossi. Then he seemed to relax and he smiled down at her. "Are you afraid of your reputation if I bed down here beside you?"

"In these mountains I have no reputation," she said.

"Good. It's an ideal way to be. A good reputation is often just as big a load as a bad one." He lay down beside her, raising a small cloud of dust, as if he were lying down in a bed that had been empty for years. She lay on her side, uncomfortable against the rough grass but hardly aware of it, happy and safe. He put out his hand and took hers. "We're all right now, I think. We'll be in Goroka by lunchtime. Then we are going to have to decide what you'll do."

"Could I get a job in Goroka?" It did not strike her as strange that, here on a high ash-covered slope, beneath a moon streaked and discolored by volcanic dust, she should be discussing the possibility of finding employment in Goroka. She looked with love at Narvo, who could make her accept New Guinea so easily that she could even forget the horrors of this morning.

"I suppose so. But you don't want to go rushing into anything."

"I have no money. I shall have to rush into something." She smiled, teasing him, and was excited to see him smile back. Already they had the intimacy of lovers, although they had not yet even kissed.

Then he did kiss her. He leaned across and she saw the moon, yellow and bent as an old king's crown, slide off the back of his head. She felt the dust on his lips, and for one horrible moment the thought flashed through her mind that she was kissing a dead man. Terror flooded through her and she lay stiff and unyielding in the grip of a nightmare in which she was fully awake. All the emptiness of the last five years came back, a vacuum that cut her off from the world: the cold dead lips on hers were the taste of past love, the acrid presage of future loneliness. She heard a scratching noise somewhere: it was the echo of the rat in the ceiling. Tears started at the corners of her eyes and hopelessness covered her like the dust that had haunted her all day. Then she felt Narvo's hand on her shoulder, warm and firm and loving, and suddenly the nightmare had gone. The tears still in her eyes, she opened her mouth under his, tasting dust but no longer finding any meaning in it, marking her love in mud, and spoke to him the language that needed no words.

Down the hill Father Shawn saw the two figures merge for the moment; and included them in his prayers. He believed in the chances of happiness for others, if he did not believe in the chances of it for himself. He counted the beads of his rosary as a man might count the days that were left to him.

16

ANOTHER *kuru* patient died during the night, a woman whose husband and sons came and stood beside her and made their last farewell as the procession got slowly under way in the yellow morning light. They left the shrunken wasted body on the slope, covered only by the ash and dust raked over it, and went on down to join the line of refugees, now already entering another gorge.

"The other *kuru* ones are dying, too," said Duggan. "This trek hasn't done any of the patients any good."

"How's Paiwo?" Narvo asked.

"I looked at him a while ago," Traxal said. "I think he is dying, too. It is difficult to tell. These natives can stand burns much better than we whites——"

"I've seen them with an arm burnt almost right off, and still live," said Duggan.

"Paiwo is burnt more badly than that," Traxal said. "But it's something else. He *wants* to die. There's nothing a doctor can do about that."

"Is there anything I could do?" Narvo said.

Traxal shrugged. He understood Paiwo's resignation, but he didn't believe there was any cure for it; he knew there was no cure for his own similar symptoms, unless it was the unraveling of time. It was one of the few things whites and blacks had in common: the defeat by time past. "You could try. But I think he gave up depending on you some time ago."

Narvo acknowledged the truth behind the jibe, but said nothing. He would talk to Paiwo when they got to Goroka. This morning he was filled with optimism. He looked at Elisabeth and smiled at her as she waited for him.

"Have the carriers bring him to the end of the line," he said. "I want him with me from here on."

Traxal did not want to sneer again, but he could not help it. "Are you showing loyalty, or looking for the return of it?"

"Whatever I'm doing," said Narvo, "I'm sure it's not a question that has ever bothered you."

He turned and went down to join Elisabeth, and Duggan said, "You had that coming, Dr. Traxal."

He looked at her, realizing she did not know the full extent of what she had said. She did not know the matter of the waterbags, and she could not know of the report he had intended to write for the UN committee. All of a sudden it came to him that, in a way, Narvo had shown loyalty even to *him:* he had kept secret everything he had learned about Traxal.

"Yes," he said, and was surprised that surrender did not always taste bitter. "I had it coming."

The long procession of refugees was now moving steadily, more quickly than yesterday, almost lightheartedly. Dust and exhaustion and thirst no longer worried them; and fear of the volcano had vanished as soon as the mountain had gone from sight over the intervening range. The Kiap had promised them food and water and safety: they had never seen Goroka, but it was the Promised Land. They did not sing, because their throats were still too dry; but they talked, and laughed when someone slipped and fell. They walked along the bottom of the gorge, walking by the side of the road as if expecting that at any moment a truck or Landrover might come hurtling around a corner, and the precipitous sides of the mountains towered above them on either side. There seemed less dust in the sky this morning and the sun shone brightly if yellowly. Everyone had a shadow this morning, something he had not had all day yesterday, and the natives seemed to find comfort in the fact. It was as if the shadows were the first living things that would soon be returning to the dead country.

Then the line began to slow and all at once came to a halt. The natives bunched up on each other, spreading out across the road, which had now climbed out of the gorge and ran along the side of a mountain, some two hundred yards above the lip of the gorge. Narvo, at the rear with Elisabeth, Traxal and Duggan, was hidden by a shoulder of the mountain from whatever had caused the halt up ahead. He went forward, accompanied by Elisabeth, pushing his way through the chattering and curious natives who now crowded the road, and came around the shoulder. And saw what had brought the procession to such a sudden stop.

The whole side of the mountain had slipped away here. The landslide must have occurred during the last violent tremor yesterday at noon. Grass, trees, ash and dust had been carried away by the slide, and the whole side of the mountain was exposed as a great ugly wound. Rocks as large as huts were poised on ledges that did not appear big enough to hold them; a whole immense field of stony earth was ready to slide down over the lip of the gorge. There was no sign of the road for five hundred yards across the face of the mountain.

"There's Neil Figgins and the trucks," Bermingham said as Narvo and Elisabeth came up to the head of the procession.

Narvo looked across the scarred mountain and saw the trucks parked where the road ended abruptly at a wall of fallen rock. He waved and saw some someone wave in return.

"Hey, Neil!" he shouted without thinking, and a moment later realized his mistake.

In the steep cleft between the mountains, the valley that was more a canyon, his voice echoed and re-echoed, magnified as if shouted through a megaphone. Then the echo was gone, lost in the first ominous rumbling. High on top of the stretch of landslide, a strip of rock and earth fell away. It slid slowly at first, then it began to gather speed and size. The rumbling grew till it was a roar that filled the steep narrow valley. Children shut their ears against it, and babies' screams were lost in it. The landslide went plunging down, between the two sections of road, cutting off Narvo and the Kundavi party from Figgins and the party from Goroka with a wall of impenetrable dust. The earth and rocks went by and down over the lip of the gorge with a crash that sounded like another volcanic explosion. The roar died away, and then there was only the rattle of stones and the crying of children. Slowly the dust lifted and the two parties, each sure of its own safety but terrified for that of the other, were relieved to see each other still living and unharmed.

"That's the silliest bloody thing I've ever done," said Narvo, and wiped his face, as if trying to wipe away with the dust the disgust he felt at himself.

"You always were loudmouth." Duggan, with Traxal, had followed Narvo and Elisabeth to the head of the procession. "I just didn't think you had the power to move mountains."

Narvo's face cracked as he grinned. "I wish I had the power to move a few more." He looked down into the bottom of the valley, still obscured by dust, then up and around at the mountains as they towered over them. "I don't see any easy way out of this."

"I don't see any way out of it at all," said Rossi. "I came over this road a couple of times with Mr. Vockler from the mission. We talked about landslides, once. He said the only way out from here, if the road was blocked, was to cut south over the mountains from the mission."

Narvo was thinking. "I'm trying to remember what's over the other side of this mountain we're on. I can't remember it from the air—all the bloody mountains up here look alike. When I first came in here to this country, I walked up this valley. It's the only way I know."

"We can't drag this mob up to the top of the mountain, no matter what's on the other side," Bermingham said. "We don't know how much more of it is gonna fall."

"While we're standing here talking," Bernice said, "we could easily be swept away. Do something, Roy, please!"

Narvo was surveying the shattered side of the mountain. "Up there," he said, pointing about fifty yards above them, "it seems to flatten out a bit. We could work our way across up there if we knew it was reasonably solid ground all the way."

"How do we tell?" Macy asked.

"I'll go across," said Rossi, and with the alacrity of youth was already on his way. He had no desire to show bravado, but he had been looking at the fallen mountain even as Narvo had been, and he had already seen the promise of a path even before Narvo had pointed it out. He knew that if he did not volunteer to go himself, Narvo would certainly do so. And he had seen enough on this trek to know that if Narvo should perish, the others might never find their way through to safety. The onus would then fall on him, and the thought frightened him; frightened him more than the immediate task for which he had volunteered. He was aware of the danger he faced, but he had the confidence of the young that death was not yet for him.

"Frank!" Narvo swallowed the shout in his throat, and called again in a hoarse whisper. "Frank!"

Rossi, already ten yards up above the road, stopped and looked back. "Yes?"

"Frank, take it easy, boy. You'll never make district commissioner down at the bottom of that gorge."

Rossi grinned, then bit his bottom lip: he recognized the real concern behind Narvo's words. He looked with affection down at Narvo, who had suddenly become his friend and not just his senior officer; he knew, too, that Narvo now accepted him as a man and not just a boy learning a job. He waved and nodded, then went on up the mountain, climbing up through the dust-dulled *kunai* till he was opposite the suggested route across the path of the landslide. He looked down once more at those below, made a thumbs-up sign, then surreptitiously raised the thumb and crossed himself on the forehead. Then he slowly and carefully took his first step out on to the fragile crust of the mountain.

The watchers below held their breath. The word had gone back down the line, and the natives had now all come forward to witness the drama. The road was packed with them, and those that could not stand in the road had climbed up the mountainside; a long frieze of them stretched up the steep slope, still as fence pickets against the orange-colored sky. No one spoke and no one appeared to breathe as the tiny figure of Rossi began to creep like a fly across the gray cracked wall of the tumbled mountain.

Rossi went across foot by foot, testing each step like a man feeling his way across a newly frozen lake. Once he slipped, and there was a loud intake of breath from all those watching him, a great gasp like the sound of a gust of wind in the deep, narrow valley. Narvo felt beads of sweat break on his forehead through the dust, and felt Elisabeth's nails bite into his arm as she held him. Father Shawn was praying softly; and so was Duggan. Harry was stroking the cassowary steadily and automatically, as if it were some magic bird that could conjure up a genii to carry Rossi safely across.

Then at last Rossi had reached the other side. Narvo and the others saw him straighten up and raise his arm, a gesture that was unmistakable: the path, if such it could be called, across the landslide was negotiable. There was an excited murmur among the watching natives, but no one shouted: their expression was usually simple and spontaneous, but they had learned to live with these mountains: the lesson of the slide caused by Narvo's shout was already learned. Then, after a few minutes' conversation with Figgins and the men on the other side of the landslide, Rossi was seen to be coming back. He moved more quickly this time, but still with caution, keeping exactly to the path he had traversed on the way across.

He came sliding down the *kunai* bank to Narvo and the others. "It's safe enough, Roy, if they take it steady. There are a couple of soft spots, but a couple of us can stand there and watch those."

Narvo had already made up his mind how the crossing was to be made. "We'll go across in batches of fifty, a hundred yards apart. That will cut down the number of possible casualties if something does begin to go. I'll take one of those soft spots, Frank, and you take the other. The patients will come last and I'll leave you to see they get across, Peter."

"I'll stay with him," Father Shawn said.

"Thank you, Mike," Traxal said. "If we get caught in a landslide together, I may seek absolution on the way down."

"Glad to oblige," said Father Shawn, and hoped absolution would not be necessary for either of them. He did not want to die, and he had only volunteered to stay with Traxal because he wanted to put off the moment of having to cross the landslide. He knew that if a slide did occur while any of the parties was crossing, Narvo would not send anyone else across; he would say prayers for whoever might perish, but he knew he would also say prayers of thanks that he himself had been spared. *God forgive me for my cowardice*, he prayed; and wondered how many saints had been cowards. Peter, one of the first of them, had been a coward; but at least he had redeemed himself by martyrdom. And martyrdom, Father Shawn told himself ruefully and a little contemptuously, had never been one of his chosen roads to sainthood.

Bermingham, carrying one of his children, and Mary, insisting on carrying the other, led the first group of natives across the landslide.

"Just tread carefully, Jack," Narvo said. "As if you were walking on eggshells."

"Or as if I was going into one of my sister's tea parties back home in my lap-lap," said Bermingham, winking his good eye, and it was the first time Narvo had ever heard him mention anyone back home on the mainland. "I'll be careful, Roy, my word, I will."

Rossi and Narvo went with them, to station themselves at the two places where Rossi thought the ground might give way and another slide start. As soon as Narvo stepped on to the loose earth he felt the uneasiness that comes when there is no feeling of solidity beneath one. This was not *terra firma:* this was a lopsided sea of earth and rock that might break into a storm at any moment.

Slowly, with the hesitancy and awkwardness of a band of blind cripples, the group edged its way across. They came to the first spot where the slide looked most treacherous, and taking each step as if it were their last, they painfully negotiated it. Narvo stayed there, and Bermingham and Rossi led the group on toward the second dangerous spot. Narvo turned and waved, and saw the second group, with the Macys, begin the crossing.

There was utter silence on the mountainside. Occasionally a stone would roll and go clattering down the slide, carrying other stones with it: the sound would be magnified in the ears of those on the narrow path, and they would all hold their breath. Down on the road a child suddenly cried aloud, and Narvo turned, like an irritable warden in church, and made a sharp silencing gesture. The child instantly shut up, as if a hand had been clapped over its mouth. Narvo, still nervous, smiled approvingly. These native mothers, untroubled by childless psychiatrists, had effective ways of dealing with their children.

Then the second group was going by him. He could see the strain on Bernice's face; she looked old and haggard. She was looking straight ahead of her, as if trying to ignore the mass of poised earth above and below her.

"You're doing all right," Narvo said as she went by him, and she nodded without looking at him. Macy was walking close behind her, and he too looked old and haggard. But he managed a grin as he passed Narvo, and the latter grinned back.

"It's no worse than operating without anesthetic," Narvo said. "You've had to do it a couple of times on the kanakas."

"Never again," said Macy, still grinning weakly. "Now I know how the poor devils feel."

Then Harry, tired and dusty but still looking as if he were enjoying some great adventure, came by. "I had to leave Wally, Roy. You think he'll be all right on his own?"

"Cassowaries are the most self-reliant creatures in the animal kingdom," lied Narvo. "I thought I'd told you that."

"Yeah," said Harry, unconvinced. "Will he be all right, though?"

"He'll be all right," said Narvo, and wondered if the cassowary would survive. He had not seen one living wild thing, except the solitary crow last night, since leaving Kundavi. The sky was deserted of birds; the swirls of dust had taken their place. The possums, rats, gecko lizards and tree-climbing kangaroos had fled from this country of the dead; the pythons and flying-foxes had died with the trees in which they had lived. If the cassowary survived, he would be king of the dead beasts.

"I hope he'll be all right," Harry said, then looked anxiously at Narvo. "You gonna be all right here, Roy? I mean, don't get hurt or anything."

"Don't worry about Wally and me," said Narvo. "We'll be all right."

"I hope so," Harry said, and went on after his parents.

The first group had now got safely across. Time dragged on, and slowly the fearful, cautious parties went by. Narvo felt his legs beginning to stiffen and grow tired as he leaned against the slope of the mountain; but there was not room to sit down and all he could do was keep shifting his feet a few inches at a time. Then Elisabeth and Duggan were going by with the second to last group. Sergeant Beraki was with them, somehow still managing to look as if he were marching up and down the parade ground with a bunch of awkward police recruits.

"The women are safe with me, Kiap," he said as he went past. "Do not worry for them."

Narvo, straight-faced, nodded in reply. "I do not worry, Beraki. You are my right arm."

For one horrible moment he thought Beraki was going to stamp his feet and salute. But the police sergeant restrained himself, nodded a little smugly, and went on. *You great wonderful conceited bastard*, Narvo thought; and loved the strutting stiff-backed black man.

Then Elisabeth was going by, wanting to stop but unable to because of the press of natives behind her. "Be careful, darling," was all she said; and Narvo smiled at her, the smile of a lover in a public place at his loved one, the smile that can never be misunderstood by the one for whom it is meant.

He looked after her as she went on, and kept looking after her till she had passed the other danger spot where Rossi stood. Then he looked back and saw that Traxal, Father Shawn and the carriers with the patients had begun their journey. There were now eight patients on stretchers, and this group would have the most hazardous crossing of all. Traxal walked at the head of the group and Father Shawn brought up the rear. Between them the sixteen carriers, the prisoners from the post stockade, walked with the stretchers, leaning in against the slope of the mountain, moving so slowly that from a distance they hardly seemed to be moving at all.

The path across the slide had been trodden down and firmed a little by the thousands of feet that had crossed it in the last hour, but it was still no more than eighteen inches at its widest part. Several stretches of it were composed of loose rock and here no amount of treading would ever firm it down. Each pair of carriers crossed these sections on their own, the others waiting till the previous pair had gone across. Most of the patients were *kuru* cases. Paiwo was the last of the patients, his carriers a thief and a murderer: Narvo recognized the slow-witted man who had killed the woman *kuru* patient in the hospital (how long ago? Here on the scarred and naked mountainside, time had stopped: nothing seemed related to this dangerous crossing of the landslide).

Traxal went past. "The last of the sheep. You may come home now, shepherd."

Narvo ignored him and watched anxiously as the first of the carriers set his foot on the section where Narvo stood. The native, a small man with a piece of cane still stuck in the septum of his nose, looked ahead to Narvo. The latter could see the sweat on the man's dust-grayed face; it ran in the dust, giving him tribal markings of fear. The man smiled at Narvo, but there was no warmth nor friendliness in it: it was the smile one saw in skulls. The native looked back over his shoulder for an instant, as if debating whether to set down the stretcher and come ahead on his own. Narvo knew then it was time to assert some authority, to get the man moving before his fear stopped the other carriers dead in their tracks.

"Come on!" he snapped in dialect, still keeping his voice low. "You were not afraid to steal from your brother. Are you afraid to walk across a mountain?"

The native hesitated, his mouth working and incoherent grunts coming from him. He put out a foot, gingerly, as if the earth might burn it off; he put it down, rested his weight on it and took another step. And forgot to balance himself against the weight of the stretcher behind him.

Narvo saw the man's foot slip, saw him stab desperately at the ground with his other foot, as if trying to drive his leg into the ground as a stake, heard him yell and saw the earth and rock begin to slide away under him.

Then he felt the earth beginning to fall away beneath himself.

2

The next few moments were something Narvo would never be able to remember clearly. Even though he had been aware of the danger for the full hour he had been standing on the landslide and had known that it could happen at any moment, all he felt now was disbelief. It was like being in a dream in which one was half-awake: all you had to do was keep your head, not panic, and the horror of the dream would pass: you would wake up safe and sound in your own bed. But he knew this was no dream, because dreams had no sound. And later the sound would be what he would remember most frighteningly. There was the scream of the two carriers and their patient as the three of them, still somehow held together by the stretcher, as if they did not want to die alone, went plunging down the mountainside in a turmoil of earth and rocks. The other carriers had shouted, and there was a long shout from Father Shawn that Narvo would remember later as a prayer. There was a slithering sound, like that of someone being dragged across a sanded floor; and a rattling sound that Narvo, even then, imagined as the death rattle in someone's throat. A rumbling began, enveloping all the other sounds, and grew into a roar. Dust rose up suddenly, as if the mountain had been abruptly cloaked in cloud. Narvo shut his eyes, wanting, for some reason he would never know, to die blind. He seemed to be trying to keep his feet on small stones that were nor more than a strip of ground in the air; something huge brushed past, but it had no weight and went by without hurting him. The dust was thick around him and he could not breathe even if he had thought about it; he had stopped breathing because it was an effort and there was no point to it if he was going to die. And all the time he kept falling, sliding down the side of the mountain as down a giant shoot-the-chute, knowing all the time that somewhere below him, only a second away, was the lip of the gorge and the final straight fall that would be his end. Out of memory and fear, out of the long-forgotten habit of religion and the always present urge to survive, in the next life if not in this, there burst a prayer: *Christ, help me* . . . !

He felt the rock slide under him and the next moment there was nothing but dust beneath him. *This is it,* he thought. And almost instantly had the breath forced out of him with lung-flattening impact as the ground seemed to rise up and smash into him. Something thumped against his head, dazing him; his hands thrashed out instinctively and grabbed, clawing desperately for something solid. And found something and held on.

The slide went on past him, still no more than a terrible thunder in the whirling dust, and a moment later he heard the exploding roar of it coming up from the bottom of the gorge. Stones continued to roll past him, their clattering sound now heard, and earth was still sliding by with a sibilant hiss. Then the dust began to clear, lifting like a gray morning mist, and he looked out on the world he had already said good-by to.

He was some fifty yards above the lip of the gorge, lying on what had been a ledge beneath an outcrop of rock; the ledge now was heaped with stones and earth, and he would have to move carefully if he was not to go sliding off. He was holding to the snapped-off trunk of a tree, his grip so desperate that his fingers were embedded like claws in the splintered wood. He released one hand and wiped the dust from his mouth and eyes;

his eyes smarted but at least he could see clearly now. The whole landslide appeared to have moved down the mountain, leaving a great gaping wound, a wide furrowed ravine, between the two sections of road. He looked up the slide and saw that Rossi and the second to last party must have made it to safety; that section of the slide didn't appear to have moved.

He turned his head slightly and saw the people by the trucks and the natives spread up the slope behind them, and without recognizing anyone in particular, he raised his arm and waved to them. Then he saw some of the whites break from the crowd by the trucks and come sliding down the *kunai* slope below the road. With his eyes still watering from the dust, he could not recognize any of them. They were three hundred yards away from him across the mountainside, and even if it had been safe, he could not have shouted to them; his throat was swollen and seemed to be full of dust, and his chest pained him. He just raised his arm, telling them to stay where they were, and saw someone wave in reply. Then he heard the soft cry of pain and a moment later the moaning.

He turned his body on the loose slope of the ledge, feeling earth and small stones slide away from beneath him. As he turned his head he was aware for the first time of something warm on his brow and then the blood began to drip down across his left eye. Till that moment it had not occurred to him that he might be injured. That he had survived at all, that he was still alive and able to breathe and see and hear, had been enough. Lying there, still gripping the shattered tree trunk with one hand, he ran his other hand over as much of his body as he could reach. He moved his legs and flexed his toes in his boots; then looked down and saw he wore no boots, that they had been stripped from him in the fall. He laughed, shaking his head a little so that his face rubbed against the rubble and the blood turned to dark mud beneath his eye; laughed both at the loss of his boots and with relief that he had no bones broken. Then he heard the moaning again, and he raised his head and looked across the landslide.

And saw the three men, the two naked whites, stripped of their clothes, and the black in his loose tangle of bandages. And he saw no one else: twenty-three men had died in the slide.

Traxal lay caught between two rocks, a smashed bloody figure that looked already dead. But even as Narvo recognized him, Traxal raised his head and another moan issued from him. He said something in Czech and his head dropped again. Beyond him Narvo saw the bandages flutter on the still figure of Paiwo, like the wing of a trapped bird. Just above and beyond Paiwo, he saw Father Shawn lift a hand and seek another grip on the treacherous earth.

"Mike!" Narvo found the word stifled in his throat; he had to call again. "Mike, are you all right?"

Father Shawn looked across; the shock on his face was evident even at the distance. "Roy! Oh, thank God! Thank God!"

"Don't start thanking Him yet. We're not out of this. Are you all right?"

Father Shawn seemed to be testing all his body without moving anything; his hands remained glued to the small rocks that were his only hold. He lay beside a large boulder, but for some reason he was not grasping it. "I think my legs are broken. I can't feel them. Are you all right, Roy?"

"Excepting for being stuck out here like a shag on a rock." They were speaking hoarse whispers, afraid of being overheard by the mountain; a slice of earth fell away, a warning. "Peter looks in a bad way, but he's still alive. How about Paiwo?"

"I can't tell from here." Father Shawn looked up, agony and despair scarring his thin face, hiding the scar that was already there. "Roy, what are we going to do?"

Narvo cautiously turned his head and looked back across toward Figgins and the others who had come down from the trucks. He thought he saw Elisabeth there, but he knew he

was only *wishing* her there: men and women were indistinguishable at this distance. Then he saw two figures edge their way
onto the slide; and risking everything, he raised himself and
waved furiously. "Go back, go back!" he whispered hoarsely,
and a moment later saw the two figures retreat.

Then he heard Traxal moan again and he turned back. "Peter,
can you hear me?"

Traxal raised his head. His face was a mess of blood: he was
unrecognizable but for the blondness of his hair. "Forget me. I
can't move. I'm smashed—" He stopped and coughed: blood
spurted from his mouth.

Narvo stared at him for a moment, then slowly he eased himself farther up on the ledge. It took him several minutes to get
himself up into a crouch, clinging to the face of the rock above
him. He looked about him, sizing up their chances, determined
now not to die. He was past fear now. He had died once and
come back: you could not die twice. *Be careful, Narvo,* he told
himself, *and you'll get out of this.* Then he looked across the
slide and knew with something like agony that the lives of the
other three depended on him. And knew he could save only one.

He looked wildly about him, looking for a miracle; for a moment his grip on the rock relaxed and he almost lost his balance.
Then he steadied himself, leaning against the rock, feeling the
chill of it against his fevered cheek. He raised a hand and wiped
the blood from his eye. He remembered his Goethe: *blood is a
juice of the rarest quality;* and wished he bled water: at least
it would not have obscured his vision as much.

Then he set out to save himself and one other. Even as he
left the safety of his own ledge he did not know whom he would
save: Traxal, Paiwo or Mike Shawn. Only in the back of his
mind, a treachery of which he was afraid, was the thought that
Mike Shawn, his friend, was the one farthest away, the one he
would have to risk more to save.

He worked his way carefully across the rubble, inches at a

time, aware with every movement he made that he lay only on the mask of the mountain, not on the mountain itself. Earth slid beneath him and he would slide with it, his heart in his mouth, wondering if the whole landslide would start once more. He put his foot on a rock, found it firm and trod on it; and had it plummet away from him, as if jerked by an invisible and ghoulishly joking hand. The silence was so vast that in his ears the grunt of his breathing and the thumping of his heart was almost deafening; he stopped once to try and ease his breathing and to slow the heavy pumping in his breast. The blood was running freely from his brow and he looked out on the world through one eye: he wondered for a moment if it looked the same to him as it did to Jack Bermingham. He lay back flat against the slope of the rubble, took his handkerchief from his pocket and knotted it around his head against the wound above his eye.

Then he moved on and was above Traxal. He rested against the upper of the two rocks that held Traxal and reached down and lifted the doctor's head by the chin. He held the smashed mess of the face in his hand and behind the cobwebs of blood tried to find some gleam in the eyes, of hate or appeal, something to help him make up his mind.

Then the mangled wound of a mouth opened, and from behind the broken teeth the broken voice mumbled: "It's no use, Roy. I'm not worth saving."

Oh, Christ, Narvo said silently, *is that the word of a hero or a sinner or a doctor? Who speaks the truth?* He looked back across the mountain at the figures on the green safety of the *kunai* slope; they now seemed an interminable distance away, beyond reach; he could not call on them to help him in his judgment. He looked down again at the face in his hand, the wreckage of a man, one against whom he felt no anger nor reproach, a man like himself, still alive and still entitled to live. He could see nothing of the eyes behind their veil of blood and now Traxal was mumbling in Czech. He lowered the face onto the bloody naked chest and moved on across the slide.

Paiwo lay twenty yards from Traxal, and Father Shawn was another ten yards farther still. By the time he reached Paiwo, Narvo's hip and knees were rubbed raw from their chafing contact with the rubble as he had crawled across. Paiwo lay with one arm caught around a pole of his stretcher; the pole itself was caught between a rock and another shattered tree trunk. The bandages had been stripped from him and blew about him like dusty tattered garlands. His face was still covered by the dressings; the rest of him was exposed. Narvo looked down on him, fighting sickness and the weakness of profound pity. Paiwo's body was just a charred hulk; he lived only because the molten rock from the volcano had not burned his heart.

"Paiwo."

Behind the dusty bloodstained dressings on the face there was a stirring of life. It was nothing Narvo could discern; he could only sense it. He stared at the closed eyes showing through the slits in the dressing, willing them to open and give him some message. If Paiwo was still alive, he deserved to go on living; here on this brittle mask of earth, where death was only a tremble away, Narvo could not condemn even this man who had been on his way to the post to kill him. It had been his credo: an equal chance for black and white. Then the eyes opened.

"Paiwo."

Narvo leaned down head first, flat against the steep slope, his arms outstretched to support himself. To Father Shawn he presented the picture of a man crucified; even the scar of the ax wound in the shoulder could have been from the thrust of the centurion's spear. *And there's a saint,* the priest suddenly thought, and wept at the bitter and too late knowledge: there were other ways to sainthood than crawling on one's knees to God.

"Paiwo."

Narvo's face was close to that of the native. He stared into the dark eyes, but they were blind. He would never learn whether Paiwo had died hating him or loving him, and it was a nescience that would trouble him forever. Paiwo was not yet dead, but he was too far gone to call back for an answer. Narvo laid his face against the earth and wept without tears.

"Roy."

He raised his head, blinking away the blood that had begun to run again, that blinded his left eye like a red tear. "Mike, I'm coming."

"No, Roy! Go back! Save yourself. We'll never make it together all the way across. I can't move my legs. Please, Roy. I'm begging you to go. Be my friend—save yourself——"

"Save your breath. I didn't crawl all the way across here to continue our arguments."

"Roy, please! My life isn't worth yours—go back——"

But Narvo was working his way across the earth and stones and rocks. His feet, as well as his hip and knees, were now rubbed raw; his toes bled freely and there was a long bleeding gash on his ankle. He had long ago lost all feeling in his fingers; they clung to the mountain, to life itself, of their own accord. His throat was thick and swollen with dust and he could not even raise spittle in his mouth.

He reached Father Shawn. The priest lay beside the large boulder, his thin naked body stripped even of its skin. The flesh of one thigh was gashed open and Narvo could see the bone sticking through. But the eyes that looked up at Narvo, though shortsighted and clouded a little with pain, were the eyes of a man who still had a firm grip on life, who couldn't give himself up to death because he hadn't the courage and knew it.

"God bless you for a stupid saintly bastard," said Father Shawn. "I'll never argue with you again."

"That makes it a dull prospect," Narvo said. "Hardly worth crawling back across the mountain for. Grab hold under my arms, Mike, and try and pull yourself up. I've got to get you away from that rock."

"That's why I didn't want you to come, Roy. The rock is barely holding."

"Bit late to tell me now. That's the way it is with you priests—always holding something back." Narvo rested for a moment, gazing intently at the boulder. Then he shrugged, and Father Shawn, clutching him, felt the gesture. It was simple enough, but it bound them together from now on, in life or death. "Here goes, Mike. Hang on tight and lift."

Slowly Narvo inched back up the slope, pulling the little priest with him. He had thought he was spent and weak; but he found reserves of the great strength that had been his. He dug with his toes and knees into the rocks; it was like dragging himself up a bed of nails and broken glass. The blood was gushing from the wound above his eye, and the muscles in his shoulders and arms seemed to be tearing. Father Shawn's hips slid past the boulder; the protruding thigh bone scraped against it like a soft stick; his feet, one still wearing a boot and sock, slithered by it. Then the boulder, as if it had done its job, relieved now of the little priest's light weight, began to move.

Narvo lay head downwards, Father Shawn stretched out below him, and watched the boulder go racing down the slide, gathering earth and stones and rocks with it, drawing the mountain after it, a stone Pied Piper racing to its death over the lip of the gorge below. Traxal and Paiwo moved like men about to stand up and walk away, then slowly, then all at once gathering speed, they slid down the slope, rolling over and over like men unable to swim in the gray rolling surf, and were gone from sight. Narvo watched the earth slide away from beneath Father Shawn, saw the little priest sink slowly into a trough. The roar and rattle of the slide came up to them, and Narvo waited for the huge field of rubble above them to follow the lower slope down into the gorge.

Then Father Shawn was looking up at him, grinning horribly but still grinning. "I don't think He wanted us that time, Roy."

"If He didn't want us then," said Narvo, "He won't want us for a long time yet."

Cautiously he slid down beside Father Shawn. He lifted the little priest onto his back, then lay flat on his stomach on the slope. Then, like a giant crab under its human shell, he began to make his way, slowly but with confidence, across the Judas face of the mountain.

17

THE CESSNA came up the gorge, under the thin cloud of smoke, and over where the airstrip had been. The young Pole took the plane down low, holding it steady against the updrafts, and they saw the huge crack right across the strip, and the boulders, streaked with cold lava, that littered its top end. The windsock still fluttered, a rag in the breeze, but its pole leaned at an angle that held little hope that it would flutter much longer.

"That strip's seen its last plane," Rossi said from the back seat.

Narvo nodded, and felt the seat belt tighten across his stomach as the pilot took the Cessna steeply around the mountain, over the quietly smoking crater, over the gray frozen flood of lava that covered Vaikaka and Benamaua, over the gorge and up toward Kundavi.

"Still untouched," Rossi said, and Narvo nodded again. "We could almost move right back in."

But Narvo did not nod to that. No one would ever move back into Kundavi. The post was a ghost station now; the mountains had claimed it. The huts still stood in neat array about the parade ground; the grass looked as if it had just been cut, except that it was gray and not green. The hospital stood ready for patients; the gate of the stockade was open for prisoners; the flagpole waited on a flag to be raised. Even the old generator, on its stand under its *kunai*-thatch roof, looked ready to be turned on. The plane flew along the bottom of the parade ground, over the House Paper and Rossi's hut and the cleft in the cliff where Narvo's own hut had stood. And that was the moment to turn his back on Kundavi forever.

"Let's go home," he said, and turned his back on what had been home.

The pilot took the plane up above the ranges and headed for Goroka. Rossi, twisting his body to look back at the vanishing patrol post, said, "Somehow no other post will ever be like that one for me. I suppose it's like the first girl you love—" Then he turned forward again, biting his lip, blushing beneath his tan. "You know what I mean."

"When you get your first post of your own, you'll soon forget Kundavi," said Narvo.

"How do you think you'll like being back on the coast?"

Narvo shrugged. He had got his new posting this morning, and that was why he had made this farewell trip out to Kundavi. Neil Figgins had called him into his office just after breakfast and he had known at once that Figgins had bad news.

"They're sending you to Samarai. A nice developed area where you can't do any harm, where it is unlikely you'll ever see a UN committee. You are to be district officer. Congratulations."

Narvo stood up, knocking his chair over, uttering an oath that seemed to disturb the regulations tacked to the walls. "What the hell are they doing to me?"

"They are rewarding you," said Figgins. "For your work in getting as many as you did out of Kundavi."

"Did you recommend me for this promotion?"

"I recommended your promotion. I didn't recommend Samaria. I told them you were a mountain man, as much as any Kukukuku. Their answer was: Samarai."

"But what the bloody hell will I do down there?" Narvo's was a cry of anguish. "The place is settled, civilized. There's nothing to do but paper work and a few patrols by boat."

"You'll have your work cut out being a husband," said Figgins, stroking his mustache with his knuckle. "That is, if you're going to go through with that idea."

Narvo didn't answer that, but shoved his hat on his head and stalked out of Figgins' office. He almost knocked down Macy and Bermingham as they came up the steps into the building.

"We're going over to see Mike this afternoon at the hospital," Macy said. "You want to come with us?"

"Duggan's feeding him up as if he was her favorite kid." Bermingham looked neat but uncomfortable in his shirt, shorts, socks and boots; Sergeant Beraki strutting across the lawn, waiting for Narvo to recognize him so that he could salute, looked more at ease in clothes. "It'll be my farewell chat with the little bloke. Me and Mary leave tomorrow for Okava."

"Somehow I can't see you running a trading store," Narvo said.

"I'm gonna give it a go. A man can do anything if he puts his mind to it. There's young Harry, going to school here and liking it. And look at Eric here. He's even got used to the idea of being here in Goroka, working behind a desk."

Narvo looked at Macy, just soon enough to catch the gleam of regret in the latter's eyes. But Macy was smiling. "We'll go out and see Mike this afternoon, then all come back to our place for a drink."

"Will Bernice mind if I bring Mary?" Bermingham asked.

"I don't think Bernice will mind anything from now on. No offense, Jack, you know what I mean. She came out of Kundavi alive and now we're living in Goroka. What more could a woman want?"

"I couldn't guess," said Narvo, and went down the steps past them. "I'll come out to see Mike with you. We've still got a lot of arguing to do before he leaves for the States next week."

"He's not going to like that," said Bermingham. "My word, he's not."

"No," said Narvo, and all at once his own disappointment seemed to be nothing. *He* was not condemned to a wheelchair for the rest of his life, to the pity of his family, to the Job-like resignation expected of a man who had once wanted to be a saint. Samarai was not what he wanted, but at least it wasn't hell. "No, he's not going to like that at all."

And now the plane was coming down on to the airdrome at Goroka, and Rossi was saying, "There's Elisabeth waiting for you. You're going to have to marry that girl, Roy."

Narvo looked back over his shoulder at the boy. "What would you do if you were me, Frank?"

"I'd marry her," said Rossi. "A man can live just so long alone."

September 1958—   *Stokes Point, Avalon,*
August 1959   *N.S.W.*